Delphine Pontvieux

ETA
ESTIMATED TIME OF ARREST

To Nicole,
So great meeting you at Sohohouse today. Looking forward to the next boozy book club!

Delphine

MISS NYET PUBLISHING™

April 17

ETA - ESTIMATED TIME OF ARREST
Copyright © 2009 by Delphine Pontvieux

This book is printed on acid-free paper. The text stock used in the printing of this book is SFI certified. It is supplied by a green initiative vendor who participates in the Forest Stewardship Council and the Sustainable Forestry Initiative programs, which are both devoted to encouraging the responsible management of the world's forests.

Published by Miss Nyet Publishing, LLC
PO Box 12436
Chicago, IL 60612
USA
www.missnyet.com

Layout and cover design by Jason Link
Cover photography: Michael Smith
Inside cover illustration by Guillermo Zubiaga
Maps, photos and inserts by Delphine Pontvieux (unless otherwise noted)

ISBN-13: 978-0-9842176-0-1 (hardcover)
ISBN-10: 0-9842176-0-6 (hardcover)

Library of Congress Control Number: 2009908991

First edition – December 2009

Printed in the United States of America

ACKNOWLEDGEMENTS
-ESKER ONAK-

I would like to express my gratitude to those who contributed their knowledge, personal experience and/or professional expertise to strengthen the substance of this novel, which resulted in creating a credible, while entirely fictitious, story.

For specific information and advice regarding the Basque country and its history, not to mention his hospitality in Euskadi, I am grateful to my friend Fermin Muguruza.

A big thank you goes to Jean-Baptiste Cappicot for sharing his passion for rock climbing and the Vallée d'Aspe, and to Jean-Luc Palacio, Pierre Puiseux, Guy Sérandour and Philippe Barrère for their knowledge and insight about the Béarn region, and the ins and outs of mountaineering in the Pyrenees.

Special thanks to Marco Rieu-Mère, Rainer Luttgens, Alberto Ansorena, Sylvie Javelas, Isabelle Leclerc, Benoit Mélen, Anju Ahuja and Patricia Sevening for answering my numerous questions within their respective fields of expertise.

I am particularly indebted to Helga Schier, my editor, for her suggestions and corrections to my manuscript, in addition to her counsel and guidance.

Thanks to Jennifer Bernsen, Peg Schneider and Judith Mayzel for their critique and valuable edits, and to Jessica Dolan and Katherine Mooney for their tremendous help during the proof reading process.

Thanks to Guillermo Zubiaga for creating the coat of arms for the book, to Fabrice Calmels for lending his striking eyes to the cover, to Michael Smith, his photographer, and to Christopher Call for his image editing and web design talents.

And last but not least, to Jason Link for creating the book design and layout.

A very special thank you goes to the people I hold dearest, Michèle, Jean-Luc, Isabelle, Tony, Mamie and the whole family.

To all the friends, past and present, who have left their indelible mark on me.

And to Momo, who I miss greatly.

ESTIMATED TIME OF ARREST

Bay Of Biscay
ATLANTIC OCEAN

France

Lyon
Bayonne
Bordeaux
Bilbao
Pau
Marseille
Spain
Barcelona
Madrid

Bilbao

San Sebastián
(Donostia)
Bia
Irun-Henday

*Vizcaya
(Bizkaia)*

*Guipuzcoa
(Gipuzkoa)*

Saint-Jean
-de-port
(Doniban
Garazi)

Vitoria
(Gasteiz)

Pamplona
(Iruñea)

*Alava
(Araba)*

*Navarr
(Nafarr*

Castilla

SPAIN

Legend:
----- - Province borders of Euskal Herria
XXXXX - French - Spanish Border

Delphine Pontvieux 2009

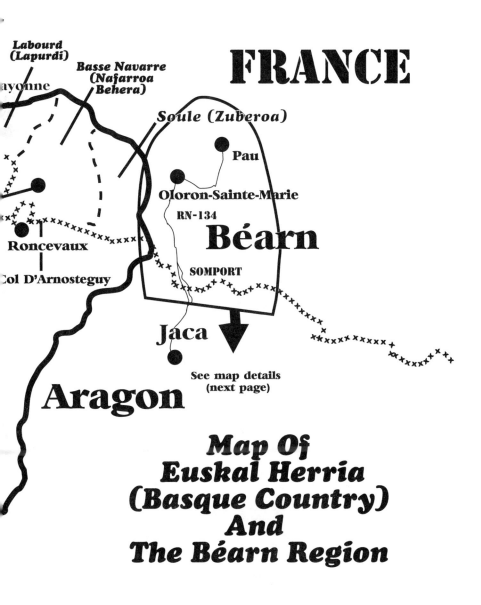

Map Of
Euskal Herria
(Basque Country)
And
The Béarn Region

TO OLORON-SAINTE-MARIE

Sarrance

RN-134

Bedous

Accous

LA GOUTTE D'EAU

Cette-Eygun

Laruns

Etsaut

Hell's Canyon -
Chemin de la Mâture

Fort du Portalet

Urdos

Lac de Bious-Artigues

GR 10

Les Forges d'Abel

Pic du Midi d'Ossau
2884 m / 9461 ft

Somport Pass
Candanchú

Pourtalet Pass

Somport Tunnel

Vallée d'Aspe
And
Vallée d'Ossau

Delphine Pontvieux 2009

PROLOGUE
– HITZAURREA –

09:37 PM ~ Friday, December 17, 1993

The passenger held out a handful of pesos to the cab driver with gold-capped teeth. He had just pulled along the curb of Avenida Lázaro Cárdenas, amidst a honking chaos of cars and a myriad of little green Volkswagen taxicabs that resembled limes on wheels. The smart beetles, or *bochos*, as they were affectionately called in Mexico City, scurried around in all directions, hustling passengers along busy streets where two lanes of traffic became three at random, and where metered cab fares varied greatly from one customer to the next. While the young man waited to receive his change, he noticed the *taxista* studying him with exaggerated attention in his rearview mirror. He was used to that kind of attention, for he had been blessed with that one-of-a-kind attractiveness that made both men and women look twice. He was tall and slender, with a lean muscular body and a mass of thick, unruly light brown hair that framed his handsome face in loose curls. His lips were full, his nose straight. His jaw was square and chiseled, and more often than not, he sported two days of beard growth.

"Something wrong?" he asked the cab driver.

The sudden question startled the Mexican, who apologized at once for staring at his customer in such a rude manner.

"*¡Con mucho perdón, señor!* I was looking at your eyes. They are *muy*—peculiar."

Indeed they were, much to his chagrin. His extraordinary stare made it difficult for him to go through life unnoticed. The young man had heterochromia iridium: one iris was a different color than the other. His left eye was deep blue and the other hazel, speckled with gold flakes.

He gave the cabbie a shadow of a smile, slammed the passenger door and got lost in the revolving tide of people walking up and down the avenue leading to Plaza Garibaldi. The twenty-three year old man had only spent three days in the Mexican capital and, already, he could not wait to leave.

Night had just fallen over the metropolis, and even though Christmas was right around the corner, the temperature was still in the high seventies. In the distance, he could already hear the cacophony of dozens of mariachi bands vying for attention and a promise of a paid gig to someone's wedding or a lucky girl's upcoming *quinceañera* party. People from all around the world were strolling around Plaza Garibaldi. Entire groups danced to the uplifting beat of "La Cucaracha," the quintessential song played upon request by every mariachi band from Jalisco to Veracruz. New lovers favored the less illuminated corners of the Plaza in order to listen to tear-jerking serenades. Everywhere, rugged Mexicans with thick handlebar moustaches and wide-brimmed hats urged the crowds to pay a visit to their watering holes.

The young man followed the instructions and walked across the Plaza in search of the statue of the great Mexican musician José Alfredo Jiménez. Dressed in the typical mariachi attire, the prolific singer carried a long wool blanket folded over his right shoulder and held a large *sombrero* in his hand. Looking straight ahead with its frozen stare cast in bronze, the imposing statue appeared unconcerned with the ebb and flow of passersby moving about at its feet, night after night, like drunken ants.

Now that he had found the spot, all the young man needed to do was wait for his contact to arrive. He leaned back against the stone pedestal and rolled a cigarette between nervous fingers. Trying hard to act natural, he lit the cigarette and inhaled the acrid smoke. Given the circumstances, this was easier said than done. Now was certainly not the time to attract any unwanted attention. A group of eight mariachis were standing just a few yards away from him. They were cracking jokes and tuning their instruments while waiting for someone willing to pay a few pesos in exchange for a *ranchera* song praising the valiant men of the great State of Mexico. The men were dressed in matching black *charro* costumes, tight straight-cut black trousers adorned with gold-plated ornaments worn along the outside of their pant legs and short fitted jackets over immaculate frilled shirts. Intricate patterns made of gold thread had been embroidered on their jacket sleeves, as well as on the outside rim of their wide felt hats. They looked brave, much like the bullfighter in his "Suit of Light." When a Mexican family walked up to them to request an audition, the band members did not waste any time in picking up their instruments and finding their allocated spot within their semi-circle formation. Before long, they were pouring their hearts out, playing and singing a colorful rendition of "Cu-cu-rru-cu-cu Paloma."

The young man never saw the person who walked up to him from behind. He jerked sideways in pure reflex, startled by the stranger who had just tapped him on the shoulder. As he pivoted on his heels, he realized the stranger was just another peddler, a street photographer. He was about to wave the man off when the Mexican, undeterred by his obvious irritation, grabbed him by the sleeve and whispered in his ear,

"Don't think. Just play along."

The young man quickly collected his wits and nodded. The Mexican he had taken for another con artist was actually the person he had come to meet. Without missing a beat, they started haggling over the price of a *muy chunga* souvenir picture from Plaza Garibaldi. The young man, unsure of what the phony street vendor was getting at, played along quite convincingly. After a short while, they settled on a reasonable price, and he gave the contact a chunk of money. Satisfied, the photographer instructed him to pose by the statue and snapped his picture with an instant film camera. When done, he pulled a thick paper stock photo frame out of his messenger bag. He affixed the photo inside with care and folded the frame cover over the snapshot. At last, he handed it to the handsome young man with a wide grin and a "Gracias."

The young man stood stock-still for a fleeting moment, his fingers clutching the cheap-looking cardboard frame. "Greetings from Mexico City" was printed over the front in silver foil lettering. When he looked up, his mysterious contact had disappeared into the crowd.

The card was unusually thick. Without a doubt, something had been inserted behind the photograph. He tucked it in the waistband of his jeans and walked briskly past the columns of the Plaza and out into the not-so-safe streets of the adjacent neighborhoods. Few tourists ever ventured in this part of town, save for small clusters of blurry-eyed club-hopping youngsters looking for drugs. Should they score without being mugged or beaten, they would keep the party going until dawn in some fancy hotel room of the "Zona Rosa." The young man ignored the lewd catcalls of street pushers advertising live sex shows at nearby cabarets. He was a tourist to them, a *gringo* whose pockets must be lined with silver dollars. Glad for the easy disguise, he kept on walking with his head down, on a mission. He needed to find a quiet place where he could rip the photo frame apart and pour over its contents.

When he was confident that no one had followed him, he walked into a dingy bar, ordered a bottle of *Dos Equis* and asked the bartender for directions to the bathroom. He followed the guy's scrawny thumb toward the back of the grimy building, pushed the door of the men's room open and locked himself into one of the stalls. He pulled the photo frame out of the back of his blue jeans and ripped it apart. Behind the over-exposed instant snapshot, he found a little booklet. Because the light inside the stall was dim at best, he had to climb on top of the filthy toilet bowl to get closer to the flickering neon light.

He examined the booklet carefully, running his fingers over the grained cover with reverence. It was a French passport. He took a deep breath before he flipped it open to learn his new name. He read it out loud, so as to imprint the name into his memory. At last, he stashed the official document in his pocket and took a moment to calm his nerves.

"¿*Perdido?*" asked the bartender as soon as his customer had returned to the bar.

Before he answered cautiously, the young man took a long swig out of the beer bottle that had been waiting for him atop the sticky Formica counter. "Am I lost? No. No, I'm not."

"We don't see too many *gringos* like you around here," the sinister-looking Mexican continued, eyeing him with a suspicious look.

"I see."

"Did you come here to score or use? Because if you did, you came to the wrong place, *amigo*."

"I've got what I asked for right here in front of me," the young man replied gruffly while pointing at his drink. "If my presence here is such a problem to you, I'll be on my way."

"¡*Que no!* ¡*Que no!*" The bartender's attitude changed at once. He gesticulated wildly for the man to keep his seat. "We've had, um, trouble with the law lately, so I had to ask. I'm sure you understand. Even though I knew all along that you were a good man!" he added with a toothy smile and a sleazy wink. "Sooo, *bienvenida, amigo!* Your hard-earned pesos are welcome here anytime! I'm Manolo, proud owner of this fine establishment!"

"And I'm Rafael," the young man replied as he firmly shook the bartender's hand. He was pleased at how easily the name rolled right off his tongue: Ra-fa-el.

12:37 PM ~ Thursday, March 24, 1994

"Safe!"

The sound of Faustine's voice echoed all the way down the stony cliff to the Fort du Portalet.

The gloomy fortress stood at the entrance of a narrow defile, past a ravine with the fitting name of Hell's Canyon, barely hanging onto the steep slopes of the mountain. It had been erected at a strategic location between France and Spain, when fortifications were built for fear of a Spanish war in the nineteenth century. If not for the steep road that zigzagged up to the main gates of the fort, one would have a hard time noticing its very existence, as the walls of the fortress blended perfectly into the dark cliff.

Despite its downright oppressive appearance, Fort du Portalet was not the sole incongruous sight in this ominous landscape. In fact, the flank of the mountain on the opposite side of the canyon, the one Faustine was climbing, bore a deep scar. As if once slashed by the giant knife of an ogre, it stretched across the entire width of the mountain's almost vertical face.

Just like the Portalet, the longitudinal fracture that cut the mountain in half was no work of Mother Nature, but the result of years of painstaking manual labor carried out by French convicts in the eighteenth century. Against the odds, with little more than pick-axes and a few barrels of black powder, these men carved a trail out of the cliff to bring the tall pine trees they harvested atop the mountain down the vertical ravine to the valley. The trees would be carved into masts in the naval shipyards of Bayonne to "hold the great sails of the flamboyant Royal vessels of the King of France." The *Chemin de La Mâture*, the "Trail of the Masts," was an admirable work of art and a blatant example of that era's delusions of grandeur.

Faustine had just reached the top of the rocky face of La Mâture after what turned out to be a demanding climb. She turned eighteen this past February, finally entering the tantalizing world of "legal" adulthood. While Faustine acted mature for her age, she still had the innocence and enthusiasm of a teenager. She was tall, lean and athletic. Her extraordinary long mane of light blond waves, which she weaved into a tight braid to keep it off her face, cascaded well below the small of her back to graze the top of her thighs.

Faustine let out an exalted scream of victory and turned sideways, beaming at the world, taking in the breathtaking view from her exposed vantage point. Spring of 1994 had come early. The air was brisk and clean, and the noon sun above was a triumphant disk of gold radiating its bright rays of light over the white-shouldered peaks of the French Pyrenees. The snow was melting atop the canopy of dark green pine forests, which blanketed the steep mountain slopes as far as the eye could see. Wildflowers were sprouting all over the open pastures in fireworks of yellow, red, purple and blue. At the bottom of the tender green valley, eighty-five vertical yards under her feet, the Gave d'Aspe dug its riverbed ever deeper into the soft limestone, carrying icy waters the color of translucent jade all the way to the Atlantic Ocean.

"Awesome job, Faustine!" Rafael's voice boomed from below. "You're on a roll today!"

"Can you believe I just climbed those three pitches on sight?" she shouted back at him, ecstatic. "Playing Hooky" was the name of the course Faustine had just climbed, a five rope length expanse of slightly angled rock in the section of *La Grande Dalle de La Mâture*, also known as "The Big Slab." Its grey-blue limestone was so smooth that it offered very few deep holds. Yet, for some inexplicable reason, hands and feet seemed to adhere to the surface like glue. "Coming down now!" she called out to him.

The stainless steel carabiners made clicking noises as she unclipped them from the permanent bolts drilled into the craggy wall on her way down. Except for the metallic sounds echoing down the canyon, silence reigned. While she abseiled down the face, Faustine savored her achievement. Just two months ago, she had not even been good at climbing trees. Thankfully, her hesitation had not deterred Rafael one bit. From the very beginning, he had been adamant about initiating her into the art of rock climbing. Under the watchful eye of her mentor, she was developing into a promising climber.

Faustine's feet made contact with the ground in a soft thud. She squatted down to gather slack from the climbing rope in order to untie herself. Rafael raised a hand in the air and high-fived her.

"Welcome back to earth, partner!" he said with a facetious grin and put a lit cigarette between her lips. "Do I have something stuck on my face?" he asked next, out of the blue.

"What?"

"You were just staring at me weird."

"No, I wasn't!" she stammered in protest and quickly looked away before Rafael could notice her cheeks redden. To Faustine, the blue and the gold of his eyes were like water and fire, two clashing elements, each one in control of a part of him. His gaze was a powerful and bewitching weapon. No matter how hard she tried to avoid it, she was inescapably drawn to his eyes.

"OK now, my turn!" he said with a laugh.

Without waiting for an answer, Rafael tensed his muscles and lunged upward to grasp a hold several feet over his head, just above the lip of the overhang. His feet dangled in the air for an instant until his left foot found a miniature ledge to rest upon. He probed the tiny protrusions of the cliff with the tip of his bandaged fingers and swung his body over the lip to recover his balance. Next, he exhaled and looked at the limestone slab towering over him. He was already anticipating the logical sequence of fluid moves that would bring him closer to the top. By the time Faustine had threaded the rope through her belay device and clipped it the proper way onto her harness, Rafael was already twenty feet above the overhang. He placed a quick draw, a short sling with a carabiner clipped to each end, through a steel bolt to his left and gathered slack from the rope, so as to hook it through the snap gate of the carabiner.

"Hey, Rafa! If you'd rather solo climb, just say the word, 'kay?" Faustine said matter-of-factly, exhaling a cloud of smoke toward the sky.

As much as she refused to admit it, Faustine never tired of watching Rafael climb. He was a man who understood the language of the stone. He would run his fingers across the rock as if reading in Braille to unlock its secrets with disarming ease. Watching him negotiate a difficult passage was like admiring a ballet dancer performing on stage. Every move he made was calculated and excruciatingly precise. Yet, his climb seemed effortless and graceful. Rafael constantly defied the laws of gravity. It was as if they simply did not apply to him.

While she paid out rope from the relative safety of the trail, Faustine's mind began to wander. Before long, she was daydreaming about the series of events that had brought her to the mountain with the object of her obsession, Rafael.

04:30 PM ~ Monday, January 3, 1994

Faustine would never forget the day when Rafael first came to *La Goutte d'Eau,* meaning "The Water Drop" in English. It was just a few days after New Year's Eve. *La Goutte,* as people called it for short, was a commune of ecological activists. Aside from the occasional visits from die-hard mountain climbers who would temporarily pick this area as their winter playground, La Goutte usually remained rather empty during that time of the year. As a consequence, Rafael's arrival created quite a commotion within the resident community, and amongst the ladies in particular. As for the men, they were thrilled to welcome another green warrior in their ranks.

That first night, they all gathered around the fireplace in the communal room in order to listen to the tale of the handsome traveler, who introduced himself to them as Rafael Vargas.

For young Faustine, it was love at first sight. Too shy to introduce herself at first, she stood at a respectable distance, stealing glances in his direction whenever he looked away. The sound of his voice, deep and slightly husky, tantalized her at once, not to mention his exotic Spanish accent which, to her, was downright sexy. He impressed her with the way he carried himself. He stood tall and proud among a crowd of complete strangers. Undeniably, he was a charismatic outsider who moved around with the deliberate swiftness of a stray cat.

The whole month of January brought nothing but miserable weather. The non-stop snow and sleet forced everyone to remain confined inside for days. Rafael was already staying at La Goutte d'Eau for five days when he finally spoke to Faustine. They got along immediately, and soon picked up the habit of talking every night after dinner. Oftentimes, other residents joined them by the fireplace to listen to Rafael as he told tales of epic mountain expeditions led by the select few alpinists he admired. Before long, Faustine became fascinated with this brave world of mountaineering.

One morning toward the end of January, when the wind finally died down for the first time in weeks and a timid sun was peeking through the clouds, Rafael decided to put an end to their serious case of cabin fever. That day, he convinced Faustine to try rock climbing for the very first time.

Faustine met Rafael by his car, a rusty powder blue Renault "4L" that had seen better days. They drove in silence the few kilometers that separated La Goutte d'Eau from the sleepy village of Etsaut with its steep narrow stone streets. From there, they followed an asphalt road for about another mile until they reached the beginning of a withering path. As soon as they got out of the car, Rafael pointed to a wooden sign that read CHEMIN DE LA MATURE in large green block letters and declared matter-of-factly,

"From this point on, we'll walk."

Faustine followed him along the icy trail, desperate to think of something clever to say. Rafael could sense her awkwardness, but, much to his surprise, he was not able to do much to put her at ease. She unlocked a storm of feelings in his mind and heart, and, clearly, he was at a loss as to how to deal with this torrent of emotion. Faustine was not bothered by the long silences between them, for she already understood that Rafael valued his solitude and quiet immensely. Still, something else made her feel uneasy. Faustine possessed a gift for reading people's thoughts. Yet, as she stared at the back of his head while they trudged along the trail, she only picked up signals that were as informative as a test pattern on a television set. Everything about Rafael seemed enveloped in a thick shroud of secrecy, almost as if he was not real.

Faustine and Rafael had been walking for half an hour when they reached a narrow point along the slippery path skirting a near-vertical abyss to their right.

"This place gives me the creeps!" Faustine said, as she pointed a finger toward the foreboding structure of the Fort looming across the precipitous canyon.

"Did you know that Marshal Philippe Pétain, the French Chief of State during the Vichy regime, was imprisoned there after World War II ended?"

"No, I didn't," she replied meekly.

"He said that Fort du Portalet was such a depressing place that, had there been no bars on the window of his cell, he would have thrown himself into the river below."

"How do you know all these things?"

"I'm just curious, I guess. I like to know things about the places I come to visit."

"You haven't even been here a month and you already know this valley like the back of your hand!" she commented admiringly. "It's like you know every single cliff and mountain trail around here."

Rafael modestly dismissed her comment with a shrug and pointed to the crag over their heads instead.

"I think this course has your name written all over it," he said with a wink.

Faustine sized up the vertical face with overt skepticism. Threatening patches of glistening ice clung onto the rock in places, and cracks and ledges were covered in snow.

"Right," she laughed carefully, "you're so funny." Nevertheless, one look into his mesmerizing eyes was all it took for Faustine to realize that he could not have been more serious. "You want me to climb—that?"

"Uh-huh! Don't worry. Piece o' cake!"

"Yeah, right."

Rafael opened his backpack and retrieved a long purple climbing rope, two harnesses and a faded blue nylon sling holding a wide assortment of carabiners and other strange contraptions. To Faustine, they all looked like twisted torture devices. She stared at the gear spread before her with apprehension. Rafael was quick to notice that she was out of her element and jumped to the rescue.

"Let me give you a hand," he said.

Their bodies were so close during that fleeting moment. Faustine repressed a gasp when she felt Rafael's fingers grazing her skin as he adjusted the leg-straps of her harness for a snug fit. There was no denying the sexual tension between them, even though they did their very best to pretend it was not there. He unclipped a carabiner from the sling with a figure eight-shaped metal device attached to it, locked it in place onto her harness' front strap and quickly stepped away from her, purposefully avoiding her gaze. Suddenly, feeling awkward, he cleared his throat and started ranting about safe belaying techniques as an abrupt means to defuse the unnerving situation.

Next, Rafael pulled out a pair of bright blue-and-yellow suede climbing shoes from his backpack and spat on the black rubber sole of the first one. He rubbed the spit onto it until it squeaked under the pressure of his hand. He did the same thing to the other shoe and tied them on to his feet. Faustine admired Rafael's obvious expertise as she watched him getting ready for the climb. At last, he tied one end of the rope to his harness with a bowline knot and then weaved it into Faustine's figure-eight belay device.

"I'm ready when you are, Rookie!" he announced in high spirits.

"Whoa, hold on! I think I've figured out how to work this belay thing, but I don't think that you should trust me with it just yet."

"There's only one way to find out, I guess!"

"Wait! What?"

Faustine held her breath as she watched the rope sliding at a fast pace through the ring of her belay device. When Rafael clipped the rope to the first anchor-point bolted to the rock, he called down to her,

"You can reel the excess slack in now; not too tight, though!"

"OK!" She hesitated for a second, not too sure of what he meant. Faustine watched him with mounting panic as he climbed past a second bolt to his left and, again, as he ignored a third one. "Rafa! You forgot to clip your rope!" she shouted at Rafael, who did not seem to care at all.

He was dangerously high above the last safety protection point when she heard him scream,

"LOCK ME OFF!"

Rafael propelled himself away from the cliff. Faustine tried to reel in as much slack on the rope as she could, but it was a waste of effort. She felt his body mass swoosh past her at massive speed while she held onto the rope with all her might. Pulled upward by a tremendous force as the rope tensed up to stop Rafael's fall, her feet lifted off the ground, and she soon found herself plastered against the frigid rock. Her legs dangled a few feet above the trail in the air. Her figure-eight device was jammed tight against the anchor points and she was still clutching the rope with both hands.

"Rafael? Are you there?" she asked in a choked up voice, too scared to look down just yet.

Rafael's excited shout came from below. "Wow, that was a scream-er! Must have been a 'forty-footer,' at least!"

Faustine's heart felt like it was about to leap out of her chest when she forced herself to look over the edge of the cliff. To her surprise, Rafael was already speed-climbing the wall like a spider. In no time, he was back by her side, slapping the snow off his pants, grinning as if nothing had happened.

"Don't—tell me that you fell on purpose," she stammered, still petrified with fear.

Rafael started laughing. "Why not?"

"You're a fuckin' idiot!" Faustine yelled before she struck him fair and square in the chest.

"Ouch! Easy, *amiga!*" he replied, now roaring with laughter, his arms wrapped around his torso in a mock protective stance.

"I could have killed you!" Fresh tears welled up in the corner of Faustine's eyes. Rafael stopped laughing at once.

"I didn't mean to scare you like that." Without thinking, he wrapped his arms around Faustine to comfort her. "Please don't cry. I'm sorry," he added in a half-whisper. Suddenly, Faustine could no longer tell whether the butterflies in her stomach were soaring because of her recent scare or because she could feel his heartbeat so close to her skin. "You must never be afraid of falling," he continued with a soothing, yet firm, voice. "Falling is an integral part of the whole learning process. The more you push yourself, the more you'll fall, but also, the better you'll get. It's when the fear of falling takes over that you can't progress anymore." Faustine nodded her understanding vigorously, even though she was too distracted to clearly register what he was saying. "In the end, it all boils down to trust. Trust in your gear and most important of all, trust in your partner. Once you've established that trust, you can concentrate on what's important, which is the climb at hand."

"I get it," she said in a small voice, "still, you could have given me a heads-up. I almost had a heart attack!"

"I know," he replied with a frank smile, "but for what it's worth, now I know that I can trust you with my life."

They remained silent for an instant, oblivious to the snowflake-sprinkled breeze stinging the side of their faces, reluctant to break their embrace. Faustine felt faint as she hoped for a kiss that never came. Instead, Rafael pulled away unexpectedly. For the second time that day, they looked away from each other, and both felt confused and ill at ease again. As she was struggling to cover up her disappointment, Faustine tilted her chin toward the cliff and announced in a defiant tone,

"So, are you going to install that 'top rope' for me, or are you taking root?"

Faustine's fingers were shaking when she tied the climbing rope into her harness for the very first time.

"Are you sure you're ready for this?" Rafael asked her out of the blue.

"Why?" she replied in alarm.

"Once you experience the high, it becomes an addiction that's tough to kick!"

"So I hear."

She clamped her hand onto the first hold above her head and pulled herself off the ground with stubborn determination. Before she knew it, she reached the top of the pitch. Rafael must have known what he was talking about when he recited his disclaimer to her moments earlier. Never mind the frozen fingers; climbing that one course was all it took. Faustine was hooked.

Acting as if the "near-kiss-incident" had not occurred, they went about their afternoon and climbed until Faustine's arms and legs were just too tired and numb. With their attraction hidden deep and their bodies exhausted from the climb, Faustine and Rafael silently packed up their gear and retraced their steps along the frozen path of La Mâture.

3
-HIRU-

Summer of 1993

Faustine Laroche and her mother Vivienne had come to the Vallée d'Aspe seven months prior to Rafael's arrival. They met with other activists from all over Europe to protest the excavation of a five-mile long tunnel under the Pyrenees, the ever controversial "Tunnel du Somport."

Back in 1988, the European Commission in Brussels had approved the construction of a large tunnel under the Somport Mountain. This was a project within the larger construction scheme of a trans-European highway called the *Axe E7*. Spain had recently joined the European Community, and, as a result, generous budgets had been approved in order to reinforce its economic ties with the rest of Europe. Inherent to the construction of the tunnel, the resolution also called for the upgrading of RN-134 to be turned into a wider and safer road. Until now, RN-134 had been a beautiful, but dangerous, two-lane mountain road that meandered through the Vallée d'Aspe toward Spain, via the Somport pass. If, or rather when, the project would come to completion, the valley would become a traffic bottleneck due to the ever-increasing number of trucks favoring that itinerary over existing roads. Not only would the whole area suffer from the irreversible effects of pollution, but the *Axe E7* junction would sever in half the homeland of the last five Pyrenean bears alive in France.

The reaction was immediate and passionate because the valley was home to many species on the brink of extinction. Large environmental groups, such as Greenpeace and the World Wildlife Federation, along with the French Communist and Green parties, joined forces to create the *Collectif Alternatives Pyrenéennes à l'axe Européen E7* (CAP) in retaliation. The CAP's collective goal was twofold. Its members wanted to protect the valley's wildlife and secondly, they hoped to find a viable economic alternative to the road and the tunnel. Therefore, they lobbied for the reopening of the, then-abandoned, Pau-Canfranc rail line.

Amidst all the political, economic and ecological mayhem, emerged a man whose name would forever be linked to the Somport tragic saga. He went by the nickname of "the Indian" after his habit of wearing a vulture's feather in his hair.

The Indian, a former student in Political Science at the University of Bordeaux in France, first came to the Béarn region as a conscientious objector in the 1980s. One year of military service was still mandatory in France. People opposed to joining the army were required to serve a two-year term in the civil service instead. The Indian had opted for the latter. He quickly fell in love with the valley and decided to settle down there.

With a handful of mountain guides and hang-gliding instructors, he renovated an unused train station in the tiny village of Cette-Eygun, located in the heart of the Vallée d'Aspe. The train station had been abandoned since March of 1970, after a train carrying a load of corn had derailed on the Pau-Canfranc line and destroyed the bridge of Estanguet in the process. The French railway company deemed the repairs too exorbitant for a line that was not profitable at the time, and opted to close it down forever. The Indian and his friends christened the train station "La Goutte d'Eau." The word quickly spread beyond the valley.

La Goutte became a gathering place where visitors and climbers alike could meet knowledgeable mountain guides, set up camp in the backyard of the train station and enjoy a good time, with a glass of beer and a plate of delicious *tapas* served at the bar. Eventually, tensions grew between the Indian and the original founders of La Goutte. As a result, many of them distanced themselves from the project, until only the Indian remained. Still, new people moved in to keep the place going.

At the turn of the 1990s, it was obvious that La Goutte had become a stronghold of rebellion against the construction of the Somport tunnel. The Indian, backed by a handful of environmental activists who took residence within the walls of the train station, decided to take the reigns of the valley's active resistance. The building became their headquarters; a self-governing place where people of all backgrounds were welcome to stay and fight for the cause.

Just like that, La Goutte d'Eau had morphed into a bastion of unrelenting opposition against the capitalist system its residents despised. This was a place where everyone valued the quality of life and preservation of nature, a place that strongly opposed the notion of productivity for profit.

Around that time, Faustine's mother, Vivienne, who had been living with her Italian boyfriend, Massimo, in Copenhagen, Denmark, heard of the situation in the Pyrenees and decided to combine ecological activism with a well-deserved holiday in the South of France.

It was the summer of 1993.

Their camper, a battered 1979 Volkswagen, survived the stress of another long road trip and found its final resting place in Cette-Eygun on a warm evening of June. The tight-knit commune accepted them with open arms, and by September, the summer pit-stop became permanent. All three decided to stay in order to lend the Indian and his growing tribe of *Aspaches* (the residents had coined the term, a self-referencing nickname, as a tongue-in-cheek reference to both the Apache Indian tribe and the word *Aspois*, meaning "resident of the Vallée d'Aspe") a hand in the fight against the tunnel.

The way of life at La Goutte d'Eau was a somewhat strange combination: at times, serene, and at times, hectic. Very few people owned an alarm clock, but everyone arose to do their chores. The Aspaches grew vegetables in a well-tended garden. A few hens provided fresh eggs in the morning. The commune maintained a campground along the banks of the Gave d'Aspe, as well as an old train car. The wagon was converted into living quarters for visitors. Everyone was expected to share the workload and to live in harmony with each other and with nature.

People met. They fell in and out of love, and babies were born. Some would leave, and others would take their place. Ecologists, bohemians, artists, alpinists, outcasts, adventurers, squatters and travelers comprised the backbone of this parallel society. There was drama, tragedy and dire disappointment. There were also victories and milestones to celebrate, not to mention a great deal of memorable parties.

As far as its political affairs were concerned, La Goutte was buzzing with activity. The Aspaches kept track of donations sent from all over France and abroad to help finance the resistance. They wrote pamphlets and articles to keep the public informed. More often than not however, the collective lacked time and resources to create the impact they wanted.

Rallying under Dolores "La Pasionaria" Ibárruri's famous battle cry ¡NO PASARAN!, they coordinated peaceful sit-ins where people of all ages would lie down in great numbers across the road to prevent trucks from getting to the construction site. Often, the Indian would pick up his guitar and get everyone to sing and dance right there in front of the machines. The eclectic horde, led by this modern-day Robin Hood, also organized raids in the middle of the night to sabotage machinery at the Somport site. While it could not be denied that they relied on random acts of vandalism to carry out their mission, they never resorted to violence against human beings. Needless to say, encounters between Aspaches and the police force were commonplace. Many a militant, the Indian in particular, had paid a hefty price for political activism and spent time in jail as a result of their hands-on desire to protect the future of the valley.

Still, in spite of everyone's efforts, the construction of the tunnel entrance was well underway, and plans to start the actual excavation had been slated for the second quarter of 1994. They were fighting a lost battle, but the Aspaches refused to give up.

By that time, Vivienne had already broken up with Massimo and moved inside the train station with her new and much younger boyfriend, Etienne. Massimo, unfazed by the situation, had promptly hooked up with another resident of La Goutte and settled in with his new lover in the bedroom adjacent to Vivienne and Etienne's. As a result of this game of sexual musical chairs, Faustine had become the proud owner of her very first dwelling, her mother's green VW camper. The half-gutted van was slowly rusting away in peace atop four cinder blocks, sandwiched between a beautiful cascading river and thick tufts of wild grass poking through rusting train-tracks.

For the first time in her bohemian life, not only had Faustine returned to her homeland, but she really felt, at long last, she had found a place to call home.

The Aspaches became family. She fought for the cause with all the enthusiasm and rebelliousness inherent to her age. She was fulfilled at last.

Then Rafael arrived, if only to make her realize that there was a lot more in life to lust for than what she already had.

4
-LAU-

06:17 PM ~ Thursday, March 24, 1994

Back in Rafael's car, Faustine lowered the sun visor to take a quick look at her face. Somehow, she wanted to see whether her facial expressions showed her true feelings for Rafael, a love that seemed unrequited, a love that seemed to condemn her to the mere memory of a few exciting seconds during a climb. To her surprise, instead of a mirror, she saw a large bumper sticker that read: *BESTAK BAI, BORROKA ERE BAI* in blood-red letters.

"What does it mean?" Faustine asked, as she pointed to the decal.

"I had no idea it was even there," Rafael replied, a genuine look of surprise on his face.

"But what does it say? I want to know!"

"It's Basque language. It means something along the lines of 'We party, but we must fight too.' Not sure what it stands for." Rafael seemed uncomfortable discussing the meaning of the slogan. "You know, I bought this car second-hand just before I came here. I didn't put it there."

"*Bestak bai, borroka ere bai,*" she repeated as she snapped the visor back in place. "I like the sound of it. It should become our motto from now on, *oui?*" Faustine pivoted her head sideways to face him, only to notice that he was staring at her intently. "What?" she blushed.

"Nothing. I'm just glad I met you," he replied a little too fast. The old Renault's engine coughed to life.

Faustine hoped to spend the evening in Rafael's company but as it turned out, he had already made other plans for the night. She tried her best not to let her disappointment show when he dropped her off at La Goutte d'Eau.

"Thanks for today, Rafa. I had a blast," she said.

"Ditto!"

"OK then. See you around later, I guess."

"Hey, Faustine?"

"Huh?"

"I'm very proud of you for climbing 'Playing Hooky' on sight today."

"Come on!" Faustine dismissed his comment with a wave. "It's not that big of a deal. You could climb it with your eyes closed!"

"Don't sell yourself short, *amiga!* I could have never done that course back when I was a beginner. You're a truly gifted climber. A natural."

"Thanks. Coming from you, it sure means a lot."

Faustine slung her backpack over her shoulder, waved him goodbye and hurried down the grassy path to her camper.

The lights were on inside the Volkswagen. A punk rock song was blaring from her old cassette tape player. The sliding door of the van opened without warning and came crashing against the stoppers of its rusty railing with a loud bang.

"Be nice to the door, for Christ's sake!" Faustine shouted from far away, wondering who might have intruded upon her home.

A young woman with a mischievous grin on her face jumped out of the gutted vehicle like a jack-in-the-box.

"SURPRISE!"

"Graziella? What the hell are you doing here?" Faustine broke into a sprint toward her. The two girlfriends kissed and hugged, giggling like prepubescent schoolgirls.

"Come on, let's get back in, it's freezing out here in the sticks!" Graziella let out a good-natured laugh and shoved her friend inside the van like she owned the place. "Seriously, someday you'll have to explain to me how you manage to live in this shit-hole!"

"Wow, I can't even believe you're here!"

"I hope you don't mind me spending the night with you. You and I have tons of stuff to talk about! Soooo, I figured we'd have a good ol' slumber party tonight, just the two of us. Whaddya say? Unless you're already expecting company later on," she added with a knowing wink.

"I have no idea what you're talking about!" replied Faustine, feigning surprise.

"Yeah, right! I've been here the whole day, waiting for you to show your pretty face! Too bad, girl, I already got all the 'intel' from your mother! She doesn't seem to like him much, which is a great sign in my opinion! Everyone else is gushing about the guy, though. So where is this stud, anyway?"

"He won't be around tonight. Don't get too excited, though. I don't know what you've heard, but we're just friends!"

"Uh-huh! Sure you are!"

"I swear!"

Graziella shot her one of her classic "Don't-you-bullshit-a-bullshitter" looks. "OK, sit tight for a second!" She disappeared to the front of the camper and came back with a bottle of cheap vodka, two plastic cups and five cigarettes of various brands that she had stolen earlier from packs lying around in the communal room. "Am I taking good care of you or what?" She unscrewed the bottle-cap and poured two stiff servings into the cups. She handed Faustine one and held the other in front of her before saying, "*Tchin-Tchin,* my friend!"

"Cheers, girl! It's good to see you!"

"Watch out, world," squealed Graziella. "It's party time in Faustine's van!"

Graziella was Massimo's only daughter, and she was the apple of his eye. She was a petite, curvy, (self-proclaimed) Italian princess with gorgeous olive skin and lustrous dark hair that was recently cut into a trendy asymmetrical bob. Forever true to her Latin origins, she was a talented drama queen who knew how to get what she wanted. Her father, in particular, found it hard to resist any of her caprices, due to the fact he had given into most of her eccentric requests since she was a toddler. Tantrums aside, no one could deny that Graziella had a heart of gold and a great sense of humor. She had grown up in a posh countryside house near the town of Nice at the Côte d'Azur, back when her father was a VP of marketing for a successful Italian clothing brand. Her parents separated when she was twelve. Massimo never took the breakup well. He suffered a nervous breakdown soon after his divorce, resigned from his position and decided to travel the world. He knocked about as far as India, New Zealand and a few other countries in-between when he decided to head back to Europe. In Copenhagen, he met Vivienne and reconnected with his daughter. In the meantime, Graziella turned out to be a gifted student. She graduated high school with honors at seventeen and enrolled in the University of Nice to study biology in the fall of 1993.

"So, tell me. Aren't you supposed to be at university?" asked Faustine.

"I'm just here for a few days. Actually, I had a big fight with Mom on Tuesday, so I figured I'd go pay Dad a visit. The good news is that I won't have to see her psycho face for the next three days, plus it'll piss her off to no end when she finds out that I came here, of all places!"

"I envy you." Faustine let out a sigh. "Sometimes, I wish I had your life; going to university and all that—"

"What for?"

"Well, duh! To get an education! To become smarter!"

"A diploma's just a piece of paper to frame and hang up on your wall. It's not a seal of intelligence! When you see the morons that have made it all the way to university, it makes you wonder sometimes. Come on, you don't need a freakin' diploma to be cultured! Take a good look at you, for example. You learn things your own way! Don't you realize how lucky you are?"

"Lucky? Hardly! Just go and ask anyone around here what they think of people like me! 'Lucky' is not the word you'll hear!"

"At least you weren't raised in a petri-dish like the rest of us!"

"But society despises people like me because we don't fit the mold."

"Do you want to fit the mold?"

"I guess not. Still, I don't want to live like an outcast either."

"Out there, you always need to prove yourself, diploma in hand or not. It doesn't matter how educated or successful you are, people will always judge you, either by the money you make, the kind of clothes you wear or the people you hang out with. Trust me, you're better off here. None of that shit matters at La Goutte."

"But I don't intend to stay here for the rest of my life!" Faustine replied with indignation.

"Amen to that! You're too pretty to be a hippie anyway!"

"I'm not a—"

"I'm just messing with you, girl!" Graziella interrupted. "Listen, you've got nothing to worry about. You're going to be just fine."

Faustine valued Graziella's friendship a great deal. Not only because she did not have too many friends her age to start with, but also because she was by far the most "normal" person she had ever known. Graziella, on the other hand, loved Faustine for the exact opposite reasons. Faustine was a bohemian soul who could call twelve countries home, a young woman who had been raised with few rules to follow. In Graziella's eyes, her friend was a quintessential free spirit, the poster-child for unconventional living. Although they enjoyed each other's company, Faustine knew that Graziella would tire of the bare-bones lifestyle at La Goutte in no time. Still, Faustine was determined to enjoy every minute of Graziella's stay, no matter how short it may be.

"OK, so tell me, have you made out with him at least?" Graziella asked out of the blue. She had just polished off her second vodka and was slurring her words a little.

"No! I told you, it's nothing like that. We rock climb together and stuff, but that's about it."

"Rock climbing, huh? Jeez, honey, you're so naïve! What do you expect from the guy? A banner that reads: 'Let's fuck?' It's obvious that he's totally into you. So, what are you waiting for?"

Faustine felt her cheeks burn red hot. Graziella's legendary bluntness toward all things sexual had always made her laugh hysterically, but she knew nothing about desire back then. This time around, however, Graziella succeeded in making her blush. In fact, her statement left her tingling all over. She could not allow her friend to see that or she would never hear the end of it.

"He's new around here, you know?" she said, trying her best to act blasé about the whole thing. "He doesn't know anyone aside from us here. He—"

"Oh, really?" Graziella interrupted again, "who is he hanging out with tonight, then?"

"I don't know! Why don't you give me a break? He and I, we're just friends, OK? He's got the right to see whomever he wants, whenever he wants to!"

"Whoa, easy tiger! Just friends, huh? Well, if that's all there is to it, I guess you won't mind if I go after him? I mean, it's open season then, right?" Graziella smacked her lips together and gave Faustine a lewd look. "I hear the guy is smokin' hot!"

"How dare you!" Faustine blurted out in spite of her best efforts to keep her emotions under wraps.

Graziella looked dead serious. Then, slowly, her pursed lips stretched into a grin. When she could no longer hold her stance, she threw her head back and roared with laughter.

"Look at you! I just knew you were in love with him!"

Faustine gave her a friendly kick in the leg to shut her up. "OK, so what if I am?" she said at last.

"I think it's awesome! I've never seen you like this before! So, what are you going to do about it?"

"I really don't know." Faustine hugged her pillow a little tighter. "I just can't figure him out."

"Don't think too much, silly! Guys aren't like us. They're pretty straightforward when it comes to this stuff."

"Not this one. What makes me crazy is that I can totally tell that he wants me, but it's like he's scared to commit to anything, even to a stupid kiss!"

"Hmmm."

"And it's not just that," Faustine vented on, "I don't know what to make of his constant vanishing acts, either." She snapped her fingers in the air. "*Poof!* Just like that, he'll disappear for days at a time, and when he comes back, he acts as if he just stepped out to buy a freaking pack of smokes!"

"And he doesn't give you any explanation?"

"Well, I'm not exactly his mother. See, the weird thing is that he doesn't even make up lies or anything. He just says that he 'had to take care of something,' whatever that means."

"Hmmm," Graziella said again pensively.

"I have no clue where he goes, but I know for a fact that he drives around, judging by the way the kilometers keep piling up on his car odometer."

"Wow, you've been spying on him?" she asked, her eyes sparkling.

"No! Of course, not! I just noticed, that's all. Graz, I don't know what's up with him. Usually, I'm pretty good at figuring people out, but not this guy. He's just odd."

"It's funny that you would say that, because that's almost word for word what your mother told me earlier."

"So what do you think I should do?" Faustine pleaded.

Graziella leaned over and gave her friend a hug.

"Follow your heart, girl, follow your heart."

10:25 AM ~ Friday, March 25, 1994

Faustine woke up the next day with a nasty hangover and a churning stomach. She roused Graziella who was snoring top-to-tail, only to find out that she was not faring much better.

Moving like zombies, they put the clothes from yesterday back on and walked outside toward the main building to fix breakfast in the communal kitchen. It was a damp, cold morning, and the sun was nowhere to be seen. Even the mountains around La Goutte seemed to have disappeared, blanketed by a thick shroud of clouds.

There were a few people moving about the house already, and a welcoming fire was burning strong at the far corner of the room.

"Good morning, ladies!" exclaimed Massimo. He was standing in front of the stove in his grey corduroy robe and appeared to be in a fine mood. He was even singing an Italian pop song off-key. As luck would have it, he was preparing the morning coffee. One could always rely on Massimo's savoir-faire to make a strong and flavorful cup of java. And that was just what the girls needed. *"Mama Mia!"* he said, looking at his offspring, "I wish someone had invited me to the party! Where did you two go last night?"

"Nowhere," moaned Graziella. He leaned over and gave both of them a good-morning kiss on the cheek. "We stayed in, but we drank a bit too much."

"I'll say!"

They looked for something edible on the pantry shelves. Faustine brought two bowls and an oversized box of corn flakes over to the table. Then she opened the fridge and peeked inside.

"Crap. We're out of milk again!"

She grabbed a bottle of orange juice instead and sat down on the bench. Graziella grimaced in disgust as she watched her friend pour fruit juice all over her cereal.

"What's your problem?" Faustine snarled with an unladylike grunt.

"OJ on corn flakes? Gross!"

"You've got a better idea? In case you didn't notice, this is not the Ritz!" she replied in aggravation.

"Whoa! Someone woke up on the wrong side of the bed this morning."

"Sorry, Graz. I just feel like shit, that's all."

"Well, that makes two of us," Graziella sighed. "Coffee?"

Faustine's fierce hangover was not the sole reason to account for her foul mood that day. As it turned out, Rafael had not come home last night.

After breakfast, Graziella plopped down onto one of the old couches in the living room and started reading a local newspaper she just picked up off the floor.

"Great," she muttered upon hearing the first drops of rain hit the glass windows, "nothing's more fun than camping in the rain."

More people came running through the door as the storm gained intensity outside. They were carrying cardboard boxes full of materials to make banners and signs.

"Morning, Graziella. Hey Faustine! Great day, huh?" Etienne said, sticking a finger in his mouth, pretending to make himself throw up.

Etienne was twenty-six years old. He was tall and reasonably fit, save for a budding beer belly getting comfortable over the waistband of his jeans. His light brown hair was braided in short dreadlocks, and his eyes, framed by deep crow's feet, seemed to be laughing all the time. He was usually mellow and calm, which made all the sense in the world given the impressive amount of skunk weed he smoked any given day.

"Where's Ma?" asked Faustine.

"Viv? She's sleeping in upstairs, I think." He dropped a bag full of spray paint canisters on top of the bar and nodded toward Graziella. "Hey, Graz, you're coming with us to the protest on Sunday, yeah?"

"Hmmm, I heard people talking about it," she replied. "What is it about, exactly?"

"We got wind that a delegation of political figures and construction companies' representatives are expected in Pau this Sunday for a public meeting. They're going to announce the launch date for the actual excavation of the tunnel to the public and media."

"Wow! Do they have a date already?"

"April 1st," he replied with a smirk of disgust. "April Fools' Day is definitely going to live up to its name this year."

"Jeez, Etienne, what a bummer!"

"The CAP called for a march in the streets of Pau. All of us at La Goutte are going to attend the public meeting in silent protest. We'll be there, rain or shine. You should come too," he added before he disappeared into the kitchen.

"Don't you find it weird that even though your mother is going out with Etienne, and my Dad's with the Danish girl, they still manage to live together under the same roof?" Graziella whispered into Faustine's ear as soon as Etienne was out of earshot.

"Don't get me started."

"Do you want to hear my theory? I think that my Dad sticks around only because he knows that Etienne's just a fling for your Mom. Sooner or later, Vivienne will get sick of his immaturity, and she'll go back to him in the end."

"You're probably right," Faustine replied distractedly.

"Hey, girlfriend!" Graziella shook her friend by the arm. "Get a grip! I'm sick of watching you stare out of the window with a long face, wondering why Prince Charming is still missing in action!"

"How do you know he hasn't come back?" Graziella did not bother to reply. She just shook her head from side to side. "I'm sorry," Faustine went on, "this is not like me, right? I just don't get it. I mean, aren't you supposed to feel all fuzzy and happy when you're in love?"

"Let me tell you something about love, girl. It's nothing but a freakin' pain in the wazoo!" Faustine could not help but chuckle at her friend's quip, which in turn caused Graziella to laugh with her. "He's quite something that guy, isn't he?" she murmured at last. Faustine's smile disappeared as quickly as it had come.

"I wouldn't know. And quite frankly, at this point, I just don't care."

Graziella flashed a mysterious smile at her and went back to reading her paper without saying another word.

When eleven o'clock struck, Faustine reluctantly decided to get on with her day.

"I'm going to take a shower," she said to no one in particular. She got up from her chair, her spirits at an all time low.

"I'll be right here," replied Graziella without lifting her eyes from her paper. "I told the guys I'd help them paint the signs."

Outside, the rainstorm had slowed down in intensity, but it showed no sign of stopping any time soon. The whole day turned out to be quite a miserable one. Then, dinner came and went. Still, Rafael had not returned.

07:25 PM ~ Saturday, March 26, 1994

On the second day of Rafael's absence, the rain was still falling.

Graziella could not take the dreary weather for another minute and asked Massimo to drive her back to the train station in Pau. With her friend gone, Faustine felt demoralized. She lay down on her old mattress, hands folded beneath her head, as she tried to make sense of the frustrating game of cat and mouse that Rafael and she had been playing for the past two months.

So what if their personalities were different on so many levels? They complemented each other just fine. The chemistry between them was obvious. What was the purpose of Rafael's recurrent disappearances? Was there another woman in his life? Curiosity was eating her alive. So was jealousy. Needless to say, the thought of asking him point blank where the two of them stood had crossed her mind more than once. Yet, every time she would stare into his eyes, her quaking heart would cause her throat to clench shut, and she would lose her courage altogether.

In truth, Faustine was so afraid that he might not return her feelings that she would rather keep things the way they were.

The knock at the door startled her. She jumped off her bed and peeked through the side window. Rafael was outside, blowing into his cupped hands to keep them warm against the cold rain.

"Damn!" she muttered under her breath. A swarm of butterflies stirred up at once from the pit of her stomach. She glanced at the mirror. She wore a faded promotional T-shirt, advertising a popular brand of rum, over a shabby pair of jeans. She was barefoot, and to top it all off, her disheveled hair looked like a rat's nest. "Shit! Shit! Shit!" she cursed between clenched teeth.

Outside, Rafael had turned around and was walking away.

"Wait!" she shouted after him.

Rafael stopped dead in his tracks and craned his neck around in time to see Faustine open the camper door.

"Sorry," he said over the icy wind, "I didn't mean to disturb you. I'll come back another—"

"Not at all!" she interrupted, waving him over. "Come on in!" Rafael followed her inside the Volkswagen. "Never mind the mess. I don't get too many visitors, you know." She pushed the covers over her bed in haste and invited him to sit down on the edge of the mattress. She backed away from him and crossed her arms against her chest. "Can I get you something? I mean, I don't have much, but—"

"Oh, please, no! I won't stay long anyway. I'm dead tired, and I don't feel too good. I just wanted to stop by and say hi."

"How nice of you," Faustine managed to reply, her nerves wound up more tightly than the strings of a fiddle.

"Are you all right?"

"What do you think?" she blurted out without warning. "You've been gone two nights and two days, although you told me on Thursday you would just be gone for the night! So, yeah, I've been worrying about you! Other than that, I'm swell, thanks." No matter how hard she tried to keep a straight face, she was feeling the unwelcome prick of tears welling up in her eyes.

"Hey, hey! Come over here, *amiga*." Faustine hesitated, so Rafael got up and approached her instead. He brushed a stray lock of hair away from her face as he confided to her, "I'm not used to people worrying about me. I'm sorry if I upset you. That's the last thing I'd want to do to you."

Faustine would not give in to tears. She slithered away from him and out of the light.

"Apology accepted, Rafael," she spoke with her back to him. "Listen, I don't care to know where you go, or why you feel the need to disappear all the time. All I'm asking of you is a little more accuracy when it comes to the overall duration of your trips. That way, I won't have to sit around, wondering whether you got run over by a car or something."

She felt Rafael's presence right behind her, yet he did not attempt to touch her.

"Thank you, Faustine," he murmured at last. "Thank you for letting me be."

She turned around to face him with a brave smile.

"You haven't forgotten about the protest tomorrow, have you?"

"Of course not. I'll have the car fueled and ready to go. Whatever you ask me to do, I'll do it for you."

"You should not be doing it for me, Rafael," she replied in a half-whisper. "Remember, you came to La Goutte d'Eau for two reasons: to fight the tunnel and to save the bears."

Rafael turned his gaze to the ground. He looked tense, uncomfortable and almost desperate all of a sudden. Faustine realized, with intense clarity, there was more to Rafael's silences than she had ever imagined.

December 1993

Rafael Vargas was born Lorenzo Lartaun Izcoa twenty-three years earlier in the spring of 1970, back when Spain was still under General Franco's dictatorship. He was born in Irun, an industrial city in the Basque country, also called *Euskadi*. It was a tiny, yet rich stretch of land in the Northwestern part of the Iberian Peninsula with the status of an autonomous community. Irun was right on the Spanish border, just across the Bidasoa River from the small seaside town of Hendaye, France. His mother tongue was Spanish, but he was also fluent in French, albeit with a thick Spanish accent. When he was a kid, his grandmother also taught him *Euskara* on the sly. *Euskara* was the language of the Basque people since time immemorial. It was the last remaining pre-Indo-European idiom in the whole of Europe, which was banned from schools for decades by Franco to oppress the Basques and to annihilate their ancestral culture and traditions.

Truth be told, Lartaun had been a fugitive hiding in Mexico for almost two years. He had no choice but to leave his family and friends behind one dire night in early January of 1992 after finding out that the Spanish authorities extended an international warrant for his arrest, for a crime he did not even commit. He fled in the hold of a cargo ship from Brittany, France to the Mexican province of Quintana Roo. As soon as he reached the Mexican shores, he met with fellow Basque exiles. They took him under their wing, and he lived among them in an ethereal Spanish colonial town nestled in a basin of rolling highlands that went by the name of San Cristóbal De Las Casas, in the remote mountainous province of Chiapas.

During those long months of forced exile, Lartaun was not able to contact his family for fear the police would trace their correspondence and track him down across the Americas. Instead, he relied on his childhood friend, Patxi, to be his liaison with his past. Patxi was a separatist activist whose friends were well-connected within the clandestine network of Basque refugees in Central and South America. Whenever possible, Patxi would manage to smuggle little packages filled with news clippings, music and treats via the well-established underground postal service running between *Euskadi* and Mexico. That was how Lartaun stayed abreast of the social and political state of affairs in *Euskal Herria*, "the country of those who speak the Basque language." Patxi's bundles were a godsend to appease Lartaun's heart-wrenching *herrimina*, "homesickness," at least for a brief instant. Still, he could hardly stand his life as the forced separation from his mother and sisters was a constant, abominable form of torture that would kill him eventually.

As a year stretched by, Patxi's parcels became few and far between. It was not long before Lartaun suspected that his friend might have gotten into a bad fix of his own. Lartaun was only too aware of the risks his old friend had taken just to keep in touch with him. When the "Patxi communication network" flat-lined altogether in August of 1993, Lartaun lost all contact with the outside world. The ensuing silence lasted for four months. Lartaun did not hear again from Patxi or anyone else until the beginning of December of 1993.

One evening, a young Mayan Indian came knocking at Lartaun's door. He had been paid a peso to hand-deliver a letter from his friend, in which Patxi stated that he wanted Lartaun to meet with a man named Iñaki. Lartaun complied with his friend's wishes. The two men had met near San Cristóbal De Las Casas in a fierce independent Tzotzil-speaking Mayan town called San Juan Chamula. Iñaki, on behalf of Patxi, had come to offer Lartaun a deal. He informed Lartaun that Patxi was planning an *ekintza*, a "secret operation," in the south of France that coming summer. Patxi needed someone, on location, to do some intelligence on his behalf, and, later on, to find a safe cache to hide something in the mountains. Iñaki went on, adding that the job would be easy and Lartaun's involvement in the overall mission would be minimal. In exchange for his services, Patxi was offering his old friend a one-time chance to start his life over with a clean slate. He would get him a French passport, complete with a brand new identity so that Lartaun could go home a free man before the year was over. Against his better judgment, Lartaun accepted the offer and took delivery of his passport a few days later in Mexico City.

He landed at Paris Charles de Gaulle airport on December 24 with a tattered duffel bag slung across his shoulder. The officer who stamped his passport wished him a Merry Christmas before he let him go through customs.

Rafael Vargas had made it to France without incident.

The last day of 1993 came and went amidst a cacophony of firecrackers and champagne corks in *Iparralde,* the "French side of the Basque country," a picture-perfect area between the Pyrenean chain to the south and the Atlantic coast to the west.

Lartaun's loyal friend, Bixente, had arranged for him to stay at a house nestled atop a bluff overlooking the seashore just outside the city limits of Biarritz, a beautiful seaside town better known as the "Surf Mecca" of France, so that he could lay low and get his bearings while waiting for Patxi's instructions.

Everyone who spent the night at the house was still snoring with abandon. The New Year's Eve party had raged on well past sunrise, with a steady stream of alcohol flowing all night like rain through gutters in a thunderstorm. If Lartaun, or rather Rafael, as he would call himself from now on, was waiting for a good reason to get out of bed before noon, he found none. He was savoring the moment and rejoicing in the simple pleasure of being back in the old country as he stretched his muscles, one by one, like a lazy geriatric cat.

The day before, Bixente had met Lartaun at the bar of a small hotel in Bayonne. On behalf of Patxi, he had briefed Lartaun on the details of his mission. Lartaun would leave Biarritz as soon as possible and move to the Béarn region of the Pyrenees chain. Bixente had given him specific directions to a once-abandoned building in a mountainous valley called the Vallée d'Aspe that had been taken over by a group of ecological militants. Its strategic location, on the road between the town

of Oloron-Sainte-Marie and the Somport pass, in addition to the unprej-
udiced state of mind of its cosmopolitan residents, made it the perfect
base camp for a covert operation. They had mutually agreed that Lartaun
would settle there under the pretense of being a green activist and await
Patxi's orders. When asked, Bixente had refused to disclose the nature of
the goods that Patxi was intending to steal. Lartaun had not insisted, for
it did not really matter any more at this point.

In truth, Lartaun did not foresee that he would have to fulfill his
side of the deal so soon. He just arrived home, and already he was being
sucked right back into the militant underworld which had caused him so
much grief in the first place. On the other hand, he found solace in the
fact that the sooner the *ekintza* would be over, the faster he could move
on with living his new life. Besides, even if the cliff house was geograph-
ically close to his hometown, it did not change the fact that he still could
not risk contacting his family for fear of blowing his cover in no time. In
fact, the proximity made him feel even worse, so much so that Lartaun
wondered what difference being back in Europe really made.

The good news was that leaving the cliff house would not be an
issue. Thankfully, the building was inhabited by transient surfers whose
interests in life revolved around the barreling waves of the Atlantic Ocean
and little else. In fact, they were so high half of the time that they might
not even notice or care that he was gone. His belongings, a few clothes
and an assortment of climbing gear that Bixente brought along per his
request, fit inside the trunk of the second-hand car he had purchased
three days earlier from a Basque surfer in desperate need of cash.

Although the thought of moving into a glorified campground
in the middle of winter and sharing amenities with a bunch of "granola
hippies" did not sound appealing in the least, Lartaun did not mind leaving his present accommodations. At least he would be in the Pyrenees.
This was a great consolation to him, because he always felt at home in
the mountains. Lartaun made up his mind. He would move to La Goutte
d'Eau within the next forty-eight hours.

"Six years to go until the year 2000," Lartaun mumbled to no
one. He wondered whether he would still be around to witness the dawn
of the new millennium.

As he lay sprawled across the mattress, he was oblivious to the
happenings taking place at that very moment. In fact, legions of Indian

rebels of the Zapatista National Liberation Army, led by an enigmatic and charismatic *guerillero* named Sub Commander Marcos, just began their uprising in the Mexican province of Chiapas, some five thousand and five hundred miles away from the Basque country.

Lartaun let out a deep sigh and said aloud,

"*Carpe diem.*"

10:30 AM ~ Sunday, March 27, 1994

Ever since the arrival of the first civil engineering company at the construction site, the general atmosphere in the Vallée d'Aspe had taken a turn for the worse. Tempers were flaring and skirmishes between "pro-tunnelers" and ecologists were commonplace. Meanwhile, the tunnel entrance was already complete. There was no stopping the process anymore. Opponents of the tunnel could only watch as truck after truck poured their loads of asphalt and concrete over the tender grass of the valley.

In spite of this, the Aspaches would not, could not admit defeat just yet. They had lost a decisive battle, but in their eyes, the war was far from over.

"Are you all right back there?" Rafael shot a glance in his rearview mirror. Four people had managed to squeeze into the back of his tiny car. Faustine called shotgun. In fact, anyone with a vehicle to his name had been requisitioned to drive the whole tribe to Pau that morning. "Let's go!" he exclaimed.

"Thanks for the ride, Rafa! We can always rely on you to save the day!" Mina cooed from the back seat.

Mina was a twenty-five-year-old French girl of Algerian descent whose grandparents had emigrated from the Valley of Soummam in

Kabylie to France after World War II. She had been living at La Goutte d'Eau longer than most. Consequently, people considered her a bona fide Somport "veteran." Mina was of average beauty, but she knew how to flaunt her best assets. She never kept it a secret that she was quite fond of Rafael. Needless to say, she annoyed Faustine to no end.

"Yes, Rafa! It's so cool of you to give us a lift!" Faustine chimed in, mimicking Mina's sultry voice before she pulled a monkey-face. Rafael smiled a little, for there was a certain pleasure in seeing a beautiful woman like Faustine jealous of another woman. Faustine's cutting remark did not deter Mina in the least, however. She carried on flirting shamelessly with Rafael.

"If only we had more people like you from the beginning, we might have stood a better chance to win." Rafael tried to protest, but she shushed him at once. "Puh-leeze! Don't act like you don't know what I'm talking about, I've seen how much time you've invested in the cause since you've come here!"

"Is that so?" Faustine muttered under her breath. She turned to Rafael with an inquisitive look on her face. Sure, he did his share of work, but, in all seriousness, could he be labeled a die-hard tunnel warrior? Hardly.

"I shouldn't say this," Mina pressed on, "but people have been talking about you lately. Spreading rumors, you know? Don't hold it against us, though. I, for one, must admit that I was just as curious as anyone else to find out what you've been up to. But, to tell you the truth, I got fed up with listening to everyone's stupid speculations, so I decided to take the bull by the horns and see for myself."

"What are you talking about? What did you do?" Rafael was careful not to show his alarm. Still, it was a taxing endeavor given the circumstances.

"Hmmm, I followed your car the other day. Call me a spy if you want."

"What the—?"

"I shouldn't have, I know. But come on, don't be mad! I mean, why wouldn't you just tell us what you were really up to in the first place?"

"What did you see?" Rafael blurted out, making everyone cringe, for they never saw him that agitated before.

"Well, I followed you to the tunnel construction site. And I saw you taking pictures and notes, um, and drawing sketches. Believe me man, I felt like a total asshole when I realized that while we were talking crap about you, you were actually the one that was out in the field, doing all the groundwork to devise our next plan of attack. I guess I owe you an apology. In fact, we all do."

"Come on, Mina, give me a break." Rafael put his poker face on, but deep inside, the adrenaline was pumping madly through his veins. "I'm the rookie here. I was just trying to get up to speed so that I can catch up with you all. That's all there is to it, really."

"You're too modest for your own good, Rafa. That's what gets you in trouble!"

All the passengers started to laugh good-heartedly, with the exception of Faustine, whose forced laugh did not elude Rafael. Within seconds, everyone in the back seat resumed talking as if nothing had happened. Rafael loosened his grip on the wheel. It was a close call.

The meeting was already in progress when they pulled up to City Hall just before noon. Faustine pushed the heavy entrance door open and peeked inside. Someone was delivering a speech behind a lectern. They tiptoed along the old, creaky wood floors toward the back of the room. It was crowded. All seats were taken and people were standing against the wall in the back. They found a spot near their friends and turned their attention to the public speaker.

"...The building of an underground tunnel under the Somport will turn the road between Pau, France and Saragossa, Spain into a unique and strategic international crossroad right here in the heart of the Pyrenean chain. The European Economic Community is fully aware of the impact such a junction will have on the commerce and transport of goods within its borders and is fully supportive of its realization."

A few people clapped. They were local political figures, as well as members of various regional chambers of commerce, who hoped to reap some financial reward from the situation.

"Correct me if I'm wrong, sir," interrupted a senior citizen, "but you are saying that our valley is going to become a major crossroad for European commerce. Will our local businesses and tourism benefit from this at all? Or should we resign ourselves to watching a never-ending string of trucks roar outside our windows? What will we get out of this other than exhaust fumes and pollution?"

A general rumble of agreement built up throughout the room, but the Deputy of the Atlantic Pyrenees region intervened promptly. He reminded the audience that Monsieur Fontaine was only speaking in the name of the civil engineering companies involved in the construction of the tunnel, and that he was in no position to discuss political or economic issues.

"Please, Monsieur Fontaine, carry on," urged the Deputy.

The speaker continued with a brief summary of the on-site and lab study of the mountain's geological composition as well as its hydrology. As soon as he realized that he was losing his audience upon mentioning words such as "Devonian" and "carboniferous antethercynian rock formations," he jumped straight into a description of the solid geometry and layout of the tunnel in relation to the actual mountain. He produced several large drawings that showed longitudinal and cross-section plans of the project for everyone to see. In conclusion, he told the audience that the tunnel would be just less than five miles in length, that it would give sufficient clearance for vehicles up to twenty-one feet high, and that the road running through it would have a two-lane wide design to allow for bidirectional traffic.

"And now, this brings me to the actual process of drilling the tunnel," he announced with a smile to the assembly.

Faustine stood on tiptoes to whisper into Rafael's ear,

"This is totally boring. Let's get out of here and join the protesters outside."

"You can leave if you want to, but I'm staying here," he replied. "I want to hear what the guy has to say."

Faustine rolled her eyes to the ceiling and started for the door, along with a handful of Aspaches. Monsieur Fontaine pretended to take no notice of the disruption and went on with his presentation.

"I am aware that the use of explosives is a concern for the valley residents as far as safety, noise and vibrations in relation to the buildings in the vicinity of the construction site are concerned." Upon mentioning the word "explosives," Monsieur Fontaine won his audience's undivided attention at once. "When drilling a tunnel with dynamite, the main objectives are first to ensure the workers' safety, second, to control the quality of the work for each blast sequence, and third, to perform the retaining work as the excavation progresses. At this point in time, we estimate that about two hundred and fifty tons of explosives will be needed to bring the project to completion."

After a few whistles of admiration, a middle-aged woman stood up and took the floor with no introduction.

"Two hundred and fifty tons of dynamite stocked at the construction site... Do you realize how dangerous that is? What if there was a fire at the Somport? Wouldn't the explosion blast us all the way to the moon?"

Everyone started talking at the same time. Monsieur Fontaine requested silence by tapping his pointing stick against the lectern.

"I understand your concern, Ma'am. However, you will be happy to hear that there is no need to worry about such a potentially tragic scenario. In fact, I was getting to that point. As far as explosives go, we never stock anything on-site overnight. The dynamite will be brought to the Somport on the day it will be used. Any leftovers are returned to an approved warehouse at the end of every workday."

A journalist raised his hand and asked,

"Sir, my educated guess is that the dynamite will be brought to and from the construction site by road, correct?"

"That is correct."

"Well, RN-134 is the only road leading to the Somport and we all know how dangerous it can be, especially in bad weather. What if there was an accident?"

"Again, good question," replied Mr. Fontaine. "As far as transport safety is concerned, the dynamite will be brought on a daily basis aboard a truck outfitted for transporting exactly this type of product. Let me point out that detonators and explosives never travel together. The explosives are kept in a special safe so that they can never come in contact with flames or any other incandescent objects. Also, the vehicle is engineered to guarantee maximum shock absorption from the road, so that the goods are not shaken or prone to getting damaged in any way. In addition, the agents who drive these armored vans carry weapons, and they are prepared to protect the cargo with their lives. So, you see, we have taken all the precautions necessary so that you have nothing to worry about."

Pressed by more questions from the audience, he moved on to other subjects, such as the removal and disposal of the rubble during construction. When he was done with his exposé, the moment that every supporter of the tunnel had been waiting for had come at last.

"Ladies and gentlemen, it is my pleasure to announce that the excavation of the long-awaited Somport tunnel will officially commence next Friday, April 1st!"

Politicians and elected representatives of the region stood up at once to congratulate each other on a job well done. They shook hands and smiled for the cameras. The tunnel would soon become a reality, and nothing would hinder its completion. They were the undisputed victors of the day, and they were intent on celebrating the moment.

Meanwhile, the clan of protesters who had remained silent

throughout the duration of the meeting unrolled a large banner that read in French and English:

SOMPORT: LE TUNNEL DE L'ABSURDE
THE SOMPORT TUNNEL: A TOTAL JOKE

Journalists and television reporters turned around as one to flash cameras in their direction. A handful of them exited the room in a hurry to cover the action unfolding outside.

Shouts of protest coming from the street became louder by the minute. The peaceful march was about to start, and a large crowd rallied to the cause. The men and women standing outside City Hall were brandishing signs and banners over their heads with slogans that read:

NO TRUCKS IN THE VALLEY!

and

NO PASARAN!

Meanwhile, sitting on the ground in the middle of the street, Faustine, Mina and the others were crying bitter tears of disappointment. So much effort, so many sacrifices carried out by so many people for so many years, all for nothing.

The tale was a modern take on the fight of David and Goliath. The underdog had fought the monster with all his might and bravado. Sadly, in the real world, David had been crushed in the end.

7
-ZAZPI-

07:55 AM ~ Sunday, April 3, 1994

Armed with plenty of information to relay to his old comrade, Lartaun was driving west. In a few hours, he would meet Patxi in the little seaside village of Guéthary, a dozen miles away from the Spanish border. They had not seen each other in over two years. As much as he was looking forward to seeing his lifelong friend again, he was also dreading their encounter. Would things ever be the same?

Patxi and Lartaun first met when they were six years old. Although they went to school together, it wasn't until three years later that their friendship blossomed, after Lartaun lost his father to cancer. Left alone with a meager pension and three children to raise (Lartaun, the eldest, his sister Soledad Haizea and their baby sister, Itxaro), his young mother had no choice but to sell the house. They moved into a nondescript apartment complex on the outskirts of Irun, where Patxi and his folks lived as well. From that moment on, the two were inseparable. Growing up, they used to spend their summer holidays together, either camping on the Biscayan coast nearby Bakio beach, or in the mountains of Urbasa in the Navarra region of the Basque country.

As teenagers, the pair started to hang out at the bars of Plaza Mosku in Irun. One could find them at Skatu, Eskina or Sunbilla, or standing on benches skirting the Plaza on any given day. There, they criticized society at large while passing bottles of cheap beer back and forth. They would hold court for hours on their curbside turf, dressed in tight cuffed blue jeans and cherry-red, eight-eye Doc Martens' boots with steel toes.

At first, their teenage rebellion shone through in the form of music. Every weekend, the pair hung out at the *gaztetxe*, the local youth center in the neighboring town of Hondarribia. There, they witnessed the emergence of the "Rock Radikal Vasco" scene front and center in the early 1980s. *Euskadi's* punk rock, ska and hardcore movement, which propelled underground Basque bands such as Kortatu, La Polla Records, RIP and Eskorbuto into the limelight, not only exposed new genres of music, but also delivered a quintessential political message in song lyrics. Some of the bands' front men would even give political speeches during their acts.

As time went on, Lartaun and Patxi started to pay more attention to the reality of the Basque sociopolitical struggle. At the turn of the twentieth century, the ever-increasing popularity of left-wing separatist and nationalist movements, generally defined as *Ezker Abertzalea* (Nationalist Left), gave rise to radical organizations that based their activist stance on the Sabinian nationalist philosophy. Sabino Arana, the father of Basque nationalism, implied then that *Euskadi* was a country in a state of moral occupation. Later on, after the defeat of the republicans in the Spanish Civil War in 1939, Basque oppression became grim reality under Franco's dictatorial regime. Of these radical organizations, ETA was, by far, the most popular. ETA stood for *Euskadi Ta Askatasuna*, *Euskara* for "Basque country and Freedom." It was a radical paramilitary separatist faction determined to win independence for a Basque state in northern Spain and southwestern France. The organization had long been classified by the European community, the United States of America and the United Nations as a terrorist group responsible for over eight hundred violent deaths since its official inception on San Ignacio de Loyola's day in 1959.

Due to the progressive radicalization of the group and a general escalation of violence caused by its paramilitary branch, ETA was losing popularity in the beginning of the 1980s. To make matters worse, its members were no longer portrayed as the valiant heroes courageously fighting Franco's fascist oppression to save their country's unique identity. Once democracy returned in Spain after the dictator's death in 1975,

ETA's past supporters no longer saw a point to their military struggle, even though their support for ETA's political arm, *Herri Batasuna* (People's Unity), remained strong. Indeed, the radical party still received about fifteen percent of the votes in every election.

As absurd and counterproductive as it may appear, it was *Zona Especial Norte* (Special Northern Zone, also called "Plan ZEN"), an elaborate plan designed to eradicate ETA and the Basque National Liberation Movement (MLNV in Spanish) that would unwittingly contribute to the restoration of ETA and *Herri Batasuna*'s reputation in the mid 1980s.

Plan ZEN was created in 1983 by Socialist Prime Minister Felipe González, implemented by the Minister of Interior José Barrionuevo and coordinated by the Spanish police forces, the army and political institutions. Paramilitary death squads known as Antiterrorist Liberation Groups (GAL) conducted a campaign of extra-judicial killings against suspected Basque activists. All in all, GAL tortured and killed at least twenty-eight suspected ETA members between 1983 and 1987. Unfortunately, about one-third of the victims were targeted by mistake. If, in the beginning, the public opinion in Spain was rather supportive of GAL's actions, allegations of corruption that had police and politicians working hand-in-hand with GAL mercenaries seriously compromised the Socialist government. The outrageous affair, dubbed the "Spanish Dirty War," was investigated, and high-ranking government officials within the PSOE (the Socialist Party), along with members of the *Guardia Civil* (the Spanish gendarmerie) and the CESID (the Spanish Intelligence Agency), were charged for their involvement with the death squads as a result.

The scandal further reinforced the Basques' contempt for Spanish security forces. Their efforts to eradicate radical Basque nationalism had backfired. Worse, the state of Spain had managed to give ETA another popular boost in the process. By the time Lartaun and Patxi were fifteen, independence for *Euskadi* was the rage once again.

While growing up, Lartaun never felt much serious attraction for any particular woman, even though there was no shortage of teenage girls with a crush on him. On the other hand, Patxi seemed determined to make up for that. His hormones shot through the roof every time he caught a whiff of feminine perfume. In the end of June of 1985, Patxi fell head over heels in love with Anabel, a skinny punk rock girl five years his senior. Her favorite pastime was to flirt with younger guys so she could bum their smokes and drink their booze. He was so smitten that he immediately introduced her to Lartaun. Lartaun, Anabel and her younger brother Bixente bonded at once. As it turned out, Anabel and Bixente were very involved with "Jarrai," a youth political organization within the Basque National Liberation Movement. The MLNV encompassed all social, political and military organizations revolving around the philosophy and agenda of ETA, with *Herri Batasuna* leading the political action front. The Spanish community, the media, police and political officials considered Jarrai an incubator for future ETA members and openly blamed the organization for being the instigator of the *Kale Borroka*, the "urban guerilla," in the streets of Spain and *Euskadi*. As far as the separatist youth were concerned, Jarrai was a completely legitimate political platform that supported the ever present Basque national liberation struggle.

Lartaun and Patxi were at the height of their angst-ridden years. Inspired by ETA's new surge of popularity and fueled by their contempt for the Spanish government, they were desperate to find a role model and a peer group. They ended up joining Jarrai in July of that same year, for better and for worse.

09:32 AM ~ Sunday, April 3, 1994

Patxi was just as anxious as Lartaun, and because of that, he arrived early in Guéthary. He was strolling past City Hall, a whitewashed building with its roof, woodwork, shutters and doors stained in deep red in the Basque tradition, when he noticed two teams of three young *pelotari* warming up on the Jai Alai court. The players were hurling a goatskin-covered ball at dizzying speed against the *fronton*, a concrete wall against which the game was played, and catching it back on the rebound inside their *xistera*, a curious-looking leather glove with a long and narrow curved wicker scoop strapped at the end of it. Their dexterity and speed never ceased to mesmerize Patxi, and the swooshing sound of the ball thrown back and forth against the wall had a soothing, almost hypnotic effect on him. Since he had time to kill, Patxi took a seat on the bleachers and followed their game for a while.

Like Lartaun, Patxi was born in 1970. He was one month his junior and would turn twenty-four at the beginning of May. With his spiky ash-blond hair, large green eyes and reed-thin body, he looked like an awkward teenage kid whose face had aged overnight without warning. At five-foot-ten, he was not quite the height of Lartaun. Still, he was taller than most of the people he knew. Patxi had learnt early on to compensate for his lack of God-given beauty. He had developed such a magnetic personality that people fell for his unusual charm pretty much on command. Yet underneath his winning personality, Patxi was as short on scruples as he was long on charm.

Patxi lifted the hood of his sweatshirt over his head and turned his face into the sun. This was going to be a strange day.

Unbeknownst to Patxi, Lartaun arrived early, as well, for their meeting. The little terrace of the café was packed with locals who had come to enjoy the sunniest Sunday morning of the year so far. Sitting at a table, a trio of teenage girls was ogling a group of young men shooting the breeze by the war memorial across the street. No sooner had Lartaun sat down at an adjacent table, three pairs of batting eyelashes zoomed in on him, fluttering like butterflies. He nodded his head and smiled at the girls. They giggled with happy embarrassment.

When Patxi showed up at the appointed time for their meeting, Lartaun raised his hand and waved him over to his table.

"*¡Me cago en la puta, txo!*" exclaimed Patxi as an unorthodox form of greeting when he spotted his old friend. "You look freakin' good for a guy who's been through what you've been through! And it looks like you've got a fan club, too!" he added with a wink, pointing at the girls whispering in each other's ears.

"I could say the same of you, *hermano!* You look great!"

"Don't let the outside shell fool you, my man. I might have inherited my mother's good skin genes, but deep inside, I'm a wreck."

They laughed and held each other in a strong embrace.

"I hope you've got time for a drink or two with me!" Lartaun said before he invited Patxi to sit down at the small wrought-iron table he had already claimed for them.

"*¡Joder!* Twist my arm!" Patxi replied with a wide grin on his face.

They ordered two glasses of the local draft.

"How's your girl doing? You are still together, right?"

"Anabel's good," Patxi said, laughing, "trying to keep me out of trouble, as usual."

"What about my family?"

"They're hanging in there," Patxi replied in a more serious tone. "It's been tough for your mother, but even more so for your sister. I mean, you and Haizea were like twins. She's been lost without you around."

"I feel the same, believe me. How did she cope with the situation?"

"After you left, she started hanging out with a bad crowd. Then I heard she started smoking smack and stuff." Upon seeing Lartaun's face decompose with worry, Patxi immediately reassured his friend. "Don't worry though. As soon as I found out, I straightened her out and warned her idiotic crew that they'd better leave her alone. It wasn't easy to convince her at first. I mean, you know her; she's got a mind of her own—runs in the family! But I told her you'd kill me if I didn't take good care of her, so she started to listen to me."

"I'll never forgive myself for letting her down," said Lartaun, shaking his head in despair.

"I know it's tough, but try not to worry about her. She's smart, she's got a heart of gold, and she's strong. She'll be okay. They'll all be okay." Patxi's eyes focused on the medallion dangling around Lartaun's neck. He extended his hand to touch it. It was about an inch in diameter, and represented the Basque cross with its four comma-shaped heads. "The *lauburu*," he said in a half-whisper, "I can't believe you're still wearing it after all these years!"

"That's because I never take it off!" Lartaun replied. "I guess I'll die with it around my neck."

"So, how does it feel to be, well, almost home?"

"Good," Lartaun replied hesitantly. "I wish I could see my folks, but other than that, it's good to be back."

"I wanted to see you sooner, but it would have been too risky, with the cops snooping around and all that. I hope you forgive me."

"Don't you even go there! If it weren't for you, I wouldn't be here today."

"Thanks for saying that. It means a lot to me, really. Anyway, for what it's worth, I just want you to know how happy I am to see you alive and well."

"Same here, *txo*. Same here." Lartaun leaned over the table to squeeze his friend's shoulder.

"I'm so sorry for all the shit that happened to you. I wish I—"

Lartaun cut him off mid-sentence. "I know you've had it rough too. Look, it's been hard on all of us. But, the past is the past. So let's put it behind us and drink to the future instead, OK?"

As if on cue, their beers arrived. They clinked glasses and guzzled down half the contents of their heavy mugs in one swig. Lartaun wiped the foam off the corners of his mouth with the back of his hand.

"Glad to see that you can still drink like a man!"

"Some things never change!" Patxi replied before he let out a cavernous belch.

"We sure did our share of crazy stuff back in the day, didn't we?"

"Tell me about it," Patxi said with a grin. "Remember the Kortatu show at the Playa del Barrio Antiguo during the *Semana Grande* festival in San Sebastián? We were what, fifteen or something?"

"Do I remember? Damn, my head still hurts just thinking about it! Now there was a band with a message. They were the real defenders of Basque independence and culture," Lartaun mused. "Oh, and what about the bar brawl at the *bodega* after the gig? I can still picture you throwing blind punches at those fascist assholes at the bar! You were bleeding like a pig when I brought you to the ER to get stitched up!"

"Yep, and I still have the scars to show for it!" Patxi swung his head around and smoothed out his hair to reveal a two-inch reddish scar at the top of his scalp. "*¡Coño!* I was so wasted, I didn't feel a thing!"

"And what about the 'run of the bulls' in Pamplona?" exclaimed Lartaun.

"Whoa, yeah! Man, you could have died that day."

Lartaun felt a tinge of nostalgia upon remembering their rambunctious teenage years. Just like that, he and Patxi reconnected at a deep level. For a brief moment, they were the two young rebels who grew up together, joined at the hip, and it felt good. Patxi signaled the waitress for another round.

"We had it made, man." Lartaun stared at his glass and sighed. "We were always up to no good, but it was all in good fun in the end."

"We thought we were invincible, didn't we?"

"Sometimes, I wish things had stayed just the way they were: the punk shows at Saindua, the *Borroka ere bai* protests…"

"Don't forget the foosball tournaments at Sunbilla with the rest of the gang!"

"We believed that we could turn this world around with a raised fist and a few Molotov cocktails!"

"And look at us now. Our innocence is long gone, and the battles we fight are very real," Patxi concluded in a somber tone. "Anyway," he quickly added to change the subject, "tell me about you. How's life in hippie lane?"

"It's been quite a rewarding experience, I must say," Lartaun replied with an enigmatic smile.

"Hmmm. You look, I don't know. Different," Patxi said after

careful examination of his friend.

"How so?"

"I'm not sure. All that fresh air, maybe?"

Lartaun fiddled with his glass for a moment, wondering whether he could still confide in his old companion. He hesitated, and mentally shrugged at the consequences.

"I've met someone, actually."

"Oh."

"Well, it's not what you think. It's too complicated. I mean, I can't even tell her my real name! But she's like no other woman I've ever met. I feel that she came into my life for a reason. She gives it a whole new meaning, you know?"

Patxi did not say anything for a while.

"I'm happy for you, *txo*, I really am," he managed to reply once he got over the initial shock. "I'd love to meet the woman who stole your heart. She must be very special."

"Her name's Faustine."

"Is she from that commune?" Lartaun nodded. "You do understand that you can't afford to be in love right now, correct?" Patxi stated in a stern tone.

"Believe me, I'm trying hard not to."

"Be careful, Lartaun. You may love her, and she may love the man that you're pretending to be, but she has no idea who you really are."

Lartaun struggled to find the right words, for he knew that Patxi was right.

"All I want is to protect her, be there for her. How do you think it makes me feel to know that I can't even do that?" he blurted out in frustration.

"You're on the run, *txo*. This relationship has no future. You want my advice? Go bang someone, anyone, except her."

"It's got nothing to do with sex."

"I know it doesn't. That's why it's so dangerous. Listen, what you decide to do with your life once you are finished with this job is up to you. But for now, you must concentrate on the task at hand. There will always be other women."

"It's a never-ending story, Patxi, and you know it. New identity or not, I'll always be a fugitive. Sometimes I wonder whether I should just turn myself in. Perhaps all will turn out well for me. After all, they're holding me responsible for a crime I didn't commit."

"You know that. I know that. But the police need a scapegoat, *txo*! They don't care whether you did it or not; they just want someone to crucify! Do you seriously think that you'd get a fair trial? Shit, they'll shoot you point blank the minute you turn yourself in."

"I'm so sick of this stupid life."

"Hang on tight! These things always sort themselves out in the end. You must keep the faith, that's all."

"Faith?" repeated Lartaun.

"We must believe that our sacrifices are not made in vain. I don't enjoy violence any more than you do, but every *ekintza* serves a purpose. Our people understand that. The Basques know that political negotiations with Madrid have never gotten us anywhere and, while it's sad, they never will. Our people understand that the only way to free our country is to keep on fighting. We must be ready to die for the cause. For some of us, bearing the cross is a deliberate choice. For others, like you, fate decided. In the end, we're not responsible for the blood that's being spilled on both sides of the fence. It's not like we were ever given a choice in the matter."

"Easy on the dogmatic speech, *txo*. I don't adhere to your ideology of martyrdom. I actually believe that we could work out a peaceful resolution of the conflict."

"If you were right, none of this would be happening," Patxi replied with a heavy sigh.

"Patxi, did you join the group?" Lartaun asked, lowering his voice to a whisper. "Did you become a *legal?*"

"It's more complicated than that. Look, I'd rather leave that topic alone."

"I have no business judging your decisions, but why? Aren't you sick of all this violence?" Lartaun searched for a spark of acknowledgement in Patxi's emerald green eyes. To his dismay, all he found was an empty stare. "Listen," he pressed on, "I can see that you have changed and I worry about you. I mean, it's never too late to turn your life around if you want to, you know?"

"Ha!" spat Patxi. "And what do you think I should do then, huh? Go back on everything that I've stood for all these years? Make a mockery of the people who have put their trust in me? No sir, no way! There's no turning back in this life. That's the choice I've made a long time ago, and I'll stand by it until the bitter end." Lartaun struck a sensitive nerve with his last comment. Patxi was struggling to keep a somewhat calm composure, and yet Lartaun could see his lips trembling with repressed anger. "You've got no idea what it's like to do what I do or why I do it or who I do it for! You know what's wrong with you? You've been gone too long, *txo*! This isn't a fucking joke anymore. We're at war!"

"No shit, Cochise! I've spent the past two years of my life on the run because of that damn war! There's a price on my head, for crying out loud! Do you think that I could forget that for a second, even if I wanted to?"

"Sorry, man," Patxi said hurriedly. "I was out of line."

"All I'm saying is that you're free, still. Take it from someone who has learnt his lesson the hard way. Freedom is a valuable thing. I hope with all my heart that you never lose yours. On that note, I brought you a little present from Mexico." Lartaun handed Patxi a little box wrapped in gold paper. "It isn't much, but I hope it'll remind you to be careful. Always."

"Thanks." Patxi reached over the table and plucked the tiny package from Lartaun's fingers. He stuffed it in his pocket without opening it.

For the first time during their reunion, they fell into an awkward silence. Neither of them seemed to want to break it. After a while, Lartaun forced the dreaded words out of his mouth.

"OK, Patxi. You brought me home, and I'm in your debt. I wish Iñaki had told me what it was you wanted me to hide in the mountains. I would have never agreed to the deal, never! And, for the record, I didn't like finding out by happenstance! I can't believe you had me come back home to store, um...well, you know, the stuff. But what's done is done, and the joke's on me for playing dumb. Now let's get this over with so that we're even."

Patxi nodded. He tucked a twenty-franc note under the ashtray to pay for the check and stood up from his chair.

"Let's take a stroll by the ocean, shall we? You'll tell me everything you've found out so far." He gestured across the street. "My car's parked over there."

Patxi hung a right past the city limits and cruised down a steep and narrow road toward the village's minuscule harbor. The old whaling port of Guéthary was little more than a sloped semi-circle carved out of the rock, so tiny it could dry dock no more than eight small launch boats at a time. Patxi parked his car just yards away from where the waves crashed against the rocky shore. Lartaun turned his face into the wind and filled his lungs with the fragrant air charged with sea spray. Nearby, a retired fisherman was resting his bones on a stone bench. As their eyes met for a brief moment, the old man tipped his beret with a furrowed hand in greeting. Aside from him, Lartaun and Patxi were all alone. They started walking side-by-side along the shore, while Lartaun wrapped up his report to Patxi.

"...The goods are sealed in an armored container inside the cargo bay, which is itself under lock and key," Lartaun explained. "On top of that, both drivers carry weapons and they're in constant radio contact with their company's switchboard. Let me tell you, this thing is more secure than a bank! I wish I could tell you that they were keeping the stuff on site, but that is not the case, unfortunately."

"So?"

"So, here is my two cents," continued Lartaun, "you'd better scrap the idea altogether, because robbing an armored truck in broad daylight on a two-lane mountain road with no alternate routes for a quick bailout is just complete freaking madness, Patxi!"

Patxi scratched the blond stubble on his chin as he processed the information. "Nothing's ever too crazy, *txo*," he said after a short pause. "There's a weak link in every chain. It's just a matter of finding out which one it is, destroy it and watch the whole thing fall apart before your eyes. It works like a charm every time."

"Good luck to you, then!" Lartaun dismissed his friend's frayed theory with a shrug.

"Luck has nothing to do with a successful *ekintza*. It's all about organization, strategy, thorough planning, a rock-solid contingency plan and meticulous attention to detail. It's when you start overlooking the small stuff that you get caught."

"So, what's your plan?" Lartaun asked with a cynical attitude.

"Well, let's think of the positive points, here. First of all, we know that the cargo is brought to the construction site every day. Since there's only one road to get there, they can't change their itinerary at random. That forces them to set a well-established routine, which works to our advantage. Second, the mountain road is full of hairpin turns and dangerous curves. In other words, it's a dream site for an ambush. Third, you've always seen the convoy drive by at the break of dawn. Road traffic is minimal at that time of the day, which means we'll have very few commuters to contend with. Basically, our only issue is finding a way to make the truck and its drivers invisible for a few minutes while we raid its contents."

"To make a truck vanish into thin air is no small Houdini move, Patxi," Lartaun countered with mounting aggravation. "These two drivers are armed and they won't hesitate to use their weapons if need be. Besides, they'll ring the alarm the second they notice that something's wrong!"

"That's why I must think of something that will happen so fast they won't realize what's going on until it's too late."

"When I said I would help you, I did under the condition that there would be no violence."

"Who says there will be?" asked Patxi.

Lartaun was having a hard time dealing with Patxi's sardonic attitude.

"Don't mess with me, Patxi."

"Listen, I was under the impression that the goods would be stored over by the construction site. It would have been a quick and easy steal, but I was wrong. Unfortunately, 'shit happens' and plans do change."

"Well, perhaps you should go looking for your shit elsewhere."

"The odds of stumbling upon several hundred pounds of free *goma* are slim to none, *txo!* I can't let this opportunity slip through my fingers."

"Jesus, Patxi!" Lartaun kicked the sand in frustration. "Don't you get it? No matter which way you look at it, it's not going to work! Not this time!"

"I thought you'd have a little more faith in me than that," replied Patxi, unfazed by Lartaun's sudden outburst.

"Faith in what, exactly?" spat Lartaun. "Faith in your twisted ability to orchestrate an impossible robbery? And what for anyway? To carry out the terrorist attack of the year?" Lartaun knew he had gone too far the second the words came out of his mouth. "Forget what I just said," he mumbled in haste. "I don't have the slightest idea about your ulterior motives. Besides, whatever it is you have in mind, I don't want to know fuck-all about it."

Patxi's lips quivered a little. When he spoke again, it was in a low voice, almost a whisper. "Don't get confused, Lartaun. Your job here is to help me with the logistics of the robbery. Not to plan it, and certainly not to comment or critique my orders. You do what I ask you to do, and you leave the rest up to me. I did not hire you to think, so don't."

"Come again?" Lartaun snarled at Patxi.

"You heard what I said. I'm the one calling the shots this time!"

"I agreed to help you only because I had no other choice! Don't think for a second that you have me under your thumb."

"Finally we're getting at the truth. You keep on telling me that I've changed, but what really kills you is that you are not in control this time around!"

"What?" Lartaun stared at his friend in shock.

"Come on, you know what I'm talking about! You were always the handsome, the brave and the smart one! I was nothing but your loyal sidekick, forever in your shadow. Once you were gone, though, people started to realize my worth. I worked hard to earn their respect, and now I'm the one they listen to!"

Lartaun's jaws dropped. "For the record, I've always loved you like a brother. And I always thought that the feeling was mutual. If it weren't so, why did you bother to come to my rescue on the night of the riots, huh? And why did you take the risk of getting caught by the police just so that you could keep in touch with me while I was stuck in Mexico? Why, if it weren't for our goddamn friendship?"

"I've always been and I will always be your friend, Lartaun. It's just that I'm no longer the person you used to know." Patxi's green eyes flickered. He pivoted toward the ocean so Lartaun would not notice the dispirited look on his face. "After the riots in Irun, after you ran away, the police came looking for me." He paused for a while, biting the inside of his lips absentmindedly. "They did horrible things to me—to make me tell them where you were. But I didn't say a thing because I knew that you would have done the same for me. Still, after they let me go, something switched inside of me. All this rage I had inside, it all came out at once. I was filled with hatred. I wanted to go back to the station and kill them all. I wanted to watch them suffer."

Lartaun clasped Patxi's shoulder. Moments later, Patxi did the same. They stood side-by-side, holding each other the way they did back when they were kids and stared at the ocean in silence.

"I'm sorry you had to suffer because of me," Lartaun said after a while.

"It was entirely my fault. Do you want to know why I asked for your help for this *ekintza*? I mean, aside from the fact that you're the one person I can trust, that you're fluent in French and an expert rock climber?" Patxi looked his friend in the eyes and gave him a melancholic smile. "I did it because I wanted to see you again. I wanted to see you again before I—"

"Before what?"

"Never mind." Patxi's face hardened again without warning. He moved his arm away from Lartaun. "After I get my *goma*, I want you to go away. I won't remember your new name, and I want you to forget mine."

Lartaun was puzzled. "What do you mean?"

"When your job's done, you'll be a free man. Want a piece of advice? Forget all about Lartaun Izcoa. Embrace the new you. Go see all the places that we once said we would go visit together. Lead a good life for the two of us and never come back here again."

"You could do that too, you know. Shit, we could do that together, if only that was what you wanted!"

"I know I could, but I don't want to." Patxi looked straight ahead in the distance, careful to avoid Lartaun's stare. "You see, my problem is that I still believe. Remember this, Lartaun. The only battle you lose is the battle you don't fight. As long as you keep on fighting, you haven't lost the war."

"Patxi, it doesn't have to be this way."

"You and I have grown apart. There's no need to feel bad about it. It was inevitable, *txo*. Such is life. Whether we choose the paths that we walk on or not, we have no choice but to soldier on and hope for the best. We don't carry enough gas to turn around anyway, so we must keep on moving forward until our tanks run dry." Patxi peered into Lartaun's eyes, as if he were trying to imprint an image of his friend in his memory. "Trust me. Some day soon, you'll wish that you had never met me at all. Life is fucked up that way." With that, Patxi pivoted around and started walking back to his car.

"Patxi!" shouted Lartaun after him. "Hey, Patxi!"

Patxi never once looked back to catch one last glimpse of his estranged friend.

Lartaun stood there alone for a while, trying to make sense of their conversation. Left alone with his own dark thoughts, Lartaun realized how incredibly naïve and foolish he had been to pretend that he could fulfill his side of the deal and come out of it with his conscience intact and his hands clean. Just because he chose to ignore the reason why Patxi was so adamant to carry out his mysterious mission did not make his own involvement in his friend's murky affairs excusable. Whoever said that ignorance was bliss must have been high. Even if he was somewhat pressured into the deal, he was still a man responsible for his own actions.

RESPONSIBLE.

Confused, angry, and with lots of free time left in his hands, Lartaun walked away from the beach. He was wandering aimlessly along the narrow streets of the village when he was suddenly distracted by a choir song drifting from the thick stone walls of the church. Deep guttural male voices mixed with the mesmerizing wails of the women as they sang a hymn in *Euskara* with all the fervor inherent to the Basque faith. The bells started ringing, indicating that Mass was over. Within a few minutes, the priest would dismiss the faithful. They would take over the church square, greeting each other and discussing the latest gossip before they would head back home to enjoy a lengthy Sunday feast. Lartaun could not help but feel resentment against the righteous, those who danced their way through life with a light heart and a pure soul.

People like Faustine.

His mind back-tracked to the day when he first laid eyes upon her. Her wild beauty captivated him right away. She was radiant. It seemed like she was forever basking in an ethereal glow of shimmering light, like the saints on the votive pictures his grandmother used to give him when he was a kid. Faustine looked so innocent, even naïve at times. In spite of appearances however, a saint she was not. She exuded sexiness without even trying. She had the power to drive men crazy, even though she had not yet mastered the use of her magic to its full extent. Never before had he experienced such a powerful attraction for someone else.

Lartaun waited for the flow of parishioners to thin out before he walked inside the church. Votive candles were flickering everywhere, creating shadows that stretched all the way to the intricate carved gilt choir at its far end. The potent smell of incense was heady and intoxicating. He could not tell what had urged him to enter the church, but somehow he had felt compelled to follow the voices. He looked up to the wooden two-tiered galleries flanking the side walls of the structure, the place where Basque men traditionally stood during celebrations, segregated from the women huddled below in the nave. Memories of a childhood lost overwhelmed him, and he suddenly crossed himself, a gesture he had not made in years. As he did so, Lartaun suddenly paused to examine his hands from every angle, as if he was looking at them for the first time. The skin was tanned and smooth on the outside, but his palms were callused, and his gnarled fingernails had a rim of black dirt. The indelible mark of years of rock climbing. He wondered if Faustine would ever allow him to touch her body with such hands.

Standing by his car, Patxi fumbled through his pockets for his keys. He felt the bulge of the box that Lartaun had given him earlier. He took the small package out of his pocket, and held it between his fingers to inspect. Curious, he bounced it a couple of times against the palm of his hand to feel its weight. When he finally opened the black velvet-lined jewelry case, he found enclosed a heavy silver medal. It was a reproduction of the famous *Piedra Del Sol*, the Aztec calendar stone. He looked at the medal with admiration for a moment, as he felt the intricacy of its carvings with the tip of his index finger. He quickly returned it to the box, closed it with a snap, looked over his shoulder to make sure that no one was around, and threw it as far as he could out into the sea.

The secret operation he had been working on for months did not include a bailout plan. Should things go wrong, there would be neither exile nor jail time. Only death. Patxi and his men were fine with that. Come to think of it, he had not bothered to ask if Lartaun was all right with that, too.

Without giving it a second thought, Patxi turned the key to the ignition and sped away from Guéthary.

06:25 PM ~ Wednesday, April 6, 1994

Faustine and Rafael sat side-by-side as their feet dangled over the edge of the drop off. They had secured the best seats in the house to watch the sun as it descended upon Hell's Canyon, setting it ablaze in fiery pink and orange hues.

"I can't get enough of this view," mused Rafael. "If there is a God, I swear he lives somewhere around here!"

"Well, why don't you ask God for a new climbing rope next time you see him?" Faustine quipped. "Ours is frayed beyond repair, and I'm not looking forward to pay my respects to Saint Peter anytime soon!"

Rafael's hearty laugh echoed through the mountains, and it suddenly filled her heart with joy.

"Smoke?"

"Sure, thanks."

Rafael took a fresh pack of cigarettes out of his fleece jacket, inserted one between Faustine's lips and lit it with a green disposable lighter. He cupped his hands against the cool breeze to light up his own. A swirling curl of blue smoke enveloped them before it vanished into the crisp air.

"Why did you come to La Goutte? I mean, really," Faustine asked out of the blue, hoping to somewhat blind-side him with the bluntness of her question.

"I could ask you the same question," he stammered after a few seconds of hesitation.

"I asked you first," she replied with aplomb, puffing away at her Gauloise Blonde.

"I was hoping to meet a cool girl like you."

"Yeah, right!" Faustine smiled and looked in the distance. "You don't like answering personal questions, do you?"

"No. Is that a problem?"

Faustine turned her head sideways to look him in the eye again. "No, I guess not."

"How about you?"

"What?"

"Do you like answering personal questions?"

"Sure. I mean, I don't mind, sometimes."

"Then I'd like you to tell me everything."

"Everything about what?"

"Everything about you." Faustine burst out laughing, only to stop when she realized that Rafael was serious. "Come with me," he said as he got back on his feet, "I have a surprise for you."

They did not head back toward the bottom of the valley. Instead, they marched in the opposite direction along GR10, the hiking trail that skirted the exposed flank of La Mâture toward the plateau. They reached a little cabin just before nightfall. It was a tiny mountain refuge, open all year round to visitors in need of shelter.

"Here we are, finally!" exclaimed Rafael, a content look on his face.

"Is that it? Is paying Mathéo a visit your idea of a surprise?" Faustine enquired without trying to hide her disappointment.

Mathéo was sort of a hermit, a bit crazy and quite smelly. His self-appointed job consisted of maintaining the cabin and playing Good Samaritan to hikers in distress. One had a good chance to find him there, since he had no real other place to live. Oftentimes though, he disappeared alone for days on end, as he stalked tracks left by the last of the Pyrenees' bears. It was not that Faustine disliked him, but rather that she had never made much effort to get to know him.

"No," Rafael replied with a mysterious smile, "the surprise is that he's *not* there."

They pushed the wooden door with no lock and stepped inside. A rancid smell filled their nostrils.

"Yikes! This place is in serious need of a woman's touch!"

Faustine opened the windows in order to let the fresh breeze in. The refuge was a one-floor rectangular building. Its four walls were made of large chunks of stone sealed in with concrete, topped by a slanted corrugated iron roof. Inside, the floor was a rough slab of poured concrete. The furnishings were minimal. A wood table held an oil lamp and a large ashtray filled with a box of matches. Two heavy benches flanked either side of it. There was a fireplace, too, and a wooden ladder led to a mezzanine that provided bed-less sleeping quarters for four to six people. No running water, no electricity.

"Tonight, I'm treating you to a feast at *Chez Rafael!*" Rafael announced to her, "but on one condition. You must stay out of my kitchen until dinner's ready!"

Faustine arched her eyebrow in surprise and gave him an amused look. "You? Cooking? Are you kidding me? I wouldn't miss that for the world!"

"Out, or the deal is off!" he said with good humor as he shooed her out the door.

When Faustine re-entered the cabin about an hour later, Rafael stood holding a bottle of wine with its neck missing in his right hand. As Faustine stared quizzically at the mutilated bottle, he felt an explanation was in order.

"I forgot to bring a corkscrew, I had to improvise."

He poured a glass of wine for her and for himself, and they sat across from each other at the massive wood table.

"Thank you, Rafa, for the surprise." She tipped her glass to him and took a sip of the wine. "What?" she said to him after a short while, as she suddenly started to feel uneasy.

Rafael stared at her in silence. It was as if he were examining every single square inch of her body. His extraordinary gaze was so piercing that she felt like a butterfly pinned to a piece of cork, at the mercy of an entomologist's magnifying glass. She had grown used to their silences, but this time, things were different.

"Rafael," she ventured, "you are a man of few words, and I can appreciate that. So many guys out there ramble on and on for the sake of filling the void and I'm glad that you're not one of them. But, sometimes, I'd really love it if you would—"

"If I would what?"

"I don't know. Tell me stories about yourself from time to

time."

"Stories about myself, huh?" he replied, slightly amused by her cautious tone. "So tell me, what kind of stories would you like to hear?"

"I don't know," she hesitated again, feeling the crimson rise to her cheeks, "stories about your youth, your friends, your family. Or things like, have you ever been in love?"

There it was, the million-dollar question. Faustine bit her lips, but it was too late. She felt so naïve all of a sudden, so young and inexperienced.

"It's funny how we're always dying to know certain things about certain people," he answered in a low voice. "We agonize over it until we finally get our answers. And when we get them, nine times out of ten, we wish that we had never asked those questions in the first place. That's why I prefer to keep quiet. It's like telling the truth, only better."

"Oh," was all Faustine could muster.

Rafael stretched his hand over the table and wiped a droplet of wine from the corner of her mouth with his thumb. He brought it to his lips and licked it, never taking his eyes off her. Faustine felt as if her whole body was wired and ready to snap under the pressure of desire. She never felt such a sensation before. She felt terrified and entranced at the same time. Rafael stood up and walked around the table. She followed him with her gaze, unable to move. He wrapped his hands around her waist and gently forced her to turn toward him. With one effortless move, he lifted her off the bench and sat her on the table. He pushed the two plates aside with the back of his hand and gently lowered her down onto it. Moving with slow and deliberate movements, he lifted her sweatshirt over her stomach, inch by inch. Faustine arched her back against the table and raised her arms above her head like a child so that he could undress her. He laced his hands around her toned waist and let them wander up toward her breasts. They were perfect, round and firm. Goose bumps crawled up all over her body. She let out a little moan and closed her eyes.

"No, Faustine. Look at me." She opened her eyes again, and Rafael saw a little fear in them. "I never thought I would find such perfection in my life. So much beauty on the inside and out," he whispered. As he leaned close to her, he removed his shirt with one hand. His skin was tight against his abdominal muscles. His waist was slim, almost feminine. He unbuttoned his jeans and let them fall to the floor. "Touch me. I beg you," he pleaded.

Faustine, petrified, was unable to move. Rafael pressed his body against hers and found her mouth. She kissed him back, taking in the electricity radiating from his warm skin against her belly. He let go of her lips and moved down her chin, discovering every tiny beauty mark on her throat along the way. Faustine trembled, her hands limp at her sides. He cupped her breasts and kissed her nipples. He followed the peachy fuzz above her belly button with his mouth and unzipped her pants. Faustine pulled her thighs closer in reflex, but his hands were already separating them in one gentle, yet insistent, move. She felt something strong pushing inside her, invading her. Faustine felt caught in the middle of a storm, lost and helpless like a castaway at sea. She was almost oblivious to it in a way, as if she was floating above her body. And yet, she was aware of Rafael's warm breath against her shoulder, of his weight pressing against her chest, of the heat radiating from her insides all the way down her legs and all the way up to her heart.

Then Rafael's muscles tensed for a brief moment, and everything was quiet again. For the first time, Faustine wrapped her arms around him in a tight embrace. She had just left her innocence behind and crossed the threshold into a brand new world. She felt drunk with ecstasy. Elated. Different. Reveling in the fact that Rafael had no idea how he had transformed her yet.

She let him kiss her forehead, her eyebrows, her eyes and her nose. His skin, speckled with tiny beads of sweat, glistened against the flames dancing in the fireplace. He was so handsome, so strong, so—everything. Faustine started to cry silent tears of joy. Rafael pulled away from her a little, wary all of a sudden.

"Are you all right?" he whispered.

"Rafael, I think I love you," she said in a quivering voice.

"I love you too, Faustine. I love you with all my heart." That was when he noticed the blood on him and on her. "Faustine! Oh, Faustine," he whispered, "I did not know. I did not know you had never—"

"Hush," she placed her index finger across his mouth to silence him and whispered back, "since when do you feel the sudden urge to talk?"

Hours later, long after they had eaten and made love again, Rafael fell asleep in Faustine's arms. But sleep did not come to her. As she moved slowly so as not to wake him, she broke away from his embrace and got up. The temperature had dropped. She shivered and yet, she did not feel the need to cover up. She poured herself another glass of wine and let the dark-red liquid slide down her throat. It was mediocre wine at best, but it was wine just the same, and its earthy texture tasted divine.

"This man loves me," she murmured to herself. "He said so. I know so. I've known it all along."

Faustine felt like the phoenix rising from the ashes. Strong, confident and beautiful. She sat down on the edge of the bench and spent a long time examining her skin, admiring the toned curve of her long legs, the roundness of her breasts, the pale color of her hair. She ran her hand between her legs and looked at her fingers in the half-light. She tasted the blood's coppery flavor on them. Life was good.

Next, she allowed herself to take a good look at Rafael. He laid out on his stomach with his head resting sideways on his folded arms. She admired his back, wide and muscular, sticking out from his sleeping bag. The pendant he always wore had turned on its chain and was now rested on the nape of his neck, tangled up in his chestnut curls. That was when she noticed the scar across his shoulder for the first time. How could she not know of its existence? It was so large and sinuous. So impressive. As she returned to their makeshift bed to lie down next to him, she wondered how he had gotten it.

Faustine jerked when the ground started shaking around her. Alarmed, she roused Rafael.

"Rafa! Did you feel that? What was it?"

"Tremors, Faustine," he replied in a sleepy voice, "tiny earthquakes. The mountains like to remind us that they, too, are alive."

"Oh," she said, relieved, before asking again, "Rafa?"

"Yes?"

"How did you get that scar on your back?"

Rafael grunted as he turned around and wrapped his arms around her. "It was a long time ago," he whispered groggily, burying his face in her hair. "I'll tell you some day, if you want."

Minutes later, Faustine was sound asleep. Everything was so perfect, so peaceful. So simple. Except for the fact that now was Rafael's turn to stare, wide awake and anxious, at the shadows of the last dying flames that stretched out along the far wall of the cabin.

9
-BEDERATZI-

Nine years ago, 06:45 AM ~ Sunday, July 7, 1985

"¡Pamploneses, Pamplonesas, Viva San Fermín! Iruinarrak, Gora San Fermin!"

Basque flags—the green, red and white *Ikurrina*—of all sizes were hanging from the wrought-iron balconies of the old pink-stone buildings surrounding the overcrowded plaza. The *Txupinazo*, a fire rocket announcing the official start of the fiestas in Pamplona every sixth of July at noon, had been launched into the sky from City Hall the previous day. At once, Plaza Ayuntamiento had erupted in chaos. Tens of thousands of excited people yelled *"¡Viva! Gora!"* in unison as they waived bright red scarves over their heads in celebration of the martyr Saint Fermin. The three angels adorning the top of City Hall had, once again, silently witnessed the drunken orgy unraveling on the streets as champagne corks popped into the air by the hundreds, spraying all over the crowd and drenching everyone in the process.

Everyone in Pamplona, locals and tourists alike, had been waiting all year for this. Lartaun, Patxi, Anabel and Bixente, Anabel's younger brother, had traveled the hundred kilometers separating Irun from Pamplona by bus in order to take part in the hugely popular celebration. Already, the stench of booze was enveloping the city in its sultry arms. The week-long party had just begun and no one in the city was expecting to get much sleep.

Bixente woke at first light and roused Lartaun with a song.

"*¡Uno de enero, dos de febrero, tres de marzo, cuatro de abril, cinco de mayo, seis de junio, siete de julio: SAN FERMIN!* Come on, man, get up! The brave rise with the sun! The *entzierroa* doesn't wait!"

Lartaun barely got an hour of sleep, if that. Where the hell was he? And where was Patxi? Lartaun and Bixente had partied all night long until they ended up crashing at some random guy's pad. He vaguely recalled losing Patxi and Anabel in the crowd just before dawn. His mind was too foggy to remember the details.

"Bixente, what gives?" protested Lartaun. "What are you waking me up for?"

Bixente was eighteen at the time, three years older than Lartaun. He had short, jet-black hair and a wiry, yet muscular, frame. He sported a tribal tattoo depicting a stylized snake wrapped around a stick on the inside of his left forearm. It was a gutsy statement for the time, as it brought the striking ETA logo to mind. According to ETA's imagery, the snake symbolized intelligence and stood for ETA's political branch, while the axe represented the armed fight, the group's paramilitary branch. In other words, the ETA logo celebrated force governed by intelligence.

Although Lartaun hardly knew Bixente then, he was aware of his reputation as a tough guy. Bixente was a popular figure and a staple at the *gaztetxe*, the youth center where everyone hung out. Historically, his family was known for engaging in the active resistance against the fascist forces of General Francisco Franco ever since the Civil War in 1936. His older brother Jose Maria, who was sixteen years his senior, had joined the separatist group in 1971 at the age of twenty. After taking part in numerous secret missions over the years, he was finally arrested a year ago in 1984, and condemned to serve a twenty-year sentence without parole.

"Don't you remember what we talked about last night? We're going to run with the bulls! It's the tradition! C'mon man, hurry up!"

Running with the bulls? It all came back to Lartaun in a flash. If it had sounded like a grand idea a few hours ago, it since had lost much of its appeal. Lartaun was still drunk, and to be perfectly honest, a little scared too. Bixente handed him a plastic cup filled with black coffee. Lartaun took a sip and spat it right back into the cup.

"I really don't feel good. I think I'm gonna puke," he said with a grimace.

"Let's split. Some fresh air will do you good. Koldo! Pepe! Are you coming or what?"

The small group stepped over snoring bodies scattered all over the floor and left the apartment.

It was not yet seven in the morning. Blinding sunlight greeted them as they stepped out onto the street. They briskly walked toward the "Casco Viejo" district. As it turned out, Pepe, a nineteen year old man as tall and skinny as they come and fit as a fiddle, was not faring much better than Lartaun. His eyes were bloodshot and his voice was hoarse and crackly. He handed Lartaun a small flask.

"Take a sip. You need the hair of the dog that bit you. Besides, a little liquid courage won't hurt." In spite of his fierce hangover, Pepe still packed a level of confidence and a congenial attitude that commanded everyone's respect.

Lartaun took a couple swigs from the bottle. "Guys, I have no idea what I'm supposed to do!"

Bixente elbowed his worried friend. "Don't worry. The *entzierroa* goes so fast, it'll be over before you even know it. It's a great high, you'll see!"

"It works like this," Koldobika offered to explain. Koldo, as his friends called him, was a stocky skinhead guy, clad in straight blue jeans held by a wide pair of red suspenders over a "Stiff Little Fingers" T-shirt. "The whole run goes on for about half-a-mile, starting from the corral and ending up at the bullring over at the Plaza de Toros. We're going to pick a section somewhere along the run and wait for the bulls there. When you hear the rocket, you'll know that the bulls have been released, and they're coming. As soon as you hear their feet clacking on the pavement, start running as fast as you can. And when you feel they're close enough to your liking, just move to the side of the street and lean against the wall, or find a spot to climb up. The bulls will run right past you and then, it's over. Pretty simple, really."

Lartaun could not see anything simple about it.

"Some sections of the race are safer to run than others," Pepe continued. "Personally, I like to run straight up Santo Domingo Street because that's where the bulls are released, so they're fast and furious! But we'll take it easy today, for your sake. I think we should hit Mercaderes. The street's pretty narrow so you'll get a good adrenaline rush. But it's also relatively safe because there's fencing along the way so you can make a quick escape to safety. What do you think?"

"Yo Pepe, Mercaderes for a first-timer, do you think that really makes sense?" asked Koldobika.

Lartaun gave them a worried look.

"Be cool man, don't scare the kid!" Pepe replied with nonchalance, before he addressed Lartaun again. "Just try to avoid the corner of Mercaderes as it gets hairy over there. The turn is real sharp, and the bulls often slip and fall at that particular spot. But I doubt you'll get that far."

Spectators were already standing behind the double-fence along Mercaderes street. Bixente was right. The race had not even started, but Lartaun was already feeling an adrenaline rush. It was almost eight. The street was crowded with runners clad in white clothing and red scarves tied around their necks. Some of them also wore red sashes around their waists.

Bixente gave Lartaun a friendly poke in the chest and shouted, "Are you ready for this?"

"My throat's drier than Jesus' sandals after his trek in the desert, but, other than that, I'm peachy," Lartaun mumbled. "Any last minute advice you can give me?"

"As long as the race is on, be aware that the bulls can cut loose from the rest of the pack. So even when you think that you're home free after their passage, always keep an eye out for them until you hear the rocket announcing that the bulls have all made it inside the Plaza de Toros."

"OK, got it."

"Oh, and one more thing... Beware of other runners. It gets pretty chaotic out there because a lot of people don't know what the hell they're doing, and sometimes they trip each other. If, for any reason you fall down, just stay down, cover your head and don't move, got it?"

The runners' faces turned solemn as they sang the prayer to San Fermín, asking their Patron Saint to guide them through the Bull Run and to give them his blessing and protection. "*A San Fermín pedimos, por ser nuestro patrón, nos guíe en el encierro dándonos su bendición.*"

BANG!

An explosion resounded somewhere north of the city. Excited shouts and gasps rose from the public gathered outside the fence.

BANG!

The thunder of a second rocket echoed into the streets.

"It's show time!" exclaimed Bixente.

"Say again, how many people get hurt every year doing this?"

Lartaun shouted back.

"It's too late for you to worry about it now!"

From far away, Lartaun sensed a low rumble swelling up gradually, like a tsunami wave picking up speed as it approaches the shore. As the seconds ticked by, it became louder and louder. Somewhere up the street, spectators started cheering,

"They're coming! They're coming!"

Lartaun felt the street vibrate. The runners were on their marks, ready to go. He called for Bixente one more time, but his voice was already drowned out by the deafening roar of the bulls' hooves approaching. He felt no more fear, just raw exhilaration, as he began to run for his life. The stampeding horde was closing in on him, even though he was running as fast as his legs would allow. Suddenly, the sash of the runner in front of him came undone. It caught around Lartaun's leg, and before he could grasp what was happening, he crashed down face first onto the cobblestones of Mercaderes Street.

There was a collective gasp, followed by shouts of consternation from the public. Lartaun, stunned by the fall, lost consciousness for a split second. When he came to, he propped himself up on his elbow and looked over his shoulder. The look in his eyes was one of disbelief and horror when he realized his impending doom. The bulls were mere yards away from him. There were six of them, stampeding flank to flank and taking up most of the width of the street. Six beasts with over a thousand pounds of brutal force each, charging onwards with horns bigger and pointier than daggers. They were running with their heads low, breathing hard through their flared nostrils. The last thing Lartaun saw before he covered his head with his arms were the long strings of saliva flying from the side of their mouths and the impenetrable blackness of their eyes.

The animal running on the outside of the pack trampled Lartaun's upper legs first and kept on going without even slowing down. The second *toro* however, which was running flank-to-tail with the other, hooked Lartaun by his shoulder blade. It lifted him into the air and carried him several yards on its left horn by the fabric of his shirt, until it sent him crashing to the ground like a broken rag doll. The jolt of pain was immediate and intense. A dark stain grew steadily across Lartaun's sweater as it soaked up the fresh blood oozing from his wounds.

Pepe stared at his friend in shock before the adrenaline kicked in again, which urged him to rush to Lartaun's rescue. He jumped down from the pole he had climbed to avoid the bulls and yelled at the top of his lungs,

"Help! Over here! He's been gored! Our friend's been gored!"

He had just about turned Lartaun on his side when he heard a loud bellowing coming from the spot where Mercaderes turns into Estafeta Street. A lone bull, stressed and disoriented, was retracing its steps toward them. It had lost its footing on the slick pavement as it took the sharp turn onto Estafeta and had fallen down as a result. The rest of the pack had continued their mad dash down the street, leaving it behind to fend for itself.

The beast, overwhelmed with the noise and activity all around, charged blindly into a cluster of runners, sending men scattering in all directions as it made its way up the street toward the spot where Lartaun had just fallen. Suddenly, it stopped in the middle of the street. It noticed Lartaun lying down on the ground and found an easy target to torment. The angry bull leaned back on its haunches and let out a blood-chilling bellow before it started to stampede toward Lartaun. In the nick of time, a group of skilled runners started yelling and jumping around in order to divert the animal's attention until they succeeded in encircling it. Meanwhile, Pepe and Bixente struggled to carry their friend to safety.

Upon seeing Lartaun getting to his feet and staggering out of harm's way, the crowd erupted in loud cheers of relief and applause.

When they got to the other side of the barricades, a medic rushed to Lartaun's side. He cut through Lartaun's tattered sweatshirt to check out the extent of his injuries, rinsed the wound and exhaled with relief. Thankfully, the bull's horn had slashed across his skin like a knife before it had caught onto Lartaun's clothing, making it look like the bull had gored him. Still, the gash was deep enough to require extensive stitching.

A few hours later, Lartaun appeared through the revolving doors of the ER waiting room with his torso bandaged up and his right arm in a sling.

"Are you all right?" Koldobika asked with concern.

"I'm in pain, but I'm fine, I swear. Aside from the cut, it's only scrapes and bruises," Lartaun replied as his cheeks flushed with embarrassment.

"*¡Coño!* I really thought that was it for you back there," said Pepe, still shaken.

"For real!" added Koldobika. "When I saw the bull dragging you by its horn, I thought to myself, the kid is toast! What a scare, *txo!*"

"The others are going to kick themselves for not waking up when we tell them what they've missed!" Bixente said with a laugh.

"How many stitches did you get?" asked Koldobika.

"Thirty-five," Lartaun replied with a hint of pride.

"Ouch!" Lartaun's friends exclaimed in morbid awe.

"You've gotta stop using your body like you're renting it! Seriously, how do you feel?" Koldobika asked again.

"You really want to know?" continued Lartaun, "way too sober for my own good!"

"All right then, let's go to where the real party's at! Off to the *txosnas!*"

Truer words were never spoken. From afar, the sky looked as if it was speckled with red dots as people kept on throwing their San Fermín scarves in the air in celebration. Punk rock music blasted from dozens of open stands that were erected in a wide circle along Yanguas street. The *txosnas* were simple booths which housed various alternative collectives, along with youth and political organizations. There, cheap food and alcohol were served to revelers in order to raise much-needed funds to keep said organizations afloat all year round. True to form, the place was jam-packed with a young crowd eager to drink hard and party harder.

Chaos reigned. The noise was deafening; the heat stifling. The sun was fierce and sticky like hot breath on the back of everyone's necks. There was no shade anywhere. Complete strangers hugged and kissed at random. Bottles of liquor traveled from hand to hand before being thrown to the ground, littering the street along with discarded food and forgotten or lost personal items such as scarves, cameras and even the occasional piece of lingerie.

"Hey!" Lartaun screamed into Bixente's ear as they were elbowing their way through the rambunctious mob. "Do you think that Anabel and Patxi will ever find us again in this crowd?"

"Don't worry!" Bixente yelled back at him. "Anabel knows where to find us. Relax! It's going to be all right."

Bixente grabbed Lartaun by the sleeve and dragged him toward a large stand buzzing with activity. An imposing banner with the word "JARRAI" stenciled in red spray-paint hung from the roof of the tent. Three guys standing behind a long folding table poured drinks at breakneck speed. Bixente ordered two beers and chatted up the bartenders for a couple minutes. He handed a plastic glass to Lartaun, and they retreated toward a sizeable group of young men holding court nearby the booth. They were all engrossed in a heated conversation. One of them recognized Bixente at once. He yelled his name and waved him over.

"Hey, Beltza! *¡Viejo cerdo!*" Bixente yelled right back at him. "*Oye,* Txatxu! Chucho! So glad to see the gang's all here!"

"Have you heard the news?" Beltza asked excitedly after giving his friend a manly hug. "We were just told that singer Imanol smuggled Piti and Sarri out of jail by hiding them inside the loudspeakers of his PA system!"

"They—wait! Imanol did what?"

The breaking news spread like wildfire throughout Pamplona. Poet and writer Joseba Sarrionandia, along with Iñaki Pikabea, ex-member of the Basque Parliament, just escaped from the Martutene penitentiary in San Sebastián, where they were serving prison sentences as convicted ETA members.

"Rumor has it that the band Kortatu helped plan their escape when they played a gig there a few weeks ago!"

Bixente took a big swig from a bottle of home-made *kalimotxo*, a concoction of cheap red wine mixed with Cola. Although quite delicious in a weird way, the drink guaranteed a painful hangover to anyone foolish enough to drink it in large quantities.

"Hey, Piti! Yo, Sarri!" he yelled drunkenly to the skies. "Here's to the sweet taste of freedom!"

"Make sure you stick around," continued Beltza, "all the *txosnas* have pitched in for the punk show tonight."

"Yeah, except for those cheap-ass "mofos" from *Juventudes Socialistas del PSOE*. They didn't chip in a cent for it!" laughed Pepe, joining in the conversation.

"With Kortatu on the bill, it's going to be off the hook! These guys are catchier than the clap in a two-bit whorehouse!" Beltza added with a big grin on his face.

"*Bestak bai, borroka ere bai!* We fight all right, but we must party too!" Bixente exclaimed at last. He locked his arms around Koldobika and Pepe's necks, and Lartaun watched them stagger toward the Jarrai stand to get another round.

Left alone amongst a group of strangers, Lartaun spoke to the man facing him and shyly ventured,

"Cool shirt."

"You like it?" Txatxu replied with pride, tugging at his T-shirt so that Lartaun could take a better look. It depicted a large Basque flag with the words *IKURRINA BAI, ESPAINOLA EZ* meaning "YES TO THE BASQUE FLAG, NO TO THE SPANISH FLAG" printed in block letters underneath. "Bixente tells me that you've been spending a lot of time at the *gaztetxe* lately," Txatxu asked Lartaun point blank.

"Hmmm, I like to go there and listen to what people have to say," answered Lartaun.

"And you agree with their views?"

"Their political views? Yes, I do. Actually, me and my friend Patxi have been talking about joining Jarrai for a while."

Txatxu's face brightened with a smile. He was a bit older than the rest of the guys, and by the looks of it, appeared to be completely sober. Judging by the respect the others clearly showed toward him, Lartaun realized he must be somewhat important.

"You're talking to the right person," he said warmly. "My name is Txatxu, and I'm one of the organization's leaders. Welcome to Jarrai!"

With a smile, Txatxu offered his hand to Lartaun. Just like the bull branded him that day, it took but a simple handshake to seal Lartaun's fate forever.

Nine years later, 09:42 AM ~ Thursday, April 7, 1994

"Where the hell have you been?" Vivienne was just coming out of the old train station when she spotted her daughter and Rafael walking back along the path, hand in hand. "I thought you'd fallen off the cliff or something! I was worried sick!"

"Hey, Ma!" Faustine let go of Rafael's hand and gave her mother a kiss.

"Morning, Viv," Rafael greeted her in his turn. Vivienne cast a less-than-friendly glance toward the young man. Still, she kissed him on both cheeks as the French do.

"C'mon Ma, don't fret. It was late when we finished climbing, so we thought that we might as well spend the night with Mathéo at the refuge, that's all. I would have called to let you know, but there aren't any pay phones up there!"

"Hmmm," she grunted, not buying her daughter's lame excuse.

"I don't know about you, but I'm starving," Faustine said to Rafael. "Do you want to get breakfast?"

"Let me unload the car first. I'll be right behind you."

"Okay!" she replied to him. "Ma, are you going back inside?" she asked her mother next.

"In a second, honey," Vivienne replied.

Faustine headed for the house while Rafael took off in the opposite direction.

"Hey!" Vivienne called after him when Faustine was out of sight. "Would you have a smoke, by any chance?"

Rafael turned around and fumbled in his jeans' back pocket. He produced a crumpled pack of Gauloises Blondes and handed her a cigarette. She straightened it with her fingers and lit it with his lighter.

"Thanks."

"Sure thing."

"Hey, Rafa?" He turned around again. "Um, nothing. Never mind."

Vivienne was thirty-six years old, and she looked way too young and attractive to be the mother of an eighteen-year-old. She stood a little shorter than Faustine and more petite, with fair skin and strawberry-blond hair that she wore in a loose bun under a colorful bandana. She hid her slim silhouette under smocked peasant blouses and ruffled skirts that reached down to her ankles. She donned a stack of silver bangles around her right wrist that jingled every time she brought the cigarette to her lips. As she stared at Rafael's back, she realized, once again, her maternal instincts had not failed her. Just as she feared, her daughter and the Latino-Frenchman had become more than friends. One look at her daughter confirmed the two were sleeping together. While Vivienne was not one to cringe about the topic of sex, it was tough for her to accept that her baby had grown up so much, so fast.

She tried, once more, to convince herself of her reason for disliking the guy. She was jealous of all the attention Faustine was throwing his way. Yet, deep down, she knew there was more to it than that. Something about this young man bothered her from day one. He looked way too mature and disillusioned for his age, and he had the distressed look of a man bearing the weight of a heavy cross on his shoulders. She messed with enough men like him in the past to know the type. They were bad news.

One of the unspoken rules at La Goutte d'Eau was not to question anyone's background, as long as there was no good reason to do so. Despite the initial gossip when he first arrived, everyone in the community came to appreciate Rafael Vargas for who he was. Thus, Vivienne thought it best to set her concerns aside for the time being. Call it a mother's intuition, but she could not refrain from thinking that their budding relationship did not bode well for Faustine's future.

When her cigarette had burnt all the way down to the filter, Vivienne stepped on it with her clog. She shook her head, absentmindedly, as if to brush off a bad thought, and walked back inside the train station, shutting the door behind her.

10
— HAMAR —

04:30 AM ~ Monday, August 22, 1994

Stéphane Pédrino and Daniel Marin arose before dawn to be on time for their shift. The armored van was already stocked with several cases of F19 NOBEL, Diameter 25/35/40, and they were scheduled to deliver the cargo to the construction site of the Somport tunnel before eight o'clock that morning.

Daniel, a die-hard bachelor, was paying the price of a long holiday of debauchery spent at a singles resort in Djerba, Tunisia. As a result, Stéphane, his long-time driving partner, generously offered to get behind the wheel that morning. They left the warehouse in Toulouse and, soon after, merged onto the highway heading toward the city of Pau. After a two-hour drive, they paid the toll at exit eleven and drove past the famed wine town of Jurançon before they hopped on RN-134 south toward the Spanish border.

They drove through the town of Oloron-Sainte-Marie around six in the morning. The beautiful mountain road heading to the Somport ran a somewhat parallel course to the Gave d'Aspe and the abandoned railway line. The road, the river and the train tracks crisscrossed each other like a braid via a succession of skillfully crafted tunnels and stone bridges along the bottom of the valley. Further down the road, past the village of Sarrance, an old man sporting Wellingtons was fly-fishing for trout in the stream, as he stood under the tall arch of an abandoned railroad viaduct. With his white moustache and his old-school wicker basket slung over his shoulder, he was a picture of perfection in this pleasant pastoral scene. Yet, Stéphane did not pay much attention to the scenery. He was too busy laughing while he explained to an exhausted Daniel how he had managed to fit the entire Pédrino family luggage inside their compact car for the return trip from the in-laws.

They had been driving for another five minutes or so when a huge boulder went tumbling down the side of the mountain and bounced right in front of the van.

"*Shiiiit!*" was all Stéphane had time to scream.

Stéphane gave the wheel a sharp turn to the right and immediately lost control of the van. The heavy truck swerved violently and began to tilt. At that particular spot, the road was curved into a sharp bend. There were no protective railings along the road shoulder to stop the truck. Daniel let out a scream as the vehicle's left tires lost contact with the asphalt. The van instantly took flight and crashed forcefully on its side at the bottom of a ravine, fifteen feet below the road. The sheer violence of the impact knocked both driver and passenger unconscious. Stéphane, who clutched the wheel for dear life, collapsed against the driver's window. Daniel's seat belt was the only thing that kept him pinned to his seat. As his arms and legs dangled limply above Stéphane's body, Daniel looked like a dead cosmonaut floating about the cabin.

From the road, the truck was invisible.

The dying engine of the vehicle hissed loudly. Save from the turbulent waters of the Gave d'Aspe, the aftermath pitter-patter of the wreckage was the only sound to be heard for miles. Suddenly, a bit of grit ricocheted onto the roof of the crumpled wreck, followed closely by the distinct sound of footsteps. Two hooded men, dressed in black fatigues and army boots, climbed down the ravine.

They circled the truck with extreme caution. The front passenger door caved in, at some point, during the accident. The bulletproof window popped out of its grooves. Once assured that the men inside were unconscious, one of them bashed the glass sheet against the side door with the butt of his Kalashnikov AK-74 assault rifle and fumbled around until his hand found the door handle. He forced the door open. It gave in with a creaking sound. He made a silent gesture to his partner and disappeared inside the toppled cabin. The second man, hiding behind a black jersey hood, spoke with a low voice into a short-range radio. In his gloved hand, he kept a Beretta 92 FS 9mm Parabellum pistol pointed toward the top of the ravine.

The intruder set his rifle against the lopsided dashboard, keeping it close enough to grab if necessary. With his hands free, he fished in his pocket for heavy-duty cable-ties. He brought Stéphane's hands together and bound his wrists with two of the ties. He ripped a piece of duct tape and stuck it over his mouth. Finally, he snatched the gun clipped to his holster and dropped it into one of his pockets. As soon as Stéphane was bound, he moved to Daniel. Maneuvering inside the flipped-over cabin was not an easy task. The man was forced to proceed with extreme caution. He produced a serrated knife and cut through the seat belt that kept the other victim pressed against the passenger seat. As soon as he was released from his binding, Daniel plopped right into his arms. Unconscious, he was heavier than expected. His fall caused the intruder to lose his footing and crash backwards under Daniel's dead weight. The man cursed under his breath and pushed him off without ceremony. Daniel landed in a heap on top of his unfortunate colleague. He repeated the same steps to bind and gag Daniel before he confiscated his weapon.

The trespasser was searching the cabin when he noticed something shiny sticking out from under Daniel's sweater. Clipped to a loop on his uniform, dangled a sturdy metal ring with the key that opened the cargo bay. He tore it off with one quick pull. He stuck his head through the opening again and dangled the key chain from his index finger so that his accomplice could see what he had found. His partner gave him a thumbs-up and spoke a few words into his radio. Meanwhile, the hooded man already slipped back inside the cabin to unlock the armored door and get inside the cargo area.

"We've unlocked the cargo bay. Over."

"Roger that. Scanning the perimeter. We're sending the team down."

"Ten-four."

A nondescript silver Citroën CX car, dragging an old camping-trailer, sat idle on the road shoulder. Two of its occupants, dressed in civilian clothing, jumped through the side door and stumbled down the ravine while the driver remained inside the car. He concealed a miniature walkie-talkie in the palm of his hand, which he used to keep in contact with the rest of his team. His radio crackled to life a few minutes later.

"Ready to send the first load up."

"Roger that. No, wait!"

The driver just spotted a large eighteen-wheeler barreling down the road in his rearview mirror. The vehicle did not bother to slow down as it passed by his car. The wind it displaced caused the trailer to rattle on its rusty axles.

"What was that?" the alarmed voice came through the radio.

"Just a truck. Nothing to worry about. Top area's clear now."

"Sending first load up. Advise if situation changes."

"Ten-four."

The two men reappeared over the edge of the ravine. They carried a large case wrapped in a thick blanket, loaded it inside the trailer and ran back down without wasting any time. As soon as all three cases had been brought back up, they jumped back into the car.

As they crouched below the edge of the asphalt road, the other two armed assailants awaited their order from the driver to return to the vehicle.

"Exit now!" ordered the driver, "go, go, go!"

Upon hearing the signal, the two men sprang into action. They ran the short distance to the trailer while holding their guns. They dropped down to the floor of the trailer and slammed the door shut, just as the Citroën picked up speed.

By the time they changed back into civilian clothing and hid their weapons and fatigues inside the false bottom of the caravan, the convoy had almost reached its destination. So far, things had gone according to plan, and the toughest and most dangerous part of the operation was now behind them. Still, they were not out of the woods yet. The man sitting on the floor with his back resting against the crates knew that only too well. He raked his fingers through his ash-blond hair and exhaled hard in an attempt to slow the wild beating of his heart.

"Do you think they were dead, back there?" the other man asked him bluntly. His name was Iñaki. He was a tall skinny Basque with an aquiline nose and a thick brown beard framing a set of thin red lips. His mousy black eyes darted back and forth behind the severe-looking rimless glasses that he just put on. His attempt at conversation startled his companion as they had not exchanged a single word since the beginning of their mission.

"How would I know? You're the one who dealt with them."

"I know that the driver was breathing when I tied him up. As for the other one," he replied, his voice unsteady, "I'm not so sure. He was bleeding all over. Kind of freaked me out, to tell you the truth, so I did not really check. One thing's for sure, though. They were out cold the whole time I was in there. When they wake up—"

"You mean, *if* they wake up?"

Iñaki knitted his bushy eyebrows. "Right. When or if they wake up, they won't even know what hit them."

"There you have your answer, then," Patxi replied calmly.

The radio clicked several times. It was a code from their accomplices inside the car letting them know that they were getting close to the drop-off. The convoy slowed down, and then came to a stop. They overheard a brief exchange of words followed by the creaking sound of an old metal gate opening. Shortly afterward, the trailer started moving again. Judging by the crunching sound of the tires on the gravel, they entered some sort of a courtyard. Abruptly, the vehicle came to its final stop. Mikel, the driver, shut down the engine and cranked the handbreak. Patxi listened to the triple bang of the car doors as his partners slammed them shut. He tensed upon hearing footsteps outside. The side door of the trailer opened wide, flooding the confined space with sunlight. Iñaki and Patxi squinted until their eyes adjusted to the light.

"I'm glad you got here safe and sound," said the man standing in the threshold. "I'm Jean-Philippe."

"*Aupa.*" Patxi stood up and swatted the dust off the back of his jeans as he exited the caravan. Without wasting another second, he started shouting orders to his men. "Koldo! Iñaki! You two are in charge of moving the crates to safety! Mikel, go unhook the trailer and switch the car plates! I want to be back on the road within the next five minutes, so crank it!"

"Where to?" Iñaki asked Jean-Philippe as he and Koldobika lifted the first case off the pile.

"The wine cellar!" he answered, pointing at a small arched doorway across the courtyard.

"Eric and, um, you," said Patxi, pointing at Jean-Philippe, "let's go in."

Jean-Philippe led them into his house. Just like Eric, Jean-Philippe was French. With his elaborate disheveled look, longish light brown hair and drowsy dark blue eyes, he was the poster boy for the "clean," upper class, grunge generation. Patxi was meeting him, face-to-face, for the first time. Even though Jean-Philippe had not given him a valid reason,

Patxi distrusted him right away. Somehow, he gave off the vibe of a phony, a poser. Down the road, that could become a real problem.

"So, how did it go?" Jean-Philippe asked them, barely able to contain his excitement.

"Everything went according to plan," Patxi replied. Jean-Philippe exhaled with relief.

"Koldo, Mikel, Iñaki and I are taking off right away. Eric is going to stay here to help you erase any evidence of our passage. Be sure to hide the weapons in a safe spot until we come back for them later. And don't forget to get rid of the trailer. The sooner, the better."

"No sweat, Patxi. We're on it."

"Contact Lartaun as soon as you think that it is safe to transfer the loot to the secret location."

"Got it. We know what to do."

"Should anything go wrong from this point on, we never met each other. You're on your own."

"Yep."

"Don't make me regret hiring your ass. Understood?"

Jean-Philippe tugged at the collar of his cropped plaid shirt as if it were suddenly choking him. "Of course, Patxi," he said, much less confident this time around.

"All right, then. Good luck to you two. *Agur.*"

Patxi turned on his heels and hurried back to meet his accomplices in the courtyard.

"Dude, this Patxi guy is scary as shit!" remarked Jean-Philippe.

"What did you expect?" Eric replied with a shrug. "You wanted to play in the big league, so deal with it. And by the way, try not to behave like a douche next time you're around Patxi, OK? For the record, I don't think that he was all that impressed with your big-time badass impersonation."

"Yeah, well, fuck you too, asshole." Jean-Philippe replied matter-of-factly before helping himself to a cold beer from the fridge.

Jean-Philippe was a single child, born to a wealthy family from Biarritz. Early on, his parents realized that their son's main source of satisfaction came from mischief and constant rebellion. While they worried about it at the dinner table, they were too wrapped up in their own dissolute lives to find time to address the problem. Jean-Philippe soon turned to drugs and alcohol to entertain his boredom, but before long, even that became a drag. He wanted to live his life in the fast lane. He was hungry for action.

As it turned out, Eric was a prominent member of ETA's French Basque counterpart, the separatist group *Iparretarrak,* meaning "Those of the North." While *Iparretarrak,* or "IK" for short, never claimed any actual terrorist attacks, it did provide ample support and logistical help for ETA on French soil. That was how Eric first met Patxi, back in 1992, via the ETA/IK clandestine network. Well over a year later, some time during the month of October 1993, Patxi contacted Eric again surreptitiously to help his secret cell with the logistics of an upcoming robbery. Eric accepted the invitation to give Patxi a hand. In his turn, Eric asked Jean-Philippe, whom he had befriended at a party, six months prior, if he would be willing to act as a temporary keeper of the stolen goods for Patxi. He knew that Jean-Philippe's family owned property in the heart of the Vallée d'Aspe, where the *ekintza* was slated to take place.

At first, Patxi was wary of working with someone he did not know, let alone trust. However, the recent arrests of ETA and IK members throughout the French side of the Basque country had left Patxi with few men to choose from. That was how Jean-Philippe eased into living the double life of a clean-cut man by day and a clandestine *guerillero* by night. He finally found the rush, the high that he yearned for all along. Now that he was in possession of several cases of stolen goods and weapons, he could no longer deny that he had jumped with both feet into the ring of fire. Additionally, while he would not admit it aloud, it was turning out to be quite a frightening experience.

Jean-Philippe looked up toward the neighbors' window overlooking his courtyard. The shutters were drawn. Thank goodness, they were still asleep. He and Eric walked to the wine cellar in the adjacent building to check on the cargo. The cases were piled one on top of the other at the far end of the room. They were hidden from view behind a metal rack filled with dust-covered wine bottles. Satisfied, they both walked to the trailer inside the garage. Jean-Philippe wiped it clean of fingerprints. In a night or two, he would drive to the local landfill and abandon it there.

At last, Eric stuffed the weapons and clothes inside a large dry bag. He planned to sink it in the old stone well in the courtyard. All the pair had left to do was to rake the gravel in order to erase the tire marks left inside the courtyard.

Once Jean-Philippe and Eric were confident with their attempts to conceal the evidence, they returned into the house for breakfast.

Meanwhile, a few minutes past seven o'clock, Patxi, Iñaki, Mikel and Koldobika crossed the Spanish border without incident. As soon as they drove past the small city of Jaca, Patxi rolled his sweater into a ball and announced calmly that he was going to take a well-deserved nap.

11
- HAMAIKA -

06:42 AM ~ Monday, August 22, 1994

Mathilde Fablier sat behind the wheel of her '85 red Renault Supercinq. As she zoomed down the road, windows down, she took in the warm morning breeze. She knew the road like the back of her hand. Every day she commuted from Etsaut to Oloron-Sainte-Marie, where she worked as a real estate agent.

As she approached a hairpin curve, she downshifted gears in order to let the engine-break slow the car down. This, in turn, caused the old exhaust pipe to backfire with two sharp explosions. She could have sworn she heard the sound of a car horn further up the road, and yet, there was no car in sight once she rounded the bend. Instead, the road was littered with large chunks of rock. Curious, she pulled over to the side of the road. Upon closer inspection, she noticed two thick skid marks imprinted on the asphalt. They looked fresh, and they led straight for the ravine.

"Sweet Mother of God!" she mumbled out loud. She choked her engine with a turn of the key, got out of the car and cautiously approached the edge of the drop off. She looked down, gasped and leaped backwards. A boxy truck lay crumpled on its side. With its wheels sticking up in the air, it looked like a dead animal. Mathilde forced herself to calm down before she called out to whoever might still be trapped inside the wreck.

"Hello?" She cleared her voice and shouted a little louder this time. "Hello? Is there anybody out there?" The horn howled twice from inside the wreck. "Can you hear me?"

Honk! Honk!

Without a doubt, someone was stuck in there.

"Can you talk?" she ventured.

Honk!

"Are you hurt?"

Honk! Hoooooooonk!

Mathilde tried to think fast while the horn went off again. "Hold on tight! I'm going to drive to the next village and get help!"

She rushed back to her car, revved the engine and took off.

Unable to move because he was sandwiched between the door and his lifeless friend, Stéphane listened to the car speeding away in the distance. Overwhelmed with despair, he started to sob. His face was caked with blood that had run down his eyes and into his nose. He could not tell for sure whether the blood was his or Daniel's. He snorted hard to clear his airways from the sticky substance that started to clot inside his nostrils. At this point, the pain radiating up and down his spine was the only thing that kept him from drifting into unconsciousness. He closed his eyes so that he would no longer have to look at the back of Daniel's cracked head.

Fifteen minutes later, Mathilde's car screeched to a halt in front of a pay phone. She jumped out and dialed "18" for emergency. Within minutes, a dark blue Renault van from the "Gendarmerie Nationale," the French paramilitary police force, picked her up. They took off, sirens blasting, as they headed toward RN-134. Firefighters along with Emergency and Resuscitation Mobile Service ambulances were also contacted. Everyone was on their way, waiting for Mathilde to report the exact location of the accident over the radio.

"Slow down, we're almost there!" she said, pointing toward the curve ahead. The uniformed driver spotted the broken chunks of stone sprawled over the road and reduced his speed. "There!" she shrieked. "That's where the truck fell off the road!"

"I need two men to stay up here and control traffic while Antoine and I go check below," instructed *Adjudant-Chef* Lionel Darvin. He turned to Mathilde next. "Ma'am, I must ask you to remain inside this vehicle for now."

The Chief was a svelte man in his mid-fifties with a short buzz cut and graying temples. He jumped out of the van and, flanked by one of his officers, started to climb down the steep slope. When they neared the wreck, they called out to the victim. There was no answer at first. They circled the van to investigate further. Suddenly, they heard a muffled shout coming from the driver's side. Chief Darvin wasted no time climbing onto the side of the truck. Proceeding with care, he peeked through the smashed-up window.

"Well, I'll be damned!" he exclaimed.

His partner hurried to the Chief's side.

"What the hell?" he said in his turn, looking down at the sickening scene inside the crumpled cabin.

Stéphane was trying to shove Daniel out of the way in a desperate attempt to see who the men were. He wanted to yell, but the duct tape was choking him. His bloodshot eyes were as big as saucers, and he was hyperventilating.

"Gendarmerie! We're here to assist you! Stay calm and conserve your energy. We're coming to you right now," said the chief. "I see two of you in there. Are there any more passengers in the back?"

Stéphane shook his head no.

"Chief, look! They're tied up!" exclaimed gendarme Antoine Servan.

"I don't like this one bit. Take his gag off. Don't worry, I've got your back." The officer slithered through the window opening. "Be careful in there and try not to disturb anything. I'm calling for back-up."

Gendarme Servan put on a pair of latex gloves before he ripped the duct tape off Stéphane's mouth. The poor man let out a scream of pain. He secured a resealable zipper bag from his uniform pocket and dropped the discarded piece of tape in it as evidence. He passed the bag onto his chief.

"Are you hurt? Do you feel pain?" Darvin asked the victim. Stéphane answered with a grimace which spoke louder than words. "Hang on, OK? The medics will be here in a minute," he said in a reassuring voice. "Can you tell us what happened here?"

"I don't know, I just don't know!" Frightened and in shock, Stéphane replied, shaking his head back and forth. "Just get me out of here! Please!"

Darvin watched on as Officer Servan checked on Daniel's pulse.

"And?" Darvin asked.

"Weak, very weak," Servan responded softly, trying not to alarm the other victim.

"Sir?" Stéphane Pédrino's voice was all choked-up. "Can you check on our cargo in the back?"

"No need to worry about your cargo right now," replied Chief Darvin. "We need to get you and your partner to safety first, and then we'll check on—"

"Please," Stéphane pleaded, "we were transporting a load of commercial explosives to the Somport. Two hundred and fifty pounds of it."

"Jesus!" Darvin muttered under his breath. "Antoine! Go take a look inside the cargo bay."

Officer Servan grabbed his flashlight and promptly disappeared into the twisted entrails of the truck. His answer came in a matter of seconds.

"There's nothing in there. It's empty!"

Lionel Darvin radioed the Colonel of the Gendarmerie Nationale's brigades in the city of Pau to request his presence along with a TIC team, the crime scene investigation unit. For all they knew, they were now looking at a bona fide crime scene.

Upon receiving word of the incident, the Colonel called for the immediate implementation of a *plan épervier*. "Operation Sparrow Hawk" was the code name for setting up road blocks at strategic locations in order to stop and search any suspicious vehicle within a predetermined grid-locked area. The instructions were to search any vehicle capable of transporting several large crates in its cargo bay. The Colonel then placed a phone call to the State Prosecutor in order to relay the preliminary details of the incident. At last, he summoned one of his Majors to tag along in his chauffeured car to assess the situation at the crime scene.

While he was waiting for the Colonel's arrival, Chief Darvin ordered his team to secure the perimeter. He himself photographed the scene above and below road level in meticulous detail.

In the distance, one could hear the wailing howl of MEDEVAC units approaching with great speed. Two ambulances stopped right behind the gendarmerie van. The medic team jumped out with their first-aid kits and gurneys and hurried down the ravine to attend to Daniel, who appeared to be in critical condition. Working with precision and efficiency, they strapped him onto a backboard to hoist him out of the vehicle cabin. As soon as Daniel was set free from the wreckage, the second team stepped in to take care of Stéphane's injuries.

When they were ready to go, Chief Darvin took one of the paramedics aside and asked,

"What's your prognosis?"

"All I can tell you is that the driver looks like he has multiple fractures. He's going into shock, but that is to be expected after such an accident. We're sending him to the hospital in Oloron-Sainte-Marie. As for the other victim, we suspect that he has sustained extensive head injuries. The 'SMUR' dispatch center has already sent a civil defense helicopter over there to transport him to the trauma unit of the hospital in Pau if needed."

"Thank you, sir. Here's my card. Have the hospital personnel contact me as soon as more information becomes available."

"Very well, Mister, um, Darvin," the paramedic said after reading the Chief's name on the business card.

"Jesus Christ, what a morning!" Darvin commented to no one in particular.

An hour later, a gendarmerie patrol car, escorting a light grey Citroën BX, stopped on the road shoulder. Four uniformed officers exited the car with Colonel Lambert leading the way. Lionel Darvin greeted him with a formal hand salute.

"*Mon* Colonel, I am glad that you could come on such short notice."

"Good morning, Darvin. Have you met Major Boréda?" he asked, pointing to the blue-eyed man standing by his side.

"Never in person, I'm afraid. However, we've spoken on the phone. Pleasure to meet you, Major." They shook hands.

"And these two men are my crime scene investigation agents, Pascal Charenton and Thierry Boisvin," added the colonel. "Please, fill us in."

"Certainly, *mon* Colonel," he said as he saluted the two other men. "We're looking at a Western-style hold-up here. Evidently, the truck and its occupants were ambushed. We assume that a large boulder was pushed down the mountain to land on the road right in front of this truck. The driver must have swerved to avoid it, and subsequently, lost control of the vehicle. They went off the road, crashed, and both driver and passenger blacked out. When the driver regained consciousness, he had a gag over his mouth and his colleague was bleeding all over him. We checked on the cargo, at his request, and found out that the commercial explosives they were transporting were all gone. So were their weapons. This looks like the work of skilled professionals."

"All of this has been duly recorded, I presume?"

"Absolutely, *mon* Colonel."

"Thank you, Chief." With that, Colonel Lambert turned to the TIC team experts. "Gentlemen, let's get to work. Retrieve every piece of evidence you can find. Dust for fingerprints and record footprints left in the mud. You know the drill. Be sure to send whatever is worth analyzing to the lab as soon as you're done." Finally, the Colonel addressed Major Boréda with a grave expression. "Jean-Claude, you're officially in charge of this investigation. Needless to say, this case is your number one priority. I will put all necessary resources and men at your disposal. We must find the culprits and retrieve the dynamite ASAP." He surveyed the crime scene perimeter one last time, a weary look on his face. It was swarming with gendarmes taking pictures, measuring and collecting evidence. "If you need me," he said, "I'll be in the car."

Boréda and Darvin watched him walk away in silence.

"No press, no cameras," Boréda ordered as soon as he had pulled himself together. "When the media call for details, tell them this was nothing more than an unfortunate traffic accident."

"Of course, Major." Darvin scratched his head, dumbfounded. "I just don't get it. Who would steal two hundred and fifty pounds of dynamite?"

"Someone who's planning one hell of a fireworks show," Boréda responded calmly.

12
-HAMABI-

05:00 PM ~ Tuesday, August 23, 1994

By the time the warm days of summer returned to the valley, Rafael and Faustine had taken up residence inside Vivienne's old Volkswagen camper, which he had fully gutted and transformed into a cozy living space for two. Massimo, tired of waiting for Vivienne, had left the valley for good. Consequently, Graziella had not returned to La Goutte d'Eau since March. While Faustine missed her girlfriend, she had little time or reason to sulk. She and Rafael were in love and on top of the world.

Faustine, Rafael and Etienne were sunning themselves on the old concrete platform at the back of the train station. Mina came to join them with a six-pack that she took out of the fridge. She sported a crocheted, jade green bikini that matched the color of her eyes, a remarkable trait her Kabyle father had passed on to her. Its hue contrasted beautifully with her complexion and the dark chocolate color of her hair, which she had braided in an elaborate pleated bun.

"Mina, come sit by me! I'll trade you a cold one for a few puffs!" Etienne had just finished rolling a joint between his fingers, and he was ready to light it up.

"Deal!" Mina replied with a laugh. He made room for her, and she plopped down on his beach towel. "Guess what happened on RN-134 yesterday?" she quizzed the group.

Etienne, who loved to push everyone's buttons for the hell of it, hummed the notes of France's national television news jingle. Everyone laughed good-heartedly because Mina, in her self-appointed role as PR person for the commune, kept track of all local and national news that referred to their collective and the Somport struggle at large. Etienne once called her "anchorwoman," and the nickname stuck ever since.

"Oh, you're so funny I could just puke!" she replied with a sarcastic pout. "Well, there was an accident yesterday morning."

"Not anyone we know, I hope?" asked Etienne.

"*Ya 'Allah*, no. Some truck drove off the road and crashed by the river. Mark my words: when the tunnel opens, this kind of news will become a daily occurrence! This road was never meant to handle much traffic."

"What kind of truck was it?" Etienne inhaled on his spliff, filling his lungs to capacity with the potent smoke.

"Not sure. To be honest with you, the article I read was very evasive. They did not say what model truck it was, or even what it was transporting. Isn't it scary though? I mean, it crashed just yards away from the Gave d'Aspe! Imagine, for a second, it was carrying chemicals or anything poisonous that could have seeped into the river!"

"I don't want to think about that. Way too freaky," commented Etienne.

"Was anyone hurt?" Rafael asked out of the blue.

"Both the driver and his passenger were injured," answered Mina. "One of them is in critical condition."

Vivienne stuck her face out the window at that moment and shouted,

"Rafael? Are you out there? There's someone here who wants to see you!"

Rafael raised his eyebrows in surprise. "Save me a beer, guys, I'll be right back," he grumbled.

He stood up and disappeared inside the train station.

Sitting by the bar, Jean-Philippe made small talk with another customer. Upon spotting the man he knew as Lartaun, he swiveled his chair around and pointed his thumb toward the main door as an invitation to go outside. Lartaun approved with a nod, and they both walked out the front of the building.

"The truck accident, that's the reason why you're here, correct?" Lartaun asked as soon as they were out of earshot from everyone else.

Jean-Philippe nodded. "They did it, all right. We need to hide the loot first thing tomorrow morning."

Lartaun shook his head in disbelief. "It's been months of peace and quiet. I was beginning to believe they wouldn't go through with it."

"So did I, but we were wrong."

"So, what's the plan?" Lartaun asked after a pause.

"Seven o'clock tomorrow. My place. Bring your climbing gear. I'll take care of the rest."

13
— HAMAHIRU —

06:45 AM ~ Wednesday, August 24, 1994

The large wrought-iron gates opened just wide enough to let Lartaun's car through. He parked his Renault "4L" out of sight in the garage and crossed the courtyard toward the old farm building. Jean-Philippe's parents had renovated the place with opulent taste. Undeniably, they came from old money and it showed.

"Jean-Philippe?" Lartaun called from the front door stoop.

"Over here, man. In the kitchen!"

Jean-Philippe was not alone. A seemingly bored young man comfortably sat in a kitchen chair, his feet resting atop a century-old oak table. He took one last drag from a rolled cigarette before he addressed Lartaun.

"So you're Lartaun, huh?" The man extended a limp hand to greet him. "At last, I can slap a face onto the name of Patxi's protégé."

"And you must be Eric. *Kaixo,* " replied Lartaun.

Lartaun figured Eric was in his early thirties. His arms and chest were quite muscular, a sign that he was working out on a regular basis. He would be a reasonably handsome man had his cheeks not been pitted with so many chicken pox scars. They added a sinister touch to his physique, and his malevolent sneer did not help make him any more likeable.

"Patxi said that you've found the perfect *zulo* for the explosives," Eric went on.

Zulo meant "hole" in Basque. The word was also used to indicate a secret place where ETA members concealed their arsenals, or even their prisoners. Indeed, Lartaun had found a small cavern no one seemed to know about, most likely because its entrance was located about two hundred and fifty feet above ground, smack in the middle of a vertical cliff and far away from any road.

"He must really trust you to let you hide his loot without even knowing the *zulo*'s exact location," Eric added with obvious skepticism in his voice. Clearly, he wanted to challenge Lartaun.

"I hope he trusts everyone he works with," replied Lartaun with a stone-cold voice.

Jean-Philippe, sensing the tension building between them, opted to defuse the situation by getting down to business.

"Guys, we need to get the dynamite out of sight as soon as possible."

"How heavy is the stuff?" enquired Lartaun. "We can only make one trip."

"Give or take two hundred and fifty pounds."

"I have about fifty pounds of climbing gear to lug around already. That makes three hundred pounds to carry between the three of us. I hope you are well rested, because this is going to be one tough hike."

They left the house and walked over to the wine cellar. The air inside was cool and a little musty. Jean-Philippe pulled on a string hanging from the low-arched ceiling near the entrance to turn on the lights. A naked bulb revealed racks and racks of dusty wine bottles stacked up high against every wall. Deep grooves imprinted onto the packed dirt floor toward the back of the room were evidence that some of them had recently been moved. Lartaun immediately made a mental note of Jean-Philippe's mistake, blatant proof that he was an amateur, but thought best to keep his mouth shut since it did not really matter anymore at this point. Jean-Philippe swiveled the wine racks around, one more time, to reveal three voluminous crates stacked up behind them.

"This is it. It looks like a lot, but once we unload the dynamite sticks from the boxes, I think it'll be more manageable."

"Where did you put the backpacks?" asked Lartaun.

"Over there." Jean-Philippe pointed to a far corner of the room.

"Let me go get the climbing gear," said Lartaun. "I left it in my car."

When Lartaun re-entered the wine cellar a few minutes later, Eric broke the seals off of the first crate. Inside were several cardboard boxes bearing the logo "NOBEL." They opened the one on top. Ten bright red sticks of dynamite came to view, wrapped up in heavy duty plastic. Each log was a little over an inch in diameter and about sixteen inches long. They looked like big sausages encased in plastic tubing that had been clipped and sealed at both ends.

"Wow!" Eric was barely able to contain his excitement. "This is serious stuff! Gelatin dynamite. No DNT or TNT or any of that crap! Excellent sensitivity and low toxicity fumes. Strong enough to blast a hole in a mountain!"

Jean-Philippe grazed the dynamite sticks with the tips of his fingers, a concerned look on his face.

"Is it safe to carry this stuff on our backs?" he suddenly asked.

"As long as the temperature does not exceed 122 degrees Fahrenheit, the explosives should remain stable. Besides, we don't carry any detonators," stated Eric, "but just to be on the safe side, I'd suggest we all refrain from smoking around it if we can help it."

"A hundred and twenty-two degrees? That's it? Do you have any idea how hot the backpacks are going to get when we carry them in direct sunlight?" questioned Lartaun.

"Take a chill pill, sonny boy. Maybe you can raid your grandma's first aid kit and grab a couple ice packs to keep your load cool," sneered Eric.

Eric's last remark sent Lartaun over the edge. He lashed out at him with all his strength and sent Eric crashing backwards to the ground. Before Eric realized what was happening to him, Lartaun had him pinned to the floor. His fist was raised above his head, and he was about to punch Eric square in the face. Jean-Philippe yanked Lartaun's arm back just before he could take the first swing.

"What the fuck's wrong with you, man?" squealed Eric, his left arm extended in front of him to protect his face.

"Quit it, damn it! Do you really think that we have time for this shit?" Jean-Philippe yelled, caught in the middle.

Lartaun was fuming. His stare alone was enough to scare Eric witless.

"By the time we get to the *zulo*, the cliff will be hotter than the hinges of hell! Can't you see that it's barely seven in the morning, and it's already hot outside?" Lartaun said, trying to contain his anger the best he could.

"I hear you," Jean-Philippe answered as he helped Eric back to his feet, "but it's not like we have a choice. The time is now or never."

"Fine. After all, I don't call the shots. As for you," he added, pointing a menacing finger at Eric, "I suggest you limit your smart-ass remarks to a minimum until this day is over."

Eric, beet-red with humiliation, uttered not a word. Instead, he brushed the dust off his pants and returned to unloading the contents of the crates into the backpacks.

Fifteen minutes later, they were packed and ready to go.

"Let's go," said Lartaun. "We've got a long walk ahead of us."

Eric slung the giant backpack over his shoulders and gasped under its weight. He secured the wide cummerbund around his waist to help him balance the charge on his back and adjusted his shoulder straps to a snug fit. Jean-Philippe followed his example with a painful grunt while Lartaun lifted his own backpack in one smooth pull, as if it weighed nothing at all.

"This is going to be painful," complained Eric, who was already struggling under the weight of his load.

"If you think that this is painful, just wait until your freakin' bag explodes in your face," Lartaun cursed under his breath.

"I wish you'd given us a ride in your car to the start of the trail, at least," Eric continued. Clearly, he had not overheard Lartaun's remark. "It would save us a great deal of time and energy."

"And leave the car in plain sight by the side of the road? While you're at it, how about we stick a map on the windshield for everyone to see where we're heading?" Lartaun blurted out in spite of himself.

"You—"

"Shut up you two, and let's go!" Jean-Philippe interrupted them. He was already at his wits' end with the pair.

They stepped out of the cellar in single file and began marching into the sun.

Lartaun led the way, followed by Eric, with Jean-Philippe bringing up the rear. The trio had been walking along the uneven path for close to two hours, concentrating on putting one foot in front of the other, when Lartaun heard a muffled cry behind him. Eric had slipped on loose stones and lost his balance. He looked as helpless as a turtle lying on its back as he struggled to get back on his feet to no avail. Lartaun freed Eric from the binding straps of his backpack and extended a hand to help him. As soon as Eric put weight on his left foot, he let out a piercing scream and slumped back again to the ground.

"I think I broke my ankle!" he cried in pain.

Lartaun dropped his backpack to the ground and kneeled beside Eric. With gentle movements, he proceeded to examine his leg. Eric's ankle had already doubled in volume. The skin around it was turning a painful shade of purple.

"I think he's right," Lartaun said to Jean-Philippe. "It's broken."

"You've got to be shitting me! What are we going to do now?" asked Jean-Philippe.

"He'll have to stay here and wait for us. This means that you'll be climbing with me."

"Are you nuts? I've never done this before!"

Lartaun ignored Jean-Philippe's comment. Instead, he improvised a makeshift splint made out of two straight branches tied together with Eric's own T-shirt to immobilize his lower leg. Afterwards, they dragged him into the shade, where he sat with his bare back resting against a tree trunk.

"Jean-Philippe will check on you when he comes back to get your bag. In the meantime, sit tight and try to relax," Lartaun said calmly.

"You're not going to leave me here alone, are you?" whined Eric, looking more frightened than a kid left alone in the dark.

"Why? Do you have a better suggestion?" replied Lartaun.

"What about bears?"

"Last I checked, there was only six of them alive this side of the Pyrenees. I can't decide whether you'd be lucky or unfortunate to see one."

"Here, take this, just in case," said Jean-Philippe, careful to avoid Lartaun's gaze. He handed Eric a nine-millimeter gun.

Lartaun stared at the weapon and challenged them both with a scornful glare.

"Shoot a bear, and I swear that I'll shoot you myself!"

The sun was hot on their backs when they made it to the foot of the cliff a little after ten o'clock in the morning. Jean-Philippe wiped his forehead with the back of his hand. He opened the top flap of his pack to inspect the load inside. Thankfully, everything looked all right. The explosives had not started to sweat. He let out a sigh of relief and pushed the bags back into the shade. Standing a few feet away from him, Lartaun spread out his climbing gear on the ground.

"I'm going to get Eric's pack," Jean-Philippe said without enthusiasm and left.

When he returned about half-an-hour later, he was sweating profusely and the canvas of his backpack was frighteningly hot to the touch.

"What now?" he panted.

Lartaun looked up. Jean-Philippe imitated him at once. The cliff was a vertical compact limestone slab. Long diagonal crevasses and dihedrals sliced through its otherwise flat features. There was a wide ledge at about ninety feet, where a couple scraggly trees managed to survive and grow. Near the top, an oblong-shaped hole carved out of the face loomed, seemingly out of reach. There it was, the *zulo*.

"See this patch of dark stone all the way up there? That's where we're going," said Lartaun. Jean-Philippe followed Lartaun's finger with his eyes.

"You can't be serious!" he gasped. "I'm scared of heights, man!"

"The course is three rope lengths to the cavern," Lartaun went on talking, unfazed. "I'll free climb it so you won't have to. Technically speaking, 'jumaring' isn't much more difficult than climbing a ladder. You'll get the hang of it quickly. Besides, you'll be tethered to a safety rope at all times. So even if you mess up, you can't fall. OK?"

Lartaun's blunt words of comfort didn't seem to help Jean-Philippe at all. Still, he forced himself to set his fears aside and listen as Lartaun taught him the rudiments of aid climbing. Next, Lartaun explained in detail what he expected from Jean-Philippe as his belaying partner.

Within the hour, they were ready to tackle the climb.

Lartaun, thirty feet above ground, paused long enough to insert a stopper inside a small vertical crack. He tested the device by giving it a gentle tug before he clipped his rope onto it and continued his ascension. He repeated those steps, several times, until he reached the ledge at the end of the first pitch. It was about three feet wide and ten feet long, with a twisted thorn bush extending its thirsty branches into the air smack in the middle. Lartaun moved with caution, so as to not dislodge any stones that could fall onto his partner below. There, he set up a solid triple anchor belay capable of holding their combined weight as well as the three backpacks. When he was done, he warned Jean-Philippe that he was about to throw the ropes down to him.

Standing at the foot of the cliff, Jean-Philippe geared up and mentally practiced the moves he would have to repeat in order to static-climb along the face. Deep inside, he knew he had no choice but to get it right the first time.

Jean-Philippe secured the first ascender. The mechanical device was designed to glide effortlessly along the rope in an upward motion and to block itself immediately upon any downward tension. He tested the device by putting on his weight. The handle gripped the rope firmly. So far, so good. He repeated the process with the second climbing aid. He slid the ascender handle up the rope and arrived at a standing position. His right foot rested inside the loop of the sling. Soon, he was off the ground. If the technique seemed awkward and confusing to him in theory, Jean-Philippe realized it was not all that difficult in practice. Before long, he was progressing at a good clip toward belay, while Lartaun reeled in the slack of the safety rope above him. When he set foot on the ledge at the end of the first pitch, he was elated he had made it all the way up there on his own. But there was no time to celebrate. The sun was already high in the sky.

Lartaun rigged the rope system with a self-blocking pulley and proceeded to hoist the bags, praying, in silence, they would not snag onto a rock and get stuck mid-face. Luckily, the operation went without a glitch, and the load promptly made it to its destination. Lartaun set the bags side-by-side along the natural platform and anchored them to the rock to ensure they could not, accidentally, get knocked off the ledge.

They repeated the same process for the second pitch. About an hour-and-a-half or so later, Lartaun prepared to tackle the final rope-length to the *zulo*.

The route followed a tricky forty-foot high dihedral formed by two planes of rock which were so sleek and smooth that the cliff looked like a giant open book. The passage to the cavern offered very few opportunities to place protections along the way, turning it into a very exposed climb.

"All right, I'm off," announced Lartaun.

"Don't fall, man, I beg you!" Jean-Philippe gripped the climbing rope with all his might. His stare darted back and forth between Lartaun and his figure-eight belay device.

"Don't take this the wrong way, but with you as a belayer, I'm not planning to!"

Lartaun placed a tiny "friend," a spring-loaded camming device used for mountaineering protection behind a narrow flake at the base of the crack. He took a long breath and went for the "crux," the toughest section of the climb. He placed his left hand and foot on one side of the dihedral and his right hand and foot on the other, applying counter pressure between the two opposing sheets of rock, as if he were trying to split them apart. He progressed that way throughout its entire length, choosing his placements with utmost precision.

Meanwhile, Jean-Philippe followed his every move in awe, cringing and praying that he would not make the one fateful mistake that would cause the two to plunge to their certain deaths. By concentrating solely on Lartaun's moves, he tried to forget he was a man with zero climbing experience, a man who was hanging off a vertical cliff one hundred and seventy-plus feet above ground. And as if that was not sick enough, he had two hundred and fifty pounds of dynamite tethered at his side for companionship.

Further up, the dihedral flattened out and turned into a deep vertical crack. Lartaun placed a large stopper at its base and clipped his rope onto it. Both he and Jean-Philippe let out an audible sigh of relief at the same moment.

"*Bravo!*" Jean-Philippe's choked-up voice echoed from below.

Even though Lartaun was not home free just yet, the toughest part of the climb was behind him. He slid his foot into the crack and balanced his weight by extending his other leg flat against the cliff. Wedging his hand further up into the crack, he locked it into a hand-jam by contracting his forearm muscles before he lifted his foot higher into it. Lartaun repeated this demanding move several more times until he buried his bleeding knuckles into a deep handhold at the lip of the cavern. At last, he swung his right leg over the edge and vanished from view.

A little after two in the afternoon, Jean-Philippe's head finally appeared through the opening. He slithered on his belly over the cavern floor, eager to put a respectable distance between him and the void before he unclipped his harness from the safety rope. At long last, he kneeled at the center of the *zulo* and took a good look around. While the cavern entrance was narrow, it was quite spacious inside. A man had plenty of room to stand up in the center of it. The hole was maybe ten feet in depth and fifteen feet wide. The floor was covered with a thin layer of sandy gravel that crunched under their feet. The air they breathed had a dusty smell, yet it felt dry and cool against their skin. Toward the back, a large protrusion in the rock gave the illusion that a platform had been carved out of the stone wall. It would make a great storing place for the explosives, hidden from view and protected from the elements at the same time.

"This place is sick!" Jean-Philippe exclaimed with admiration.

"Jean-Phi, help me out here, please. The bags are coming," Lartaun grunted, utterly exhausted.

As soon as the backpacks were hauled inside the *zulo*, Jean-Philippe and Lartaun set out to work. With utmost care, they arranged layers upon layers of dynamite sticks over the rock platform. When finished, they removed their latex gloves and discarded them into one of the empty bags. For the first time that day, Lartaun allowed himself to take a quick break. His muscles burned and ached. The skin on his fingers was raw, and both the palm and the back of his hands were scratched.

"Are you ready to head back down soon?" he asked after a couple of lapsed minutes. "I'll feel better when this day is over."

"I'm ready whenever you are," replied Jean-Philippe. "You did all the work, man. I just came along for the ri—"

His answer was cut short by the clacking sound of a gunshot fired somewhere close by.

"Eric!" they exclaimed in unison.

"Let's go!" Lartaun said, hurriedly. He sent Jean-Philippe abseiling down the face first. He cast a final glance at the cavern to double-check that everything was in order and followed suit, zipping down the cliff at lightning speed.

Once they were back on the ground, they ran down the path as fast as their legs would allow toward the spot where they had last left Eric. When they arrived, Eric was nowhere to be found.

"Are you sure this is the right spot?" Lartaun asked.

"Positive!" Jean-Philippe panted.

Lartaun crouched to inspect the ground around him. "Oh, no— look!" he half-whispered.

"What?"

"There." Lartaun pointed his finger at a moist, fertile patch of soil in front of him. He removed a couple dry leaves from the area so that Jean-Philippe could get a better view. "See that? Bear tracks! And they look fresh." Lartaun quickly investigated his immediate surroundings. He found more grooves imprinted onto the dusty soil, probably made by Eric as he tried to crawl away. At first glance, nothing indicated that a fight had taken place. Most importantly, there was no blood. "Let's get back on the path and see if we can find him!" Lartaun ordered.

Jean-Philippe followed him, all the while calling out for Eric.

They found their unfortunate partner two hundred yards away from the spot where they originally left him. Eric was crawling along the trail, dragging his damaged leg behind him like a useless appendage.

"Eric! Stop right where you are!" shouted Lartaun.

Eric looked over his shoulder. As soon as he saw Lartaun, he stopped dead in his tracks and dropped his forehead to the ground in a gesture of profound relief and utter exertion.

"I never thought I'd be that happy to see you, man," he panted as soon as Lartaun had caught up with him.

"What happened to you?"

"A bear! It was a bear, I swear. It came out of nowhere!"

"A bear?"

"I heard noises and cracking branches. I thought that it was you guys. I called your names, and before I could even realize what was going on, there was this big, huge bear coming right at me! It was—oh God, it was so—sick! And it was not scared of me, man, I swear it wasn't!" he babbled, still reeling with fright.

"I just can't believe it!" exclaimed Jean-Philippe. "What did you do?"

"I had your gun in my hand the whole time I was alone. I fired a shot, but—"

"Did you hit the bear?" Lartaun interrupted him.

"No! I was so fucking scared man, I could have had that beast on top of me and still, I would have missed it! Thank god the noise scared it away. Shit guys, I almost crapped my pants out there!" Eric grabbed Lartaun's sleeve in an attempt to sit up, but it was in vain. He grimaced and screamed in pain.

"Don't make any unnecessary moves and save your energy. It's not going to be a walk in the park, but we're going to bring you home," Lartaun said reassuringly. "Jean-Phi, come around this side and help me carry him."

Jean-Philippe locked arms with Lartaun to create a human chair for Eric to sit on, and the two proceeded to carry their injured companion back to Etsaut.

09:34 PM ~ Wednesday, August 24, 1994

Jean-Philippe handed Lartaun a glass of fine Cognac that he just poured from a Baccarat crystal decanter and said,

"I just checked on Eric. He's passed out in the guest bedroom. Ugh, talk about a harrowing day!"

"I'm glad you were there. I couldn't have done it without you." Lartaun swirled the honey-colored nectar onto the side of his glass, observing the Cognac's oily legs as they slid down the smooth surface of the crystal snifter. "So what's the game plan now?" he asked reluctantly.

"We sit tight and wait for Patxi's instructions. I'll be in touch with you, when the time comes, to retrieve the loot."

"Any idea of how long it will take?"

"Not sure. A few days. A week, perhaps?"

"What are you going to do when this is all over?"

"I'm going to make myself scarce for a while. I don't care where, as long as it's a far away place!" Jean-Philippe took a sip of his Cognac and let its pleasing flavors roll over his taste buds. "What about you? I assume that you're not going to stick around here for too long either, right?" he said.

"Obviously, I'll move on at some point, but I don't want to raise any red flags by leaving too soon either."

"If I were you, I'd stay away from La Goutte d'Eau. The police are bound to stop by sooner or later to investigate the robbery."

"Why would they come over to La Goutte?"

"C'mon man, everyone knows why! Whenever shit gets stirred up in the valley, La Goutte d'Eau is the first place the police check out. Trust me on that one. The last thing you want is to be there when they come sniffing around."

"I should get going then. Thanks for the drink and the piece of advice, Jean-Phi." Lartaun drained the contents of his glass in one gulp and stood up from the sofa.

"Anytime, man. Drive safe."

Lartaun shut the front door behind him and stepped into the courtyard. Bathed in the eerie moonlight, the paint on his old car was shining as if it were brand new. Still, it was only a mirage, an illusion, just like his own naïve belief that he could get a fresh identity and start anew. Lartaun was learning the hard way that it took more than a falsified passport to get another lease on life. Granted, he had returned home, but he still could not contact his own family for fear of discovery. Worse, it was clear to him now that he would never be truly safe anywhere near his old stomping grounds, especially with Patxi's plans in full swing. The police would soon descend upon the residents of the valley like vultures upon the remains of a decomposing carcass. Eventually, someone would recognize him. Jean-Philippe was right. The time had come for Lartaun to rush headlong into the unknown again. He had no choice. He had to go. Yet, the mere thought of abandoning Faustine like he had once left his family, overnight and without a proper explanation, made him feel nauseous. Why did he have to fall hard for this girl at the worst possible time? Life was too cruel. Deep down, he doubted he could find the strength to leave loved ones again.

Lartaun revved the engine, switched on his headlights and headed for RN-134. As he peered into the darkness, the present started to crumble into tiny grits of extra temporal matter tumbling down the chute of an imaginary hourglass. Lartaun traveled back in time, revisiting the events that forced him to go into exile and vanish off the face of the earth overnight.

06:35 PM ~ Saturday, January 4, 1992

Marching side-by-side in tight ranks, the formidable crowd filled the avenue. It was Saturday, the 4th of January, 1992. Thousands of people, of all ages and walks of life, had gathered from all over the Basque country to participate in the national demonstration in Irun. They were protesting the extradition of Basque refugees living in France, following a massive roundup operation of ETA members by the French police.

EZ, EZ, EZ, EXTRADIZIORIK EZ!
NO, NO, NO, EXTRADITIONS, NO!

The chant galvanized the assembly. At the head of the parade, hundreds of people carried signs bearing photographs and names of ETA prisoners. Behind them, a Basque flag floated over the protesters' heads. A gigantic banner, held by dozens of demonstrators, read in large painted letters:

ERREFUXIATUEK EUSKADIN BIZI BEHAR DUTE!
BASQUE REFUGEES HAVE THE RIGHT TO LIVE IN THE
BASQUE COUNTRY!

Others, demanding immediate and unconditional amnesty for all

ETA members behind bars, brandished hand-painted signs which said:

PRESOAK KALERA, AMNISTIA OSOA!
RELEASE THE PRISONERS, TOTAL AMNESTY!

As the crowd marched on, residents looked out their windows and waved in support while a few others drew their shutters and hid as the protesters took to the streets below.

The protest remained peaceful for several hours. As the majority of people broke off the ranks to head back home, only the hardcore militants remained. By sunset, they were pumped-up and ready for action. It was prime time for the *policía nacional* to send in their troops, heavily clad in anti-riot gear.

The police stood off in a tight line across Paseo Colón with bulletproof shields raised in front of their chests. They remained still while they sized up the crowd of protesters yelling just a few arm-lengths away. On either side of the invisible demarcation line, demonstrators and anti-riot policemen awaited one false move. A glass bottle, thrown at an officer, was all it took for the riot to start.

The first tear gas canisters tore through the air, and the police blindly charged into the masses. They started shooting at people with rubber pellets in order to disperse the crowds. Within a matter of minutes, it was bedlam. Several cars parked along the neighboring streets had already been overturned by rioters. Fires raged in garbage cans, and deadly piles of glass shards from smashed storefronts littered the curbs. In their haste to escape the mayhem unharmed, protesters shoved and tripped each other, while others tumbled to the ground amidst screams of panic. Sirens blasted through the night. They screeched louder and louder as ambulances, police and fire trucks converged downtown toward the riot zone.

The sound of a sudden explosion echoed amongst the commercial buildings lining up Paseo Colón. A dissident just threw a Molotov cocktail at an empty bus stationed along the curb. The young man, facial features unrecognizable under his hood, was about to fire up another one when his instincts somehow compelled him to look over his shoulder. He stopped dead in his tracks. Five anti-riot policemen closed in on him in a semi-circle, their side arms pointed straight at his chest. As soon as he realized there was no way to escape, he placed the bottle and lighter side-by-side on the ground in slow motion, dropped to his knees and surrendered, raising his hands high above his head.

In the blink of an eye, two officers jumped on him and pummeled his body with jabs and kicks to the kidneys and chest. When the rioter was completely incapacitated, they dragged him by his feet along the asphalt toward a paddy wagon stationed nearby at the corner of Colón and Aldapeta Street. They patted him down and confiscated his wallet. At last, they threw him inside the anti-riot truck and locked the doors behind him.

In the meantime, the dissident's friends had managed to elude the police by hightailing it up the steep slope of Pikoketa Street.

"Where's Lartaun?" yelled one of the hooded men.

"The pigs got him!" shouted another youngster wearing a red and black "Negu Gorriak" hooded sweatshirt.

"We have to go back for him!" he screamed again.

"It's too damn dangerous, Patxi! They'll catch us too!" exclaimed a third.

"We can't leave him behind!" Patxi replied, stopping dead in his tracks. "Did anyone see where the cops took him?"

"They threw him into a police truck around the corner of Aldapeta Street!"

"Let's go, then! Come on, move, move, move!" Patxi exhorted them.

"How will we get him out of there?"

"Do we have any Molotov cocktails left?"

"Just one! Do you think it'll be enough?"

"We'll make it enough!" shouted Patxi. They all fell in behind him without uttering a single word of complaint, for they would not dare challenge Patxi's orders in times like these.

The back doors of the paddy wagon reopened with a bang. Another protester was just arrested, and two policemen struggled to shove him inside the truck. Just as they were ready to shut the doors behind him, the panicked man managed to leap outside, escaping their grip in the process. The officers immediately ran after him and tackled him to the ground, mere yards away from the vehicle. Those few precious seconds of inattention were just what Patxi and his gang had been waiting for. Under the cover of darkness, two hooded men slithered soundlessly through the open doors of the police truck. Inside, Lartaun was lying on the floor, semi-conscious. They dragged him out and swiftly carried him away. One of the two policemen, who had been busy handcuffing the other rioter, looked up, just in time to witness Lartaun's escape.

"WATCH OUT! The other one is getting away!" the patrolman yelled at the top of his lungs to the officers sitting inside the cabin, oblivious to the scene unfolding behind their backs. Suddenly, he noticed a third man standing by the anti-riot truck. Dressed in black from head-to-toe, the man was holding a flaming bottle of cheap whiskey, filled with gasoline, over his head.

"¡La madre que lo parió!" the policeman mumbled in complete disbelief.

Time stood still as he realized with horror what was about to happen. His transfixed eyes watched the ball of fire, traveling in a curve through the darkness, disappear inside the truck and shatter into a thousand shards. A curtain of flames engulfed the police wagon at once, rising high up into the inky sky.

"GET OUT! The truck is going to explode!" screamed the stunned policeman. The front doors of the truck opened violently, and two officers jumped out of the cabin. They hit the ground with a hollow thump, scrambled to their feet and hurried to safety around the street corner. The other agents followed suit, dragging the handcuffed rioter along with them.

The explosion was tremendous when the flames hit the gas tank. The truck seemed to levitate off the ground under the force of the blow. A blast of warm air buffeted the shocked men in uniform and their prisoner.

Patxi had created the diversion his group needed to beat a hasty retreat into the night. By then, Lartaun had regained consciousness and mustered just enough strength to stand on his own. They scurried off into narrow streets, only stopping to hide behind dumpsters as police patrol cars sped by with their blaring sirens.

"The cops are everywhere! Let's get the hell out of here!" someone screamed.

Patxi stopped long enough to unzip his sweater and tear the bandana off his face. He discarded his clothes in a trash can. The others followed his example.

"What are we going to do now?"

"Everybody be cool!" ordered Patxi. "I know a safe place where we can hide for a while. Follow me!"

They turned a couple more street corners and ran across Plaza San Marzial. They tumbled down a flight of old stone steps to the left of City Hall before they stopped in front of a nondescript door in the middle of Jesus Street. Patxi frantically rang the bell. They were buzzed in a few seconds later, ran up the stairs, banged at the door of apartment 2A, and barged inside the tiny dwelling, pushing the bewildered owner against the wall in their haste to get to safety.

"Holy crap! That was a close call!" Patxi leaned against the wall inside the living room. He panted hard. "Thanks for letting us in, *txo*. I'll explain everything to you in a second."

"*Joder*, Lartaun, who beat you up like that?" Bixente exclaimed upon seeing his friend dragged by the armpits into his flat.

"Fuckin' *txakurrak* did it, man!" said Patxi, answering on Lartaun's behalf, "bastard cops!"

"Shit." Bixente walked up to Lartaun, who was already lying down on the couch. He lifted up his friend's sweatshirt to look at his injuries and shook his head with concern. "You need to see a doctor," he stated at last.

"No dice. Cops are after him. Can you turn on the local news?" Patxi asked in haste.

"Sure, Patxi, hold on." Bixente pushed a button on the remote control. The small television set sprung to life.

"...Things are heating up, once again, in downtown Irun as a non-violent pro-ETA march turned into a raging riot. What had started this afternoon as a relatively peaceful protest against the extradition of Basque etarras living on French soil turned sour after nine o'clock tonight when alleged members of separatist organizations belonging to the Basque National Liberation Movement confronted members of the Policía Nacional. Cars were overturned and storefront windows smashed along Paseo Colón. Vandals suspected to belong to Jarrai set a public bus on fire by throwing a Molotov cocktail through one of its open windows. Thankfully, there were no passengers inside the vehicle. The police have strengthened their forces in an effort to regain full control of the situation. Stay tuned for more news..."

Bixente hit the mute button.

"I'm screwed, Bixente," mumbled Lartaun, struggling to enunciate clearly. His lower lip was cracked open, and his right cheekbone had swollen to the size of a goose's egg. "Cops took my wallet. They've got my ID. They know who I am."

"Hey, wait! They—WHAT?" Patxi stared at his friend in disbelief.

"Will someone just tell me what happened, for fuck's sake?" exclaimed Bixente.

"The pigs caught Lartaun after he threw the Molotov cocktail at the bus," explained Xanti, a fellow Jarrai member from the neighboring town of Hernani.

"So, the bus pyromaniac, that was you, huh? Nice!" Bixente said to Lartaun. His face was not smiling one bit.

"They beat the crap out of him, and they threw him in the paddy wagon," Xanti continued. "When we realized that Lartaun was missing, we came back for him. And, er—"

"And then we blew up the freakin' truck to get him out of there," finished Patxi.

"Shit, guys. Why would you do something that stupid when the cops had already confiscated his ID?" Bixente scolded them.

"I didn't know that, back then!" Patxi protested. "Oh man, looks like I really fucked up this time."

"All right, everyone stay calm! Did anyone follow you over here?"

Xanti and the others shook their heads "no."

"OK, that's good. Did the cops see your faces? Could they identify anyone of you, aside from Lartaun?" Bixente questioned further.

"No. We were wearing bandanas and we had our hoods on. We tossed our clothes in a dumpster on our way here."

"All right, listen to me! All of you, go home, separate ways. That goes for you too, Patxi. I wouldn't be surprised if the police were already over at Lartaun's house as we speak. Soon, they're going to find out that you're his best friend. They'll want to ask you questions, no doubt. So, think about getting yourself a rock-solid alibi and no matter what they do to you, keep your mouth shut. You got that?"

"Yes. Yes I do," replied Patxi.

"All right, guys. Now beat it. All of you."

"What about Lartaun?" asked Patxi.

"He's going to stay here with me until I come up with a plan. In the meantime, I'll try to patch him up the best I can," replied Bixente.

Patxi staggered over to Lartaun. He hovered above his friend, afraid to touch any part of his body for fear of causing him any more pain. The whole left side of Lartaun's torso was bruised and swollen. The same went for his arms, which he used to shield himself from the policemen's brutal assault.

"I don't know what to say, *txo*," Patxi muttered to his friend, "if only I could turn back time—"

"You heard the man, *hermano*." Lartaun tried to smile. Instead, his face contorted in a rictus of pain. "You have to go before you get yourself in trouble, too. Don't worry about me, I'll see you soon, 'kay?" Lartaun waved his friend away. "Now go, man, GO!"

One after another, they left the flat in two-to-five-minute increments, so as not to raise suspicion.

Bixente's apartment became eerily quiet. Bixente helped Lartaun into his bedroom and attended to his friend's wounds. He was about to turn off the lights and leave the room when Lartaun grabbed him by the sleeve. One look into Lartaun's eyes made his heart sink. Bixente never saw him in such distress or consumed with so much raw fear.

"Should I surrender to the police?" Lartaun asked Bixente in sudden panic. "Maybe they'll go easier on me if I turn myself in? I mean, I never meant to hurt anyone. I knew the bus was empty before I set it on fire. I can explain!"

"*Hombre*, I don't know what to tell you. You're going to need a great lawyer, that's for damn sure." Lartaun nodded feebly. "Listen, why don't you lie down and rest for an hour or two? We'll figure something out when you wake up, OK?"

"Don't leave me alone, all right? Please!" Lartaun asked with imploring eyes.

"Of course not. I'm right here with you," Bixente whispered back. He slowly freed his forearm from the clasp of Lartaun's desperate grip. "Don't you worry about a thing."

Bixente returned to the living room. As he prepared to strike a match and light his cigarette, the image on the muted television screen caused his lower jaw to drop in horror. The unlit Ducado fell from his lips and rolled under the couch. He did not even bother to pick it up. Lartaun's driver's license picture was displayed in the upper right corner of the television set. Filling up most of the screen, a stern-looking anchorman was delivering a special news flash. Bixente pounced on the remote to turn up the volume. What he heard was devastating.

"Lartaun! Lartaun! Wake up!" Lartaun half-opened an eye. The cocktail of painkillers that Bixente made him swallow, less than an hour ago, propelled him into a mind-numbing daze. "Listen to me!" he said urgently. "We've got to leave right now!"

Upon noticing the chilling tone of alarm in his friend's voice, Lartaun propped himself up on one elbow and turned around to face his friend.

"Leaving? Where? What's going on?"

"A bomb exploded an hour ago at the central police station on Plaza Ensanche. Fuck man, they think you did it! I saw your freakin' picture on TV!"

"But, but I was here!" Lartaun stammered, still haggard and disoriented.

"I know that! They also said that a cop died in the attack, and there might be more casualties. They're accusing you of *murder*, man! They say they have proof! They called you a *terrorist!*" The dreadful news began to sink in. Lartaun immediately sobered up, as a tidal wave of panic surged from the pit of his stomach. All of a sudden, he felt like he was going to throw up. "You can't stay here, it's not safe!" Bixente urged him on. "You've to get the hell out of here, and fast!"

"Where should I go? To the police?"

"Are you nuts? The station's been vaporized, man! A cop died! If they see you now, they're going to make you pay for it, *txo.* They'll kill you!"

"What am I supposed to do, then?"

"I already made some calls. I'll drive you to the *Puente Internacional.* You'll cross the bridge on foot. Some friends of mine will be waiting for you on the French side of the border in about thirty minutes. They'll take care of you and arrange for your escape out of Europe."

"Out—of Europe?" Lartaun stared at his friend in disbelief.

"There's a price on your head! The police will be looking for you everywhere. Come on, get up! There's no time to lose."

"But—wait! What about my folks?"

"I really hate to tell you this, but they're the last people that you'd want to contact right now. The police are most likely at your house already. This is not a game, Lartaun. Nothing's ever going to be the same from now on. You must understand that once you're gone, you'll never be able to come back here again—ever."

Lartaun's world was crumbling around him, and there was nothing Bixente, or he, could do to stop it. He was tumbling headfirst, straight to hell.

"Bixente, I'm scared!" Lartaun whispered, struggling to keep his composure.

"I know. I'm scared for you, too," Bixente replied in earnest.

Bixente gave Lartaun some clean clothes and a wad of cash.

Fifteen minutes later, he started the drive toward the Villas de Mendíbil in order to reach the drop-off point at the edge of the *Puente Internacional*. Lartaun was hidden in the trunk of his car.

When the time came to part, Lartaun shed the tears that he could no longer hold back.

"Tell Patxi to take care of my family while I'm gone. Have him tell my mother and sisters that I love them. And that I am so sorry for the pain that I'll be causing them."

"Lartaun," said Bixente, "don't you ever forget this, no matter what happens to you from here on out. You are innocent. You hear me? You are innocent!"

Lartaun snorted loudly and nodded. He said goodbye to Bixente, then he reluctantly set out for the other side of the bridge, limping away as he gripped the handrail for support.

Lartaun was only twenty-one years old, and his life was shattered. Fellow students would not see him on campus the following Monday. They would already know the reason for his absence. Before the first recess of the day would be over, his name would be dragged through the mud. His mother and sisters would cry, and he would not be there to comfort them or tell them what really happened. Overnight, Lartaun turned into a fugitive. A broken man with no future.

10:24 PM ~ Wednesday, August 24, 1994

Lartaun caught sight of the hand-painted road shoulder sign depicting a blue water drop in his headlights. He glanced at his speedometer and realized that he was driving way too fast for his own good. This particular curve had been christened "the marble curve" by the locals for a good reason. At once, he slammed his foot on the brake and downshifted gears. The tired transmission box screamed in indignation, and the tires screeched loudly as they bit into the steep bend. Lartaun struggled to keep control of the vehicle, but the back tires slid sideways, moving him dangerously close to the edge of the road. The back of the car hit a tree, causing it to spin out of control until it finished its crazy course into a shallow ditch on the opposite side of the road.

Against all odds, the motor was still running and the tape player still blasting inside the vehicle. Lartaun, stunned by the suddenness of the accident, slowly reached for the ignition key and killed the engine. Silence returned. He wrapped his arms around the wheel, dropped his head against it and, for the first time in months, allowed himself to cry.

Faustine was already asleep by the time he finally returned to La Goutte d'Eau.

Lartaun, or rather, Rafael, took off his clothes in the dark, careful to make as little noise as possible, and slipped under the covers next to her. Stirring from her slumber, Faustine burrowed her face into his neck and wrapped her long legs around his.

"Where were you all day?" she mumbled in a drowsy voice.

"At the Somport," he whispered in her ear.

"Ugh! So sick of hearing that word."

"Me too. Let's get out of here!"

"What?"

"Let's go on a little vacation, just you and me."

Faustine propped herself up on her elbow. "Are you serious?"

"Dead serious. How about first thing tomorrow?"

With a smile so big that he could see it through the darkness, Faustine's face lit up. The vision filled him with so much joy that he could have cried again. He chose to laugh in gratitude instead as Faustine's smile was the most beautiful thing he had seen all day.

15
-HAMABOST-

08:13 AM ~ Thursday, August 25, 1994

"Ma!" Faustine exclaimed the second she barged into Vivienne and Etienne's bedroom, "wake up!"

"What's wrong?" Vivienne moaned. She half-opened a glassy eye, and covered her face with her pillow to shield herself from the bright sunlight. "Can't it just wait 'til I'm awake?"

"No it can't! I came here to tell you that Rafael and I are going away for a few days."

"Wait, what? Where?"

"We're going on a climbing trip in the mountains!"

Etienne groaned like a bear at the unwelcome disturbance, especially at such an ungodly hour. He rolled to the other end of the bed, taking the covers along with him. Vivienne fought back for her share of the blanket with a swift move.

"Whoa, not so fast, Missy!" Vivienne sat upright on the bed. "What climbing trip? What time is it anyway?" Vivienne rubbed her throbbing temples. Last night's wine was not agreeing with her body this morning.

"Almost eight. Here, I brought this for you. I figured you'd need it." Faustine handed her a glass of water with a fizzing tablet of aspirin. "Anyway," Faustine pressed on, "it's no big deal. We'll only be gone for a few days."

"I imagine that Rafael knows what he's doing, but you, m'dear, have zero experience with mountaineering. It's not a place for novices like you."

"I'm a good climber!" she exclaimed in protest.

"I don't doubt that for a second. But in the mountains, the climbs are much more demanding than those on the cliffs around here. You also have to contend with altitude, unpredictable weather, not to mention—"

"Ma, please don't start!" Faustine said, rolling her eyes.

"Oh, and don't forget hypothermia, avalanches and sudden rocks falls," Etienne chimed in from under the covers.

"Etienne, leave it alone!" warned Faustine.

"What if you get lost? Or hurt? This is way too dangerous!" Vivienne went on.

"Come on, Ma, you know I'll be careful! Besides, Rafael would never let anything bad happen to me."

"Sure, when he finds the time to be around, that is."

Vivienne had the knack to open the proverbial can of worms at the most inopportune times.

"Ma," Faustine snarled, "if you have something shitty to say about Rafael, just say it, for Christ's sake!"

"You're moving too fast, too soon! I know you hate it when I say that, but you're still very young. Rafael, on the other hand, is older than you, and he's been through a lot."

"Rafael loves me, and I love him back!" Faustine blurted out. "What's wrong with that? Why can't you just be happy for me once in your life, instead of trying to break us apart anytime you get the chance? Just because you're jealous of him doesn't give you the right to make my life miserable!"

"Who, *me?* Jealous of Rafael? Why would I?"

"Because you're afraid that he's going to take me away from you, and you just can't stand the idea of being left alone!"

"Guys, can you take this somewhere else? Some people are trying to sleep here!" moaned Etienne.

"Oh shut it, will ya?" Vivienne snapped back at him. "I'm talking to my daughter!"

"Sounds more like screaming to me," he replied.

"Gee, dah-ling," Vivienne said condescendingly, "maybe you want to enlighten the both of us with your outstanding parenting skills, then?"

"Ugh!" he replied, too groggy to even bother with an articulate answer.

"Listen," Vivienne turned back to Faustine, "I have nothing against Rafael. I just don't want him to put your hopeful little heart through the wringer, that's all."

Faustine and her mother had always shared a very strong bond, but Faustine was maturing fast and, just like any mother, Vivienne had trouble accepting the fact that, with each passing day, her offspring needed her less and less. Vivienne knew she had no choice but to let nature run its course. "Pick your battles carefully" had become her motto lately and, perhaps, this was not a battle she should fight.

"Come here," Vivienne said with a resigned sigh. "I'm not in the mood to argue. Give your old mother a hug." Faustine, stubborn as she was, did not budge at first, but she soon gave in and sat down on the bed beside her. Vivienne ran her fingers through her thick blond tangle of hair that had never been cut. "Oh, honey. I know you're grown up, but nothing will change the fact that you'll always be my baby. I could never forgive myself if anything bad ever happened to you."

"I know, Ma. I'll be careful. I promise."

"So, where did you say you were going?" Vivienne asked meekly, accepting defeat.

"I don't know for sure. It's a surprise."

"I hope you realize that I'll be sick with worry until you come back!"

"*Maaaaa!* Spare me the guilt trip," she joked, "gotta scoot now. Bye!" Faustine gave her mother a quick peck on the cheek, jumped off the bed and ran out of the room before her mother could have a change of heart.

"Love you too, honey!" Vivienne called after her. She let out a guttural moan and slumped back into bed, physically and mentally exhausted.

Rafael and Faustine left La Goutte a half-hour later. They drove along in silence. Ever since he awoke that morning, Rafael had looked dispirited. When Faustine asked the reason for his brooding mood earlier, he blamed it on the car accident. Needless to say, she did not buy his excuse for a second. It was not in Rafael's character to lose sleep over a bit of scraped metal.

"You know what?" Faustine told Rafael abruptly. "I'm not sure whether this is a good idea after all. I don't think I'm ready to tackle a mountain just yet."

"Why not?"

"I'm scared, Rafa." Rafael slowed down and pulled the car over to the side of the road. "What are you doing?" she asked tentatively.

Rafael shifted sideways on his seat to face her. "You're a strong woman, Faustine. You just don't know what you're truly capable of."

Whenever Rafael stared at her that way, Faustine forgot about the world around her.

"If you think I can do it, I'll do it," she said with a quivering voice. "The truth is... I would do anything if you asked me. That, perhaps, is what scares me the most."

"*Maite zaitut*, Faustine. I love you," he whispered. "Always."

16

-HAMVASEI-

09:07 AM ~ Thursday, August 25, 1994

At first, Vivienne thought the muffled shouts of surprise and screams of protest coming from the garden were part of her dream, but when she heard the banging at the front door downstairs, she realized they were real. She roused Etienne and went to take a look outside her window. She had seen her share of police action in her life, but the scope of the activity down below was new, even to her. Uniformed gendarmes were spread out in a circle formation across the front yard, blocking every possible exit of the old train station. They were closing in on everyone inside the building. Another contingent of patrolmen ousted campers from their tents and RVs scattered about the property.

"What's going on?" Etienne propped himself up on the bed. He looked disheveled and dazed in the bright morning light.

"I don't have the slightest idea," she whispered.

They heard the unmistakable noise of stomping boots coming up the stairs toward their bedroom. Seconds later, someone banged at their door. Etienne sobered up at once and jumped off the bed.

"Who is it?" he shouted.

"Gendarmerie Nationale! We have a warrant to take you all to the station for questioning. Get dressed immediately and follow us out!"

Vivienne and Etienne had no choice but to comply with the orders.

Minutes later, they stood at the foot of the stairs, joined with the rest of their house mates. The confusion in everyone's eyes was obvious. What was going on?

The gendarmes relied on the "surprise factor" in order to minimize resistance during the massive arrest. About thirty people, residents and campsite guests alike, most of them still in their pajamas, were rounded up and ordered into the patrol cars. Save for outraged shouts of protest and abundant cursing, there were no incidents. La Goutte had been cleared in less than ten minutes.

11:50 AM ~ Thursday, August 25, 1994

"Miss Laroche! Come to the desk, please."

The gendarme, dressed in a dark blue uniform, sat behind a long reception desk facing the police station entrance. He cast a bored, and somewhat disgusted, look at the confined crowd in the smallish waiting room. Painstakingly, he rubbed his forehead. Marco Fernandez, of the Gendarmerie Nationale in Pau, was not having a pleasant day.

He stood up from his chair for the umpteenth time to ask the assembly to keep the noise down. The deafening racket echoed well past the reception area and beyond the main hallway, backed up by the frantic "tac-a-tac" of every typewriter in the building.

Young men and women, some with toddlers in their arms, sat on the faded orange plastic chairs that lined the sterile walls of the waiting room. Those without a seat sat Indian-style on the linoleum floor or stood with their backs against the wall. Amongst them, La Goutte's permanent residents seemed unfazed by what was going on. After all, this was not their first raid, and they were used to being rounded up. Still, they speculated the reason they were arrested this time. Had the police found out about their backyard cannabis plantation? Were they being subjected to collective punishment for acts of vandalism perpetrated at the tunnel construction site? No matter how hard they tried to pry information from police officers passing through the waiting room, no explanation was offered. One by one, the Aspaches were called into the offices to be deposed. Once interrogated, they were not allowed back inside the gendarmerie. They would just have to wait for an explanation.

As the number of people in the waiting room dwindled, the atmosphere grew exponentially tense.

"For the last time, is there a Miss Laroche here?" Officer Fernandez asked in a monochord voice. Vivienne stood up and identified herself, at last. The gendarme escorted her to an office down the hallway and waved her in without ceremony.

Sitting behind his desk, Major Boréda unlocked a drawer, the one where he kept his firearm overnight whenever he was too tired or lazy to lock it in the main safe. He popped the cap off of a bottle of painkillers and poured two caplets in the palm of his hand. With a swig of tepid coffee, he swallowed them.

The lack of evidence at the crime scene had failed to jump-start Boréda's investigation. That was until he received intelligence regarding a fugitive suspected to belong to ETA, a man who went by the name of Lorenzo Lartaun Izcoa. Spanish secret service had reason to believe that he might be hiding in, or near, Pau. It was a long shot. With no other lead to follow, let alone a viable suspect to interrogate, the Major had received instructions to cast his net wide and investigate any lead that came across his desk. As a consequence, he had contacted Lionel Darvin, the *Adjudant-Chef* from the brigade of Oloron-Sainte-Marie, late the night before. Oloron was the first sizeable town at the foot of the Vallée d'Aspe. Its principal claim to fame was to be the capital of manufacturing for the world famous, woolen, pancake-shaped, *béret Basque*. As soon as Major Boréda exposed his intentions to implement an expanding search pattern for the ETA suspect, starting from where the robbery had taken place, Darvin was quick to propose a blitz raid at the commune. Together with Colonel Lambert's blessing, they decided to deploy forty officers from both brigades in a joint effort to raid La Goutte d'Eau, and take everyone they could find on site to the gendarmerie in Pau for thorough questioning.

"Please, come in and shut the door behind you," said Major Boréda.

He motioned the woman to a seat across his desk. Vivienne did as she was told. She sat down without saying a word.

The office was about twelve-by-twelve feet and furnished in a typical 1970s administrative style with nothing but light grey metal furniture. The clutter over the desk provided a bit of a personal touch. Behind the Major's desk sat a large metallic file cabinet. The bottom drawer was half open. Vivienne noticed that it was full of overstuffed hanging files. Closed cases, perhaps, judging by the yellowish hue, indicating the passing of time, of some documents. Piled high atop the cabinet sat several pamphlets and printed forms. The wall opposite the window was plastered with pictures, newspaper clippings and printed notes.

"Let's see what we have here."

Major Boréda perused through a pile of documents stacked on a corner of his desk. He pulled out a thin manila folder from the middle of the pile and opened it in front of him. Vivienne recognized a picture of herself clipped to the top left corner of the folder. It was her driver's license photograph, dating back from when she was eighteen years old. The Major took a moment to read through her file, and Vivienne seized the opportunity to get a good look at him. He seemed to be about her age, a few years older maybe. His frame was muscular, which made her think that he must have been an athlete in his youth. Years spent sitting behind a desk had somewhat softened his physique, but he was still in fine shape. His skin was tanned, and the dark blue of his uniform made his blue eyes all the more striking. They were so clear and transparent, he almost looked blind. Much to her chagrin, Vivienne had to admit that he was very attractive.

"Vivienne Laroche, born in Paris on July 12th, 1957. Your father is Lucien Laroche and your mother Françoise Laroche, maiden name Lesclun, blah, blah, blah." He lifted his eyes off her file and gave her a thin-lipped smile. "So, Miss Laroche, what do you do at La Goutte d'Eau?"

"I live there."

"Right, that was my understanding. But what brought you there in the first place?"

"The fresh air, perhaps?" She folded her arms across her chest and leaned back on the chair, a childish look of defiance passing over her smart hazelnut eyes.

"Let's be clear on one thing, Miss Laroche," he said in a mildly irritated tone, "I don't want you here anymore than you want to be here. All I need from you is an answer to a few simple questions, and I'll send you on your merry way. So, don't feel pressured to put on a one-woman-show just for me. When it comes to performances, I'm hard to please."

Vivienne, taken aback by his curt comment, took a few seconds to regain her composure. She was not about to be intimidated by a gendarme.

"Since when do you have the right to trespass on our property, kidnap us and treat us the way you did today without any valid reason to do so?" she lashed at him.

"Oh, but we do happen to have an excellent reason for bringing you all here, believe it or not."

"And what would that be, if you don't mind my asking?"

The Major blatantly ignored her question and moved on with the interrogation instead. He produced an eight-by-ten inch black-and-white photograph from a drawer inside his desk. Vivienne, curious all of a sudden, leaned closer to the desk to take a look at it.

"Miss Laroche, have you ever seen this man?"

He placed the portrait of a young white male in front of her, tapped the face on the picture with his index finger and looked her straight in the eyes. Vivienne struggled to contain her surprise. She was staring at a photograph of Rafael. She feigned to inspect the head shot some more while she tried to keep a poker face. Then she settled back in her chair.

"Nope." She pursed her lips and added in a voice she hoped was firm enough to convince him, "I've never seen that guy in my life."

Major Boréda seemed bothered by her answer. "That's too bad." He grabbed the picture and made it disappear inside his desk. "I was counting on your cooperation. Mind you, I am a little surprised by your answer because many of your friends seem to know him rather well."

Vivienne shifted uncomfortably in her seat. He just caught her in a lie, but she knew that this could be a trap. She could not imagine that anyone at La Goutte would denounce their friend to the police without knowing what they wanted him for in the first place.

"If that's the case, you should spend time with them rather than me."

"Damn squatters!" Boréda muttered under his breath. So far, every single person they interrogated denied knowing the man in the photograph. "I guess I must thank you for your cooperation, Miss Laroche. Sorry again for the rude awakening this morning."

"Can I go now?" Vivienne tentatively arose from her chair, ready to head for the door.

Boréda was prepared to dismiss her when something in her file caught his attention at the last moment. "One more thing, Miss Laroche," he said. "Please, remain seated." She slumped back into her chair. "I didn't know you had a daughter?"

"So what if I do?" she hissed at him.

"Well, for one, I'd like to know where she is."

Fleeting images of Faustine and Rafael hiking together on a mountain trail flashed through Vivienne's mind. She better think of an answer... fast!

"She's in Paris, visiting relatives."

"Relatives in Paris, huh?" he repeated, absentmindedly flipping through her report. Boréda had a colleague and good friend who worked for the *Direction Centrale des Renseignements Généraux*, the domestic intelligence service of the French police, whose mission was to search for and centralize any data of interest to the government. Upon his request, his friend faxed the Major all the information he found on Vivienne and the residents of La Goutte d'Eau. There was very little to report about Vivienne, aside from an arrest in 1973 for drinking and disorderly conduct. According to her file, she had no family to speak of. Vivienne's mother died when she was very young, and her father took care of her until she left the domicile at age sixteen.

"She's staying with her grandfather." Vivienne hoped the gendarme would buy the specifics of her lie.

"You mean, your father Lucien, correct?" Vivienne nodded. Boréda lifted a finger in the air as if to interrupt their conversation while he read a short paragraph at the bottom of her file. He seemed lost in his thoughts for a moment before he returned his attention to her. "Ah, Paris! What a great city! How old is your daughter now? About eighteen, right? I bet your father has a tough time keeping up with all that youthful energy!" he added with forced enthusiasm.

"I'm sure they're doing just fine."

"Why, haven't you spoken to your daughter since she left?"

"I have, but I don't think this is any of your business."

Boréda's expression changed. His eyes seemed to take on a darker hue, as if a storm was brewing behind his retinas. He frowned and shot her an annoyed look.

"You must explain the following to me, then. How could your daughter be staying with your father when it says right here…" He turned the file around so that Vivienne could read it with her own eyes. "…that your father, Lucien Laroche, was admitted to the Pitié-Salpêtrière's hospital in Paris on December 4, 1991, where he was pronounced dead on arrival at 08:47 in the evening following a fatal car crash."

"Huh?" Vivienne gaped in stupefaction.

"Your father died two-and-a-half years ago, Miss Laroche."

Vivienne could do little more than stare blandly at the Major. As her mouth dropped open, she gasped for oxygen like a fish out of water.

"Did you assume we didn't know?" Boréda asked again, his irritation obvious. "The police know pretty much everything, Miss Laroche."

"No, it's not that," Vivienne whispered as two big tears rolled down her cheeks and splattered on the document, "*I didn't know.*"

Jean-Claude Boréda hesitated for a split second. He reached into a drawer and handed her a box of paper tissues. Vivienne grabbed one and pressed it against her mouth. Boréda wondered if the tears were honest, or if this woman was putting on a show to distract him from his task.

"What a terrible way to find out about your father's death," Boréda said with genuine empathy. "I am terribly sorry. Please accept my sincere condolences. However, you do understand, Miss Laroche, that under the circumstances, I'll need you to stick around a little while longer."

Vivienne was beginning to understand the enormity of her mistake. Not only had she failed as a daughter for not being by her estranged father's side when he died, but she had also failed to protect her own daughter from the police.

"Please come with me." Boréda walked around his desk and offered Vivienne his arm for support. "I'll show you to a different room where you'll find peace and quiet for a moment. I'll come and get you in a while, when you feel you are ready to talk again."

He led her to a windowless office located a little further up the hall from his own. Vivienne slumped in a chair facing a metal desk similar to that of the Major's.

"Make yourself comfortable, Miss Laroche. I know it's not much of a room to look at, but you've got my word that no one will bother you here." Boréda fished for a pack of cigarettes in his uniform pocket. He took one out for himself and placed the open pack in front of her. "Help yourself if you wish to smoke. The lighter is over there, by the ashtray. I'll see you in a bit."

"OK," replied Vivienne in a robotic voice.

Boréda was on his way out when he turned to face her one more time.

"I don't know why you felt compelled to lie about your daughter's whereabouts. But now, more than ever, I need to know where she is. And most importantly," he added, as if he could read her mind, "who she is with."

Vivienne twisted the fabric of her long gypsy skirt with her fingers as she stared vacantly at the August picture of a 1994 firefighters' calendar pinned to the wall. Never before had she felt lonelier than this, but she couldn't dissolve into tears. She grabbed a cigarette absentmindedly, lit it and inhaled deeply.

Back in his office, the Major got off the phone with the State Prosecutor's office. Cooperation between the Gendarmerie Nationale and the *Direction de la Surveillance du Territoire*, the "Directorate of Territorial Surveillance," was deemed necessary for the continuation of the robbery's investigation. The DST, as it was called in the business, was France's domestic intelligence agency, which specialized in counterintelligence, counterespionage and counterterrorism. The bureau in Paris just informed Boréda of the imminent arrival of two senior inspectors. They were scheduled to land at Pau airport later that afternoon. While he was not sure what to make of the recent turn of events, one thing was certain. Whenever the State Prosecutor requested DST's active involvement in an ongoing investigation, it meant they were onto something big.

The Major could only hope that the team coming his way did not have a bad case of "DST syndrome," a propensity to suffer from an incurable superiority complex compelling DST inspectors to act like condescending jerks toward fellow law enforcement agents. They were expected to cooperate and to keep each other informed about the details of their parallel investigations with the least amount of bickering and drama. However, Boréda was painfully aware that communication between the two entities was usually a one-way street.

Marco Fernandez stepped into Boréda's office to announce Officer Carignan's return from the hospital.

"Afternoon, Major. I have good and bad news for you," said Carignan.

"Humor me, André. Start with the good," replied the Major.

"Stéphane Pédrino, the armored truck driver, is recuperating well. In fact, I managed to take his deposition this morning. Here it is." He handed the Major a typed transcript. "Unfortunately, he does not remember a thing."

"Is that the bad news?" asked Boréda.

"I'm afraid not. Daniel Marin, his colleague, just died an hour ago. He fell into a deep coma after extensive emergency surgery."

"Aw, shit," said the Major.

"Yes, a mess," Fernandez commented in his turn. "No prints, no evidence, no clues and now a dead victim!"

"Well, we do have a potential suspect. A fellow by the name of

Izcoa," continued Boréda. "Problem is, we have no clue where he is. All we can hope for is that the DST has 'intel' to share with us."

"They've put the DST on the case?" Fernandez asked with surprise.

"As of today. I sent the preliminary reports and evidence to Paris on the day of the robbery. The Prosecutor in Pau referred the matter straight away to the XIIIth prosecution chamber of the Paris' Court."

Fernandez let out a whistle. "I guess they're sticking with the terrorist theory, huh?"

"We can't rule it out," replied Boréda. "Until then, our number one priority is to find Izcoa."

"What do we know about him?" asked Carignan.

"He's a Basque fugitive. The Spaniards have had an arrest warrant for him for the past two years. He's being accused of vandalism, destruction of public property, arson, rioting, resisting and escaping arrest. And that's just the beginning. Their secret service not only suspect that he's an active member of ETA, but that he was also instrumental in the '92 bombing of the downtown police station in Irun."

"That was quite a bloodbath."

"Indeed. The attack claimed the life of a police officer and injured five others. The case is still pending. ETA claimed responsibility for the terrorist attack, but no arrests were made at the time, and they have been stalking Izcoa ever since. Back then, they followed him all the way to Central America, but they lost his trace there. Reportedly, he resurfaced on our shores not too long ago. Don't ask me how they found out, but they have proof that he's back, all right. And they believe that he might be hiding in the area."

"Well, well, well! A dangerous *etarra* is on the loose, and just like that, two hundred and fifty pounds of explosives go missing in the Vallée d'Aspe. Coincidence? I think not." Carignan seemed agitated.

"It is too early to tell. We raided La Goutte d'Eau this morning. We figured it would be a good starting point, given its proximity to the crime scene and the type of radical activists who live there."

"And?" asked Carignan.

"At first, *nada*. Izcoa wasn't there, and everyone we've interrogated denied ever meeting him. Still, I got the feeling that they were all lying through their teeth. And low and behold, I have someone in the office next door that seems to know a lot more than she cares to admit. But I was ordered to wait for the DST agents' arrival to question her further."

"These guys don't trust anyone, do they? *Pff!* I bet you that the second they step in, they'll keep the meat to themselves and leave the rest of us in the dark."

"We'll see how it goes. I'd rather not start off on the wrong foot with them, especially because I have a hunch that this lady could lead us to our suspect. She's the kind of person who seems way too honest to be a good liar. Anyway, thanks for the report, André."

Boréda stood up, a sign to Fernandez and Carignan that their meeting was over.

17
-HAMAZAZPI-

04:27 PM ~ Thursday, August 25, 1994

Vivienne had spent most of her day at the police station. By four o'clock in the afternoon, Boréda's pack of cigarettes was lying in front of her, crumpled and empty. She was about to call for someone to bring her more when Boréda walked through the door with a fresh pot of coffee and a sandwich for her.

"I haven't done anything wrong, and neither has my daughter!" she blurted out without warning. "Why are you keeping me here?"

"Miss Laroche, agents from Paris will arrive shortly to ask you questions. I can only encourage you to cooperate, for you and your daughter's sake. No more telling lies."

"Are you threatening me? Is my daughter in danger?"

"I suppose you know the answer to that question better than I do."

"What is that supposed to mean?" Vivienne was indignant. "As a mother, I know that every teenager is in some sort of danger, but beyond that, I have no clue what's going on here. So I'd like you to fill me in. Perhaps I'd be more willing to cooperate if I knew what I am supposed to cooperate about—"

There was a quick knock. A female officer slipped her head through the door to warn the Major that the DST agents just walked in.

"Thanks, Isabelle. I'll be right behind you." The Major turned sideways to face Vivienne. "Please, Miss Laroche. This is not a game. Eat something. Perhaps you'll feel more responsive on a full stomach." He handed her the saran-wrapped sandwich.

"Did you even hear what I just said?" Vivienne shouted to Boréda's back, knowing full well he would not answer.

The door closed with a soft thud, and she heard him turn the lock. Vivienne threw the sandwich against the door: a gesture of frustration and despair. It bounced and plopped limply onto the ground, hardly making a sound. The pathos of the situation angered her even more. She stared at the food with both disgust and want. When she could not stand it anymore, she rose from her chair, plucked the sandwich off the linoleum floor and took a ravenous bite out of it.

A few minutes later, the Major greeted the visitors in front of his office. They introduced themselves as Frédéric Blanchard and Didier Vilorain. While Vilorain seemed the conservative type with his creased trousers, light blue shirt and uptight look behind his tortoise shell glasses, Blanchard's appearance threw Boréda for a loop. A man in his mid-thirties, he was of average height with broad shoulders and muscular biceps which protruded from his form-fitting polo shirt. He wore his sun-bleached hair in a spiky hairdo, and his demeanor seemed rather laid-back and friendly. He appeared a smart man, savvy and determined. Boréda caught himself thinking that, had the circumstances been different, he could easily strike a friendship with Blanchard.

As he invited them to step into his office, Boréda exhaled with relief. He felt hopeful that they would work well together. He briefed them on what had transpired in today's round of interrogations. As he anticipated, they were eager to speak to Vivienne Laroche.

"I hope that you won't object to the fact that we would like to conduct the interrogation ourselves, which means we would appreciate it if you would refrain from asking Miss Laroche any direct questions. You are welcome to join us in the room, if you agree to remain silent," Vilorain stated with an air of authority that ticked Boréda off, but he had enough tact to hide it.

"I'd be happy to stand back and watch you work your magic, gentlemen. Now if you would follow me."

Boréda led the way to the interrogation room.

Vivienne was ushered in a few minutes later. She looked pitiful in her mismatched clothes. Earlier that morning, she grabbed the first skirt and T-shirt that she could find. The raid did not give her the time to brush her teeth, take a shower or even comb her hair. She could smell the alcohol coming through her pores, and she reeked of cold tobacco. Even though she felt ugly and dirty, she was well aware that her grooming issues and fashion faux-pas were the least of her problems.

Frédéric Blanchard gestured for her to take a seat. Without further ado, he punched the red button on the recorder placed between them on the small square table. He asked her to identify herself and added,

"All right Miss Laroche, tell me everything you know about this man."

He pulled out the same photograph of Rafael that Vivienne looked at earlier.

"Why don't you ask your colleague over there," she pointed haughtily toward the Major who was standing with his back to the door. "I already answered him."

Blanchard leaned over the table and hit the "stop" button with an impatient finger.

"Vivienne. You don't mind if I call you Vivienne, do you?" She scratched the side of her nose nervously and shook her head. "Good," he said. "So listen to me, Vivienne. You look like crap right now, but I would bet a hundred francs that you clean up real nice. Under ordinary circumstances, I wouldn't mind you playing 'hard-to-get' with me, but we happen to be in a hurry here. So, listen to me and listen carefully, because I'm not going to repeat myself. I'm the one who asks the questions here. And, when I ask a question, I expect an answer. Not just any answer, I expect the truth. Do you think you can handle that, sweetheart?"

Without awaiting her answer, he punched the "record" button again and leaned back against the metal chair. Vivienne, intimidated by the man's brusque manners and his rude attitude, recoiled in her seat. She instinctively turned to Major Boréda for protection, but he purposefully detached his gaze from her to instead examine an imaginary scratch on his shoes. In the meantime, the cassette tape kept rolling, recording the heavy silence inside the room, until Blanchard spoke again. Except this time, he did not bother to switch off the recording device.

"Just so that we're clear on one thing, Miss. I am not planning to let you out of this room until I get the answers I'm looking for. I know you know the man in the picture. So why don't you tell me his goddamn name so that we can all move on?"

Vivienne understood from the very beginning that she stood no chance against this man. She took a big breath and said,

"His name is Rafael. Rafael Arcas, or Barcas or—oh God, I don't even know his last name."

"How about Izcoa?" Boréda could not help but to interject, in spite of the promise he made to remain silent.

"What?" Vivienne turned to the Major, genuinely surprised. "Izcoa? No, that's not it. I'm positive."

"Bear with us, OK?" Blanchard said rather curtly to Boréda. "We'll talk about that later." The Major mouthed the word "sorry," and Blanchard returned his attention to Vivienne. "OK, Miss Laroche, so we've established that you know the man in the picture. Now, tell us when you met him for the first time."

"He came to La Goutte d'Eau right after New Year's," she replied with a resigned voice. Distraught that just a bit of pressure was enough to make her give in and cooperate, Vivienne realized the only thing that mattered, at this point, was protecting her daughter.

"Did he offer any explanation as to why he wanted to move there in the first place?"

She shrugged her shoulders, as if the answer was obvious. "He came to protest the construction of the Somport tunnel, just like the rest of us."

"I see. Say, why did you lie to the Major about your daughter's whereabouts this morning?"

"Because," Vivienne choked back her tears, "because I wanted to leave her out of this mess."

"So where is she now?"

"She went on a mountain climbing trip. I'm not sure where."

"Your daughter also knows him, doesn't she?"

"She—well, yeah, she does, just like everyone else who lives at La Goutte!"

"Where is he?"

"I don't know. Frankly, I don't care, either." She tried to remain strong, as her lips started to tremble.

"Is there a chance that, maybe, they are together as we speak?" asked Blanchard, ever so calm and composed, and yet, so cold and emotionless.

"Why are you looking for him? If I knew, perhaps I could be of better assistance?" she suddenly said in spite of herself. "What on earth could he possibly have done?"

"Answer my question, Miss."

"Yes! I mean, no! They're not together!" she snapped back defensively, "and even if they were, I believe that my daughter is free to hang out with whomever she damn well pleases!"

"Is that so," he stated coldly, "really? You wouldn't mind if your daughter hung out with, say, a wanted terrorist?"

"What?"

Vivienne felt the ground give way under her feet. She wavered in her seat. The Major, who immediately noticed her distress, took a step forward, ready to come to her rescue. One tense look from Blanchard made him stop dead in his tracks.

"She's fine," said Blanchard between clenched teeth. He turned to face Vivienne again. "You're fine, aren't you?"

"Yes—yes," she stammered.

Boréda's attempt to help did not elude Vivienne. She felt deeply grateful for the Major's deliberate demonstration of humanity and compassion toward her. It gave her the strength to recover, somewhat quickly, from the blow. She straightened in her chair and muttered,

"A terrorist? What makes you say that?"

Inspector Blanchard was not about to tell her any more, but he changed his tactics and spoke in a more soothing tone this time around.

"Vivienne, it is of the utmost importance that you tell us exactly where this man and your daughter are."

18
- HEMEZORTZI -

"The feeling of extreme tiredness that one endures during a quest of great interest actually rejuvenates and strengthens oneself more than it does bring one to the brink of exhaustion."
Words attributed to Guillaume Delfau upon reaching the summit of the Grand Pic d'Ossau in 1797.

05:30 PM ~ Thursday, August 25, 1994

Rafael and Faustine had taken their time to reach the Vallée d'Ossau, which was a valley adjacent to the Vallée d'Aspe. They had stopped here and there to climb a few cliffs they discovered along the way. It was already late in the afternoon when they parked their car at the edge of the Lac de Bious, a beautiful blue ice-water lake at the foot of the impressive Massif d'Ossau. While the peak was not one of the highest summits of the Pyrenean range, it was definitely one of its most famous. This was due, in part, to its unmistakable shape. With its two distinct summits separated by a big cleft in the middle, the mountain jutted majestically toward the sky, isolated from the neighboring peaks of the chain.

Rafael spread their gear on the asphalt of the parking lot. He wanted to do one last proper inventory of their supplies before the journey ahead. To his left, Rafael set the gear they would not use for climbing: a lightweight tent, a torch, a little gas stove with a spare gas cartridge, tea bags, sugar cubes and water-purifying caplets in a clear resealable bag, an assortment of canned food, two banged-up metal water bottles, two rolled-up sleeping bags, several trash bags and a roll of toilet paper. To his right, he laid out a coiled 165-foot-long climbing rope, two climbing harnesses, two descenders and other mechanical stoppers, plus several screw gate carabiners, quick draws and a small assortment of camming devices, which were clipped according to size onto a heavy-duty nylon sling. Although this equipment would not be required for the direct ascent via the *voie normale*, "the ordinary route," Rafael had his heart set on climbing a couple buttresses along the face of the Petit Pic. He looked forward to ascending them with Faustine later on, provided she would get hooked on mountaineering the same way that she had loved free climbing.

He divided the load between the two backpacks and secured the bulky climbing rope under the top flap of his own while Faustine looked over the preparations with great interest. When they were ready to go, he flashed Faustine an exhilarated smile.

"Hey, rookie! Ready to rock n' roll?"

"You bet your sweet ass I am!" she replied with a laugh.

Rafael locked the car and helped Faustine lift her backpack onto her shoulders. They took off along a well-marked hiking trail which meandered along the lake's bank toward the edge of a forest. They trekked along a tiny water stream for a while before the grade of the slope started to intensify. After a while, they reached the plateau de Bious and traversed several grazing fields toward the Lac de Peyreget.

Given the fact that this part of the itinerary posed no particular difficulty, Rafael set a fast pace for them. Before long, Faustine was breathing hard, and she began to wonder what she had gotten herself into. Oblivious to the magnificent landscape surrounding her, she locked her eyes onto Rafael's shoes instead. Left, right, left... His legs were like two pendulums swinging with the timed precision of a metronome. She was forced to focus on them in order to keep up with his stride. Every once in a while, he reminded her to take a look at the majestic scenery. She then mumbled something along the lines of "yay!" or "wow!" without even bothering to lift her head up. At some point, Faustine's obvious lack of enthusiasm got under his skin, so Rafael stopped dead in his tracks. Faustine, unprepared for the sudden halt, almost bumped into his backpack.

"What's up?" she panted, out of breath. Rafael turned around and gently took Faustine's pouting face in his strong hands.

"Aren't you enjoying yourself?"

"It's not that. It's just hard keeping up with you. You're going way too fast for me."

"Then why don't you say so?" he asked softly. "We have all the time in the world."

"Look, I know that you could be climbing with the best right now, tackling all these hard climbs that you dream about. But instead, you take me along. I am very flattered, but I also feel like I'm slowing you down."

"There is no one in the world that I would rather be with right here, right now, *maitea.*"

"OK then, if you say so!" she replied with a coy smile. Faustine loved it when Rafael called her *maitea*, not only because it meant "my love" in *Euskara*, but most importantly because no one ever called her "my love" before him, regardless of the language.

"You know what?"

"What?"

"People say that beauty is in the eye of the beholder."

"So?"

He gently turned Faustine's face around so she could take in the breathtaking view, at long last, and whispered in her ear,

"So, behold."

They reached their destination at a quarter to eight, before sunset. All things considered, the hike had been short. It took them less than two hours to reach the lake.

"We'll camp here for the night," Rafael said with contagious enthusiasm. "Princess, tell me where you would like me to build your castle?"

Faustine scanned the area surrounding the lake. At last, she pointed her finger toward a green patch of fat grass right between her two hiking shoes and declared,

"How about right here. I think it'll be perfect."

She dropped her backpack to the ground with a satisfied grin. The tent was up just before it started to drizzle.

"I'm starving!" exclaimed Rafael. "You?"

"If I find enough strength to remove my shoes, I might think about cooking us some dinner."

Faustine lit the stove and made some tea while Rafael opened a can of ready-made tuna salad. He folded the edges of the metallic lid flat one atop the other and bent it at an angle, creating a makeshift spoon. They ate with voracious appetites while they listened to the hypnotic sound of rain splattering against the fabric of their collapsible shelter.

In time, the rain slowed down and soon stopped altogether. Rafael unzipped the tent and took off for a short walk outside. When he returned, he could not help but smile at the sight of Faustine, buried so deep inside her sleeping bag that not even a strand of her long blond hair was sticking out.

Her breathing was slow and regular. She was fast asleep.

19

— HEMERETZI —

05:45 PM ~ Thursday, August 25, 1994

Vivienne was in the grip of a nightmare. Her daughter was at the mercy of a supposedly dangerous criminal, and she did not know where to start looking for her. Pressed by the inspectors, and scared witless by the fact that the man she knew as Rafael was presumably Lartaun Izcoa, a wanted terrorist, Vivienne struggled to remember every bit of information that Faustine had given her about their planned destination.

Within the hour, every police station across the Pyrenees received photographs of Rafael—or Izcoa, or whatever his name was—and Faustine, along with their vehicle description. All the brigades were given the express order to check every single parking lot at the start of any existing hiking trail in their respective jurisdictions and to report any positive identification.

While they huddled inside Boréda's cramped office, awaiting feedback, the DST agents and the Major took advantage of the relative lull. They compared their parallel investigations in search of clues that may have eluded them thus far.

Inspector Blanchard helped himself to a fresh cup of coffee and plopped down in a comfortable chair.

"I like it here," he said to Vilorain with a wink. "The air is pure and the coffee doesn't suck."

"So, tell me, Inspector Blanchard, how did you stumble upon Iz-coa in the first place?" asked Boréda. He was dying to hear how the DST came upon their prime suspect, given the blatant lack of evidence or eye-witnesses in the case.

"Well, it was a combination of circumstances, to tell you the truth. From the beginning, we suspected that the hold up had been set up to benefit some terrorist group. I mean, who in his right mind would go through so much trouble to steal two hundred and fifty pounds of dyna-mite? I mean, even if Joe Shmoe had decided to carve out an Olympic-size swimming pool in his backyard, what the hell would he do with this much TNT?"

"Our counter-terrorism experts analyzed the pattern of the rob-bery," added Inspector Vilorain. "While they couldn't overlook the possi-bility that Muslim terrorists would be implicated in this affair, it was pretty obvious that this kind of blitz operation had ETA, or its French Basque counterpart *Iparretarrak*, written all over it. Plus, due to the fact that the holdup took place a few kilometers away from the Spanish border, we had to contact CESID, the Centre of High Studies and Information on De-fense, Spain's military and foreign intelligence agency, to tell them about the robbery. A couple hours later, a senior agent from CESID called us back with an interesting story. He informed us about a kidnapping attempt orchestrated by ETA against a rich industrialist that took place in San Se-bastián on the same Monday as our attack, even though the date is purely coincidental and irrelevant at this point. At any rate, that operation took a turn for the worse when the industrialist's bodyguards opened fire on the intruders at his property. They ended up shooting one of the kidnappers. While the others managed to escape, the Spanish police were able to iden-tify the body left at the scene. It was a man named Bixente Zubizarreta."

"This is quite interesting, but I don't see how it relates to this case," Boréda commented with a perplexed frown.

"Patience, Major," interjected Blanchard.

"The San Sebastián detectives obtained a warrant to search Zubi-zarreta's apartment," Vilorain continued. "They tore the place apart, but they couldn't find many personal effects aside from a couple of photo albums and his address book. Of course, everyone was listed under a code name. But he made a mistake."

"What mistake?" Boréda could hardly stand the suspense.

"Well, they looked through the photo albums. There was nothing interesting in there, just family crap and stuff. But then they found a series of loose photos tucked between two pages at the back of one of the albums. That caught their attention. The snapshots pictured Zubizarreta and another man who looked somewhat familiar to one of the agents, even though he could not quite figure out why. According to the print date on the lower right corner of the picture, the photos had been taken on December 30th of last year. They brought the albums back to the station for closer examination. Someone was quick to notice that the mystery man's eyes were two different colors. That pointed to the *etarra* wanted for the bombing of the Irun police station for well over two years now! They made some calls, and sure enough, the guy who was all smiles in the picture next to Zubizarreta was no other than—"

"Lorenzo Lartaun Izcoa!" exclaimed Boréda.

"In the flesh! Their experts analyzed the background of the snapshots to find out where they were taken. As it turns out, the two *compadres* were hanging at the Hotel Monbar, in the city of Bayonne."

"Oh, I know that place," continued Boréda. "It's a regular hangout for Basque refugees. It made the headlines back in '85 after two mercenaries, belonging to the Marseille's Mafia, opened fire from the street into the bar, killing four suspected ETA members. The craziest part was that they casually left the scene, on foot, after the carnage."

"On foot? After a shoot-out? What were your colleagues doing?" Blanchard interjected rather condescendingly.

"Members of the GAL were behind it. They were connected with the police. But they had not even considered that patrons inside the bar would go after them and actually manage to stop them. The police had to make the arrests after all. In court, the murderers claimed that they had been promised a reward of fifty thousand francs for each wounded target and two hundred thousand francs for a kill." Boréda shook his head in disapproval. "Those were not glorious times."

"Hmmm," said Vilorain as he sipped his coffee, "at any rate, the guy the Spaniards have been looking for in vain for two years finally decided to return home. Can you believe the nerve? Izcoa and Zubizarreta were parading around town right under everyone's nose! By the way, the 8x10 head shot we sent you was a blow up of one of those pictures. Pretty photogenic, our guy, wouldn't you say?"

"Yeah, I'd imagine him working as a model rather than a terrorist, but whatever rocks his boat, I guess." Blanchard added with a shrug.

"Still, what's his connection with our case?" ventured Boréda.

"As soon as the San Sebastián police identified Lartaun Izcoa as the man in the picture, they alerted their agents on location in the French Basque country in hopes of tracking him down," explained Vilorain. "Turns out an informer-slash-surfer burnout from Biarritz ratted him out right away to save his own butt from being thrown to jail for cocaine possession. He claimed that he had sold him his car back in January, except that he knew Lorenzo Lartaun Izcoa as Rafael Vargas."

"Well, I'll be damned!" exclaimed Boréda.

"The surfer told the police that Izcoa had offered to pay for the car in two separate payments because he didn't have enough cash on him at the time. While he was not too thrilled with the idea, the man had agreed to the deal because he was broke. Izcoa ended up giving him half the money up front, and promised to send him the remaining balance a couple weeks later. Sure enough, the guy received the rest of his cash by mail. There was no return address on the envelope, but the letter was postmarked in Pau."

"Thanks to Miss Laroche and the surfer's testimonies, we not only have plenty of circumstantial evidence that Rafael Vargas and Lorenzo Lartaun Izcoa are indeed one and the same," concluded Boréda, "but also, that Izcoa has been hiding all this time at that commune in the Vallée d'Aspe."

"Granted, we have no hard evidence, at this time, that Izcoa has taken part in the attack on the dynamite truck a few days ago, but now you understand why we're itching to have a conversation with him just the same," Blanchard said at last.

Vilorain slammed his fist on the desk. "I'll be frank with you, Major Boréda. We're not going to get much sleep until we find this man!"

Around five o'clock in the evening, Marco Fernandez poked his head through the door. He informed his superior that, in the past few hours, people from La Goutte d'Eau placed several calls to the switchboard. They were demanding explanations regarding Vivienne's detention. He added that their tempers were flaring, and they were even threatening to send a delegation over to the gendarmerie if they did not get answers soon. Inspector Blanchard cocked an eyebrow in surprise and turned to the Major with a quizzical look on his face.

"Oh, crap," mumbled Boréda. "I had already forgotten about those damned Aspaches."

"Those who?"

"Miss Laroche's friends. They're the green activists who live at the community we raided this morning. She was the only one left behind after we sent them all back home. So now they believe that they have the right to stick their noses into our business."

"Let's ignore them for now," Blanchard said with a dismissive wave.

"I wish we could, Inspector. Trust me, it would be easier on all of us if we'd allow Miss Laroche to contact them. If she tells them to stay out of it herself, they might listen to her. If not, please don't come complaining to me tomorrow that you couldn't sleep because a few of them were yelling outside your hotel room all night."

"I can't allow her to talk to them. This is all classified information," Vilorain pointed out.

"She doesn't know anything, really." Boréda contradicted. "What can she tell them that is considered classified info?"

"Didier is right," interjected Blanchard. "We can't let her tell them who their friend Rafael really is. On the other hand, since we all know that Miss Laroche is not going anywhere tonight, we could think of an excuse for her absence, if only to keep them quiet. We need something totally unrelated to Izcoa. Let me think about this for a second." He rubbed his forehead with the tip of his fingers. "These people were all shown a picture of Lartaun Izcoa. Obviously, they know that we're after him. What if—"

"I've got an idea!" exclaimed Boréda. "Miss Laroche didn't know that her father had passed away until I told her this afternoon. How about we have her announce the sad news to her friends and tell them that she must go to Paris for a few days in order to sort out his affairs? That way, no one will ever know that she's in custody, and they'll stay off our backs until we find Izcoa and her daughter."

"Sounds good to me," agreed Blanchard after a short pause. "Didier, thoughts?"

Vilorain nodded his approval.

Only a few minutes later, Inspector Vilorain handed the phone to Vivienne. Before he released his grip, he spoke to her in a stone cold voice,

"Go ahead, place the call. Remember what you were told to say and stick to it, word for word. I'll be right here, listening to the whole conversation. Do you understand?"

Vivienne did not respond immediately. Deep inside, she was grateful for her friends' concern. It was comforting to know that they would put up a fight for her. More than ever, she needed their support. Even if she had been estranged from her father for many years, she was devastated over his loss. She would never get another chance to hug him or to apologize for all the harsh words between them. He was gone forever, and any chance to make up was gone with him. As if that was not enough, the fact that Faustine was gallivanting off somewhere in the mountains with a presumably cold-blooded murderer was not especially comforting either.

"I said I'd do it. So I'll do it, OK?" Vivienne shot Vilorain a hateful look and added, "I'm not sure what you've been told about the kind of people we are or what we stand for, but for the record, none of us knew who Rafael really was or anything about his agenda. Rest assured, we have no more sympathy for terrorists than you do, and that includes this man in particular, if, in fact, he *is* a terrorist." She paused for good measure and glared defiantly at the three men. "We may be activists, *Monsieur*, but we aren't criminals."

With these words, she took the receiver from his hands and dialed La Goutte d'Eau.

Etienne came to the phone right away. Judging by the noise in the background, Vivienne could tell that everyone was huddled in the common area, anxious for an update. In a few words, she told Etienne the lies she had been instructed to repeat. Because he had no reason to believe that their conversation was tapped, Etienne spoke without restraint.

"What a way to hear about the passing of your father! It's awful, Viv. Just downright shitty. It's good to hear your voice, though. We were thinking that the *képis* had locked you up! Man, what a crazy day! Did they ask you about Rafael too? I wonder what they want from him."

"I have no idea," she lied.

"We didn't say shit, of course, but now we're kind of wondering what the hell is going on with him. I mean, I'm kind of worried because he's with Faus—"

Vivienne interrupted him quickly. "Listen, I'm calling you from a pay phone at the train station, and I'm running out of cash, so I'll need to get off soon, 'kay?"

"Viv? Why didn't you come home first to pack and to, uh, tell me all this face-to-face? You know that I would have gone with you."

"I know you would have, honey, but I'd rather go on my own. Besides, I need you to be there when Faustine gets back. I'll only be gone for a couple of days at most."

"I understand," he stammered, even though his tone of voice betrayed his state of confusion. "Everyone here sends you their love, Viv. We're very sorry for your loss."

Vivienne felt like a traitor, but she couldn't tell him the truth. She had to protect her daughter, at all cost. "Thank you. I love you. I love you all," she managed to say before her throat clamped shut.

"Call me as soon as you get to Paris, promise? I love you t—"

The line went dead with a click as Vilorain's index finger pressed down the button on top of the phone. Vivienne handed the receiver back to the inspector and wiped her eyes with the back of her hand.

"There. Happy now?"

From then on, Vivienne was officially in police custody so she could be subjected to further questioning. Major Boréda escorted her to one of the cells where she would spend the night. Upon locking the door behind her, he felt compassion mixed with surreal feelings of attraction to her. This was a woman consumed by grief and worry who remained strong in adversity. He could not deny that she had made quite an impression on him.

20

-HOGEI-

07:55 PM ~ Thursday, August 25, 1994

"Since we have some time to kill," Blanchard suggested as soon as the Major had returned to his office, "how about dinner?"

"Good idea, I'm starving! I wouldn't mind sampling the local cuisine," replied Vilorain, rubbing his stomach for emphasis.

"I know the perfect place."

The Major took them to a quaint hotel-restaurant, just down the street. The owner, a feisty woman in her forties, gave the inspectors a warm greeting before she kissed her friend on both cheeks.

"Hello Jean-Claude! I see you have company tonight! Welcome, welcome, *messieurs!* Let me offer you something to drink! First round's on the house!" She winked at Boréda and poured the contents of a bottle of Jurançon into four glasses. One for each one of them and another for her. "Will you be staying for dinner tonight?"

"We sure are! I told my guests this was *the* place to taste the fine cuisine of the Béarn region!" Boréda replied.

They took their seats at a quiet table toward the back of the dining room. A young waitress sauntered over to take their order.

"What would you recommend?" Vilorain asked her while he was perusing the menu.

"The *Garbure*, sir. It's our traditional soup. It may not be the most refined dish in the world, but here in the mountains, we like hearty food that sticks to our bones!" She uncorked a second bottle of Jurançon and handed it to the Major before she left to take care of their food order.

"I'm a little concerned that we haven't received any feedback regarding our suspect's whereabouts," Blanchard said as he took a sip of the wine. "How about you?"

"It's still early. Most gendarmerie stations around here are understaffed. Give them a bit more time," replied Boréda.

"I'm sure you're right. We Parisians are always so impatient, aren't we, Didier?" Blanchard said, tipping his glass to his colleague. "The thing is, I checked in with the bureau just before we left for dinner. Rumor has it, Prime Minister Felipe González Márquez's cabinet did not take the news of the robbery too well. As a result, everyone has their panties in a wad, and they're all breathing down our boss's neck. So, you can imagine who's going to start feeling the heat real soon!"

"It's the same old story. The Spaniards want heads to roll into the basket," continued Vilorain, "not just those of the actual robbers, mind you. For them, incidents like this one are a great excuse to request the extradition of all suspected ETA members living on French soil. Anytime something similar occurs, they play the 'See what-happens-when-you-don't-do-what-we-asked-you-to?' card. Don't get me wrong, I understand that they are under a tremendous amount of pressure, with the rampant terrorism sweeping their country and what not, but we need to be rational here. We must keep a cool head and consolidate our respective resources and intelligence to solve this conundrum."

"What Vilorain is alluding to," said Blanchard, "is that many ETA leaders and refugees have kept their reins on the Basque terrorist organization from the relative security of the French side of the Basque country. For decades, the Spanish have been resenting our government, in particular, that of current Socialist President François Mitterrand, for treating ETA members as political refugees within the French borders and for granting continuous amnesty and protection to ETA members imprisoned in France. Historically speaking, France has always considered ETA more as an anti-Franco organization fighting for the rights of the Basque people rather than a terrorist group per se."

"Well," ventured Boréda, who was aware that he was treading a dangerous path, "ETA is a terrorist group, no doubt, but you can't deny that from the time of its inception in 1959, it was the sole organization to actively oppose Franco's fascist regime. Think of the bombing of the city of Guernica by the *Luftwaffe* in 1937, when the Germans tested their "burnt-earth tactics" with Franco's blessing. They ended up killing and wounding thousands of Basque civilians during the Spanish Civil War, not to mention the ensuing massive Basque exodus. Franco was cooperating with Hitler at the time, because he was absolutely determined to annihilate the Basque way of life, their freedom of speech and their culture altogether! I mean, once World War II was over, everyone felt that the defeat of the Germans would result in the automatic demise of the fascist Franquist regime, and therefore, bring forth the return of a Republic in Spain. But the end of the World War led to the Cold War between the United States and the USSR, and Franco's regime took advantage of the situation. Clearly, the existence of a profoundly anti-communist state in Spain served the Americans well. In 1950, it led to the United States' recognition of the Franquist regime and its subsequent integration into the United Nations. *Euskadi* became a martyr nation, with no one to turn to for help. That was when ETA, *Euskadi Ta Askatasuna*, was created. The organization's members believed that the only way of reclaiming their freedom was to fight to the death for the independence of *Euskadi*, and that it was everyone's duty to fight against Franco. Which naturally leads one to wonder, if ETA had not carried out the assassination of General Franco's appointed successor, Admiral Luis Carrero Blanco, in 1973, who else would have delivered Spain from prolonged fascist oppression?"

"I will concede that there was a purpose to the group's existence and struggle back then," replied Blanchard, "but once King Juan Carlos replaced Franco after his death in 1975, the process of transition to democracy was underway. For the Spanish, it meant free elections and the ratification of the Constitution. The Basque country was accepted as an Autonomous State. *Euskara* was recognized as the official language and all that. Hell, the government even signed a decree of general amnesty for ETA prisoners and for all imprisoned persons guilty of crimes carried out before the initiation of the transition to democracy. From that point on, you would have thought the group would disintegrate and die off, considering that democracy was restored and Basque fundamental rights had been reestablished." Blanchard paused for a moment, shaking his head in disbelief. "But instead, ETA morphed into a paramilitary organization, very similar to the IRA in Ulster. They have been responsible for countless murders, extortions and violent activities ever since. Their members might have once passed for heroes, but to me, they are nothing but dangerous terrorists. They need to come to grip with the fact that the tables have turned, thanks to the fact that both our socialist governments in France and Spain have found common ground in their efforts to crack down on the terrorist network operating from France."

"That is true," Vilorain agreed. "We took our sweet time, but for the past couple of years our government has taken a fierce pro-active stance. Not only by going after alleged members of ETA and *Iparretarrak*, but also by organizing fast-track transfers of ETA detainees serving their sentence in France so that they could be judged on Spanish soil for the crimes they perpetrated.

"This, of course, is terrible news for *etarras*. Extraditions to Spain mean tougher trials for them and exponentially harsher sentences compared to those that they would have served had they stayed in France," chimed Blanchard.

"There is no question that France is no longer the safe haven it used to be." Vilorain cupped his hand over his mouth to cover a yawn. "Sorry. Long day."

"I still find it hard to believe that ETA is responsible for our robbery," Boréda said in reaction to Vilorain's earlier statement. "I mean, we all agree that the organization was pretty much dismantled after the Bidart arrest, correct?" he continued, referring to the massive arrest of ETA's *cúpula,* back in March of 1992, when the top three ETA leaders, the head of the military branch, Francisco Múgica Garmendia, a.k.a. "Pakito," the political leader, José Luis Álvarez Santacristina, a.k.a. "Txelis," and their logistics man, José María Arregui Erostarbe, a.k.a. "Fiti," were caught and extradited to Spain.

"Yup," agreed Vilorain.

"So how could they have recovered so soon from such a blow to their structure? How could they be capable of planning a major terrorist coup?" continued Boréda.

"The problem with ETA's structure," replied Vilorain, "is that it is a hydra-headed monster. As soon as an *etarra* falls, another member is ready to take his spot. Obviously, the fall of the *cúpula* seriously disabled the organization, but it did not wipe it out entirely. In fact, for the past two years, ETA has taken advantage of the ensuing truce to quietly regroup and strengthen its core. Who knows what they are capable of this very minute?"

"There is no doubt in my mind that ETA has the resources to carry out a major act of terrorism as we speak," interjected Blanchard. "However, I don't think that it fits within the group's current political and tactical agenda. A bomb attack would only further undermine ETA's popularity, which is already at an all time low. That is why ETA's new military leaders have been favoring the urban guerilla warfare strategy. They want to keep the population on their toes rather than resorting to the more radical actions they've been notorious for."

"Are you referring to the *kale borroka*?" asked Boréda. Blanchard nodded in agreement. "On that note, what's your take on the 'Y' group? Do you think that it exists for real, or is it just a hoax?"

"Well, it depends on whom you ask. According to the Spanish Intelligence, ETA would have turned to minors to create havoc in the streets. Spanish secret service alleges that the group trains young people to start riots and to initiate sabotage missions all over. That way, ETA leaders can keep their war of terror going while they wait for a more auspicious time to resume their activities. This is a sneaky tactic, but it is just as potent as a large scale attack that puts the 'fear of God' into people's hearts," explained Blanchard.

"On the other hand, the very existence of the *talde* 'Y' as an organized phenomenon is being contested by the supporters of the Basque National Liberation Front," Boréda countered. "They claim that it is nothing but a trumped-up excuse by the Spanish authorities to give longer prison sentences to those convicted of street violence. The youngsters who get arrested for taking part in the *kale borroka* maintain that they act on their own, and ETA does not pay them to raise hell."

"Either way, it does not change the fact that these young rebels are a threat to the nation. If you ask me, they deserve to be punished for their actions, to the full extent of the law. Plain and simple," Vilorain stated. "Izcoa is the perfect example. He was one of them in his teenage years, and look at him now!"

"'Y' group or no 'Y' group, it all boils down to the fact that the Spanish authorities are totally overwhelmed by the situation," Blanchard continued. "The population is scared because it seems like the violence can't be contained. Everyone lives in fear of future terrorist attacks. We all know that it is not a matter of *if*, but a matter of *when* and *where*. Everyone is angry, fed up and scared. And this, my friends, is how ETA ultimately wins the game of terror, regardless of the measurable strength of its structure at any point in time."

"Don't get me wrong, I can totally understand why the Spanish cabinet is going berserk right now," Boréda said, as he helped himself to a piece of baguette.

"I don't think that it is even a matter of 'whodunit' as far as they're concerned. Their number one concern is to locate and recover the explosives. Without dynamite, there's no explosion." Vilorain took a sip of his wine. "That is why we must capture Izcoa and hope that he was involved in the robbery, so he can provide us with answers to the riddle."

"*Insha'Allah*," concluded the Major, before he excused himself to place a phone call. When he returned, just a minute later, he had good news. The police station in the village of Laruns had established a positive identification on Izcoa's car.

"Sorry for cutting our dinner plans short, gentlemen, but we have to go!"

Blanchard and Vilorain jumped from their seats, and the trio rushed out of the restaurant.

Izcoa's vehicle was indeed recovered in the parking lot of the Lac de Bious, near Laruns, a small town in the heart of the Vallée d'Ossau. The lake was the start point of a classic hiking trail leading to the Pic du Midi d'Ossau, the Béarn region's famed mountain peak.

Blanchard relayed the news to the DST in Paris without delay. The whole team was aware they had a small window of opportunity to catch the suspect by surprise while he was oblivious that the police were after him. Up in the mountains, Izcoa was like an unsuspecting rat just about to be caught in a giant mousetrap.

It was close to midnight when the Major drove the inspectors to their hotel. After a lot of brainstorming, they finally agreed on a plan to implement the next morning. Their strategy was two-fold. "Plan A" called for dispatching gendarmerie squads, dressed in civilian clothing, at every existing hiking trail leading to the Pic du Midi. In addition, two pairs of specially trained mountain rescue officers would hike up the plateau toward the base of the Grand Pic. Their specific job would consist of spotting Izcoa and his girlfriend from afar and relaying their every move to the teams waiting below. In the meantime, the officers would sit tight and wait for the pair to come down the mountain via one of the marked trails, since they had no choice but to go down the mountain at some point. They would ambush and arrest them the second they walked past the undercover gendarmes.

The scheme was brilliant in its simplicity. If all went well, it would be a zero-violence raid. Nevertheless, they could not underestimate their suspect. The man could be armed. He could decide to take his girlfriend or an innocent hiker hostage should he realize, at any time, he was under surveillance. After all, he was a terrorist and considered to be very dangerous. Boréda and the DST agents also understood that, should he slip through their fingers, they would lose their one and only prime suspect in the explosives' robbery. With that in mind, they eschewed a thorough contingency plan, "Plan B."

"Plan B" would be paramount to the operation's success should things take a turn for the worse. As a consequence, Major Boréda contacted the GIGN unit in Paris, the "National Gendarmes' Intervention Group," to be put on active standby as of five o'clock the next morning. They would be prepared to dispatch an elite team at a moment's notice in case the situation got hairy. These highly skilled gendarmes, who underwent extensive cross training in a variety of specialties including scuba diving, rock climbing, long range marksmanship, parachuting, explosives handling and hand-to-hand combat techniques, were able to handle anything from hostage situations and prison mutinies to an airplane high-jacking. They were a force to be reckoned with. Jean-Claude Boréda felt more confident knowing he could count on their support should it become necessary.

The Major slipped under the covers, eager to get a good, albeit short, night's sleep. Unfortunately, as soon as he switched off the bedroom lights, dark unsettling thoughts started swirling through his mind, hindering his efforts to sleep.

21
-HOGELTABAT-

05:50 AM ~ Friday, August 26, 1994

Rafael awoke Faustine to still-dark skies.

"Wake up, *maitea!*"

Rafael's smiling face appeared through the opening of the tent. He was in great spirits for someone who arose that early.

"I'm so sore!" moaned Faustine from the depths of her sleeping bag. She unzipped it a little and stuck an arm out to feel the outside temperature. "Yikes, it's cold!" she shrieked and propped herself on her elbows to take the hot cup of tea from Rafael's hand. "Do we ever get to sleep in during boot camp? It's still dark outside!"

"We'll have all the time to sleep when we're dead. Come on, Rapunzel, we have a big day ahead of us! No time to waste, the sun will be up soon."

Faustine grabbed her pants and wrestled to put them back on. She looked for her shoes in the dark, laced them onto her feet and crawled outside. After a light breakfast of tea and a cereal bar, she helped him fold up the tent. Soon, they were on their way.

They hiked among an expanse of dry grass and medium-sized stone boulders until they reached a second lake. When they arrived at the base of a steep stone field, Faustine started to walk inside Rafael's steps so as not to slide on the wet and unstable rocks. They cleared the zone in forty-five minutes and reached the Col du Peyreget, a pass 7,612 feet above sea level, soon after sunrise. Fighting against a crest wind that threatened to push her over the edge, Faustine crouched down behind a boulder to admire the south flank of the Ossau. The pointy face of the Petit Pic seemed to be tearing a hole through the grey sky. Behind it, she could barely make out the summit of the Grand Pic. She said a small prayer to the Mountain Gods for the weather to clear up soon. It seemed impossible to her that, should everything go as planned, she would be standing up at the top around noon.

"Let's get moving before the wind blows you off the mountain!" teased Rafael, holding his hand out to her. "Do you see that toy-like house straight down the slope?" Faustine squinted in the direction he was pointing with his finger. "That's the Refuge de Pombie. If we walk straight down the slope instead of following the classic route toward the Soum de Pombie pass, we should get there in half an hour. It's a little more of a challenging path, but not too bad. Just watch where you put your feet, OK?"

When they cruised past the refuge, Faustine noticed the chalet looked quite modern. There were solar panels installed below the top roof, and the place seemed cared for.

"I'd give anything for a hot shower and a meal!" she exclaimed, eyeing the cozy building with envy.

"Patience!" replied Rafael. "We'll come back here tonight, I promise. That will be our reward for surviving the climb!"

"Hmmm. OK." She reluctantly shifted her gaze toward the Col de Souzon, the last pass before the climb up the peak. From the refuge, the trail meandered between an impressive mass of boulders bearing the name of *Grande Raillère de Pombie*, the "great stone field of Pombie," and continued past through a grassy slope to the saddle ridge of Souzon. The path veered west until it stopped abruptly at the foot of the immaculate andesite flank of the Grand Pic.

They finished the approach trek. Faustine touched the rock with both hands to make sure she was not dreaming. She tried to let out a whistle of admiration, but her mouth was too dry to push sounds past her lips. Her legs felt like butter, and the knot in her stomach had grown to the size of a fist. The mountain she had stared at all morning became taller and steeper with every step she took. Now, it towered over her, impassive and menacing. Faustine tried to put on a brave face as she sized up the first chimney.

"Don't let this chunk of rock play tricks on you," Rafael said to reassure her. "It looks more impressive than it really is. Knowing the kind of climber you are, I would not even bother with a rope, but since it's your first time on a big mountain, we'll play it safe."

He counted sixty feet of rope and tied it around Faustine's waist. He then coiled the excess rope in neat loops over her shoulder and across her torso. Next, he paid out another forty-five feet and attached it in the same manner onto himself.

"Let's get going while we have the face to ourselves. It gets pretty crowded around here this time of year."

The first chimney was a short climb, fifty feet at the most. It was almost vertical, but there were many deep holds and ledges to grasp. They cleared it without difficulty. The second chimney was taller by forty feet. The rock there was yellowish in color. It flaked in places and crumbled to the touch. While Faustine consciously knew a fall would be fatal without a safety rope, she had no fear because she was in good hands. Besides, she was elated by the sheer size of the face and the magnanimity of the view. The higher she ascended, the more she felt exposed, but somehow less apprehensive. She was on a natural high. She could not get enough of this amazing Temple of Nature.

Once they cleared the second chimney, they followed a narrow trail on a northwest course. There were a couple of passages where Faustine had to use her hands and feet to move forward, but nothing was too complex. Later on, they veered south in order to climb a large mass of fallen rock. This, in turn, led to the start of the third and final chimney at 8,595 feet. While the third chimney was the tallest, about a hundred and thirty feet, it was an easier climb than the previous two. The sun suddenly came out from behind the clouds, and Faustine welcomed its glare with a big smile. The day turned perfect after all.

They eventually reached a slim iron cross bearing the name of La Croix du Portillon, before they broke free onto the Rein de Pombie, which was an impressive scree-laden slope that went all the way to the summit.

Faustine and Rafael made it to the top around noon. It culminated at 9,462 feet above sea level and was surrounded by precipitous drop-offs on all sides. Up there by the cairn, the ominous silence would have suited a Carthusian monastery. The sky was clear and the view breathtaking in every direction. As far as Faustine's eyes could see, jagged peaks, dark-looking stone fields, vertiginous ravines, twisted needles and towering buttresses filled the scenery. In places, narrow patches of blackish ice stuck to steep couloirs that forever remained in the shade. At a lower elevation, the grassy fields of the plateau exploded in a glorious patchwork of color. They were peppered with wildflowers, bright-green fir trees and inviting crystal-blue rivers and lakes.

She spotted the Refuge de Pombie, which was flanked by a beautiful heart-shaped lake glistening in the sun. Rafael pointed out the Aiguilles d'Ansabère and the Aspe Mountains to the east. The massive wall of the Peña Telera spread over the Spanish border to the south. To the west, the Pic de Lurien, the majestic pyramid of the Pic du Palas, the Arriel, the Balaïtous, and, further in the distance, the Pic d'Enfer and the Vignemale were also visible.

"Thank you for bringing me here," Faustine whispered in awe.

Rafael produced a small flask from his backpack, unscrewed its twist-cap and offered it to her.

"Here's to you, my love, standing tall and proud on the roof of the Béarn chain!" he offered as a toast. Faustine took a generous sip from the bottle. The gentian liquor burnt her lips and tongue at first. She savored the flavor of alcohol as it lingered on her taste buds like a bittersweet afterthought.

"Are you trying to get rid of me by getting me drunk before the descent?" she said with a facetious look on her face. They both laughed and fell silent again, mesmerized by the splendor spread before their eyes.

"Now what?" she said after a while, still lost in contemplation.

"It never ends, does it?" he murmured.

Faustine turned sideways to get a good look at him. Rafael looked frightfully sad, all of a sudden. It made her heart sink.

"Is that wrong?"

"Sometimes, yes, it is."

They took one last look around. The time had come to head back down the mountain.

They just retraced their steps back to the old iron cross when they heard voices coming up from the chimney below. Rafael suggested a short break to allow the group of climbers to clear the wall before their own descent. They sat down on the ground with their backs resting against their backpacks and turned their faces toward the sun. Faustine let the warm rays burn her skin with unabashed pleasure. When she spoke, she did so with her eyes closed.

"You know what's strange, Rafa? We spend so much time together and, come to think of it, I realize that I don't have the slightest idea who you are."

"You know me, Faustine. You know me better than anyone," he replied evasively.

"Don't give me that 'you-know-me' crap!" she blurted out in sudden aggravation. "You know exactly what I'm talking about! Your entire life is nothing but a big mystery to me!" Rafael kept silent. "I try hard not to let it bother me, but it's tough, you know? Sometimes, I feel like I'm living with an amnesiac!" she pressed on. "It's not like I'm dying to know all of your darkest secrets or anything... I just wish that you would learn to confide in me, that's all. So what if people have hurt you before. You know that I'm not one of them!"

They were interrupted before Rafael had a chance to answer her. They turned silent, listening to the sound of voices and heavy mountain boots scraping the rock just beneath them.

"Hey, there!" A jovial face emerged from the chimney, followed by two more. "Nice day for it, huh?"

The group of climbers consisted of two men and a woman.

"You must have woken up really early!" said the woman, an energetic-looking lady who introduced herself as Sylvie. She extended her hand in greeting. "We thought we were the first team on the mountain this morning. I guess you beat us to the top! Did you two start from Anéou?"

"No," replied Faustine, "we got here last night. We started from Bious. Glad to see human beings at last. You're the first people we've seen around since yesterday!"

"Well," Sylvie replied with a wink, "enjoy it while it lasts. We all come to the mountains for the peace and quiet, right? Well, not so much today, I'm afraid. When we reached the parking lot of Anéou this morning, the place was swarming with cops!"

Rafael's body stiffened imperceptibly.

"Cops?" Faustine repeated in surprise.

"OK, I might be exaggerating a bit when I say 'swarming.' At any rate, there were a couple of patrol vans stationed at the start of the trail. We thought they were there for mountain rescue practice at first, but they stopped us to ask where we were going!"

"Yeah, where the hell did they think we were going, dressed the way we are?" one of the men added with a chuckle, "to check the summer sale at the 'Galleries Lafayette,' perhaps?"

They all laughed at his joke, save for Rafael.

"Seriously, they checked our IDs!" continued Sylvie. "They told us they were doing random identity checks or some crazy bullshit like that. Can you believe this nonsense?"

"That is screwed up for sure," said Faustine, shaking her head with empathy.

"So what's your name, man?" the funny guy asked Rafael.

"Rafael. *Lo siento, pero casi no hablo francés,*" he replied, feigning a confused look, as if he were unable to communicate with them.

"Oh, you're Spanish?"

"Uh-huh!"

"Nice to meet you Rafael. *Como se dice…* Oh yes, *encantado!* Anyway, I'm Pierre." Pierre was a very good-looking man in his early thirties, his eyes as blue as the sky they were hiking toward. "And who's the gorgeous French lady to my left?" he asked, shooting Faustine a flirtatious smile.

"Faus—er, Florence," Rafael answered with a thick accent before Faustine got the chance to answer herself. She gave him a puzzled look but kept her mouth shut.

She turned to the group again and managed to ask casually,

"How about you, guys?"

"This is Chris, my partner in crime," said Pierre, "and you've already met Sylvie, his lovely wife. Where do you guys live?"

"Madrid," Faustine lied. "We're on holiday."

"Well, we hope to see you later at the refuge."

"Sounds fun! We'll catch up with you this evening, then!" Faustine wished them a safe climb and off they went.

As soon as they were out of earshot, she yanked Rafael around to face her. "So now you don't speak French, *huh?* What was that crap all about? And since when is my name Florence?"

"Those people were way too nosy."

"What are you talking about? They were only asking for our names! Actually, I thought they were cool, and I'm kind of looking forward to hanging out with them tonight at the ref—"

"Suit yourself, then." Rafael's curt tone indicated, beyond any doubt, he would rather not take their conversation any further.

"What is wrong with you? Why are you so mad all of a sudden?"

"I came here to be alone with you. Is that so hard to understand?"

"Fine. Whatever."

Faustine snatched her backpack and took the lead down the chimney without adding another word.

22
—HOGEITABI—

12:49 PM ~ Friday, August 26, 1994

Jean-Philippe parked his car at the end of a narrow dirt road overgrown with nettles and blackberry bushes on either side. He came to check on Eric, who just returned home, the previous day, from the hospital in Oloron-Sainte-Marie.

A little over six months ago, Eric moved into a modest chalet on the edge of the small village of Urdos, about three miles south of Jean-Philippe's house in Etsaut. Urdos was the last settlement along RN-134 before the Spanish border at the Col du Somport. Just as it was for Lartaun, this was only a temporary relocation, only meant to last until the *ekintza* was over, and the explosives were turned over to Patxi and his men.

The front door stood wide open. Jean-Philippe let himself in and called Eric's name. No answer. He pushed the wooden door closed behind him and checked out the Spartan living quarters from afar, careful not to touch anything. The log-and-stone cabin was tiny. Still, the air was agreeably cool inside in comparison to the stifling heat outside. The home consisted of a main floor with a basic kitchen, a small living room with a wood-burning stove and a bathroom. A steep set of stairs led to the attic which had been converted into a bedroom. This was where Eric worked and slept. The appliances and amenities were rustic, at best, and in dire need of thorough cleaning and massive overhaul.

"Hello?"

"Jean-Phi, is that you?"

"Yes, where are you?"

"I'm outside! Get us a couple beers from the fridge and come over!"

Jean-Philippe, with two ice-cold beer bottles in his hand, opened the screen door leading to the back porch. Eric was sitting in the shade on his rocking chair, as he tried to stay cool. He wiped the sweat off his brows with the front of his T-shirt and waved at Jean-Philippe.

"Whoa, that looks painful!" Jean-Philippe commented upon spotting his friend. Eric's left leg was plastered in a cast that extended from the middle of his thigh all the way to his toes.

"Tell me about it, not to mention that it's a bitch to move around! The doc gave me these," he said, pointing at a pair of crutches lying on the ground beside him. "But they require some serious getting used to. Anyway, I'm glad you came over. You saved me a trip to the pay phone, which is a long way away in my condition."

Jean-Philippe popped the cap of his beer bottle with a lighter.

"Why? What's up?" he asked.

"I guess you haven't heard the news, huh?" Eric took a long sip of his beer. He was trying to act cool with his cavalier demeanor, but his attitude did not fool Jean-Philippe for a second.

"What news?" Jean-Philippe asked again, his voice rising with sudden concern.

"Cops raided La Goutte yesterday. They're after Lartaun."

"*What?* Says who?"

"Etienne. He stopped by this morning."

The news hit Jean-Philippe like a ton of bricks.

"How could the cops know to look for him? He was not even there when the *ekintza* took place!" he struggled to say, still reeling from the shocking news. "No one could have seen us carrying the load to the *zulo*, either!"

"No one said that they wanted him for the robbery. It's not like Lartaun never broke the law in the past," Eric replied matter-of-factly.

"But why now? Don't you think that this is just a little too creepy to be a coincidence?"

"Yeah, I know. Talk about terrible timing on their part."

"Shit man, could it mean that the *képis* are after us, too?"

"I don't know, but for what it's worth, Etienne told me that they only asked about Lartaun."

"What are we going to do? Fuck, I'm starting to freak out here! Shouldn't we all scram while we can? I mean, I can look into flights for the both of us. If we leave in the next couple of hours, that would put us at Charles de Gaulle airport by—"

"We're not going anywhere, Jean-Phi," Eric cut him off. "I already spoke to Patxi."

"You did—what?"

"He asked to see me, but since I can't go anywhere because of this damn cast, you'll meet him instead. He'll be waiting for you at Plaza Urdanibia, ten o'clock tomorrow morning in Irun."

"Why me?" Jean-Philippe shrieked in spite of himself.

Eric ignored his question and said,

"He'll be sitting on a bench across from a building with a blue fa-çade. You can't miss it. Oh, and when you spot him, don't signal or wave to him. Just pay attention to where he goes and follow him at a respectable distance until he decides that it's OK for the two of you to make contact. He doesn't want to take any chances, should the police be on your tail too."

"Shit." Jean-Philippe drained the rest of his beer in one gulp. "That's just fucking *great!*"

"Don't worry. All you need to do is listen to what Patxi has to say and then report back to me." Jean-Philippe started to pace the room fre-netically, looking distraught. "Hey, Jean-Phi?"

"What?"

"Keep your cool. So far, we have nothing to worry about. We're golden, all right?"

"Oh, but of course, if you say so!" Jean-Philippe shrugged his shoulders and stomped out of the chalet.

"Come see me tomorrow as soon as you're back from Irun!" Eric called out after him.

The front door rattled on its hinges as Jean-Philippe slammed it shut.

As soon as he arrived home, Jean-Philippe made a beeline for his father's study. He helped himself to a highball full of whiskey and drank half of its contents in one swig. He grimaced, drained the rest of it, and immediately poured himself another one. He hoped the alcohol might numb his mind and fears.

23

- HOGETAHIRU -

01:16 PM ~ Friday, August 26, 1994

Non-climbers tend to assume that an ascent ends when one has reached the summit. That is far from the truth. Any mountain climber will agree, one is not in the clear until he has retraced his steps all the way down the face, back to base camp, or better even, back home. With this fundamental rule in mind, Faustine elected to stash her immediate concerns in the back of her head and focus on the descent instead. Still, as she progressed down the crag, she found it more and more difficult to ignore the little voice inside her head screaming, "something is horribly wrong!"

She silently mouthed the questions over and over, "Why were there cops on the mountain? And why did Rafael lie to those hikers?"

Two more chimneys to go and they would clear the face. The pair took advantage of a flat ledge to sit down and take a short break. Rafael dug into his backpack and removed a beat-up metallic water bottle. He handed it to Faustine, who gingerly took a sip. Wiping her mouth with the back of her hand, she passed it back to Rafael. As she stared at his profile from the corner of her eye, she watched his Adam's apple move up and down as he drank the water. His eyes sparkled as if he were about to cry. He, who was so happy not even an hour ago, looked discouraged and beat. She watched him stare at the ground, and wondered what could be of so much interest to him. He was transfixed by the sight of a tiny Rock

Jasmine. The frail plant was growing on a minuscule patch of soil encased in a crack between two sheets of rock, right by the tip of his hiking shoe. Whatever miracle had caused this little seed to travel all the way up there and find a piece of earth to call home seemed like a true wonder. It was so ironic and yet, it made Rafael think about the Basque country. The flower was just like his people, fighting an ongoing battle against all odds so that they could flourish and grow on their small piece of land. He resisted the urge to crush the delicate plant under his foot in frustration. Instead, he poured a few drops out of the water bottle onto the soil to quench the puny mountain flower's thirst.

"Faustine, I am so, so sorry." Rafael's body suddenly tensed up against Faustine's. Unable to look her in the eyes, he buried his face into her hair. He breathed in her scent, as if it was the very last time. He recognized a faint trace of perfume mixed in with her sweat and the bittersweet smell of mountain dust. Rafael knew, all too well, that once again, he was on the verge of losing something irreplaceable. The pain was unbearable. "I have lied to you, *maitea*," he said, "over and over, right down to my name."

Upon hearing his words, two long streams of tears carved a path down Faustine's dusty cheeks. They splattered onto a round pebble resting at her feet, giving it a light sheen. Rafael picked up the small stone and stashed it in his pocket. Faustine did her best to remain stoic as she watched her perfect little world crumbling to pieces around her. Somehow, she had known all along that it would end up this way. Together, they had created a parallel universe to shield themselves from reality, but it caught up with them at last. Still, one thing remained tried and true, the love they shared for one another. That, too, was about to be put to the test.

"The police... Are they here for you?" she reluctantly asked.

"I think so," he answered in a voice so low that she could hardly hear the words coming out of his mouth.

"How bad is it?"

"I don't know. That is God's honest truth. I wish I'd never had to put you through this mess. Of all the people, you are the last person I would ever want to hurt."

"Maybe, someday you'll tell me your story." Faustine resolutely wiped her tears with the back of her shirt and stopped crying at once. "For now, I just want to know your name."

At last, he lifted his head and locked his extraordinary eyes into hers. "My name is Lartaun Izcoa. Lorenzo Lartaun Izcoa," he said.

"You *do* love me, don't you?"

"I love you with all my heart."

"That, *señor* Izcoa, is all that matters to me right now." After a moment of silence, Faustine stated with determination, "I don't give a damn about the rest."

Even if it made no sense, Faustine felt somewhat relieved, almost at peace. At last, the fantasy was stripped of all its bright colors and special effects. Underneath it all, the black-and-white rendition was just as striking.

Stationed just below the Col de Souzon, two agents of the mountain rescue police force, dressed in civilian hiking clothes, kept track of Lartaun's every move on the face through their long-range binoculars.

Earlier that morning, two undercover teams, each with two officers, met with the Major and the DST agents upon their arrival at the parking lot of Bious. Boréda briefed them with the details of their mission before he sent them on their way to the base of the Pic d'Ossau via the hiking trail cutting through the Cirque de Moundelhs. As soon as they reached a spot with an unobstructed view of the *voie normale* meandering up the Eastern face of the Ossau, the first team set up shop to scan the mountain, while the second pair pressed on toward the Refuge de Pombie to establish their own surveillance camp on the other side of the Souzon pass.

These men were Boréda's eyes and ears on the mountain. Their job did not require them to make the arrest, but rather, relay real-time information about the suspects' progression down the face. They would stalk the pair from a respectful distance until they could establish with certainty which trail they would pick to walk down the mountain. Once established, they would confer with the squadrons of undercover gendarmes, who had been dispatched at the start of the trails of Bious, Caillou de Soque and Anéou, all potential gateways to the Massif d'Ossau, and let them proceed with the capture.

The mountain rescue gendarmes zoned in on Lartaun and Faustine thirty minutes ago, when they were on their way down the second chimney. Since, they tracked their every single move. It was clear the suspects were unaware of their predicament, since the gendarmes did not detect any strange behavior on their part. The undercover officer adjusted the focus of his lens to get a crisp close-up of Faustine. She was wearing a pair of loose-fitting khaki pants that she had rolled up above her knees. He was quite taken by the sight of her calf muscles and tendons undulating under her tanned skin. Her forearm muscles were just as impressive, bulging and tensing under the effort. He admired how strong and attractive she was.

"Check out the girl's hair, Gilles!" He passed the binoculars to his partner so that he could take a look. "See how her braid is folded in two and it still reaches down the middle of her back?"

"Whoa man, picture her naked with that hair undone! I bet she looks just like the chick in that painting, you know the one I'm talking about?"

"The 'Birth of Venus' by Botticelli?"

"Maybe. Is that the one with the broad standing on a shell who acts all prudish while hiding her pussy with her hair?"

"Jesus, man, you've got no class," his partner replied with a shrug.

"What? Did I say something wrong?"

"Forget it, Gilles. Just give me back the damn binocs!"

The officer zoomed in on Faustine one more time, and shook his head in bitter disappointment. He wondered in silence why the girls who had it all always fell for the bad guy. With reluctance, he darted his binoculars onto Lartaun again. The young man wore a pair of gun-metal grey climbing pants. Because of the combination of heat and effort, he had stripped down to a sleeveless T-shirt. The gendarme clicked on his radio to relay the suspect's current position on the face to his superiors.

"Base camp, come back!"

"Condor 1, this is Base camp. Do you copy, over?"

"Receiving loud and clear."

Boréda was sitting inside a patrol van stationed at the parking lot of Anéou with Vilorain and Blanchard by his side. "What's the status?"

"We have an unobstructed visual on the pair. The bird-watching decoy tarp was a great idea. They don't suspect anything. Has the other team reached the refuge already?"

"That's affirmative; we spoke to the refuge keeper a few minutes ago. They're in position. Where's our guy?"

"Climbing down the face. I expect he should be back on the ground within the next half-hour."

"Keep us posted with any new developments, over."

"Ten-four, Major. Over and out."

Lartaun and Faustine set foot on the grass. The ascension of the

Pic du Midi d'Ossau proved to be a success, but they were in no mood to celebrate. Lartaun became even more preoccupied upon realizing that they were all alone, which was very unusual during summer's peak season. He spilled the contents of their backpacks onto the grass and began to sort out items with record speed. He would only take what was strictly necessary, since traveling light would be paramount for what he was setting out to do. Meanwhile, Faustine coiled their climbing rope. No matter how many times she looked over her shoulder, the plateau was desperately devoid of people.

"Can't you see that nobody is around?" said Faustine. She was still holding onto the naïve hope that Lartaun had nothing to fear after all. "Those guys up there must have been confused! Perhaps this whole thing is just a big misunderstanding!" Lartaun did not reply. Instead, he secured the climbing rope under the top flap of his backpack in silence. "You can't take off just like that!" she pleaded. "It—it's all in your head! There's no one coming after you!" Lartaun slung the pack over his shoulders. Faustine grabbed him by the arm, her last effort to detain him, but she knew it was in vain.

Lartaun freed himself from her grip, but held onto her hand and squeezed it hard. "My life was shattered until I met you," he said, "but you've made me a happy man again, *maitea*. I can never repay you for that."

"Don't leave me then!"

"Don't ever let anyone bring you down, you hear? Just remember that you're stronger than they are."

"But I want to go with you!" she exclaimed, choking back the tears.

"You know that it is not possible. *Ez larritu, maitea.* Don't worry, my love. I'll see you again, I promise." Lartaun looked away. He could not bear looking at Faustine any longer. It hurt too damn much. "You must go home, now. Go!"

He pivoted around and broke into a sprint down the steep slope heading toward a massive scree field, aptly named Chaos de Pombie. Faustine, paralyzed by the sheer violence of her emotions, dropped to her knees, unable to even yell his name.

The gendarme, thoroughly bewildered, dropped his binoculars. He reached for his walkie-talkie and urgently pressed down the "call" button.

"Base camp, we've got a situation! The pair has just separated!"

"What do you mean, they've separated?" Blanchard barked into the radio.

"The target is running away! He left the girl behind on the ridge."

Blanchard turned to the others inside the van. "Damn it! He must have suspected something after all. How the hell could he figure out that we're here?"

"They must have met with the group of climbers who saw our men getting in position earlier this morning," Boréda offered as a plausible explanation.

"What group of climbers? Didn't we give specific orders to turn everyone away? Didn't I say 'nobody is allowed on that freaking mountain today?' Didn't I say, 'no exceptions for freaking anybody?'" Blanchard was getting so riled up with frustration that Boréda thought he was going to have a heart attack. Meanwhile, he answered as calmly as he could,

"They arrived very early, before the patrol was fully briefed and the order to restrict the whole area was given."

"Well, if this shithead thinks he can escape us, he's got another thing coming!" Blanchard spat back in a rage. He picked up the radio again. "Condor 1, do you copy?"

"Loud and clear."

"Do you still have a visual on the suspect, over?"

"I'm just about to lose him over the ridge, but Condor 2 should be able to spot him soon. He's running in their direction."

"Base camp? This is Condor 2. I see the suspect. I repeat, I—"

"Copy that, Condor 2. Don't let him out of your sight, not even for a second!"

"Roger that. Over."

"What about the girl?" asked Vilorain.

"What do you mean, 'what about the girl?'" Blanchard blurted out in spite of himself.

"Ask them what she is doing."

"Condor 1, do you copy? Where's the girl right now?"

"This is Condor 1. She's on the move. She's coming down the trail toward us."

"Stay in position. Follow her moves, but don't blow your cover."

"Ten-four," concluded Condor 1 over the static.

"Perhaps it's a blessing in disguise that Izcoa and the young lady have separated," commented Vilorain. "It'll be easier for us to get to Izcoa without her in the line of fire."

Faustine walked down the trail cresting the Souzon pass at a slow pace. Her face was marred with tears as she stumbled like a drunk. Her heart was filled to the brim with anger and resentment against the whole wide world. How could she ever summon the strength to go on with her life without her lover? Then and there, it felt downright impossible.

She was cursing at the skies when, out of the blue, some movement caught her attention further down the path. She wiped her eyes and peered into the distance. It looked like a camouflage-patterned tarp flapping lazily in the gentle breeze, the kind that wildlife photographers use to approach animals unnoticed. As she walked, wondering why she had not seen it earlier, she suddenly stopped dead in her tracks, petrified by the tragic revelation that just washed over her. The POLICE! Could it be that they were here all along, tracking their progression from the safety of their flimsy lair? And, if she had not noticed the tent until she almost stumbled upon it, how many more of them could there be hiding, right this moment, on the mountain? She could hardly think straight, but knew for sure she would not let Lartaun fall into their trap.

"LARTAUN! WAIT!"

Faustine dropped her backpack right in the middle of the trail and started running after him.

03:01 PM ~ Friday, August 26, 1994

"Base camp! Base camp!"

"Now what?" Blanchard yelled.

"This is Condor 1! The girl's gone bonkers too! She just veered off the trail at full sprint. She's now headed in the same direction as our male suspect!"

Blanchard gripped the radio with both hands and shouted into the receiver, "Condor 2, do you see the girl?"

"This is Condor 2! Yes, I can see her now. She's running fast. Base camp, I'm afraid we have a problem."

"What's the matter?"

"They're both headed straight to the Chaos de Pombie."

"What the hell is that?"

"The great stone field of Pombie. Nobody goes there and for a good reason. It's dangerous and very easy to get lost in there."

"Well, that's just fantastic!" Blanchard slammed the radio mouth-piece against the dashboard. Like a yo-yo, it bounced up and down at the end of its twisted cord. He took a second or two to cool off before he picked it up again. "Condors 1 and 2, you know the area better than any of us do. How would you proceed to catch a fugitive hiding in the stone field?"

"It all depends on how much time we've got," Condor 2's voice crackled amidst the static. "If we were in no hurry, I say we stay put and wait for the fugitive to surrender of his own volition. It's a fact. There's nothing in the Chaos but stone. Sooner or later, hypothermia, combined with lack of food and water, would eventually force the suspect out of his cache. Even if your guy managed to escape this place unnoticed, he would stand no chance of breaking free. I mean, all possible exits off this mountain are blocked off. The downside is that the siege could take days."

"Time is a luxury that we can't afford right now. We must catch Izcoa today!" he fumed.

"If we had access to an aerial view of the Chaos, we'd have the upper hand," Vilorain admitted, thinking out loud.

Boréda sized up both inspectors with a penetrating ice blue stare and said with determination,

"That's it, Gentlemen. Let me call the GIGN. It's time for "Plan B.""

03:19 PM ~ Friday, August 26, 1994

As much as they hated to admit it, "plan A" had failed. It was time to bring in the big guns. Major Boréda called the GIGN headquarters in Satory, near Paris, where GIGN's SO3 team had been on standby all morning. Now that their assistance was requested, the highly trained members of the Gendarmerie Nationale's elite Special Operations Force were ready to spring into action. Within minutes, they were aboard a Transall plane of the French Air Force en route to Pau military airport.

As part of the plan, Jean-Claude Boréda requested a Puma helicopter to be dispatched from Toulouse Francazal to Pau in order to fly the GIGN team to the Massif d'Ossau. In addition, the gendarmerie in Bordeaux offered an Ecureuil chopper, smaller and more maneuverable than the Puma, to conduct the aerial search.

Boréda radioed the keeper of the Refuge de Pombie. Earlier, at dawn, the guardian was instructed to close down the chalet for the day and send all guests away until further notice. They planned to use it as their temporary headquarters. Within the hour, Boréda, Blanchard and Vilorain would hike there with a patrol of gendarmes.

Faustine could see the refuge, clear as day, at the foot of the Wall of Pombie. Earlier on, she and her lover hoped to stop there on their way back to enjoy a celebratory glass of homemade moonshine. How quickly things took a turn for the worse! She felt a ripping pang of nostalgia for time and hope lost.

In the distance, a mass of fallen rock stretched from the imposing East face of the Massif d'Ossau almost all the way down to the valley. It appeared as if half of the mountain had crumbled onto itself, leaving a fantastic avalanche trail of boulders and stones piled high against its flank. La Grande Raillère de Pombie loomed large, like an impassable obstacle. Past the refuge on the plateau, the *Raillère* changed its nature into the Chaos de Pombie. The Chaos was nothing but a vast expanse of mineral desolation, a contained desert made of precariously stacked brown andesite stones.

Lartaun carved a path in a straight line toward the refuge. He was little more than a dot in the distance from where Faustine stood. He had already entered the maze when a faint noise caught his attention. He stopped dead in his tracks and strained his ears. The wind carried Faustine's voice to him. He climbed to the top of a large rock to get a better view. Sure enough, she ran, stumbling over the first stones of the Chaos. Behind her, further away in the distance, he could make out two men standing atop the cresting trail.

Faustine bridged the gap between them in fifteen minutes.

"Why did you follow me? You should not be here, Faustine. It is way too dangerous!" Lartaun's voice was harsh and emotionless, his gaze impenetrable.

"Don't be mad at me!" His demeanor made her stop a few paces away from him. "I don't know what I'm doing. All I know is that I want to be with you!" She put her hands on her knees and struggled to catch her breath. "I saw some people hiding in a tent on the other side of the pass. I freaked out! I think they're from the pol—"

"They're standing right behind you, Faustine. Turn around and take a look over the ridge."

She followed his gaze in shock. "Oh, no! I wanted to warn you about them, but I led them to you instead!"

"Maybe."

"I am so sorry, I didn't—"

"Listen," he interrupted, "do me a favor. Turn around and go home!" Lartaun didn't want her to leave, but he couldn't bear the thought that she might expose herself to danger. "The gendarmes won't do anything to you. It is me they're after."

"No way! I'm not going anywhere without you!"

"Don't be stupid. You have no idea what you're getting yourself into." At times, Faustine could be more stubborn than a mule. Her defiant stance made it quite clear she had made up her mind and would not budge. Because he did not have the strength to fight his own desire, not to mention Faustine's stubbornness, he relented far too quickly. "Fine," he said at last, admitting defeat, "as long as you realize that this is a very, very stupid idea!"

"So what are we going to do?"

"We're going to hide in the Chaos. Toward the middle of it, the boulders are so big that we can hide underneath them. They won't be able to find us there. Once we find a safe cache, I will hack out a plan of escape."

They hurried in silence. Faustine did her best to keep up with him. Her shirt, soaked with sweat, was glued to her body. She was thirsty beyond belief, but there was no time to stop. She was well aware that she was slowing him down, and she appreciated that he did not complain about it. The deeper they plowed through the scree field, the larger the salient-angled stones turned out to be.

Before long, boulders became the size of cars, and they were forced to use their hands and feet to climb over them. They pushed across this hellish obstacle course for two hours. While the sun was getting lower on the horizon, its heat still radiated off the dark rocks all around them. Faustine's arms and legs were scratched, and the salt of her sweat made her cuts burn. She ignored the pain.

Lartaun leaned over the edge of a tall slab of rock and extended his hand to help her climb past its overhanging lip. Faustine crash-landed at Lartaun's feet. She rested on her stomach for a few seconds, completely motionless, save for the heavy rise and fall of her thoracic cage.

"Courage, *maitea*, we're almost there," he said softly.

"There, where?"

"Where we want to be."

Faustine staggered to the other edge of the sloping rock. She let out a surprised "Oh!"

The opening of a narrow trench, at the base of monstrous boulders, stood before her.

"Follow me." Lartaun dropped down on his stomach and started crawling into a crack which veered at a ninety-degree angle to his left.

"Are you sure it is safe down here?"

"In our situation, it's as safe as can be," she heard him say in a muffled voice.

Faustine felt the panic mounting inside her, but it was too late to turn around now. Besides, Lartaun's feet were already disappearing from view. "Hey, wait for me!" she called out before following Lartaun into the dark passage.

In the darkness, light pierced through in some places. The air was musty and thick with dust. Above their heads, gargantuan rocks shielded them from daylight most of the time. Faustine made out countless galleries and pathways meandering in and out of the jumbled structure. The place looked like a giant underground labyrinth born from the complex accumulation of mighty chunks of rock stacked high one on top of the other. They crawled, due east, along the Chaos' entrails for another hour or so, keeping their bearings by checking the position of the sun whenever it came into view. Faustine started to shiver. At first, she welcomed the mild temperatures at the bottom of the maze, especially after what had felt like stepping on hot coals for the better part of the day. Subsequently, her shirt, now drenched with sweat, was quickly whisking away her body heat. To make matters worse, her lungs continued to burn from inhalation of fine dust rising up in the clouds around them as they crept along the bowels of the Chaos. At last, they reached a wider pocket where the two of them could sit side by side in relative comfort. Narrow beams of light descended through small openings above them, allowing them to see each other.

"Let's stop here," said Lartaun.

"OK!" she panted, not caring either way.

Lost in their own thoughts, they extended their tired legs in front of them and remained motionless for some time. Out of the blue, Lartaun turned to her and asked,

"Where's your back pack?"

"I left it on the trail so I could run faster."

"So you don't have any water."

"No, sorry." She bowed her head down in shame.

"Don't be." He shook his water bottle. "There's a little water left in this one. You can have it."

What about you?"

"I'm not thirsty," he lied. "Look at you, you're shivering with cold!"

Lartaun rummaged through his bag and unfolded a light nylon waterproof jacket from its carrying pouch. "Take your shirt off," he said. He handed her the dry garment and proceeded to give her a brisk back rub to warm her.

"I don't know about you, but I'm feeling a tad claustrophobic in here," Faustine commented after a short while. "Where are we, exactly?"

"We've been crawling along the natural drainage system of the Chaos de Pombie."

"Is that your politically correct way of saying that we're hanging out inside a big sewage pipe?" Lartaun smiled. He admired Faustine's unshakable optimism, no matter how dire the situation. "So what's next?" she asked more seriously this time.

"First, you should eat something." He handed her a cereal bar from his backpack. "And rest for a while. In the meantime, I'll think of a way to get us out of here."

07:10 PM ~ Friday, August 26, 1994

The refuge keeper did not enjoy the disruption caused by the arrival of the gendarmerie squad, but he knew better than to voice his complaints aloud. He helped them set up their temporary headquarters inside the main dining room. The team brought long-range light strobes that they were busy installing outside the building. Thankfully, with these, they would be able to sweep the area, even after nightfall.

In the meantime, the two undercover officers, who were stationed under the camouflage tarp at the Col de Souzon, escorted the group of climbers who slipped through the gendarmes' net earlier that morning, back to the parking lot of Anéou. It was paramount that no civilians remained on this side of the Massif prior to the GIGN's arrival. As for team Condor 2, they were still standing guard by the edge of the stone field, even though they had long lost the suspects' trace. A foray into the *Raillère* on foot was not deemed necessary. Instead, the inspectors preferred to wait for the GIGN helicopter to conduct an aerial search.

Everyone was anxious for the Special Operations team to arrive. They were ready for action.

07:24 PM ~ Friday, August 26, 1994

Faustine roused herself with a jolt.

"What was that?" She shook Lartaun's shoulder in alarm. "Lartaun, what's that noise?"

A faint rumble could be heard in the distance. Lartaun touched a forefinger to the tip of his nose to signal her to remain quiet. The foreign noise started to amplify, bouncing off the peaks of the Massif.

Lartaun looked up and said without loosing his calm,

"The cavalry has arrived."

25

— HOGEITABOST —

07:27 PM ~ Friday, August 26, 1994

"Here they come!"

Inspector Blanchard exhaled a sigh of relief. The Ecureuil was the first to touch down. The pilot kept the chopper's Turbomeca Arriel 1D1 engine idling while his copilot exited the machine. A large helicopter from the French air force immediately followed. In a deafening roar that sent clods of earth and grass flying in every direction, the Puma, painted in Army grey and bearing the inscription *ARMÉE DE L'AIR* across its tail in white block letters, landed on the other side of the building. No sooner than the impressive machine touched ground, a group of armed men dressed in full raid regalia ducked under its rotating blades and broke into a run toward the chalet. Once inside, the GIGN operators lined up along the far wall of the dining room.

Special Operations leader Guillaume Parillaud stepped forward and saluted the Major as well as the DST agents. Like the rest of the non-commissioned officers of his team, Parillaud was dressed in navy blue fatigues, reinforced with padding at the knees, tucked into high-top black leather combat boots. He wore a bulletproof vest over a matching dark blue top featuring double snap pockets sewn above its padded elbows. On the left shoulder, the top was emblazoned with the round GIGN's insignia depicting a parachute atop a flaming grenade interlaced with a snap gate carabiner against a blue background. He set his heavy helmet, complete with a wide visor and a clipped-on neck guard, onto one of the large communal tables of the room. With caution, he placed his FAMAS assault rifle mounted with an OB-50 night vision scope to the side of it. He carried a sidearm as well, a Manurhin MR-73 357 Magnum revolver, along with a set of handcuffs, speed loaders and spare magazines, as well as a can of tear gas around his waist belt.

"Listen up, team!" Parillaud said to his men. "This is DST Inspector Blanchard. He is going to give you the scoop on our fugitive's behavior and personality traits as they have been relayed to him by the Spanish secret service."

Blanchard stepped forward to brief the assembly.

"Izcoa is a twenty-four year old Caucasian male. He is Spanish, but he also speaks fluent French. He is strong and won't hesitate to use violence if he feels cornered, so use caution if you find yourself in a hand-to-hand combat situation with him. Also bear in mind that he could be armed at this point. While we deem the risk of a potential hostage situation to be minimal, given the fact that the person who is traveling with him is his girlfriend, this is not a man whose actions should be underestimated at any given time. He is a master of escape and a mountain climbing expert. Even though we have the upper hand with the GIGN troops and the two helicopters at our disposal tonight, he still might find a way to slip between our fingers if we aren't vigilant. Do not forget that he is wanted in Spain for the attack of a police station which resulted in the death of several officers in the line of duty. In other words, he has no respect for the authorities and certainly would not hesitate to hurt anyone if he felt it might help him escape. Any questions?"

The Special Operators, lined up against the wall, shook their heads "no." They were accustomed to dealing with the toughest criminals, and they were experts at it. For them, this was just another day on the job. Next, one of the Condor 2 patrolmen described the spot where he last saw the suspect and his partner. When he was done, GIGN leader Parillaud reviewed the plan he hoped would ensure the successful capture of the fugitive.

"One team will fly *recon* aboard the Ecureuil over the stone field. That team will be composed of a negotiator, two snipers, and three additional men for tactical support. They will search the Chaos in a crisscross pattern. Simultaneously, they will establish communication with the fugitive via the helicopter's speaker system in order to offer him the chance to give himself up. Now, should this strategy fail to yield positive results, we will send the rest of the team to the stone field aboard the Puma."

Condor 2 patrolman turned to Parillaud with a concerned frown and said,

"Our main concern is the setting sun. Our chances of finding Izcoa will decrease exponentially with the loss of natural light."

"I don't foresee this to be a major issue. Both helicopters are equipped with powerful searchlights, and my men are equipped with night-vision optics. Should it become necessary, they will be able to conduct their search well into the night. Their thermal imaging goggles are able to detect a person up to two hundred yards away. Even if our target is hidden from view, I am quite confident that his body heat will give his position away in no time."

"Thank you for the clarification, sir," said the patrolman.

"Please proceed," added Blanchard.

"Once spotted, we should recover the woman first in order to get her out of harm's way. Then, and only then, should we proceed with the arrest of the male suspect. Based on what Inspector Blanchard told us about the person who's with Izcoa, I would evaluate the risk of a potential hostage situation to be minimal. However, should the fugitive resist arrest by opening fire or taking the woman accompanying him hostage, we will retaliate with force, though only after all other non-violent options have been considered and implemented."

"I must also reiterate that it is imperative that Izcoa be caught alive," added Vilorain.

"Inspector, my men are experts at marksmanship, and they are trained to aim for non-vital body parts. I am confident that we will capture Lartaun Izcoa tonight and alive, regardless of the circumstances of his surrender," Parillaud concluded with a confident tone.

As soon as the briefing was over, the advance reconnaissance team climbed aboard the Ecureuil. The chopper lifted into the fading twilight, flying as close to the ground as safety would allow. The pilot turned on the helicopter's powerful light projector, and the snipers, sitting on either side of the open cabin, began to meticulously scan the stone field below.

07:50 PM ~ Friday, August 26, 1994

Lartaun crawled out of his hiding place and poked his head through a small opening between two rock slabs to assess the situation. In front of him, the Pic du Midi Mountain shimmered in the dimming light. It looked as if it were made of gold. It was majestic in its grandeur and impervious to the drama unfolding at its feet. In the distance, he saw a helicopter traveling across the Chaos. Its powerful searchlight swept every nook and cranny of the stony field. Lartaun's "Houdiniesque" move had worked well. The chopper continued to search for them in the vicinity where they had first crawled under the boulders of the *Raillère*. At the very least, Lartaun's clever hoax bought them precious time. Regardless, he was not confident about their chance of escaping from this hellish place unnoticed. Even if he still refused to openly admit the brutal truth to himself, he was well aware that they were scurrying along the punishing walls of a formidable mouse trap with no way out but the cat's gaping mouth.

"What did you see?" Faustine asked the second he crawled back into the recesses of their cache. Lartaun did not have the heart to tell her how desperate the situation was.

"We're not too far from the edge of the field. The chopper is looking for me further up the plateau. So far, they have no clue where we are."

Faustine let out a little sigh of relief. "What should we do now?"

"We wait until it is dark outside. Then we will get moving. First, we must reach the edge of the Chaos unnoticed. Then, we will run across the clearing until we reach the forest. That's the toughest part because we'll be in the open."

"How long does it take to get to the forest?

"If we run fast, about ten to fifteen minutes. Beyond the forest, we're still about seven miles away from the border. We'll cross it near the Col du Pourtalet. If we steer clear of the main road, I think we'll be OK."

Faustine looked at him through the semi-darkness, shaking her head in defeat. She knew that Lartaun was not giving her the whole truth. She summoned all her courage to state the obvious:

"We're never going to make it, are we?"

The helicopter continued to work its way down the sloping Chaos and was now closing in on them. The roar of the blades deafened Faustine and Lartaun when it made its first pass above their heads. Then, without warning, a thundering voice seemed to descend straight from the sky.

"HALT, GENDARMERIE! STEP OUT INTO THE LIGHT WHERE WE CAN SEE YOU! PUT YOUR HANDS ABOVE YOUR HEADS AND NO HARM WILL BE DONE TO YOU!"

A violent shudder rocked Faustine's entire frame. She recoiled against the rock in reflex upon hearing the booming voice and covered her ears and face in panic. She shone the desperate look of a cornered animal. Lartaun looked at her and immediately realized that he should never have allowed her to follow him into the stone field. Faustine did not deserve to suffer through this ordeal any longer. He needed to find a way to bring her back to safety. He had to let her go.

"Look, Faustine. I don't think that my plan will work if the two of us stick together," he said with sudden urgency. "I'll stand a better chance if I try to escape on my own."

"I see what you're trying to do, but you're wasting your time if you think that I'm going to leave you now!" she replied.

"I don't know what these people out there are capable of, but I'd never forgive myself if you got hurt!" he said in desperation. "This is not a game, Faustine!"

"What if we never see each other again, huh? What then?"

"Let me tell you about my past. You ought to know why the police are after me. Then, you will decide, in your heart, whether you even want to see me again."

Faustine listened with undivided attention as Lartaun hurriedly re-capped the night of the riots in Irun, the subsequent time he spent exiled in Mexico, and how a friend had helped him out so that he could return to Europe, only to find out, that very day on the mountain, that the police caught up with him again. Somehow, she felt as if he had already told her everything before, albeit in abstract, indirect ways. She simply never made the effort to read between the lines.

"RELEASE THE HOSTAGE NOW AND STEP INTO THE LIGHT WITH YOUR HANDS ABOVE YOUR HEAD!"

"Hostage? Are they out of their fucking minds?" shrieked Faustine.

"You need to go. Now!"

"But I don't want to go out there alone! I'm too scared!"

"When you step out, put your hands over your head and do not move! Wait for them to come to you first. It'll be all right, *maitea.*"

"I love you!" she murmured, her voice hoarse with affliction.

"*Nire maitasun handia zara.* You are my one and only love, Faustine," he replied.

Lartaun kissed her, one last time, and started crawling away into the darkness. Faustine held onto the leg of his climbing pants in a futile attempt to hold him back, but he plowed onwards, digging his fingers ever deeper into the dust.

Once he was gone, Faustine was all alone, blind in the dark. She forced herself to count to two hundred before she crawled backwards through the narrow passage. Her head emerged between two flat boulders. She raised her arms up toward the sky.

"Over here!" she screamed into the night, "I'm over here!"

"I've got a visual on the female," the pilot said into his radio.

Within seconds, the Ecureuil was hovering above Faustine, bathing her in a sea of artificial light.

"DO NOT MOVE! I REPEAT, DO NOT MOVE! WE ARE COMING TO GET YOU!"

Faustine buried her face into her hands in order to protect her eyes from the spotlight's blinding glare, in addition to the flying debris due to the chopper's rotating blades above her.

Like a pirate's flag flying from the maintop of a ghost ship, Lartaun's jacket flapped madly around her torso.

26

-HOGEITASEI-

09:22 PM ~ Friday, August 26, 1994

Inside the refuge, Major Boréda looked eagerly out the window, his knuckles pressing hard against the glass. Behind him, the radio scratched to life.

"We've zeroed in on the girl. No sign of the suspect, but we are confident that he is close. Requesting permission to proceed with the female's evacuation toward the refuge and to send in the rest of the team to perform a search on foot for the fugitive in the area."

"Roger that. Permission granted." Boréda heard the GIGN team leader's voice coming through the speakers. "We're ready for take off. See you there."

The roar of the Puma drowned Parillaud's voice almost instantly as it flew over the roof of the mountain refuge.

Two snipers, sporting AI/AW (Accuracy International/Arctic Warfare) caliber 308 Win rifles, dangled from either side of the massive helicopter's open cabin near the spot where Faustine was standing. They covered their teammates as they repelled down a steel cable dangling from the belly of the Puma. The armed men set foot, one after another, atop the jagged boulders of the Chaos de Pombie. One operator, armed with an HK MP5, approached Faustine with caution. His partners spread out around him to form a protective circle.

"Are you alone?" the hooded man shouted to Faustine over the roar of the two helicopters.

"Yes!"

"Where's your partner?"

"I don't know!" she yelled back.

"Is he armed?"

"NO!"

The operator communicated to the rest of his team with a quick series of hand motions. He reached Faustine just in time to catch her fall. Her legs gave way. Her remaining strength just abandoned her, and her face was as pale as the moon. She wanted this nightmare to be over.

The man secured a harness under Faustine's armpits and attached it with a screw gate carabiner onto his own. He grasped the end of the steel cable dangling underneath the Ecureuil and tethered himself to it before he gave the pilot the "OK" sign for lift off. The small helicopter swept them off their feet, sending them twirling through the air. They proceeded in a mad waltz back to the Refuge de Pombie.

With Faustine in his arms, the Special Forces operator entered the building. Boréda wrapped her in a blanket to keep her warm, and offered her some water to drink. Her teeth chattered and her muscles started cramping. She was in shock. After a short inquiry about her physical and mental state, they ushered Faustine to one of the dorm rooms. An officer stood guard beside her. A couple minutes later, Vilorain stepped into the room to proceed with her interrogation.

"One down, one to go," Boréda overheard Blanchard say upon reentering the main room of the refuge.

The Major returned to the window. He stood motionless, hands crossed behind his back, and peered through the crisp moonlit sky.

The rest of the GIGN team deployed across the stone field. They shoved their rifles into every crevice in sight, looking for any potential hiding hole. Less than twenty-five yards away from where Faustine had been found, Lartaun was concealed, lying face down, his body wedged under a protruding slab of andesite.

He had hoped that Faustine's surrender would create enough of a diversion to give him the chance to escape the Chaos and sprint toward the safety of the forest. Evidently, he had not factored in the deployment of the whole GIGN team onto the stone field to happen so quickly. With their infrared goggles, they would spot him soon. He needed to make a move or his capture would be imminent. He crept on his belly between rocks that were getting smaller and smaller. Soon, he would be in the open field. A good few hundred yards separated him from the dense forest and safety. If he could reach it in time, he had a chance to get away.

The path ahead was clear, and the moon bathed the clearing with a dim eerie glow that smashed his hopes to blend into the shadows. Lartaun shot one last worried glance over his shoulder. He sprung to his legs and sprinted toward the trees. Immediately, one of the GIGN operators scouting the stone field caught the glowing outline of Lartaun's silhouette from the corner of his night vision goggles.

"Target is running to the east!" he yelled at once into his transmitter.

Lartaun was about a quarter of the way to the forest when the Puma caught up with him and pinned him down with its harsh spotlight. This did not stop him from running away. If anything, Lartaun increased his speed and continued his mad dash down the slope.

"This is one suicidal son-of-a-bitch!" exclaimed the Ecureuil's pilot over the radio. The maneuverable chopper was about to overtake the Puma to the right. "I've got the suspect in my sight. I'm ready to take over the chase whenever you are, Puma!"

"Roger that. He's all yours. Good luck!" The Puma made a wide turn to the left in order to retrieve the GIGN team still deployed on the Chaos.

"HALT, GENDARMERIE! FREEZE! PUT YOUR HANDS OVER YOUR HEAD RIGHT NOW! THIS IS YOUR LAST WARNING!"

Lartaun seemed to hesitate for a split second, but he did not stop.

"The suspect is ignoring our warning," the pilot said over the radio. "If we let him get to the forest, we can kiss his ass good-bye. The canopy is too thick for us to track him from up here. You have three minutes to make up your mind."

Blanchard and Boréda huddled around the refuge keeper's radio, following the action as it was unfolding.

"Fuck it. Tell them to open fire," Blanchard said without hesitation.

Officer Parillaud's voice crackled over the static. He relayed his orders to the snipers aboard the Ecureuil. "Scare the guy with a salvo of shots. Just make sure you don't touch him."

Faustine jumped out of her cot upon hearing the sound of gunfire echoing through the mountains.

"NO!" she screamed, "NO!" Without warning, Faustine charged into Inspector Vilorain like a fury, pounding and kicking him as hard as she could. "You cold-blooded bastards! Why did you shoot him? He was unarmed! *Bastaaaaards!*"

Vilorain did his best to protect himself while he tried to control her. Alarmed by the commotion, two other gendarmes promptly barged into the room. They restrained her in no time, but Faustine continued cursing at the top of her lungs.

"You killed him, you heartless fucks!"

"You'd better cool off and fast, young lady!" Vilorain warned her as he readjusted his glasses. "You've put yourself in enough trouble as it is!"

The two officers grabbed her by her clothes and dumped her unceremoniously, face first, onto the cot. Vilorain thought it best to postpone the interrogation. As he straightened his appearance and composed his bruised ego, the DST inspector promptly exited the room.

09:42 PM ~ Friday, August 26, 1994

Lartaun ran in a zigzag pattern, in and out of the helicopter's spotlight, cringing and ducking as stray bullets ricocheted against the stones around him. The forest was so close. He could already breathe the sticky smell of pine resin. Yet, the distance that separated him from its edge seemed insurmountable. The voices in his head screamed for him to stop and surrender, or consequently, he would certainly die. Eight months ago, he would not have hesitated for a second. Better dead than in prison! But today, Lartaun did not want to die, not in front of Faustine. Still, his legs did not stop moving.

"What's going on out there? Ecureuil, come back, over!" Blanchard demanded over the radio.

"The snipers just fired a round of warning shots. We thought it would bring him back to his senses."

"And?"

"The target is still on the run."

"I can't believe this," muttered Boréda. Next to him, Blanchard paced the room like a caged animal.

"Tell your sniper to shoot him in the leg and let's be done with it! He's going to slip through our fingers if we don't act right now!" Blanchard exclaimed in frustration.

The Major knew that Blanchard was right. Izcoa had to be neutralized one way or another. He also knew that the operators out on the field had tried every viable non-violent option. They had to up the ante.

"We're going to try one more thing. It's risky, but it's worth a shot. Over." Boréda wondered what the Ecureuil's pilot had in mind.

The chopper looked as if it was suddenly falling from the sky. An operator clung onto its side, his feet resting on the helicopter's legs, while a sniper kept his rifle aimed at Lartaun. The Special Forces agent slid further down the side of the helicopter until his foot rested inside the loop of a sling rope that was tied to the belly of the cabin. He wrapped his right arm around the Ecureuil's leg and held on tight while the pilot executed a ballsy maneuver in order to catch Lartaun from behind.

Deafened by the shattering noise of the blades and blinded by the dust flying into his eyes, Lartaun bowed his head and slowed down. Had he turned and looked over his shoulder, he would have found himself eye-to-eye with a modern-day ninja. The operator let go of the helicopter and landed squarely on Lartaun's back, pushing him head first to the ground. The force of the shock knocked the wind out of Lartaun and stunned him long enough to allow the special operator to neutralize him before he could attempt to fight back.

"Suspect is down! Suspect is down!" the pilot informed the rest of the team over the radio. "We've captured your man. He is conscious and unharmed!"

Inspector Blanchard slammed his fist into the palm of his hand and let out a boisterous shout of victory. "Great job, everyone!" he shouted into the radio.

"Thank God it is over," Boréda muttered.

09:54 PM ~ Friday, August 26, 1994

"Where's my girlfriend? Where is Faustine?" Lartaun painfully moaned as the hooded operator turned him over on his back. "Whatever you do to me, please don't hurt her," he pleaded. "She's innocent!"

"Shut up!" the SO agent blinded him with the beam of his flashlight to get a closer look at Lartaun's face. He immediately recoiled in surprise. As the black disk of Lartaun's pupils contracted in reaction to the sudden glare, the tiny flakes of gold, which speckled his right iris, refracted the light and started to glow, as if a fire was burning behind his retina. His other eye remained as cold and forbidding as glacier water. The GIGN officer, spooked by the destabilizing sight, swiftly moved his light away and proceeded to read Lartaun his rights.

By eleven in the evening, everyone had left the Massif d'Ossau. The GIGN SO3 unit boarded the Puma, back to Pau Pyrenees airport. In Pau, they would board the Transall plane, awaiting them on the tarmac, to fly back to Paris. Meanwhile, Lartaun, in shackles, left aboard the Ecureuil with a three-gendarme escort in tow. Lartaun would spend the night in a cell at the gendarmerie station in Pau. As for Faustine, she was en route to the exact same location, albeit via the back seat of Boréda's patrol car. Despite her pleading, they did not allow her to see Lartaun one last time.

Alone again on the plateau de Pombie, the refuge keeper reorganized the dining room tables and chairs the way they were before the gendarmes took over the place. In just a few hours, hikers and climbers would reclaim the mountain.

He needed to be ready for their arrival.

27

- HOGEITAZAZPI -

09:25 AM ~ Saturday, August 27, 1994

Jean-Philippe barreled down the Corniche Basque, his knuckles white from gripping the wheel so tightly. He had tossed and turned in his thousand-thread-count sheets for the better part of the night, dreading his encounter with Patxi. He rolled down his car window and forced the salty, fishy smell of the air into his lungs in an effort to calm down.

Mighty waves pounded into the black stone cliffs. They foamed white as they struck the edge of the precipitous bluff. Further in the distance, the watery expanse of the Atlantic Ocean scintillated like the sequined dress of a disco star. To the left, stern forests of sky-high pine trees grew across the two-lane road that skirted the jagged coast. Jean-Philippe zoomed past the Fort de Socoa, imposing with its fortified tower, and reached Hendaye in a matter of minutes. At the other end of the bridge over the Bidasoa River, a sign read: IRUN.

Jean-Philippe had arrived in *Euskadi*.

Patxi sat on a bench in the middle of Plaza Urdanibia. He was wearing a plain white T-shirt with a tattered forest-green bomber jacket tied around his waist. He looked sullen, lost in his own dark thoughts. As soon as he recognized Jean-Philippe from afar, he stood and started to walk away. As arranged, Jean-Philippe followed him, at a respectful distance, through the quiet streets until Patxi stopped in front of an old six-story stone building on Cipriano Larrañaga street. He paused long enough for his follower to take a mental picture of the location and walked through the front door.

The edifice must have been an opulent *hotel particulier* back in the day. Now, the half-timbered façade, built in the old Basque tradition, was in serious need of renovation. The stucco covering the side structures of the building crumbled in places and the dark red paint covering its exposed wood beams was barely noticeable anymore.

Jean-Philippe pushed the heavy entrance door and walked inside. Patxi stood waiting for him at the end of a very dim hallway. They walked up a flight of stairs. The special knock brought a young woman to the door. She ushered them into a small living room and motioned for Jean-Philippe to sit down on an old sagging couch. He did as he was told. Patxi took a seat on an equally derelict sofa across a wooden coffee table riddled with scratches and countless ring marks.

Jean-Philippe got the impression that no one had inhabited the condo in quite a while. An impressive amount of dust laid atop the mismatched second-hand pieces of furniture. The bookshelves against the far wall appeared bare. In fact, Jean-Philippe noticed that there were no personal items at all in the entire room. The air itself was stagnant and sooty. He instantly hated the place and was desperate to leave.

"Can I get you anything?" the woman asked Jean-Philippe.

"I'm fine. Unless you've already made coffee?"

"All I have is instant."

"Great."

"Patxi, coffee?"

"No, thanks. Can you leave us alone? We need to talk," Patxi requested impatiently.

As soon as the woman returned to the kitchen, Patxi looked intently at Jean-Philippe. The Frenchman could not hold the stare for long and lowered his gaze to the ground. In that split second, Patxi easily established himself as the alpha male. Jean-Philippe was nervous. He spoke fast when Patxi asked him to report.

"...What bothers me isn't so much that the police are after Lartaun," Patxi commented after listening to Jean-Philippe with attention, "but that he ignores that they're after him. If he was aware of the situation, he would know to be extra careful."

"I wish we could warn him, but no one knows where he is for sure.

All we know is that he is climbing somewhere in the Pyrenees! Trying to find him right now would be like looking for a needle in a haystack!"

"I want you guys to retrieve my dynamite as soon as he's back in the valley. The longer we wait, the riskier it'll be, and I can't afford to take any more chances. Oh, and make sure that he steers clear from La Goutte d'Eau at all costs."

"But...what if he gets arrested before we can warn him?" Jean-Philippe blurted out.

"We cannot let that happen. We need his help to climb to the *zulo.*"

"I know that, but what if he gets caught and denounces all of us? What if he tells the police about the explosives? Don't you realize that we'll be fucked if that happens?"

Patxi pondered his question with aplomb. At last, he said,

"Lartaun won't talk. He's not a rat."

"Come on Patxi, you know as well as I do that the police won't give him a break until he gives us all away!" Jean-Philippe shrieked in spite of himself. "These guys, they have ways to make a mute sing!"

"If it comes to that, we'll just have to give Lartaun a good incentive to keep his mouth shut. Even under torture."

"Like what?"

"This is not something for you to be concerned with," Patxi retorted haughtily. He tore a piece off an old magazine lying on the coffee table, scribbled a phone number on it with a blunt pencil and handed it to Jean-Philippe. "Go back to the valley. If you hear that the cops have caught Lartaun, call this number right away and leave a message on the answering machine. Just say: 'We can't make it to the party.' I will know what you mean. Got it?"

"Yes, Patxi." Jean-Philippe stuffed the piece of paper into the pocket of his ragged plaid shirt with trembling hands. "And if that were the case, then you want Eric and me to get the hell out of Dodge before it's too late, correct?"

"Nobody goes anywhere until the dynamite is back in my hands, or until I decide that it is fine for you to disappear. In the meantime, you two stay put and wait for my instructions, no matter what goes down. Am I making myself clear?"

"Are you for real?" Jean-Philippe stared at him in utter disbelief. "You have no back up plan or protection to offer Eric and me should we need help, and yet you're asking us to remain on the front line?"

The woman chose that very moment to reenter the room. She handed Jean-Philippe a cup of coffee. "Here," she said, "I wasn't sure how you liked it, so I made it black."

"He won't need it anymore," Patxi snapped. "He was just about to leave."

The woman shot Patxi and his guest a hateful glare and slammed the cup onto the table regardless, spilling most of its contents onto the grimy coffee table. Patxi watched her stomp out of the room, speechless. In a matter of seconds, the anger that had made Patxi's green eyes flicker dangerously, disappeared. Instead, his eyes filled with grief and heartbreak. It bothered Jean-Philippe enough that he felt compelled to ask,

"Are you all right? You look terrible all of a sudden."

"Aside from the great news that you've brought me, I have shittier issues to deal with at the moment, believe it or not," Patxi replied somberly.

"Anything I can help you with?" he ventured.

"Do you know how to bring people back from the dead?"

"Excuse me?" retorted Jean-Philippe, taken aback by his schizoid question.

"Yeah, I didn't think so." Patxi let out a heavy sigh. "Look, just head back to the valley and pass on my instructions to Eric. Hopefully, we'll be able to avert the crisis before it spins out of control. Now, if you'll excuse me, I need to check on my girlfriend. I'm sure that you can see yourself out."

Patxi got off the couch and went out the door before Jean-Philippe could say another word.

11:17 AM ~ Saturday, August 27, 1994

Jean-Philippe exited the house just as the first flash of lightning tore up the sky, followed by a menacing roll of thunder. Fat rain drops started splattering on his head. He took off running at full speed. By the time he opened the door to his car, he was soaked.

"What a waste of time," he sneered between clenched teeth.

He had come to Patxi, their self-proclaimed leader, in search of concrete answers and solutions to their problem. Naïve as he was, he had relied on him to save the day before the situation grew worse. In reality, the man he met with that morning was not the brilliant strategist whose fame and reputation preceded him. Instead, Patxi had come across as evil, unconcerned, and borderline paranoid. Worse, the man was sending him right back to the valley to fend for himself with zero ammunition.

Jean-Philippe turned the windshield wipers to maximum speed and took off. Back to France, back to the godforsaken Vallée d'Aspe, the very last place he wanted to be! Fear traveled with him. On more than one occasion, he had to fight against the nagging urge to veer off the highway and vanish for good. It might only be a matter of days, hours even, before the police would arrest Lartaun. They would come sniffing at his door next. Jean-Philippe was not going to take a stand in the trenches while Patxi watched the cookie crumble from afar. No, Jean-Philippe would save his own ass first.

28

— HOGEITA ZORTZI —

05:15 AM ~ Saturday, August 27, 1994

Lartaun had spent the better part of the night locked up in a small room without any windows. The bright overhead lights had been on all night, keeping him awake. The heavy metal door bore a square peep-hole at eye level, and except for a concrete bench built against one of the walls, there was no furniture. A thin mattress had been laid out on top with a rolled-up blanket. There was no pillow. The toilet, opposite the bench, was no more than a "hole-in-the-ground."

Upon his arrival at the gendarmerie station, late Friday night, Lartaun was stripped of his shoelaces. The gendarmes who had escorted him during the helicopter ride forced him to remove the silver chain around his neck. They emptied the contents of his pockets into a manila envelope and even confiscated his cigarettes.

The long and harrowing day on the mountain had taken its toll. Lartaun's sore muscles and achy bones were begging for mercy. All he wanted was to lie down on the cot and sleep for a while. The time to worry about his future would come soon enough. However, the DST agents decided otherwise. In fact, Frédéric Blanchard left very specific orders with the officers on sentry that night. They were to keep the suspect awake, no matter what. This was part of his strategy to weaken Lartaun Izcoa, physically and mentally, before his interrogation. As a result, a never-ending stream of gendarmes came and went into his cell, at regular intervals throughout the night, to check on him and wake him up should he dare fall asleep.

Soon, it would be daylight, but Lartaun had no idea because his windowless room did not have a clock. He had already lost track of time and was drunk with exhaustion. However, the gendarmes' marvelous performances as human alarms were not the only reason he could not sleep.

No sooner than he would close his eyes, images of Faustine, alone and scared, would haunt him. Where was she? Had they sent her home, or were they holding her prisoner in a cell just like his? She did not deserve any of this. Faustine was a good person. She still believed that life was beautiful. Her optimism was contagious. By her side, he always felt strong and brave, ready to conquer the world. For her sake, he needed to resist them. Keeping silent at all costs was the only way he could do this.

07:12 AM ~ Saturday, August 27, 1994

The strident buzz of the alarm clock gave no mercy. It took Boréda a little while to realize that he was in his own bed. He pushed back the covers with a yawn and walked naked toward the window in his bedroom. He drew open the curtains to check the weather outside. The sky was overcast and gloomy. The asphalt below, wet and shiny.

"Perfect weather for a crappy weekend," he mumbled to himself.

The bright red numbers on his digital clock read: 07:12 a.m. He retraced his steps and felt for the light switch along the bathroom wall. The crude luminescence of the vanity light above the medicine cabinet made him cringe. He stared at his reflection in the mirror. His five o'clock shadow had grown into a scrawny beard and his pale blue eyes were bloodshot from lack of sleep.

"Disgusting. If this is really what I look like these days, I'll be single forever."

He fumbled through the bathroom cabinet to find his razor and prepare for the day ahead.

On his way to the gendarmerie, Boréda recognized Vivienne at the last possible second. What could she be doing out there? He suddenly remembered that Blanchard had ordered his colleagues to let her go last night while they were on the mountain. They received all the information they needed from her, which in turn, led to Izcoa's successful arrest. As a result, they saw no reason to detain her any longer. Besides, Blanchard was not particularly fond of having Vivienne Laroche hanging around the station when her daughter would be brought into custody later on that night, along with her terrorist boyfriend. Boréda backed up alongside the curb and stopped in front of her.

Sleeping atop a piece of cardboard, she was huddled up against the threshold of a recessed door looking onto the street, a stone's throw away from the station.

"Miss Laroche? Is that you?"

Surprised upon hearing her name, Vivienne lifted her head. Her body stiffened as soon as she saw the patrol car idling in front of her. Boréda hastily rolled down his window.

"Miss Laroche, it's me, Major Boréda! What the heck are you doing here?"

"Your colleagues kicked me out of the station last night. I guess your guys could not come up with any good reason to keep me under lock and key any longer, so they let me go." She stood up as fast as she could, looking mortified. "I asked permission to wait there for my daughter, but they wouldn't let me! Funny how yesterday you were all over me, but I guess that since you've caught your guy, I'm no longer worth a plugged nickel to you!"

"For God's sake, Miss Laroche, look at you!" Vivienne bowed her head in shame. She proceeded to comb her hair with nervous spindle fingers in a vain attempt to straighten her miserable appearance. "Why didn't you go home last night?"

"I won't go anywhere without my daughter!"

"Jesus, Miss Laroche. What would your daughter think if she saw you like this, sleeping in the rain like a bum?" Boréda exited the car and stepped onto the curb. Against his better judgment, he extended his hand out to her.

"Where is my daughter?" she demanded with insolence.

"She's fine. She's at the station."

"I want to see her! I have a right to see her!"

"I'm sorry, but that is impossible right now. Your daughter is in custody."

"Why? She has done nothing wrong!"

Boréda chose not to react to this obvious truism. "Listen, why don't you go home and prepare for her return? I could have one of my men give you a lift back to La Goutte d'Eau if you'd like."

"I can't." She plopped down on the curb.

"Why not?"

"Everyone will be all over me, asking questions. After all, I lied to them. They think I'm in Paris, sorting through the effects of my late father, remember?"

The sarcasm in Vivienne's voice cut deep under Boréda's skin. An inappropriate sense of guilt washed over him, even though he had done nothing wrong. After all, he was a police officer who simply said and did what he needed to apprehend a fugitive. However, he knew that he had compromised the integrity of this woman. Not exactly a move to be proud of.

"Perhaps it would make more sense for you to stay in town for a day or two. I can recommend a hotel."

"A hotel?" She laughed at him. "You don't know the first thing about me, do you? I don't have that kind of money, *Monsieur*." She wiped her nose with the back of her hand. In other circumstances, Jean-Claude Boréda would have been turned off by her manners, but he somehow felt compelled to protect her, to care for this wild child.

"Don't worry about the money." Boréda had no idea what compelled him to say that. Regardless, he helped her back on her feet and opened the passenger door for her. "Jump in. The hotel is right around the corner."

"Isn't it rather unusual for a policeman to be so nice to a woman he harshly interrogated just a day earlier?" She stared at him with her intelligent eyes as they pulled out from the curb.

"I was just doing my job," Boréda replied, staring at the road straight ahead.

"Of course you were," Vivienne replied, smiling.

Boréda hated himself for blushing like a teenager.

Boréda glanced at his watch as he finally pulled up in front of the gendarmerie, if only to confirm that he was running late for his meeting with the DST agents.

"Good morning, Major." The officer, who had stood guard overnight at Faustine's cell, greeted the Major at the front door. "I'm glad I could catch you before the end of my shift."

"Morning, Max. What's up?"

"About the young lady who came in last night."

"How's she doing?"

"Not so great, I'm afraid. One minute she is catatonic, and hysterical the next. She didn't sleep the whole night. Oh, and she also refused to drink or eat anything."

"Thanks for the heads up, Max. I'll take it from here."

"All right. Have a nice weekend, Major."

"Enjoy it for the both of us!" Boréda replied, sounding gruffer than he had intended to be.

"Excuse me, Major?" Officer Fernandez rushed through the front door of the station.

"What is it, Marco?"

"The woman just passed out in her cell!" the gendarme said, point blank.

"Shit!" Boréda rushed down the hall with Fernandez at his heels.

Inside the tiny room, Faustine laid unconscious, her body curled into a ball.

"Call an ambulance!" Boréda yelled over his shoulder. He kneeled down next to Faustine and checked her vital signs. Her breathing was shallow and irregular, her skin chalky and dry to the touch. Behind her semi-closed lids, her sunken eyes rolled to the back of her head, revealing an all-white stare. "Miss Laroche! Can you hear me?" Her long lashes fluttered a little. She gazed at the Major with glassy eyes. He grabbed Faustine under her legs and shoulders and carried her over to the cot.

The paramedics arrived within minutes. Boréda looked on as they assessed Faustine's condition.

"She is dehydrated, sir," one of the medics stated after a quick examination. He inserted a saline I.V. into her arm.

"I've been told that she has refused food and water since she was brought up here late last night," Boréda said.

"She needs medical attention. We must take her to the hospital."

"I'll dispatch a patrol to escort you right away. Tell the doctors that I'll be over there as soon as I can." The Major watched helplessly as Faustine was gently moved onto a gurney and wheeled out of the station.

Suddenly, it dawned on him that he had to inform Vivienne about the condition of her daughter. "In a little while, just not now," he told himself. He was not quite ready to be the bearer of more bad news.

Meanwhile, Lartaun sat across from two DST agents: Inspector Didier Vilorain and Inspector Frédéric Blanchard. Between them, the red light on the tape recorder blinked atop a stainless steel table, signaling that every word they spoke was being recorded. The ashtray, already filled to the brim, counted no less than two cigarettes burning at any given time. A thick layer of blue smoke hovered above the three men like a bad omen. Things were not going well. Much to Blanchard's dismay, Lartaun had been answering most of their questions in monosyllables. A couple hours had already gone by, and they had not made any significant progress.

French law allowed for a suspect to be in custody for forty-eight hours. Lartaun had already been there for more than twelve. The guy was tough, but even if they had to spend the remaining thirty-six hours inside that cramped room, Blanchard and Vilorain were intent on getting answers.

When noon rolled around, Blanchard called for a one-hour lunch recess at a nearby brasserie. He wanted to debrief Boréda.

"What's your take on Izcoa so far?" Boréda asked, halfheartedly digging into his *croque-monsieur*.

"He's not the chattiest guy on the planet," replied Blanchard. "Getting 'intel' from him is like pulling fingernails. I'm talking figuratively here, of course," he added with a dry chuckle. "Anyway, I want to find out who robbed the truck, where the explosives are, who stashed them and for what purpose."

"What if he had nothing to do with the robbery after all?" Boréda ventured.

"I know he knows something. My gut is always right. No one dodges bullets and resists arrest the way he did without a good reason."

"It's only a matter of time before the Spanish secret service demands his extradition," Vilorain chimed in, pushing a forkful of quiche into his mouth. "Obviously, they are anxious to nail him for the bombing in Irun. However, we simply cannot afford to lose our number one suspect."

"You're damn right, Didier," said Blanchard. "We will deliver Izcoa to the Spanish authorities in due time, but for now, he is our prisoner."

"Well, if we don't get the answers we want by the time his custody is up, we will find a motive to arrest him for something he is liable for on French soil," continued Vilorain. "This moron is not going anywhere."

"Finding a motive for his detention won't be too tough of a task. Use of a fake passport, resisting arrest, the list goes on and on," argued Blanchard.

"I'm a bit concerned that the station is not secure enough to keep a man like Lartaun Izcoa behind bars," said Vilorain. "According to the CESID, he is quite the master of escape. Who knows whether he has accomplices nearby? What if they are already aware of his capture and are in the process of hatching a scheme to get him out of there as we speak? I mean, we already know that these guys are no strangers to bombing police stations."

"That same thought has crossed my mind," replied Boréda. "I'll start working on the suspect's transfer to the jail in Pau as soon as we head back to the station."

"How long will that take?" asked Vilorain.

"I could get the paperwork sorted out first thing on Monday."

"Monday? Isn't the jail a stone's throw away from the station? I could drive him there myself right about now!" Vilorain exclaimed, unable to contain his impatience.

"That's the French prison system for you. Unlike us, they'd rather not work too hard on weekends," Boréda replied with a shrug.

"I have a bad feeling about this," Vilorain mumbled.

01:57 PM ~ Saturday, August 27, 1994

Soon after she checked into her room, Vivienne took a long hot bath. She hoped to get a few hours of sleep, but not after tossing and turning in bed all morning. Aggravated, she kicked the sheets back and watched television instead. Although no matter how hard Vivienne tried, she was too restless to focus on anything. After staring at the phone for a while, she called the Major.

"*Monsieur* Boréda?"

He recognized the voice as soon as he brought the receiver to his mouth. "Miss Laroche, what can I do for you?"

"I want to speak with my daughter. I know that I would feel so much better once I get to hear her voice. And don't say no. I know she has the right to place a phone call, at the very least."

"Vivienne," the Major replied with an audible sigh, "I have already told you, several times, that it is not possible right now. I was going to call you later on, but now that I have you on the line, you ought to know that your daughter was transferred to the hospit—"

"What?" Vivienne pressed her wrist against her mouth, instantly consumed with worry. "What happened?"

"Nothing serious, I assure you. She was tired and dehydrated. We didn't want to take any chances, so we called EMS. She's in good hands now."

"Where is she? I need to know so that I can be with her!"

"Even though she is at the hospital, she is still in our custody. You are not permitted in the room."

"This is insane!" Vivienne yelled into the receiver.

"Listen, I'm going to check on her this afternoon. I'll call you at your hotel to let you know how she's doing. How does that sound?"

"How does it sound? Fucked up, that's how that sounds! I demand to see my daughter now, or I will make sure you are in serious trouble!"

"Miss Laroche, I promise that you'll visit your daughter soon. In the meantime, why don't you walk downstairs and tell the lady at the bar that I sent you. She's got the secret recipe for a cocktail that will make you forget all your troubles. Have two of them on me and go straight to bed. Trust me, it works." For the second time that day, Boréda couldn't believe what he just said.

"You're kidding, right?" Vivienne said with all the dignity she could muster.

"I could not be any more serious. You take care, now." Boréda hung up, feeling anything but proud of himself.

Vivienne started pacing the room like a rat in a cage. All things considered, a drink or two did not sound too bad. She was about to head to the bar when a much better thought crossed her mind. Without further hesitation, she sat back down on the edge of the bed and dialed the number for La Goutte d'Eau.

29

—HOGEITABEDERATZI—

01:45 PM ~ Saturday, August 27, 1994

After the stressful drive back from Irun, Jean-Philippe desperately needed a drink. Even though he knew Eric was anxiously awaiting his detailed report, arriving an hour late would not make such a difference. If anything, a stop at La Goutte d'Eau did have its strategic value. Someone there might have heard from Lartaun or his girlfriend.

He walked into the old train station and secured a stool at the end of the bar. The place was eerily empty and quiet. Mina sat alone by the window, reading a newspaper.

"Afternoon, Mina. Damn, where is everybody? Have you seen Etienne around, by any chance?"

Mina immediately stood from her chair and headed toward him.

"Hey JP, what's up? He's upstairs, I think." Mina ogled him with a concerned frown on her face. "No offense, but you look like shit. Can I get you a cup of coffee?"

"I think I'll have a beer instead, thanks."

Mina rolled her eyes at him. "It's in the fridge. Help yourself while I go get Etienne."

Jean-Philippe followed her with his eyes as she walked around the bar and up the stairs. She was wearing an indigo tunic embroidered with silver thread in arabesque patterns around the neckline and sleeves. She was barefoot, as usual. He noticed a silver bracelet with tiny bells tied around her right ankle. He immediately pictured her whirling about the room like a Dervish, naked except for her tinkling anklet. The sudden fantasy made him want to run after her. "And then what?" he asked himself. He shook the erotic vision out of his mind and stumbled to the kitchen to get a drink instead.

The old floorboards above his head creaked, and soon the rhythmic *thump-thump* of someone coming down the stairs followed.

Jean-Philippe quickly retrieved his beer and walked up to his friend to give him a hug. Etienne was disheveled, bare-chested and unshaven.

"How are you holding up, buddy?" Jean-Philippe asked with concern. "I came over to make sure you were all right. I still can't believe that they raided the place, man."

"Whoa, you haven't even heard half of the story yet," Etienne sighed and took a seat by the counter. "You're drinking already?" he said, pointing at the beer in Jean-Philippe's hand. "Hell, might as well."

"What story?" Jean-Philippe tried his best to keep his tone casual, but he could already feel the onslaught of another anxiety attack. Thankfully, Etienne seemed not to notice the tiny beads of sweat forming on his upper lip.

"Faustine called a little after midnight last night. Guess where from? The gendarmerie in Pau! She wanted to speak to Viv, of course, but since she is in Paris, I took the call instead. She sounded relieved to get me on the phone because she said she was only allowed one call before they would take her in custody."

"Faustine was arrested?" Jean-Philippe's jaw dropped.

"Yeah, last night, on the Pic du Midi, of all places! Can you believe that shit? Even though I think they only arrested her because she was with Rafael. I bet she'll be out in no ti—"

"Rafael was arrested, too?" Jean-Philippe shouted in consternation.

"Well, it's really him they are after, don't you know?"

"Where is he?" Jean-Philippe's voice trembled.

"She didn't know. The cops would not tell her. I feel so bad for her. Hell, I feel bad for the both of them."

"Shit!" was all Jean-Philippe could muster. Mina came back down the stairs and immediately joined the conversation.

"Did Faustine say why the police are after Rafael?"

"No, she didn't mention anything about it. I doubt she knows," replied Etienne.

"I wonder what he could have done to deserve this." Mina shook her head in disbelief.

"What a mess, man, what a mess!" Jean-Philippe guzzled the rest of his beer. "Do you mind if I place a quick phone call?"

"Is it local?" enquired Mina, thrifty in all circumstances.

"No, but I can assure you I'll keep it short."

Jean-Philippe jumped off his seat and rushed toward the communal phone. He leaned sideways against the wall, facing the opposite direction from his two friends at the bar. He pulled the torn piece of paper from his wallet and dialed the number that Patxi had given him. After a couple of rings, the sterile voice of a pre-recorded message instructed him to leave a short message after the beep. "We can't make it to the party," he half-whispered into the receiver so neither Mina nor Etienne could hear.

Less than three hours passed since his meeting with Patxi and he already had to place the dreaded call. He was well aware that he should drive to Eric's house without delay to deliver the devastating news of Lartaun's arrest, but Etienne had just happened to refill his glass while he was on the phone. His hopeless alcoholic-self rationalized, "I'll drink that one and then I'll be on my way."

02:00 PM ~ Saturday, August 27, 1994

The strident ring of the phone resounded throughout the house.

"La Goutte d'Eau, *j'écoute*?"

"Etienne, is that you?"

"Vivienne!" Etienne screamed into the phone. "I was worried sick! Are you calling from Paris?"

Vivienne chose not to answer that question. She could not even begin to tell her lover that Faustine was in police custody, or that, she herself, had never left for Paris.

"Faustine was just admitted to the hospital in Pau!" she said instead.

"The hospital? What the hell happened?"

"I heard she passed out from exhaustion and dehydration after the climb."

"Viv, that's terrible! Is she going to be all right?"

"They said so, but I'm worried to death!"

"Please, don't shoot the messenger, but whoever contacted you about Faustine did not tell you the whole story. I don't really know how to break the news to you, so I'll tell you straight up: Rafael and Faustine were arrested last n—"

"I already know that!" she hollered into the phone, cutting him off mid-sentence.

There was an awkward pause at the other end of the line. When Etienne spoke again, he sounded very confused.

"How could you possibly know that? Did the police call you? How did they know where to contact you? I don't even know how to reach you myself!"

"I—They—" Vivienne bit her tongue. She had just been caught in her lie, and Etienne would soon find out that she never left for Paris, nor ever planned to go there. She could not even remember why she was calling him in the first place. Regardless, she quickly reasoned for it did not matter anymore, and she did not feel like explaining herself. In fact, she suddenly realized she wanted nothing to do with Etienne or any of La Goutte's residents. In truth, Major Boréda stayed in her thoughts all morning. No matter how inconceivable and nauseating the mere concept of being infatuated with a cop seemed, she simply could not help herself.

"Viv! Hello? Vivienne? Tell me what's going on!" Etienne demanded in alarm. "Where are you? Vi—"

The line went dead with a click.

Vivienne replaced the receiver. She searched under the bed for her missing flip-flop, opened the door to her hotel room, and headed down the staircase toward the bar. After all, there was no problem a stiff cocktail could not solve.

Back at La Goutte, Etienne stood by the wall, dazed, staring at the receiver in his hand. He raked a hand through his short dreadlocks before finally hanging up the phone.

"What happened?" asked Mina.

"Vivienne said that Faustine was taken to the hospital in Pau." Mina and Jean-Philippe gasped in unison. "I guess she collapsed from exhaustion."

"Oh Etienne, sorry to hear that."

"She'll be OK, Mina. Right now, it is Vivienne that I'm more worried about. Something about that call was just not right."

04:37 PM ~ Saturday, August 27th, 1994

Dark clouds, heavy with rain, were rolling into the valley when Jean-Philippe left Eric's chalet, in Urdos, to return home. His visit to Eric became a short one. In just a few minutes, Jean-Philippe relayed the staggering news of Lartaun's capture to him. Even though Eric could tell that his friend was under the influence of alcohol, he was concerned with Jean-Philippe's volatile temper and erratic behavior. It took Eric a great deal of energy to bring him back to his senses and to convince him to go home and stay put until they receive further instructions from Patxi. Needless to say, the news was an ominous sign that did not bode well for their respective futures. A knot of fear grew in the pit of Eric's stomach. No matter what he did, it would never go away.

When Jean-Philippe stopped the car in front of his house to unlock the gates, he noticed that they were already open. A sobering knot of fear started to form in his throat. Did someone let themselves in while he was gone? He reasoned that he must have forgotten to padlock them in the morning, considering he had so many things on his mind. By the time he made it to the front door, the rain started to fall hard. He dropped his keys atop a stone pedestal in the foyer and staggered down the hall with a rolling gait.

He blindly felt for the two-way switch along the kitchen wall when the lights came on. Jean-Philippe screamed in surprise and gripped the door frame for support as he sized up the two intruders in front of him.

Patxi and a man he had never seen before were standing in the middle of the room. Patxi dropped a half-eaten apple onto the table. His stone-cold voice ripped through the silence, sharper than a razor.

"Here you are, at last. I was starting to get a little worried."

It took Jean-Philippe a few seconds to regain composure. He peeled himself from the kitchen wall and exclaimed with inebriated indignation,

"How did you get in?"

"Through the door, fool," Patxi replied. "You didn't lock your house. In this day and age, you ought to be a little more careful. Don't worry though, we've been good guests. We didn't touch a thing in your absence. Well, except for that." He pointed to the apple, which was beginning to oxidize where Patxi had bitten into its core.

Next, Jean-Philippe turned his stare toward the Goliath towering over him. Patxi was quick to notice his uneasiness and said,

"This is Santutxo. We jumped in the car as soon as we got your message."

"I didn't know you had a bodyguard," Jean-Philippe commented with dismay.

Santutxo was built like a wrestler, with hands the size of a catcher's mitt. His head was as bald as a cue ball, and everything from his thick jaws to his Machiavellian dark eyes reinforced the fact that he was not the type of man one would ever want to mess with.

Patxi let out a dry laugh. "Santu is no bodyguard. He is here to help us."

"Help—help us do what?"

"Help us acquire our wild card for delivery later," he replied with a mysterious grin.

"I'm not following you," Jean-Philippe replied.

"You will in a sec. Are you really a hundred per cent sure that Lartaun has been arrested?" Jean-Philippe could do little more than shake his head in agreement. "OK, then. Tell me where I can find Lartaun's girl-friend."

"Why?"

"Answer me!" Patxi sneered.

"She's at the hospital in Pau."

"What the hell is she doing at the hospital?" Patxi did not expect that kind of answer, and his surprise showed.

"Something about her collapsing from exhaustion," stammered Jean-Philippe.

Patxi quickly collected his wits. "What's the girl's last name?"

"Laroche, I think. Yeah, Faustine Laroche, that's it. Why do you care?"

"We have come to kidnap her."

"What? Why?"

"Because she is the key that locks Lartaun's lips. I trust him, I sure do, but I also know what those *txakurrak* are capable of. A little extra incentive to keep quiet can't hurt. Plus, I was told she is an accomplished rock climber. She's the only person I can think of who can retrieve the explosives from the *zulo*, now that Lartaun is out of the picture." Santutxo approved with a silent nod. As much as Jean-Philippe hated to admit it, Patxi's logic was impeccable.

"But how will he find out that his girlfriend has been kidnapped?

He's in police custody!"

"This is where you step in, my friend." Patxi showed no emotion. "I will handle the kidnapping. Meanwhile, you think of a way to communicate with Lartaun. Let him know that if he talks, his girlfriend will die."

Jean-Philippe stared blandly at Patxi. He straddled the kitchen chair closest to him and collapsed on it. His head was spinning and not just because he was drunk, but because things were getting out of control. Patxi was a madman. A dangerous madman.

"Listen, Patxi," he pleaded, "I don't know what Eric told you when you guys recruited me for the *ekintza*, but whatever he said, he must have exaggerated. I'm a nobody! A "B-list" fringe activist at best! The sole reason why you guys wanted to work with me was because of the location of my parents' house here in the valley. I never had any affiliation with ETA or IK or anything like that!"

"Well, that's perfect, because neither do we. I'm the sole and only organization you'll ever need to answer to, my friend," Patxi replied with a smirk.

"I don't understand!" Jean-Philippe's eyes darted back and forth between Patxi and Santutxo. "What's going on, here?"

"See, I once believed in ETA. But the truth is, ETA has become weak. Its leaders do not have the foresight and courage to act on a grand scale. Sure, I could have joined the fold and become another cog in the machine like the rest of them, but I had too much drive to ever let that happen." He paused, mostly for the dramatic effect. "So, I took it upon myself to create a new *talde* and—"

"What do you mean by *talde?*" Jean-Philippe interrupted him.

Patxi rolled his eyes at Santutxo. With a condescending tone, he went on explaining what a *talde* was to the drunken clown sitting in front of him. "It means 'group' in *Euskara*. You see, ETA's paramilitary branch is subdivided into organized clandestine cells, which are each composed of about a half-dozen members, whose objective is to conduct attacks in a specific geographic zone. Those cells are called *taldeak* or again *komando*. Anyway, forget about that. What you need to know is that we created our own separate group. No one knows of our existence. Not even ETA."

"Why are you telling me about it if it is such a secret?"

"Because, even though I wish you weren't, you've become a part of our operation whether you like it or not, *cabrón*. I like my people to know what they're risking their lives for. Mark my words: 'We're going to make history!' When we carry out OPERATION ASKATASUNA, the whole world will learn that we will stop at nothing in our fight for independence."

"I don't want to be part of your plan. I don't even want to know anything about it!" Jean-Philippe's voice took on a falsetto tone, but he was too petrified to care. "Just let me off the hook Patxi, please! I swear I'll disappear, and you will never hear from me again!"

"Shut up! A proud man does not beg!" Patxi scolded him, eyeing him with disgust. "Your job is not over until I say it is over. Now, either you comply with the orders I just gave you, or Santu will show you what happens to those who don't."

Jean-Philippe did not need to take another look at Santutxo to make up his mind. "OK, Patxi, OK! I will talk to Lartaun."

"Excellent!" Patxi concluded with a satisfied smile. He reached over the kitchen table and squeezed Jean-Philippe's shoulder with mock affection. "You do what you need to do, and we do what we need to do. We all stay put until I say it is time to vanish. Then, and only then, we will go our separate ways and pretend that we never met each other. See? It's not that complicated, really."

Patxi started for the door with Santutxo on his heels. Before he left the room, he turned around to face Jean-Philippe one last time and warned,

"I don't trust you, Jean-Philippe. Working with you has been a good lesson for me not to ever take chances with an outsider again. Don't ever forget that my eyes are on you. You should fear me more than you should fear the cops."

Jean-Philippe reached the sink just in time to throw up.

30

—HOGEITAHAMAR —

06:17 PM ~ Saturday, August 27, 1994

Faustine was fast asleep, aided by heavy sedatives. Outside her hospital room, nurses and physicians were scurrying up and down the hallway, eager to complete their six o'clock rounds. While some of them would curiously cast sideways glances at the policeman stationed in front of room 207, the majority just carried on with their jobs without giving it a second thought. Officer Kaziewski sat on a molded plastic chair, hunching over a copy of the French sports magazine *L'Équipe*. He, too, became oblivious to the buzzing activity surrounding him. He was bored and sleepy.

Koldobika, the driver who had accompanied Patxi and Santutxo to Jean-Philippe's place, made a turn onto the main avenue and entered the hospital compound. He drove, at a slow speed, on the brand new asphalt road, flanked on both sides by manicured lawns and modern buildings. The fourth person in Patxi's car was a woman. She continued to test the reception/transmission quality of her miniature walkie-talkie with Santutxo, who sat beside her in the back seat. Once they were assured that everything worked fine, Santutxo signaled the driver to pull over. He got out of the vehicle and took off toward the hospital. Meanwhile, Koldobika drove until he found a secure parking spot where they could sit and wait without disturbance.

The woman produced a pocket mirror from her purse. She combed the bangs of her shoulder-length brown wig and checked her makeup one more time. While she waited for Santutxo's signal, she proceeded to bite off what was left of her fingernails. All the while, she kept her eyes riveted on the walkie-talkie resting on her lap. Fifteen minutes later, the tiny device clicked to life.

"Alpha-Zulu, do you copy?"

"Ten-Four, Sierra-Tango. Come in," she replied, her lips pressed against the microphone.

"Faustine Laroche, outpatient ward, room #207. Everything is in place."

"Where's the gear?"

"Walk past the reception desk in the main hall and take the elevators to the second floor. You'll see the nurses' office to your right. Walk past it when no one is looking. Go straight toward the ladies' room. You'll find it a couple doors down the hall on your left. Look inside the janitor's closet. Good luck. Over and out."

"Roger that. Over."

Patxi reached between the seats to squeeze the woman's hand before she slipped out of the car.

The woman followed the sidewalk toward the entrance doors of the hospital. Immediately, upon entering the facility, she bowed her head to elude the surveillance cameras and briskly headed for the elevators. As soon as the doors opened to the second floor, she spotted the nurses' office.

A pudgy uniformed lady sat with her back to the sliding glass window. She chatted on the phone and paid no attention to the hallway. Anabel took advantage of the situation and tiptoed down the corridor into the rest rooms. She exhaled hard after closing the door behind her. Anabel was reasonably sure that her presence was not detected. She checked every stall to ensure they were vacant before opening the utility closet at the far end of the room.

Sitting atop a tower of industrial-size toilet paper rolls was a bundle of clothes rolled in a ball. She grabbed it and stepped into one of the cubicles. Anabel hastily stripped off her clothes and put on a white top with matching scrub pants. A pair of comfortable sandals added a credible touch to her nurse get up. She smoothed the wrinkles from her uniform and tucked the walkie-talkie, along with her compact Glock handgun, into the elastic band of her underwear. Anabel slowly reopened the stall door with caution. She buried her skirt, top and shoes at the bottom of a large trash can next to the sink. She wiped the handle and toggle clasps of her purse clean before discarding it as well.

She cracked the bathroom door open to assess the situation. The hallway was deserted. She stepped out and followed the signs to room # 207, careful to make as little noise as possible. As Anabel turned the bend, she froze. A gendarme was sitting on a chair, not even ten yards away from her. She retreated behind the corner. For several agonizing seconds, she waited before mustering the courage to stick her head out again. The officer was so engrossed in his reading that he did not notice her. She stared at him for a while, wondering what to do next. Just as she was about to send Santutxo a signal to create a diversion, the officer lifted his head from the magazine and cleared his throat. He looked at his watch, stretched his arms high above his head and let out a loud yawn. He stood up, dropped his rag onto the chair and headed down the hallway, whistling a popular tune. Anabel knew she had little time to act.

Due to lack of time, the kidnapping was not planned well. She would have to play it by ear. Her idea was to let herself into the room and tell Lartaun's girlfriend that she needed to take her temperature or something along those lines. With her scrubs on, the girl would have no reason to feel suspicious. When she got closer to her, she would point her gun at her face and order her to follow instructions without making a scene, or else. It was risky, but she did not have too many options.

Anabel peeked through the window and saw that the young woman was sleeping peacefully. She entered room #207. The door closed behind her with a swoosh-like sound. She approached the bed and pressed her Glock against Faustine's temple. Much to her surprise, Faustine did not react at all. Puzzled, Anabel wrapped her fingers around Faustine's wrist and lifted her arm in the air. She let it go and it fell back limply by her side. Faustine did not even flinch.

"She's all drugged up," she told herself. "That's good. It'll make my job a lot easier."

Anabel spotted a wheelchair in the far corner of the room. She unfolded it and wheeled it over to the side of the hospital bed. Next, Anabel slid her arms under Faustine's armpits and, gathering all of her strength, she pulled her off the bed and into the chair. Faustine opened her eyes half-way and mumbled something incoherent, but she slipped back into her twilight daze almost immediately. Anabel detached the I.V. bag from its stand and hooked it onto the back of the chair. She positioned Faustine's feet against the foot rests and covered her hospital gown with a blanket. At last, she placed pillows under the bed sheets to create the illusion that the patient was still in bed. She struggled to open the door with one hand while she wrestled Faustine in her wheelchair over the threshold. She had almost reached the corner of the hallway when she heard the officer's footsteps clack against the linoleum. Frantic, Anabel forced herself to maintain a normal pace and refrained from looking over her shoulder. She dreadfully awaited the gendarme to summon her to stop.

Officer Kaziewski was fuming because the coffee machine down the hall had malfunctioned. Sure, it swallowed his five-franc coin and prepared his piping hot *café au lait* in a plastic cup, but somehow failed to spit up his change. After several attempts to collect his money by kicking the distributor failed, he had no other choice but to kiss his francs good-bye. He shot a glance through the door window to check on the prisoner inside. Everything looked normal, so he sat back down and drank his coffee, longing for his shift to come to an end.

Anabel rushed past the nurses' office and reached the elevators undetected. When the doors glided open, after what seemed like an eternity, she wheeled Faustine inside, hit the basement button and prayed the doors would close quickly. They did before anyone else stepped inside. Her heart was hammering away in her chest when the doors reopened below street level. She instinctively reached for her gun, just in case. Even though the metal piece had already warmed up against her skin, the unique sensation of feeling it so close to her body was enough to send chills up her spine. She checked that the hallway was clear before she pushed Faustine out of the elevator. Nobody was there. It seemed as if the young woman's absence had gone unnoticed. Straight ahead, she saw an emergency exit sign with the word *SORTIE* painted in large, white, block letters against a dark grey door at the end of a concrete walkway. She was almost out of danger.

Without warning, a set of revolving doors opened with a loud bang somewhere to her left. Anabel gasped in reflex and ducked behind a large metal container under a trash chute, leaving Faustine exposed and unconscious in the middle of the hallway. Santutxo, looking flushed and agitated, leapt from the shadows.

"Over here!" Anabel half-whispered in his direction. He pivoted around with his gun cocked, eyes bulging with stress. "Don't shoot, Santu! It's me!" In slow motion, her head appeared from behind the trash can.

"I never got your signal! We thought you were in trouble, so Patxi sent me to find you!"

"I'm fine. Come help me carry the girl. Quick!"

Santutxo plucked Faustine from her wheelchair as if she weighed nothing and carried her over his shoulder beyond the emergency door and up the stairs.

Anabel and her partner shoved Faustine in the back seat of the car waiting for them outside. They took off at a normal speed, so as not to attract unwanted attention. Upon leaving the hospital grounds, they merged onto Boulevard de Hauterive. Before realizing what they just accomplished, Koldobika collected his pass at the toll-booth. Now that they had reached the relative safety of the highway, they could finally afford to relax a little. Traffic moved at break-neck speed along the left lane of the *autoroute*. If all went well, they would reach the farm by nightfall.

"Anabel, how's our prisoner doing?" Patxi swiveled the rearview mirror to catch a glimpse of Faustine asleep in the back of the car. He was the first passenger to break the heavy silence ever since their departure from the hospital.

"She's out cold, and there's still plenty of solution left in the I.V. bag. I don't see her waking up anytime soon."

"Tie her up anyway."

Anabel turned to Faustine and proceeded to bind her wrists together with a heavy-duty cable-tie, then blindfolded her with an eye mask. The young woman was slumped against the car door with her head tilted at a weird angle. Anabel straightened her up the best she could before adjusting the blanket over her hospital gown. When she was done, she admired Faustine's beauty for a moment. The young woman's lips were slightly parted, and a small strand of blond hair was moving in sync with her breath. So this was the woman who had stolen Lartaun's heart. In spite of herself, Anabel was stung by a sudden pang of jealousy.

"What happened out there?" Patxi asked. "Did your radio crap out on you?"

"No," Anabel replied, "the cop ended up leaving his post on his own, so I took advantage of the situation."

"That was a risky move, baby. You had no idea what he was doing." Patxi and his companions were still reeling from the fright she had given them. Deep down, it made her smile a little.

"It was a chance I was willing to take. Hey! It all worked out, so what's the problem?"

"There's no problem. No problem at all," replied Patxi. "You did a great job."

"You've got *cojones,* lady," Santutxo agreed in his turn. "Your brother would have been awfully proud of you."

"Thanks, Santu."

They all fell silent again, out of respect for Anabel's late brother Bixente. Anabel tried hard not to let tears fill her eyes. Bixente's death was hard on her, but she could not afford sentimental thoughts in the middle of an operation. She owed it to Bixente, Patxi and everyone in the *talde* to give her best to the cause, no matter what the repercussions may be.

Anabel removed her wig and let it drop between her feet. Underneath, her auburn hair was styled in a short pixie cut. She changed into a pair of brown cargo pants and a black spaghetti-strap tank top. When she returned to her normal self, she stuffed the nurse uniform and the wig inside a plastic bag. She rolled down the window and threw it out of the car without giving it a second thought.

As she finally reclined into her seat again, she realized that Patxi had been staring at her the whole time in the rearview mirror. After all these years, the deep love they had for each other remained as strong as ever, in spite of all the hurdles they had to overcome in the process. Anabel thought of all the things she and Patxi had sacrificed for OPERATION ASKATASUNA. They had worked on the *ekintza* for well over a year now. They were so close to initiating the chain of events that would forever alter the course of Spanish history. They hoped they would bring Madrid to its knees so that, some day soon, *Euskadi* would finally be set free.

Anabel had expected exaltation born from the promise of great things to come. Instead, with the fateful date of "Operation Freedom" rolling closer with every passing day, her conscience grew heavier with doubt and skepticism. Even Bixente's death had not succeeded in fanning the flames of her hatred against the imperialistic state of Spain. It was as if her will to fight had died with him. Because she did not have the courage to voice her concerns to Patxi, she chose to numb herself to the outside world instead. That way, she could go through the motions without thinking about her actions, like a well-programmed robot.

31

-HOGEITAHAMAIKA-

06:45 PM ~ Saturday, August 27, 1994

"Goddamn you, Roman!" Jean-Claude Boréda screamed into the receiver. "What do you mean, 'she's gone?'" Boréda struggled to think of a rational explanation for Faustine's disappearance. "Did you search every-where inside the room? Could she have jumped out the window?"

"Impossible. She was on the second floor, and the window in her room is sealed shut!"

"Roman," he said again, trying his very best to remain calm and composed, "people don't just vanish into thin air. When someone leaves a room, more often than not, he or she walks out the door. Now, did you, or did you not leave your post at any point in time throughout the course of this afternoon?"

There was a short pause on the other end of the line. "Well, I ran to the coffee machine about half-an-hour ago, but I couldn't have been gone for more than five, seven minutes at the most!" he admitted meekly to his superior.

"She must have woken up while you were gone, then. With a bit of luck, she might still be wandering about the hospital. Get the security per-sonnel to search for her at once. I don't want her to leave the premises!"

"Right away, Major."

"Don't go anywhere; I'm on my way over!" Boréda slammed the phone down and hurled a string of profanities while he fumbled through the mess atop his desk to find the keys to his patrol car.

When he arrived at the hospital, Kaziewski was waiting for him by the reception desk.

"Show me the way to her room!" Boréda demanded without slowing down.

The nurse, who had rung the alarm, was standing outside Faustine's room. The Major stormed right past her with Kaziewski at his heels. He kicked a bed pillow to the ground in anger.

"Innocent, my ass! She must have been in with Izcoa the whole time! I cannot believe she tried to escape!" Boréda exploded in a rage. If there was something he simply could not deal with, it was being taken for a fool. Meanwhile, the nurse took the liberty of entering the room. She lightly drummed her fingers on the wall to get the gendarmes' attention.

"I'm not sure what you think happened here, and I certainly don't mean to interrupt, but just so you know, the patient was heavily sedated. The amount of medication would not have allowed her to get up, let alone walk out of here."

Aggravated, Boréda turned around to face the intruder. "I'm sorry, come again?"

"The patient was pretty combative when she was admitted here, so the doctor prescribed Ativan in free serum form to calm her down. It's a benzodiazepine with CNS depressant, anxiolytic and sedative properties. Considering the dosage, there is no way she would have been capable of leaving this bed on her own."

"What do you mean?"

"All I'm trying to say, sir, is that given the circumstances, someone would have had to carry her out of this room."

Boréda pondered her statement. If Faustine could not have left on her own, someone had to have known to find her here. And that was a deeply disturbing thought. Boréda addressed the nurse one more time.

"Could you get me a list of all the personnel working in this wing? We'll need to question everyone. If this girl had to be carried outside in broad daylight, someone must have seen her, for Christ's sake!"

"I'm on it, sir," the nurse replied and left in a hurry.

"Contact the hospital security office and seize every surveillance tape that was recorded after Miss Laroche's admittance," Boréda instructed the officer, "and have someone bring them to the station so that a team can screen them right away. Also, call for back up. I want the perimeter around the room blocked off immediately. Make sure that no one sets foot in here until an investigation unit is dispatched. Do you think you can handle that?"

Kaziewski was staring at his boots in shame, shaking his head in consternation. "I feel terrible for abandoning my post, Major. If only I had known—"

"What is done is done, Roman. I will deal with your incompetence later. For now, I just need you to follow my orders!" he snapped back at the gendarme.

Kaziewski stood at attention and acquiesced sternly before his superior exited the room.

Boréda returned to the gendarmerie at a quarter past seven in the evening. Inspector Blanchard pounced on the Major the second he spotted him walking down the hall.

"How could you let this blunder happen?" he exclaimed. "Do you realize the jam that we're in now?"

"Spare me the guilt trip, I know," Boréda replied with a wary sigh as he held the door to his office for him. Vilorain was already waiting inside.

"So, what would you bid your next paycheck on?" Vilorain called out to them before they could even get to their seats. "Kidnapping or clever escape scheme? Is the girl clean or in cahoots with Izcoa?" He balanced his hands as if he were weighing their options on an imaginary scale. "Has our girl fallen in the clutches of dangerous terrorists, or is she one of them after all?"

"Frankly, I don't know what to think anymore. I hope the guys in our TIC team find the answers we're looking for at the hospital," Boréda admitted with a shrug.

"All right, here's the situation. We know that Miss Laroche was sedated to the point that she could not have walked out on her own, which implies that someone would have had to carry her out of her room," said Vilorain. "Someone who knew to find her at the hospital, of all places. Now, how could that happen, when no one else, but us, was aware that she'd been sent there in the first place?"

"Well, her mother knew," Boréda pondered. Inspector Blanchard lifted a quizzical eyebrow in his direction. "I had no choice but to tell her!" he added defensively.

"Damn, could the mother be in on it as well?"

"Either she is, or she has been innocently relaying information to people on the outside," argued Blanchard.

"It makes no sense, though," reasoned Boréda. "We've pretty much established that the mother knew nothing of Izcoa's schemes! Besides, why would she put her own daughter in harm's way?"

"I think that we made a huge mistake by underestimating the acumen of the players involved in this affair," commented Vilorain. "When is Izcoa scheduled to be transferred to the jail in Pau?"

"I called the State Prosecutor as soon as we came back from lunch. The transfer has been approved for Sunday. The bad news is that it will have to happen late at night." Boréda's mounting concern was obvious.

"This means that we're on our own until tomorrow night. We must reinforce security around Izcoa's cell immediately. Hell, around the whole station. Who knows what Izcoa's accomplices could do to this place if they decide to get him out next?" Vilorain looked at them, one after the other, from under his tortoise shell glasses, before he mouthed the word, *"BOOM!"*

An unpleasant shiver went up Boréda's spine. Things were taking a dangerous turn and they had to put a stop to it. He pointed at the telephone on his desk and announced,

"Let me call Vivienne Laroche to find out whether she has spoken to anyone about Faustine this afternoon. Who knows, she could lead us to the snitch."

"Go ahead," Blanchard handed him the receiver, "but don't say a thing about her daughter's disappearance. Let's see how she behaves on the phone, first."

Vivienne answered the phone on the sixth ring. She sounded a bit tipsy.

"I followed your advice about the special drinks you prescribed to me, Major. You were right! So right, in fact, that you just woke me up!"

When the Major inquired as to whether she had spoken to anyone earlier in the afternoon, she immediately told him the truth.

"Was Etienne alone?" he asked next. "Or is it possible that someone else might have overheard your phone conversation?"

"I couldn't say."

"Thank you, Vivienne." The Major hung up. "She has no clue what's going on," he told the inspectors.

Vilorain agreed. "Someone else is behind this."

"Let me call her boyfriend, Etienne, right now."

A minute into their conversation, Boréda motioned wildly to the inspectors for a pen and a piece of paper.

"And?" Blanchard asked as soon as the Major hung up again.

"That boy Etienne said that a woman, called Mina, and a male friend of his were present when Vivienne called. They, too, heard about Faustine's collapse and subsequent transfer to the hospital. He also mentioned that he and his friend got so drunk afterwards that he passed out on the bar. So, he never got the chance to mention Vivienne's call to anyone else."

"Did you happen to get the friend's name?"

"Jean-Philippe De Lancastaing. Sounds posh, I know. Etienne described him as a standard 'good guy.' He said that his family owns a place in Etsaut, and that he hangs out at La Goutte a lot. Apparently, he knew Izcoa too. As for the woman, she lives at the commune. We interrogated her the other day."

"Let's go see this fellow," said Blanchard at once.

07:30 PM ~ Saturday, August 27, 1994

Jean-Philippe was freaking out, and that was putting it mildly.

How did Patxi and his henchman expect him to get in touch with Lartaun while he was locked up at the station? And, based on the remote possibility that he would indeed find a way to talk to Lartaun, what would he say to him? That the very people Lartaun was trying to protect had just kidnapped his girlfriend? That Patxi was a rambling lunatic and a dangerous psychopath who had crossed ETA to create his own über-secret cell so that he could carry out his own vision of Armageddon?

Jean-Philippe was at a loss for what to do next. The only thing he knew for sure was that he would not go anywhere near the gendarmerie for all the gold in the world. He would rather lie to Patxi and pretend that he had succeeded in passing the message to Lartaun than risk being caught. Better yet, he would bypass his orders altogether and get lost while he still could. Come to think of it, Jean-Philippe knew some people in Paris who could give him protection. And when push came to shove, they could even help him out of the country unnoticed.

His decision was made. Jean-Philippe dumped the rest of his whiskey in the sink and rushed upstairs to start packing.

32

-HOGEITAHAMABI-

09:02 PM ~ Saturday, August 27, 1994

The patrol car stopped in front of the gates of the De Lancastaing's estate in Etsaut. The gyrating blue lights of the vehicle cast an eerie glow against the medieval walls. Inspector Blanchard stepped out of the car to check the name on the mailbox.

"De Lancastaing. This is the place."

He yanked the chain hanging from the wall, and a little bell rang on the other side of the gates. A few houses down the narrow street, a dog started barking. The inspector waited a few minutes before he pulled on the chain again. From where he stood, he could only see the second story of the house. Everything looked quiet. There were no lights burning inside. Somewhere to his right, he heard heavy wood shutters being pushed open. A dark silhouette leaned over the windowsill.

"Who's there?" a matronly voice asked above his head.

Blanchard looked up, surprised. "We're looking for a Jean-Philippe De Lancastaing!"

"Good Lord!" The woman crossed herself against her ample chest. "Did something happen?"

"No ma'am, we just want to talk to him."

The older lady called to someone inside her house. "Come over here, René, quick! The gendarmes are over at the De Lancastaings!" She motioned for the inspector to stay put. "Don't go anywhere, I'll be right down!"

She appeared at her front door a minute later. She wore a faded baby blue terry cloth robe and matching slippers. The woman was in her seventies, a little on the heavy side. She had gathered her thinning gray hair in a tight bun for the night. A skinny, jaundiced-looking man craned his neck, from behind her, to see what was going on. Her husband, no doubt.

"Please excuse our appearance, officer. We were ready to retire for the night. I'm Irène Sarrat, and this is my husband, René." She extended her chubby hand to the inspector, giddy with excitement to be receiving such an unexpected visit on a Saturday night.

"I'm sorry to disturb you at such a late hour, ma'am. Inspector Blanchard, *Direction de la Surveillance du Territoire*. Do you happen to know the De Lancastaings?"

"Do we know the De Lancastaings?" she repeated, beaming. "My, of course, we do! We have been neighbors for years! We take care of their house when they're away. Fine people, aren't they, René?"

"Yes, fine people, indeed!" her husband acknowledged right on cue, feigning to match his wife's excitement.

"Do you know if anybody's home tonight?" asked Blanchard.

"Well, you just missed Jean-Philippe, Inspector. Jean-Philippe is the De Lancastaings' only son. He left tonight, I'm afraid."

"Gosh, you're dogged by bad luck! He was here for well over three months, too!" her husband chimed in.

"He handed me the keys to the house at around eight this evening," she went on. "I don't mean any disrespect, but can you tell us what this is about? Nothing serious, I hope?" She had that peculiar look in her eyes that betrayed the fact she was hoping to hear something juicy.

"No, nothing to worry about, ma'am. I just wanted to ask him a few questions. Do you mind if I talk to you instead?"

"Please, Inspector, go right ahead."

"Did Jean-Philippe tell you where he was going?"

"Let me think a minute. He said he was leaving the country." She leaned a little closer before adding, as if in confidence, "You know, the De Lancastaings are very wealthy people. They own places everywhere, and they travel all over the world!"

"I see. Did he mention how long he would be gone for?"

She pondered his question for a while. "No, but he mentioned that his parents should be back some time in September."

"Can you think of anything else he told you before he left?"

"Hmmm, no. He wasn't very talkative, to tell you the truth. Now that I think about it, he looked quite frazzled tonight. Wouldn't you agree, René? It kind of struck me as odd. But then again, and please, Inspector, you didn't hear it from me, promise?" She lowered her voice to a whisper. "He's quite an expert at throwing back his head, if you know what I mean. See, everyone around here knows that he's an alcoholic. But he's hiding it from his parents, and since we talk to them all the time, that would probably explain why he was acting all strange around us earlier."

"Did he drive?"

"Oh, Lord, no! A taxi picked him up around eight thirty. My guess is that he went to Pau to catch a train, but then again, I could be wrong about that. I'm so sorry. I wish I could be of more help to you."

"You've been very helpful, Mrs. Sarrat. Oh, one last thing, any idea how I could get in touch with him or his parents?"

"Of course!" She pivoted around to face her husband. "René, go get the number for the De Lancastaings. It's in my black agenda by the phone!"

"Sure," he said, obeying his wife's command with a resigned voice.

"Are you sure there's nothing to be worried about?" she asked the inspector again as she scanned the street with a suspicious look.

"No ma'am, you can sleep tight! The streets have never been safer," he replied with a congenial smile. Irène's husband came back with a folded piece of paper, and handed it to Inspector Blanchard. "Thank you again and sorry for the trouble."

"Feel free to come see us again anytime! I know everything that is going on in this village. As the saying goes, 'small town, big inferno,' right?" Irène added with a knowing wink.

Upon hearing this, her husband rolled his eyes behind her back. Frédéric Blanchard gave him one of those "I-know-how-you-feel" looks and said,

"You have a good night now, Mr. and Mrs. Sarrat."

The old man and his wife waved good-bye. Inspector Blanchard heard them locking the door behind him as he retreated toward the patrol car.

10:00 PM ~ Saturday, August 27, 1994

Sitting atop the back of a bench with a large duffel bag wedged between his legs, Jean-Philippe was fiddling with the zipper on his luggage. As he waited on the platform for the Pau-Paris overnight train to come, his latest gadget, the revolutionary GSM mobile phone, rang. He fished it out of his breast pocket and pressed the green connection key.

"Jean-Phi *chéri?*"

"Mother?" he exclaimed in surprise. "Where are you? Are you back in France?"

"No, we're still in Bangkok, darling," she answered in her over-medicated voice. "Gosh, I'm so relieved to hear your voice! I just got off the phone with our neighbors, the Sarrats. They told me the police came around tonight asking for you. Irène called me right away, of course, being the gossip that she is! Are you OK, *mon ange?* You haven't done anything stupid, have you?" Jean-Philippe felt like the wind had been knocked out of him. "Jean-Philippe? Are you there? Can you hear me?"

"Yes, mother. Something was—wrong with the phone, but I can hear you fine now. So, what's up?"

"What do you mean, 'what's up?'" Her voice morphed into a high-pitched shriek without warning. "I hear that the police are looking for you and you're the one asking me 'what's up?'"

Jean-Philippe felt like he was going to throw up again. Had Lartaun denounced him already? As he fought the nausea, he managed to reply.

"C'mon, Mother, no need to get all bent out of shape because our senile neighbors are ranting again! I have no idea why the police might be looking for me. I'm sure it is nothing to worry about. That old woman is crazy anyway. Maybe the police did not even come at all."

"You would tell me if you were in trouble, wouldn't you?" Jean-Philippe's mother sounded on the verge of tears. "Did you have one of those parties again? Did you drink and drive?"

"I don't remember, Mother. Maybe. Anyway, it's no big deal, you hear? No need to cry over this or even tell Dad about it, 'kay?"

"If you say so, honey," she sniffled. Her son, powerless and scared witless, waited patiently while she blew her nose in a tissue from half-a-world away. "Gosh, I wish I had been a better mother to you."

"Hush, Mom, of course you're a great mother. Listen, I'm on my way to New York for business," he lied. "I'll call you when I get there, all right? I love you."

"Sure. I love you too, sweetie. Don't forget to call me as soon as you land."

Jean-Philippe ended the call and stared at his phone for a moment in utter disbelief. God bless insanely rich, half-crazy mothers with hopeless addictions to benzodiazepines and Bordeaux wines. His train of thought immediately shifted to Patxi. Should he contact him to let him know that the police might be after him too? Frantic, he punched the keys on his phone, only to hold his index finger in mid-air as he was ready to connect the call. After all, was he not running away from Patxi in the first place? No, he wouldn't call. From now on, it was every man for himself and God for them all.

Above his head, a metallic voice informed travelers of the immediate arrival of the night train to Paris on platform number two.

Jean-Philippe managed to find a seat in an empty compartment aboard the train. It was a good thing he was alone, because no matter how hard he tried, he was unable to relax and was acting all jittery. In fact, he was experiencing firsthand what it felt like to be a wanted person, an outlaw, a felon. He cringed with fear every time he heard voices outside his compartment. One minute, he was picturing policemen coming in to arrest him. The next, he was fantasizing about Patxi's men shooting him in the back of the head without the slightest trace of hesitation. Before long, he gave up on the idea of getting any sleep at all. Instead, he popped a couple of pills and washed them down with a swig off the fifth of whiskey he brought along for the ride. Then, he started thumbing through a trash magazine.

The next morning, the night train would reach Gare Montparnasse, located in the heart of the French capital. His plan was to meet up with two acquaintances that lived in an inconspicuous pad near Place de la Bastille. These guys were the go-to people for men who happened to be in trouble with the law. Maybe he would go to Morocco and lay low for a few months until it was safe for him to return to France. No matter what his ultimate destination was, Jean-Philippe knew he had to put as much distance as possible between himself, Patxi, and the authorities.

The dice were loaded and Jean-Philippe was praying for a lucky seven at life's craps table.

Meanwhile, back in Pau, Major Boréda had issued a nation-wide search warrant for Jean-Philippe De Lancastaing, effective immediately. As far as he was concerned, another rabbit had dug a hole under the chicken wire, and he was responsible for bringing it back to the holding pen.

33

-HOGEITAHAMAHIRU-

10:49 PM ~ Saturday, August 27, 1994

Faustine emerged from her daze with a pounding headache. It was as if her brain was playing drums with her eyeballs. She tried to swallow but could not, as if her swollen tongue had fused with her palate. Even the air she breathed tasted stale and lacked the proper amount of oxygen. She coughed violently. That was when she realized that she was unable to move. Overcome with sudden panic, she started to squirm and fight in a futile attempt to set herself free from the thick ropes binding her ankles and wrists.

"She is awake," Anabel said in Basque. Faustine felt a foreign hand brushing against her thigh. She tried to scream, but the only sound coming out of her mouth was a painful croak. *"Cálmase! Silencio!* You no worry!" commanded the female voice in a mix of broken French and Spanish.

"Who are you? Where am I?" Faustine began to hyperventilate under the heavy canvas potato sack someone had wrapped around her head and torso. The harder she breathed, the more the fabric stuck against her nostrils, further aggravating her claustrophobia.

"She's not breathing well," Anabel addressed a hulk of a man standing in the shadows.

"Tell her to shut up, and she'll breathe fine again," the male guard responded without a sliver of emotion.

"We no here to 'urt, OK? Just calm!" the woman told Faustine. Still, Faustine put up a fierce struggle and Anabel had to use all her strength to pin her down to the cot. "*Joder,* just—stop moving, *coño!*" she panted. "You're in safe place here! No problem!" Faustine, who was still very weak, exhausted herself in a matter of seconds. Anabel felt her limbs go limp under her weight, and before long, she stopped moving altogether. "You stay calm, then we talk. You thirsty?" Faustine nodded. "Bring some water and soup!" Anabel ordered the watchman in her cryptic tongue.

Faustine heard a door open and close with a wailing squeak, followed by the muffled sound of heavy-duty boots hitting the packed dirt outside. "They're talking in Basque," she thought to herself. She tried hard to recall the recent past, which was a taxing endeavor at the time. Little by little, memories started to come back to her, like a patchwork of jumbled flashbacks: the roar of helicopters flying above her head, the stainless steel toilet inside her cell at the gendarmerie, the bumpy ride in the back of an ambulance, the tantrum she threw upon her arrival at the hospital… Then, nothing. Complete blackout.

The armed man walked back inside the room. Faustine felt hands grabbing at her sides and she recoiled in disgust. The woman finally managed to bring her to a seated position. She removed the potato sack covering her head, revealing a second blindfold underneath.

"Here, water for you." Anabel held a plastic goblet to her lips. Faustine took a tentative sip and spat half of it over herself. "Slow, slow," Anabel encouraged her so that she would take another sip. "Good! You hungry, too? Here, soup for you." She brought a spoon to her lips. The smell of thick potato and leek soup made Faustine's stomach gurgle with hunger. She had not eaten anything for days, and she was ravenous. Faustine swallowed the spoonful in one gulp and opened her mouth wide again, like a starving chick. The spoon rattled in the plate, and she ate another one, then another. The more she ate, the hungrier she seemed to be. "Enough now or you sick," said Anabel, at last.

Anabel took the plate away and Faustine protested. She wanted more of it. Before Faustine even realized what was happening, the rancid smell of the sack filled her nostrils again. She gagged as she felt it sliding down over her shoulders. She yelled for them to stop, but they were not paying attention to her.

"You relax. You rest now."

"Don't leave me alone!" Faustine shouted into the darkness.

"Sleep!"

The door closed with a *bang!*

Silence returned, even more terrifying than the dark. Before long, claustrophobia began to rear its ugly head and started to mess with Faustine's mind. She was imagining that these strangers had buried her alive inside a hermetic box and set her adrift into a never-ending vacuum. She suddenly feared that she would go crazy unless she screamed in order to break the oppressive silence. So, she screamed, at the top of her lungs, until her stomach churned and her voice was too hoarse to yell anymore.

01:40 AM ~ Sunday, August 28, 1994

A dirt bike with no headlights sputtered up the narrow trail toward the *baserri*. The moon cast a cool glow over the farm, giving just enough light for the man to find his way in the dark. Upon reaching the isolated building, the enigmatic rider turned off the engine and put the motorcycle on its kickstand. He removed his helmet and raked his fingers through his blondish hair, breathing the fragrant mountain air for a moment. The front door swung open, and Anabel walked outside to meet him. She wrapped her arms around his waist while she looked over his shoulder, more out of habit than out of actual concern.

"You're sure that no one followed you?"

"Positive." He kissed her on the mouth. "How's the prisoner doing?"

"She woke up soon after you left. She seems to be recuperating quite well. She even ate soup around eleven."

"Excellent. I need her in good shape for Monday." Patxi caressed Anabel's short hair. "How come you're not in bed? It's late!"

"I couldn't sleep if my life depended on it. Did you talk to my mother? What did she say about the funeral?"

"I did. Baby—there's something you ought to know. Your mother, she—she buried Bixente yesterday afternoon. At the *pueblo.*"

"She—*what?*" Anabel exploded in an instantaneous outburst of anger. "Yesterday was my brother's funeral, and nobody told me about it?" The sudden grief-stricken expression on Anabel's face was too painful for Patxi to witness. He tried to turn away from her, but Anabel was quick to grab him by the nape of the neck. She shook him hard, forcing him to look her in the eyes again. "I just asked you a fucking question!"

"Your mother didn't want you, or anyone else, to come! She was aware that Spanish secret service would crash the ceremony to see who'd be in attendance, so she chose to keep the time and place of the burial a secret. Don't be mad at her, baby. She did it to protect you! She knew that you'd never listen to reason, and that you would have come, regardless of the risks, just to be by her side."

"So *Mamá* was all alone to bury my brother?" Anabel burrowed her face into Patxi's sweatshirt and burst into tears. "Oh, Patxi, she's old and blind in one eye, and no one was there for her!" Patxi let her grieve in his arms for a long time. He would stroke and kiss her hair lovingly, ever so often, murmuring words of comfort in her ear.

"You're the bravest woman I know," he whispered after a while. "It is people like you, and people like both your brothers and your mother who make our country proud and strong."

"I'm sick of this shit, Patxi!" Anabel scooted backwards and shivered despite the warm night. "I just can't sit back anymore and wait for every person I love to either die or end up in jail! Aside from *Mamá,* you're the only person I have left in my life. Can't you see that I'm nearing the bottom of my most-loved-people's list, here?"

"Hush. Don't say things like that, baby."

"How am I supposed to keep on fighting for an ideal when there's no one left to make it worthwhile?" She took her head in her hands and sobbed harder. "I'm too tired, Patxi. I just want it to be over. I want to go home!"

"You and me, we've taken the hard road. Remember though, we're not alone. Your brother died a martyr. He is a hero who perished because he refused to give in to oppression. He defended his ideals until the bitter end. He died a happy man, because he knew that his death was not in vain. You know why? Because people like us keep on fighting in the name of all the freedom fighters who have met their fate before us."

"I envy you, at times," she said between sniffles. "You stand firm in adversity. Your faith is unwavering."

Patxi shut his eyes tight. If only she knew how he really felt at times. Right this fleeting moment however, he knew he had to be their rock, had to remain strong and focused, no matter what. He put his arm around Anabel's shoulder and said, "Come with me, baby. Let's go for a walk. Just you and me."

They crossed the dirt courtyard and walked side by side under the moon. They strolled up a steep grassy field, which led to the ruins of an abandoned shepherd's refuge. When they reached it, they looked down toward the farm, some five hundred yards below their feet.

The *baserri* had been built on a flat terrace at the center of a sloped grazing field on the southern side of the mountain. It consisted of a one-story building with an adjacent barn, built centuries ago out of crudely cut gray stones which had been laid one on top of another by a Basque family from the province of Navarra. The front door of the house faced the rising sun. Its windows were scarce and narrow in order to offer the best protection against the elements. In the past, the barn was used as a tool shed and a stable to house animals during winter. The house and the barn were topped by a slanted roof made of irregular sheets of slate. To this day, the *baserri* was still standing, rugged and almost unchanged since it was built.

"Do you see all this?" Patxi slowly extended his arm in front of him. "This is the land of our forefathers. They built these homes and broke their backs digging the earth to protect and sustain their families. They herded flocks of sheep across these mountains to provide for their loved ones. This place may not seem like much, but it has weathered the passing of time. It is strong and beautiful in its own way…and it will still be standing long after we're gone. This *baserri* is the very symbol of who we are: *Euskal nazioko seme-alabak gara*, 'the children of the Basque nation.'"

"Patxi?" Anabel wiped a tear from the corner of her eye. "Promise me that you won't die before me."

"Please, don't—"

"Just promise me."

Patxi took her hands into his and said,

"When the time comes for us to die, baby, we'll die together, side-by-side. But I won't let it happen until we're so old and wrinkled that death will actually sound like a good idea." He bit her chin gently and succeeded in coaxing a smile from her, at last. "I want you, baby," he whispered in her ear, "I want you so bad."

Anabel, too, wanted to forget, if only for an instant, about the brutal death of her brother and the reason why they were at the farm in the first place. She wanted to enjoy the moment and savor the taste of her own life while she was still able to. She pulled her head back, exposing her throat to Patxi's kisses while she unbuckled her leather belt. Patxi spun her around slowly. She placed her hands flat against the crumbling wall and spread her legs out as much as the bunched up pants around her ankles would allow. Breathing hard with anticipation and need, Anabel tensed and flexed her body as he entered her from behind. Patches of dry moss and lichens thrived on the dusty stones of the derelict wall, inches away from her face. She filled her nostrils with their musky aroma, inhaling the potent scent of the earth with abandon, while Patxi made love to her.

34
– HOGEITAHAMALAU –

07:07 AM ~ Sunday, August 28, 1994

The train slowed down as it approached the terminal. The nasal voice of a steward came through the speakers, announcing the final destination, Paris-Gare Montparnasse.

Jean-Philippe slung his duffel bag over his shoulder and walked down the aisle toward the end of the car. As the train entered a tunnel, his reflection appeared before him against the glass window. With his blotchy face and unshaven cheeks, he was not much to look at. His eyes were bloodshot from the lack of sleep and the binge drinking he indulged in over the past few days. He tried to smooth out a couple cow-licks from his unruly hair, but the train exited the tunnel at that moment. His reflection disappeared, and was replaced by a grey urban landscape. Jean-Philippe fumbled through his pockets in search of a piece of gum.

A deafening screech as the brakes started to bite into the tracks announced the train's arrival at the station. The train came to a full stop just a few yards away from the massive rubber stoppers that marked the end of the line. Jean-Philippe joined the swarm of sleepy passengers spilling out of every car, walking toward the main concourse. Beyond the gigantic hall, the subway maze of the *Metropolitain* awaited its subterranean passengers. Past the station's main façade of glass stood the unique, bewitching and infuriating city of Paris.

Jean-Philippe had almost reached the end of the platform when he spotted a group of uniformed policemen eyeing passengers as they walked through a bottleneck they had created with crowd-control barriers. With trembling hands, he slid a pair of dark sunglasses up his nose and kept on walking, doing his best to ignore the beads of cold sweat that started to trickle down the small of his back.

The barriers created an impressive traffic jam of pedestrians. In true French fashion, people verbally complained, while they kept pushing and shoving their neighbors mercilessly in a futile attempt to get to the front of the line. Jean-Philippe found himself propelled into the mêlée. Whether he liked it or not, there was no other way to go but to walk through the restriction. Standing to his right, he noticed an old lady who was struggling to keep her ground among the stampeding crowd. He jumped at the chance to come to her rescue. As he had anticipated, the grateful woman thanked him with effusion. Minutes later, Jean-Philippe was walking past the policemen with a grin on his face and a beaming grandmother hanging onto his arm.

"Hey! You in the glasses! Come back here!" Jean-Philippe's body tensed up, but he kept on walking as if nothing had happened. "Hey, *Monsieur!* Are you deaf?" Jean-Philippe heard a commotion somewhere behind him. He looked over his shoulder just in time to see four policemen breaking from the group and hurrying toward him. "You! Yes, you with the lady! Stop right here!"

In the blink of an eye, Jean-Philippe dropped his duffel bag to the ground and broke into a mad sprint among the dense crowd of travelers. The old woman screamed when one of the policemen rushed past her, nearly knocking her off her feet in the process. Helpless, she clutched her purse and watched them running after the gentleman who had just been so kind to her.

Adrenaline pumped through Jean-Philippe's body. He ran as fast as his legs would allow across the vast hall and down the escalators, shoving strangers out of the way when they impeded his progress. The officers were so close that he could hear them barking into their shoulder radios for back up.

The entrance doors finally came into view. If he could make it to the street, he stood a good chance of escaping them. He bolted through the Porte Océane and hung a left onto the Boulevard de Vaugirard. As he peeked over his shoulder to measure the distance between him and his pursuers, he stepped off the curb and never saw the RATP bus coming right at him.

The passengers standing in the center aisle tumbled on top of each other when the bus driver stepped on the brakes with both feet, locking the tires. There was a desperate honk, followed by a splattering of crimson blood across the windshield of the bus. Out on the curb, witnesses of the gory scene let out bloodcurdling screams of terror. A young mother pushing a stroller covered her mouth, only to throw up through her fingers.

Without warning, traffic came to a screeching halt. Oblivious to the cause of the sudden hold up, impatient drivers were honking their horns furiously further up the street. The policemen stopped dead in their tracks as soon as they reached the rapidly forming crowd on the sidewalk. They tried, in vain, to disperse the onlookers. Everywhere, people were shouting and yelling. Sirens could already be heard blaring in the distance. It only took an instant for all hell to break loose on the boulevard.

Just a few yards away, Jean-Philippe's mangled body lay crumpled under the double back wheels of the city bus. The force of impact had killed him instantly.

07:22 AM ~ Sunday, August 28, 1994

If only Faustine had a clue where she was being held captive. Somehow, her gut feeling told her that she was in the mountains still, though not in the valley she knew. The air, for starters, smelled slightly different than back home. It was a little thinner, less pollinated, and had a faint smell of resin. Also, the sound of insects and other flies buzzing outside was not quite as pronounced as what she had grown accustomed to in the Vallée d'Aspe. These elusive clues led her to think that she was at a high elevation on a mountain, somewhere near the junction where green pastures meet dense forests of Scot pine trees and juniper bushes. Undoubtedly, it was a remote location, far away from any roads, and worse, far away from other people.

Faustine heard a faint noise of clanking bells and working dogs barking in the distance. All her senses went on high alert. She strained her ears. A flock of sheep was on its way to, or coming back from, the pastures. In the Pyrenees Mountains, the coming and going of livestock was a reliable clock to clue people in on the time of day. Even though Faustine could not tell whether it was morning or evening, she made a mental note of it, nevertheless, in an effort to keep track of time. She wondered whether the shepherd would be able to hear her screams for help. She yelled at the top of her lungs, again and again, but it proved to be a waste of effort. The clatter of bells started to fade away as the sheep kept marching on valiantly beyond the mountain's ridge.

No one acknowledged her desperate SOS. Not even her kidnappers. Faustine realized, with a heavy heart, that nobody would ever find her here.

11:40 AM ~ Sunday, August 28, 1994

Patxi and Anabel took their seats around the rustic wood table facing a sooty stone chimney with a mantelpiece carved out of a massive oak tree. Santutxo, Mikel, Koldobika and Iñaki followed suit shortly after.

"We have serious business to discuss today, but first things first. Where are Otsoa and Eric?" asked Patxi as soon as he had their undivided attention.

"Not sure," replied Santutxo, "Otsoa took the van early this morning to meet Eric at the train station. They must have been delayed. I'm sure they'll be here soon."

"All right, let's get started without them, then," Patxi retorted. "So here's the situation. While I'm still baffled as to how and why Lartaun got arrested in the first place, it doesn't change the fact that he is now at the mercy of the authorities. If they coax him into revealing the *zulo*'s location, not only will we lose our cargo, but they'll use it as evidence to charge him for the robbery. And you know damn well that if he falls, it's only a matter of time before we all go down with him."

"Evidently, the cache isn't safe anymore," said Mikel.

"That's why our number one priority is to retrieve the explosives," Santutxo replied.

"Easier said than done. Lartaun was the only person we knew to be capable of climbing to the *zulo*," Patxi continued. "With him gone, I have been wondering where I could find a new lead climber. Granted, they are a dime a dozen in the Vallée d'Aspe, but how can you convince a perfect stranger to bring two hundred and fifty pounds of dynamite down a cliff and expect him to keep his mouth shut about it forever? Realistically, it would never work."

"But yesterday, we found the solution to our puzzle. That is part of the reason why the girl is out there in the barn," Santutxo chimed in.

"Lartaun once told me that his girlfriend was a gifted climber. If she's half as good as he claims, she'll save the day for us all," said Patxi.

"That's a valid concept in theory, but what if someone recognizes her? It seems way too risky. Her face must be plastered on 'missing posters' all over the Pyrenees by now," pondered Mikel.

"Not if we give the girl a drastic makeover. I'm sure Anabel can take care of that." Anabel nodded. "Besides, I don't intend to parade her around town. It'll be an 'in-and-out' type of mission," continued Patxi.

"OK," Mikel relented, even though the expression on his face still betrayed his skepticism about the plan's chance for success, "but what if she refuses to help?"

"When Anabel tells her that Lartaun faces life in prison for a robbery that he did not even commit, I bet you she'll agree to help us get rid of the evidence, just to save his ass. If these two love each other the way they claim to, she will do it."

"*Touché*," Mikel agreed with reluctance. "So, who's going to climb with her? Evidently, Eric's out of the picture with his broken leg."

"Jean-Philippe will," Patxi replied without a pause. "As much as I hate the guy, he is the only person left who knows his way to the cache. Besides, he's already climbed up there once. He can do it again."

"That's settled, then," concluded Santutxo.

"We'll go get the dynamite tomorrow at first light. I have the whole battle plan pretty much figured out, but I need Eric's input to iron out the last details. Where the hell are those guys, anyway? It's not like Eric to be late!" Patxi exclaimed in a sudden burst of anger.

"Keep your cool, Patxi. They'll be here soon," promised Santutxo.

"All right. Let's take a break until they get there, then." Patxi sighed warily. He turned to face Anabel next. "Since we have time to kill, how about you go work your magic on the girl?"

"Sure thing." Anabel stood up and left the room.

Minutes later, the other men trickled out the door, one after the other, with the exception of Santutxo who kicked his giant legs up on the table and started to roll a cigarette between his beefy fingers. He casually threw it at Patxi, who caught it in mid air, and rolled another one for himself. They lit them up and smoked in silence. Out of all his men, Patxi respected Santutxo the most because he was unemotional in every crisis. Santutxo was like the eye of a hurricane; calm and quiet, but he made people tremble with fear about what was yet to come. One look into his dark brown eyes was all it took to realize that he could snap a man's neck without thinking twice.

Patxi could not help it; he was a bit jealous of him.

35

-HOGETTAHA MABOST-

11:58 AM ~ Sunday, August 28, 1994

Faustine jerked awake. Someone was rattling the heavy lock of her jail door outside.

"Who's there?"

Although still blindfolded by the bandana and the potato sack, Faustine craned her head toward the stranger who had just entered the room. To her relief, the footsteps sounded like those of the woman who had fed her earlier. The gritty bits of loose stone crunching under her soles gave her position away, and she was headed straight for Faustine.

"Hush! It's me. Be quiet. We've got a lot to do today and very little time for it."

"Wait! Who—who are you?" Faustine stammered in confusion.

"The same person you spoke to yesterday!"

"You barely spoke any French, yesterday!"

"We were never alone before. I didn't want that other guard to know I could communicate with you. Now pay attention. I'm going to untie you and uncover your face. For your own sake, don't even think of doing anything foolish! I'm armed and so is the guard watching the door outside. Can I trust you to do the right thing?"

Faustine, petrified with fear, could do little more than agree with a feeble nod. The serrated edge of a knife sliced through the ropes that bound her wrists and ankles to the cot. The bindings snapped free, allowing the blood to rush to Faustine's numb limbs. Anabel freed her from the nauseating canvas bag and removed her eye-mask. The narrow beams of light, piercing through scattered holes in the roof, blinded her at once. She squinted until her tearing eyes adjusted to the sudden glare. For the first time since her abduction, Faustine was able to take a look at one of her kidnappers.

Her first reaction was surprise. The woman did not fit the picture Faustine had painted of her captors in her mind. She was no GI Jane, with the exception of the heavy assault weapon strapped to her shoulder. Her frame was petite in relation to her height, and she was so skinny that the barrel of her Kalashnikov looked wider than her wrist. Had the situation been different, Faustine could have easily taken her out in a fist fight. Unfortunately, the odds were clearly stacked against her at this moment. Anabel wore a low-rise pair of cargo pants with a clingy long-sleeved T-shirt on top. A wide brown leather belt held her pants up around her narrow hips. Her face was hidden under a jersey hood with two narrow holes cut out in front of her eyes. For a split second, Faustine dared to glance at them. They were blacker than a raven's wing, and they glittered like polished onyx marbles.

As soon as Anabel felt Faustine's inquisitive stare on her, she barked,

"Look at the dirt between your feet unless I tell you otherwise!" Faustine complied at once. "I brought a washcloth and a basin of hot water so you can bathe," Anabel added in a lighter tone, "and here are clean clothes for you."

Faustine followed the hand of her kidnapper pointing to a folded pair of forest green fatigues and a plain white sleeveless shirt folded atop a rickety chair. Her fingers were long and thin, elegant like those of a pianist, except that she had gnawed her fingernails down to the core, making the tips of her fingers look like leprous stumps.

"Could you turn around?" Faustine asked with all the courage she could muster.

"No. Come on, hurry up!"

Faustine promptly obeyed her orders and removed her hospital gown. She sunk the sponge in the water, wrung it between her fingers and proceeded to clean herself. All the while, she stole furtive glances at her prison. The barn was maybe thirty by fifteen feet in size. It consisted of a single open space with a high ceiling and a ten-foot high partition wall, which prevented her from seeing the far left side of the room. Above her head, massive worm-eaten wooden beams stretched across its entire length, supporting a deteriorating roof structure. With the exception of a wide door with an ancient looking beaten-iron lock, there were no other openings within the four thick stone walls. Aside from a few bales of hay, her cot and a chair, the room was bare.

Faustine grabbed the small towel hanging from the tin handle on the basin and toweled off. Then, in a hurry, she put on her clothes. While the stretchy fabric of the small-sized shirt was forgiving enough to fit her, the pants she had been handed down were a couple sizes too large for her waist. They would not stay up.

"Here! Wear this." The woman removed her own belt and threw it at her feet. Faustine reached for it and threaded the belt through the fatigues loops.

"Much better," Anabel commented after studying her prisoner from head to toe. Faustine stood in front of her, ill at ease and wondering what was in store for her next. Even if she could make out the shape of her abductor's lips stretching out the hood fabric whenever she spoke, she could not decipher her expressions. It was unnerving because she could not tell what was going through the woman's mind.

"Can I ask you a question?" Faustine uttered at last. The woman did not answer, so she took it as a yes. "Why are you being kind to me?"

This was one of the last questions Anabel expected her to ask, and she was taken aback for a moment. She appeared to give Faustine's inquiry some thought before she replied matter-of-factly,

"Because you're an innocent person who happened to get caught in the crossfire."

"Why did you take me here?" Faustine asked again with a quivering voice. "What do you want from me?"

"We need your help. Rafael's been arrested by the police, but he's innocent."

"His name's not Rafael!" Faustine hissed at her between clenched teeth. "It's Lartaun!"

She caught Anabel off-guard once again. If Lartaun had told her his real name, Anabel realized that he might have let her in on other secrets as well.

"Tell me everything you know about Lartaun's past!" she barked at Faustine, suddenly aiming at her chest with her Kalashnikov. Faustine cringed at her abrupt mood swing.

"I don't know anything, I swear!" she stuttered the lie in terror, arms outstretched in front of her in supplication. "He told me his name just before we got arrested! He—he never said anything else to me!"

"What did he tell you about his friends?" Anabel's eyes were not flinching, her hands not trembling. Her aim was rock steady.

"Lartaun had no friends that I knew of!" she sputtered with urgency. "He never talked about his past, or present, or anything he was ever up to for that matter! I don't know anything about his life. Nothing! All I know is his name!"

"And you were OK with that?" Anabel's nose wrinkled up in wonder under her mask.

"NO! Of course not!"

"So why didn't you do anything about it, then? Why didn't you ask him questions?"

"Because I fucking love him, that's why!" Faustine snapped out the words, allowing months of built-up frustration to escape her body at once.

The latch on the front door rattled and someone started banging at the door outside.

"Hush!" Anabel said in haste.

"What's with the yelling in there? Is everything OK?" It was Koldobika. He sounded worried.

"Yes, everything's under control!" Anabel shouted back in Basque.

"All right, just checking."

Anabel let out a short sigh of relief. Because she knew Lartaun so well, she believed that Faustine was telling the truth.

"Listen." Anabel dropped the gun by her side and reached for the towel so that Faustine could wipe her tears with it. "We can help Lartaun out of this mess, but we can't do it without you. If you're willing to save him from a lifetime behind bars, you'll do what we ask you to do."

"Like what?"

"Lartaun hid something for us in the mountain, something that belongs to us. We want you to climb to the cache, first thing tomorrow morning, and bring it back down, since he obviously can't do it himself anymore. That's what the police are looking for. When it is gone, they will have no choice but to release him for lack of evidence. If you help us, we'll let you go too, of course."

"How do I know that you're telling the truth?"

"You'll just have to trust us. It might not be the answer you're looking for, but I have no other to give you."

"What if I refuse to help?"

"That's not an option, I'm afraid. Just remember that Lartaun's fate is in your hands. Besides, think about it. All is not lost! When this is over, you and Lartaun still have a shot at happiness. In time, you can put this all behind you. So what is it going to be?"

"I'll do it," Faustine whispered at last.

"Good. Let's get moving, then." Anabel produced a pair of heavy scissors from her thigh pocket. Faustine recoiled against the wall as soon as she eyed the sharp object in her hands. "Sit down and stand still."

Faustine was beginning to understand the woman's intentions. "No! Please, don't!"

"I'm sorry for what I'm about to do, but I have no alternative."

With a snip of her scissors, Anabel cut a thick lock of Faustine's long blond hair. She looked at it in shame for an instant before she let it fall to the ground between their feet. Then she cut another. And another.

Faustine held back the tears as the hooded woman shredded her beautiful mane into a short uneven bob. When she was done, she grabbed the basin filled with what was left of the water, dumped it over Faustine's head and smothered her scalp with a gooey paste the color of dark mud.

"Now we must wait for the dye to take," she said.

Anabel dragged the chair over and sat down six feet across from Faustine with her rifle balanced on her lap. They did not talk for a while. After fifteen minutes or so had lapsed, Faustine broke the silence with the question she had been dying to ask her kidnapper,

"How do you know Lartaun?"

Anabel exhaled forcefully under her hood. "You know where Lartaun was born, don't you?"

"France."

"No, he was born in Irun."

"Is he Spanish, then?"

"Wrong again! He was born in Irun, *Euskadi!* Lartaun's a *Euskaldun*, a Basque citizen!"

"Right, I knew the difference."

"Well that's the whole point! Your boyfriend has always been denied the right to live in his own country! The imperialistic forces have robbed him and his peers of their very identity for centuries with impunity! Wouldn't you fight for your basic human rights if you were in his shoes?"

Faustine's heart sunk into the pit of her stomach upon hearing her words. Had she fallen into the hands of one of those dangerous separatist groups she had heard about on the eight o'clock news? The masked identities, the weapons, the kidnapping… It was all just too terrifying to be real.

"You have every right to feel confused and betrayed right now," Anabel continued, "but you must understand that if Lartaun ever lied to you, it was only to protect you. You must trust that what he's done, he's done it for the right reasons."

"Is Lartaun part of your organization?" Faustine murmured in spite of herself. "Is Lartaun a—*terrorist?*"

Anabel pondered the question for a moment. "Lartaun is not a terrorist. He's a separatist who's sympathetic to our cause. He needed something from us, and we happened to need his assistance in return. We struck a one-time deal together. An exchange of courtesies, if you will."

"What about you? Who are you?"

Anabel clutched the barrel of her Kalashnikov and looked her straight in the eye, as if she was trying to read her mind.

"If a person should understand our struggle, it is you. You're an activist, a militant in your own right, aren't you? You've been fighting tooth and nail against the construction of that tunnel in your valley. In a way, your struggle is similar to ours. You want to right something that is wrong, yet no one cares to hear your voice. For years, you follow protocol. You spend all your energy debating and mediating with politicians. Until one day, you realize that peaceful negotiations lead you nowhere. So you decide to take the matter into your own hands and you retaliate. You agree with what I'm saying, don't you?"

"We don't kill people, though."

"Whatever. You kill machines. You kill the system that brings them to life."

"Maybe so, but machines are what they are. They're lifeless devices. They have no families and no souls. What kind of human being has the heart to watch innocent people die?"

"When you put it bluntly like that, it sounds horrible, I'll give you that. Violence in all its forms is inexcusable. Still, wherever there is a war, there are casualties. It is unavoidable."

"How does someone like you become a terrorist?" Faustine blurted out the words too fast for her to swallow them back in time. She cringed, helpless, waiting for a beating to come, if only to punish her insolence. Yet, Anabel did nothing of the sort. Instead, her eyes shone with brimming emotion. Faustine could have sworn that her chin was trembling.

"Imagine a family whose father was killed during the bombing of Guernica by the German *Luftwaffe* in 1937," she spoke in a low voice. "Imagine a child watching soldiers of the Republican army cry as they drag the remains of her father from the smoldering ashes of what used to be her home, while she hides in the folds of her grieving mother's skirt. Now, picture this kid all grown up as a mother during Franco's dictatorship. She clandestinely teaches *Euskara* to the village kids, in a schoolroom provided by a generous teacher, every Sunday. Time goes by, until one day a handful of fascists find out what she's been up to, and they denounce her to the *Guardia Civil.* As a result of their actions, a squad shows up at Sunday school. They burst into the classroom, upsetting desks and knocking books to the ground as they march down the aisle toward the lectern. They drag the woman into the courtyard by her hair. They beat her up so badly that she loses an eye. And all the while, her students are watching in horror from the classroom window. Now, imagine that her son was one of those kids. Don't you think that this young boy is going to grow up with hatred in his heart for the people who tortured his family? Do you think that he will ever have any respect for the fascists who denied him and his family their fundamental right to be Basque?"

Faustine silently stared at her hair lying on the ground, too shaken to utter a word.

"Again, imagine a twenty-two-year-old man who is accused of a crime he did not commit. Say, the bombing of a police station." Faustine flinched imperceptibly. "In order to save his own life, he has no other choice but to run away. So he does, with the help of his friends. The very next morning, the police come banging at his best friend's door. They drag him out of his house without deeming it necessary to give his family a single word of explanation. They take him to the *comandancia* to interrogate him. They beat him up, and then take turns sodomizing him because he refuses to tell them the lies that they want to hear. Do you think that this broken young man is ready to forgive?" Faustine shook her head "no" in agreement with her kidnapper. "We aren't bad people. We were taught to turn the other cheek at church, just like everyone else," she went on in a melancholic voice, "but there comes a point when the heart cannot forgive anymore. Then, it becomes an eye for an eye. It's a vicious circle."

"The woman you told me about, um, the teacher. Did you know her?" Faustine felt compelled to ask.

Anabel was not willing to tell her that the woman from the story was her mother and the young boy, her older brother, Jose Maria.

"Time's up!" she exclaimed instead. "Let's look at the new you!" Anabel jumped out of her chair to fetch a bucket of fresh water and proceeded to rinse Faustine's hair out. After Faustine toweled her hair dry, Anabel took a couple steps back to inspect her work. "Why don't you—*oye*, what's the word in French?" Anabel pretended to run her fingers through imaginary hair atop her jersey hood.

"Fluff my hair?" Faustine chanced.

"Yes, that's it, fluff it a little."

Faustine diligently complied with her request. Even with the hood masking Anabel's facial expressions, Faustine could tell she was pleased with the result. Faustine's cropped hair had taken a dark auburn hue. Had she known what Anabel looked like without her mask, she would have realized that they were now sporting the same hair color. Her head felt surrealistically light now that the weight of her tresses was gone. The warm air caressing the nape of her bare neck was a brand new sensation.

"You look pretty," Anabel said at last.

Faustine etched a pitiful smile from the corner of her mouth. She was too confused to know whether to smile or cry.

Koldobika's banging on the door made them both jump in surprise.

"Come out! It's meeting time!" he shouted through the door.

"I'll be right out!" Anabel pivoted around to face Faustine. "Sorry, but I must tie you up again."

Faustine did not resist this time. She laid down on the cot, waiting for Anabel to bind her wrists and ankles, then to blindfold her once again. There was just one more thing she needed to understand.

"Why did you tell me all these things?"

"Perhaps I want you to know that we're not always the heartless monsters the media portray us to be." Right when she was ready to leave the room, she added, "Don't worry about tomorrow, it'll be over before you know it, I promise."

"Hey! Wait, hey!" Faustine heard the door swivel shut on its rusty hinges. "Hey!" she repeated, her voice now a murmur. "I don't even know your name..."

02:15 PM ~ Sunday, August 28, 1994

When Anabel and Koldobika joined the rest of the group for

the meeting, they knew right away that something was wrong. Patxi was hunched over at the head of the table, massaging his temples. When he spoke, his voice was hoarse and betrayed his dismay.

"Eric, tell us what you heard."

Seven pairs of worried eyes turned to Eric. He took a big breath and announced,

"Jean-Philippe's dead." The ensuing oppressive silence was almost palpable throughout the room. "I missed the train this morning because Jean-Philippe never showed up at my place to give me a lift to Oloron for the 7:20 westbound train. I figured that, as usual, he must have gotten drunk and passed out. So, when I realized that I was going to miss the meeting if I didn't get moving soon, I thought I'd take my chances and drive, cast and all, to his place to wake him up."

"How did you manage to do that?" asked Mikel.

"I pushed the driver's seat as far back as I could, and I used a broom handle to operate the clutch. It was not pretty, but I made it. Good thing that his house is only a few kilometers away from mine."

"All right then, go on," Koldobika urged him, eager to hear the rest of the story.

"Just when I was about to turn into Jean-Philippe's street, I saw two patrol cars blocking the way. Needless to say, I didn't stick around, but I had to find out what was going on."

"How?" someone inquired.

"You know, gossip travels at the speed of light in tiny villages like these. The best place to hear it firsthand is either at church or at the bar, so I headed straight for the village café. Sure enough, some old folks walked in around eight. One of them had just heard the story straight from the gendarmes' mouths, and he was eager to repeat it."

Eric went on telling the weary assembly the morbid details of Jean-Philippe's untimely demise. Before long, volleys of questions shot from all sides. Anabel wondered, out loud, what Jean-Philippe was doing in Paris in the first place. Koldobika asked, point blank, if Lartaun could have possibly denounced the Frenchman to the police. Mikel worried that the gendarmes would find the stash of weapons hidden inside the well on the De Lancastaing's property. Iñaki went as far as suggesting that his death might be a sign for them to cut their losses and abort OPERATION ASKATA-SUNA altogether.

Everyone at the table talked over each other as tempers flared. Patxi, all the while, shut himself off from the argument. He was gnawing at the inside of his cheek to the point of drawing blood, a stress-fighting habit he took on at a young age, until suddenly...

"SILENCE!" Patxi slammed his fist hard on the table. Everyone instantly shut up. "Have you all lost sight of the big picture?"

Mikel was first to speak up. "We've all put our lives on the line to plan this operation, Patxi. We're not going to back out now. But we must accept the fact that the robbery, no matter how well prepared, was a bust. The police know too much. It would be suicidal to head back to the valley and try to get the dynamite back at this point. It's just too risky."

"Don't you realize that without the *goma,* there is no *ekintza?*" replied Patxi. "You know damn well that we'll never find free explosives in such quantities ever again, and we can't afford to buy it from illegal runners! The stuff inside the *zulo* is all we have. I'll be damned if we don't get it back!"

"Look, Patxi, we want the *goma* as much as you do, but how can we get it? Out of three men who went to stash the loot inside the *zulo,* one never got to see it in the first place," Mikel jabbed his forefinger at Eric as he said those words, "and as far as the remaining two are concerned, one is in custody, and the other is dead!"

"We're up shit creek without a paddle," Iñaki mumbled to no one in particular. "We want the pirate's booty, but we've lost the treasure map with the 'X' marking the spot."

"I can show you the way up to where I fell," Eric ventured. "If luck is on our side, we might be able to stumble upon the cavern."

"Don't you talk about freakin' luck to me right now!" Patxi snapped at him before he turned to Anabel. "Any remote chance that the girl would have heard about the cave?"

"Forget it, she has no clue."

Patxi scratched the blond stubble on his chin, seemingly lost in his thoughts. When he spoke again, his intelligent eyes flickered.

"Eric, you being French and all, tell us what you know about custody laws in your country. I'm curious to hear what is going to happen to Lartaun next."

"Lartaun has nearly reached the maximum legal amount of time that the police can hold him. Forty-eight hours is the law. Technically speaking, either they must release him tonight or they'll charge him with some crime or another to keep him behind bars while the investigation continues. If they choose the latter, they'll have to organize his transfer to jail. Either way, something will happen tonight."

Patxi let the information sink in, and then, without warning, he blurted out,

"We must free Lartaun!"

"Have you lost your freakin' mind?" Anabel shouted as soon as she recovered from the initial shock.

Patxi's icy stare silenced her at once. After her gutsy outburst, no one else dared to say a word. Patxi studied each and every member of the worried assembly with his piercing emerald eyes before he spoke again.

"I don't give a damn if you all think I'm crazy," he said haughtily, "but I just thought of a fail-proof plan to organize Lartaun's escape. So what is it going to be? Are you with me or not?"

"Let's get Lartaun out or die trying!" Santutxo exhorted the assembly. As always, he was the most determined of the bunch. One after the other, the others agreed, albeit with varying degrees of conviction in their voices. The fleeting shadow of a smile passed across Patxi's lips.

"I knew I could count on all of you," he spoke with renewed confidence. "Now let me tell you what I have in mind for tonight. We must seize this small window of opportunity while we can!"

36
- HØGEITAHAMASEI -

06:55 PM ~ Sunday, August 28, 1994

For the first time since she had been abducted, Faustine finally felt capable of processing rational thoughts. Even though she was still at the mercy of her kidnappers, she, at least, had the chance to see and interact with one of them. No matter how radical or twisted the woman's convictions were, she actually was somewhat decent. That alone was a comfort to her. Faustine thought about her mother and wondered whether she knew what had become of her. It made her sad because nothing would ever be the same. The days of innocence belonged to the past. They slipped through her fingers, never to be enjoyed again. And Lartaun… She wanted to hate him so much for being the catalyst of all these misfortunes, but instead, she longed for him with all her heart.

The woman promised that Lartaun would be set free if she would help them tomorrow. Even though it was a promise made in the sand, Faustine was holding onto it with all her might.

07:20 PM ~ Sunday, August 28, 1994

Frédéric Blanchard's patience was wearing thin.

His tried-and-true strategy to pry a confession out of suspects, or at least some key information, failed miserably with Lorenzo Lartaun Izcoa. To make matters worse, another promising suspect, Jean-Philippe De

Lancastaing, was dead, and Izcoa's girlfriend was kidnapped right before their eyes. The viewing of the hospital surveillance tapes brought forth the visual of a suspicious-looking female. Unfortunately, the video quality was poor, and they could not match her portrait to any known criminal in their database. While the investigation was stalling, the scoldings from their respective superiors proved relentless.

Jean-Claude Boréda marched into his office, brandishing a stamped form signed by the examining magistrate of the Court in Pau.

"Izcoa just returned from his hearing. We've got the authorization for his transfer!"

"It's about time!" Vilorain replied with a grunt. "When?"

"Eleven o'clock tonight. The prison director isn't thrilled. He argued that his workforce is spread thin enough as it is on Sundays, but we've got it all sorted out."

"Great. Hopefully I'll sleep better tonight knowing that Izcoa is under lock and key in a proper jail."

"I want to have one last talk with him before he goes," Blanchard announced without bothering to lift his head from the document he was perusing. "I want to strike him right where it hurts and let him simmer overnight."

"What's your trump card this time?" enquired Boréda.

"The cold hard truth. I'm gonna wait till the last minute before I break the news to him that his lovely girlfriend has been kidnapped and may very well be in peril. See, the man has never gone to jail before. I think that a sleepless night in the can will help him understand his predicament. If I play this well, I bet you that by tomorrow he'll be singing like a canary."

"It's worth a shot," Boréda commented unconvincingly.

"Oh, by the way, Vivienne Laroche left a message for you while you were gone," Blanchard spoke again. "She asked me to thank you again for all you've done for her, and she would like to return the favor by inviting you for a drink, if you've got the time one of these evenings. I think she likes you!" he added with a wink.

"It must be another one of her clever tricks to finagle me into granting her the right to visit her daughter," Boréda quipped, doing the best he could to hide his embarrassment. "Believe me, the day a radical woman like Vivienne falls for a cop like me, pigs will fly!"

"With sufficient thrust, pigs fly just fine," Vilorain was quick to answer.

Boréda laughed. Vilorain could be funny when he set his heart to it.

10:57 PM ~ Sunday, August 28, 1994

When the escort patrol walked over to Lartaun's cell, with Boréda in the lead, they found him pacing in circles like a caged animal. Boréda knew just by looking at Lartaun Izcoa's face that Blanchard had found his Achilles' heel. Telling him of Faustine's abduction opened a deep wound from which the young man might never recover. Lartaun looked sick with ire. The second he saw the gendarmes approaching, his anger flared with a vengeance.

"Liars!" he screamed in their direction.

Blanchard shot him a sardonic smile and waved good-bye. "Sleep on it, Izcoa! We'll chit-chat in the morning!"

Izcoa glared at him, but he knew better than to say anything.

"Time to go, sir," the officer sternly said as he placed him in handcuffs. Lartaun did not resist. Flanked by two gendarmes, one holding him by the collar of his sweater, Lartaun headed down the hall toward the exit doors.

Two dark blue vehicles with the word GENDARMERIE stenciled in white block letters on their sides were parked in front of the building. Five gendarmes stood close by waiting for the prisoner. They all wore the same uniform, a light blue short-sleeved shirt and navy blue trousers with a black stripe down the side of the leg, shiny black leather shoes and a *képi*, which they held in their hands in lieu of their heads due to the muggy summer heat. The group broke off as soon as Lartaun came into view. Two officers jumped into the front seat of the escort vehicle leading the convoy while Lartaun Izcoa was ushered into the back seat of the second car. A gendarme sat down next to him, and the remaining two sat in the front. Everyone expected the transfer to take less than fifteen minutes since the prison was only located a mile and a half away from the station downtown. The small convoy took off quietly down the Cours Léon Bérard. The cars veered to the right onto the deserted Avenue Dufau and steadily picked up speed toward their bleak destination.

The lead car just turned onto Rue Viard, two blocks away from the prison. A black station wagon with its lights off came barreling down the tiny one-way street they had just passed on their left and smashed into the second vehicle at full speed. It T-boned the patrol car squarely on the driver's side, causing it to skid sideways and sending it crashing against the curb on the opposite side of the street. The driver of the first car was so stunned by the scene he just witnessed in his rearview mirror that he realized, a second too late, he too, was on collision course with another van coming straight at him in the middle of the street. He braced himself for the inevitable impact, his facial features distorted by dread. Next to him, his partner let out a shrill scream of panic and covered his head with his arms in reflex.

There was a hair-raising din of crushing metal and glass when the hood of the police car folded into a concertina under the station wagon bumper, and the car windshield imploded into a thousand pieces. The violence of the shock in both crashes was tremendous, stunning all passengers inside.

Patxi and his gang jumped out of their vans like jacks-in-the-box. In two shakes of a lamb's tail, they knocked out, disarmed, gagged and tied up the five policemen with their own sets of handcuffs. In the mayhem, none of the policemen even had the chance to radio the station for back up or draw their weapons.

The loud noise of the pile-up caused the neighborhood to stir from its sleep. One after another, little squares of light appeared behind closed windows, lighting up the dark street like candles in a Christmas tree. Santutxo pulled Lartaun out of the car and dragged him toward a third vehicle idling twenty yards down the side street. The rest of the posse followed suit.

Somewhere up the second floor of the building across from where the getaway car stood, a window opened with a bang. A bare-chested man stuck his head out and proceeded to shout a string of expletives at the vandals causing the ruckus below. As soon as he caught a glimpse of Santutxo's black shadow pointing a rifle straight at him, he slammed his window shut in haste.

The four men and Lartaun piled into the car and took off into the night, tires screeching. Lartaun, sandwiched between two hooded men in the back of the car, was too stunned from the accident to fully grasp what was going on. He clutched the brown paper envelope containing his personal belongings in his cuffed hands, ignoring the blood dripping onto it from a deep gash above his right eyebrow.

Within minutes, they reached an industrial zone in the outskirts of town. Streetlights were few and far between. The driver stopped the vehicle at the end of a narrow alleyway ending in a cul-de-sac. The area was dark and deserted with the exception of a lone car parked in front of a loading dock fifteen yards away from them.

"Everyone, step out," someone mumbled in Basque.

"Who are you?" Lartaun asked the group.

"How about a 'thank you' for starters, for saving your sorry ass once again from a trip to the can?"

Lartaun would always recognize that voice in a million. "Patxi? What the—?"

"Listen carefully," Patxi interrupted. He pointed to Mikel, the driver, and Iñaki, the hooded man sitting to the left of Lartaun. "These two must head back to *Euskadi* right away." He signaled to Santutxo, who was sitting to his right. "Meanwhile, the three of us are going to drive to Eric's place to spend the night. We will head out for the *zulo* tomorrow at first light."

"Do you realize what you just did to those cops, back there?" Lartaun said in sudden panic. "Do you want to get us all killed?"

"Shut up! You aren't the ringmaster in this operation," Patxi snapped. "We got you out of this mess because I want my dynamite back. You still have a job to complete, don't you know?"

Lartaun stumbled out of the vehicle along with the other men, who did not waste any time changing back into civilian clothing. He felt dizzy. The left side of his body throbbed as a result of the accident. Patxi leaned against the same wall Lartaun was holding onto for support and casually lit a cigarette.

"Do you want me to take a look at it?" he said, pointing at Lartaun's forehead. "You're pissing blood, *txo!*"

"Don't you touch my fuckin' head," Lartaun said menacingly. He turned around slowly to face his friend. "I want you to answer this, though. Did you, or did you not, have anything to do with Faustine's disappearance?" Patxi did not reply. "Don't make me ask you twice!"

"Yes, we've got her!" Patxi blurted. "She's fine! We took good care of—"

Lartaun sucker-punched him, mid-sentence, with all the strength he had left. Patxi slumped onto the pavement. He could not even let out a scream of pain because Lartaun had knocked the wind out of him. He lay at Lartaun's feet, doubled over on the asphalt with his arms clutching his abdomen.

"*Sasikumea!*" cursed Lartaun. He spat on the ground next to Patxi, who was still reeling in pain. "You're nothing but a sick bastard!"

Santutxo was ready to throw himself at Lartaun when Patxi stopped him dead in his tracks with a firm wave of the hand.

"But, Patxi!" he began to protest.

"Leave us. Leave us alone," Patxi groaned, barely able to breathe. "Go help the others prep the car."

Santutxo reluctantly stepped away from Lartaun, but not without shooting him a killer glance first.

Mikel and Iñaki were almost finished erasing the fingerprints and cleaning the blood left by Lartaun inside the stolen car. They quickly switched the plates and added a couple decals to change the general appearance of the vehicle. They were ready to drive it back to Irun. Within a few seconds of their departure, there were no traces of their fleeting presence in the dirty backstreet other than a faint whiff of gasoline lingering in the stifling August night.

Patxi, Santutxo and Lartaun had to get moving, too. Patxi slowly got back on his feet and asked his accomplice,

"Did you double check that all the gear is in the trunk?" Santutxo nodded affirmatively. "All right, then," Patxi added somberly, "come on, Lartaun, we've got to go."

The trio hurried toward the second vehicle further up the alley. Upon approaching the car, Lartaun froze in his tracks.

"Hey! What about my stuff?" he asked the others.

"What the hell are you talking about?" Santutxo exclaimed without slowing down.

"Those—those guys that just left," Lartaun mumbled in consternation, "they took off with my envelope!"

37

— HOGEITAHAMAZAZPI —

04:45 AM ~ Monday, August 29, 1994

Anabel shook Faustine awake.

"Eat this," she said rather curtly, pointing at a bowl of cereal with milk. "You don't want to climb on an empty stomach."

Faustine rubbed her eyes and accepted the food. She, much like her warden, was not in a chatty mood this morning. Besides, they were not alone today. Otsoa stood guard inside the barn with a nine-millimeter handgun aimed at Faustine. As soon as Faustine finished breakfast, Anabel tied her wrists again. She sat down in front of Faustine and inspected her face with great attention. She dipped a sponge into a small vial of liquid make up and proceeded to apply a thick coat of foundation all over Faustine's face, ears, neck and arms in order to darken her complexion. She worked with the industriousness of an ant. Anabel was so close to her at times that Faustine could smell her scent. It was a combination of the perfume that she wore the day before, lingering on her skin like a sweet afterthought of spices and exotic woods, mixed with the unmistakable smell of fear. Her ebony eyes shone behind the narrow slits of her hood. They darted back and forth in a desperate effort to elude Faustine's stare. She began to wonder whether Anabel was dreading the day that loomed ahead as much as she was.

Anabel blindfolded her once again before she and Otsoa led her out of the barn. Faustine would never know where she had been held captive. A male voice ordered her to climb into the backseat of a foul-smelling truck.

"No move!" Anabel unfolded a plaid blanket over Faustine's lap to conceal the cable ties around her wrists. "Pretend you sleep! All trip!" she instructed her.

The watch guard took a seat next to her and poked her in the ribs with the barrel of his gun, a reminder to keep on her best behavior. The worn-out suspension of the truck creaked one more time as someone else climbed into the driver's seat and started the engine.

"Good luck!" Anabel whispered to Faustine.

"Wait! You're not coming?" Faustine asked in sudden panic.

"You fine. You no worry. *Agur.*" She slammed the door and stepped away from the vehicle as it started to move. Faustine bit her lips in despair. There she was again, lost and helpless inside a mysterious vehicle, jolting along an unknown dirt mountain trail, with two armed strangers whose language she could not understand.

Three quarters of an hour into the trip, they stopped for gas.

"Shush!" the driver ordered Faustine, even though she did not make the slightest noise the whole trip. The pump attendant knocked at the driver's window and asked,

"*J'vous fais le plein?*"

"Yes. Fill'er up," replied the driver.

In spite of her anxiety, Faustine felt a sudden wave of relief wash over her upon hearing someone speaking her language. They were back in France.

The van reached its final destination two hours later, around nine o'clock in the morning.

"Follow, er, diz man. Him know road," the driver explained to Faustine in broken French. Otsoa unlocked her side of the truck and pulled Faustine out with little consideration. He held her by the forearm while they waited for the vehicle to drive away and slip out of view. At long last, Otsoa removed Faustine's eye mask with his free hand.

He was about the same size as she, with a stocky build and brawny arms. A red beanie was pulled down his head all the way to his bushy eyebrows. He had tied a black bandana over his nose and mouth to further conceal his identity.

"Where are we?" Faustine mumbled in French. The man seemed confused. He spread his hands in front of him and shrugged his shoulders to communicate that he did not understand her language. Before she could say anything else, he gave her a "look-at-me" signal with two fingers pointed toward his eyes and lifted his shirt just enough for Faustine to see the gun tucked into the waistband of his pants. He showed her the way to go. She quickly nodded her understanding and started walking ahead of him up a narrow hiking trail meandering through a thick forest.

After trekking for a while, the sound of a branch cracking in the distance startled them. They stopped dead in their tracks and strained their ears to locate the source of the noise.

"What was that?" whispered Faustine, her senses in full alert.

Otsoa put a finger to his lips to tell her to keep quiet while he kept on listening. This time around, they heard the unmistakable sound of footsteps on dry leaves. People were headed their way, and they were close. Otsoa drew his gun from under his shirt. He grabbed Faustine, covered her mouth with his free hand and forced her to crouch down behind the thick roots of an oak tree. She stifled a cry of surprise, but knew better than to struggle. They stood still for what felt like an agonizing amount of time, their breaths shallow. Meanwhile, the noise they heard instants before stopped altogether. Whoever the strangers were, they must have felt their presence too. In bear territory, one had better be cautious. Otsoa let out two short whistles. Within seconds, someone whistled right back at him in the same fashion. It was a code. Otsoa let out a sigh of relief and relaxed his grip on the gun handle.

"What's going on?" Faustine whispered again through his fingers.

"OK," he murmured into her ear, "come!"

He helped her back on her feet, and they stepped back onto the trail. Faustine made out the silhouette of a man hurrying toward them through the foliage. Even though she would never hear his name or see his face, Faustine was about to meet Patxi for the first time. She craned her neck to take a better look at the two men following him and nearly fell over in shock. Lartaun was among them. In fact, he was the only one of the three who had not covered his face to mask his identity. He, too, looked in her direction. He gaped at her, stupefied, as soon as he realized who she was.

"Faustine!" he shouted. He elbowed Patxi out of his way and hurried toward her. As soon as they met, he drew her tight against him, and she buried her face into his chest. "What did these sick bastards do to you?"

Lartaun looked at Faustine with a pain-stricken expression while he ran his fingers nervously through her freshly chopped hair. Faustine, fighting back tears, slowly lifted her chin to look him in the eyes. She let go of him, and before Lartaun could see what was coming, she punched him in the mouth with her bound fists as hard as she could. Lartaun took the blow without flinching. A rivulet of crimson blood started to flow from the corner of his mouth, staining the brown beard growing on his chin.

"How could you," she hissed, "how could you do this to us?"

"Faustine—" Lartaun was going to say something, but he shut his mouth instead. There were no words of excuse or explanation. What happened to her was entirely his fault. The suffering he caused her was inexcusable, and nothing would make up for it.

"Just look at us, Lartaun! Look at me!" She lifted her wrists right up to his nose so that he could see the dark laceration marks and bruises on her skin, which were inflicted by the cable ties. "Look at what you let them do to me!" she cried in desperation.

Patxi picked that particular moment to separate the pair.

"I think you've made your point, lady," he said calmly. He grabbed Faustine by the shoulder to pull her away from Lartaun. "Now let's go. We don't have all day."

Faustine swiveled around in a flash, her eyes filled with hatred.

"Eat shit!" she yelled to his face. She spun her head toward Patxi's giant henchman and screamed, "And fuck you too! And you!" she added, jutting her chin at Otsoa, "Yeah, you—"

"I said that's enough!" Patxi cut her off, mid-sentence, and yanked her by the hair. Lartaun was about to lash out at Patxi's throat when he felt the cold pressure of a gun against his temple.

"I suggest you stay out of this," Otsoa said behind him in a stone-cold voice.

"Put down that weapon," Patxi ordered Otsoa at once. He wrapped his hand around the barrel of the gun and pushed it away from Lartaun's head. "All right, *txo,*" Patxi addressed Lartaun next with a wary sigh, "let's get this over with once and for all. Show us the way to the *zulo.*"

Lartaun started up the trail in silence, with the small group falling in a single file behind him.

11:55 AM ~ Monday, August 29, 1994

Faustine and Lartaun progressed at a good clip up the slick lime-stone cliff leading to the cavern. They both cleared the first two rope-lengths of the course and hauled the four empty backpacks in record time. During the strenuous climb, they paused just long enough to allow their muscles to relax so as to keep up with the sustained pace they set. Once rested, they moved further up the forbidding crag toward the *zulo,* two hundred and fifty vertical feet from where Patxi and his acolytes stood.

Faustine was at second belay, monitoring Lartaun's progression along the treacherous dihedral, one hundred and eighty feet above the forest canopy. This one last segment was proving to be an even more chal-lenging climb than what she feared upon first sighting. She was painfully aware that she would have no option but to free climb it, for the gear rack they were provided did not contain any climbing aids to help her through the toughest passages. So she could mimic them later when her turn came, she studied Lartaun's fluid moves with an eagle eye.

"Safe!" Lartaun shouted moments after he had disappeared into the *zulo.*

"You're off belay!" Faustine's voice echoed against the mountain.

"OK, climb up whenever you're ready!"

Faustine was anxious. She was not ready to leave the security of the belay just yet. She perused the vast expanse of rock towering above her, suddenly feeling inadequate and skeptical of her climbing abilities. She scanned the horizon with the futile hope of finding someone who would see an SOS. Aside from a pair of bearded vultures riding the high winds in large circles near the top of a distant summit, the mountains were deserted. A feeling of loneliness overwhelmed her. This time, more than ever, she needed to hear Lartaun's shouts of encouragement because they always helped her regain her confidence, but Lartaun's voice could not be heard that day.

"Hey, you! What's the hold up?" Patxi shouted impatiently from below, after he watched her procrastinate at belay for several minutes. For Faustine, that was the last straw.

"Do you want to meet me here and give it a try yourself?" she yelled back at him.

Patxi was not accustomed to being verbally challenged like that. Stunned by her gutsy statement, especially given the amount of stress she was under, he could not think of a smart reply right away. Lartaun, who just listened to their tense exchange, urgently called down to Faustine.

"Don't pay attention to them!" he shouted. "Clear your head and forget your fears! I know that you can do this! Piece o' cake!"

Upon hearing Lartaun's familiar expression, an immediate surge of determination overtook Faustine. She shook her limbs and breathed deeply to re-oxygenate her body. She unclipped the quick draw that was tethering her to the face and, with renewed confidence, went on the offensive against the cliff.

When Faustine swung her legs over the lip of the cavern with one last grunt of effort, Lartaun extended his hand. She refused his help. She crawled to the center of the cavern and let her eyes adjust to the dimly lit space. Lartaun saw her body stiffen as soon as she noticed the logs of dynamite stacked one on top of the other atop the flat stone outcropping.

"You've got to be shitting me!" she whispered in awe, unable to pry her eyes away from the incongruous pile on display before her eyes. "What are they going to do with all this?"

"I don't know, and I don't want to know," he replied in a dispirited voice.

She turned around and stared at Lartaun defiantly. "Don't you get it? They're going to blow something up! Those guys below, they're crazy-ass terrorists! And don't you pretend you didn't know that!"

"I don't know what their plans are, Faustine," he continued with the same disheartened tone. "I sympathize with their struggle, but that's where it ends. I'm not one of them."

"Oh yes—yes you are! By helping them, you help their cause, and that makes you a terrorist too!" Faustine kneeled in front of the mound of explosives and covered her mouth in revulsion. "We can't hand them the dynamite just like that! We just can't!"

"It's not like we have a choice."

"Oh, really? Why don't we let them come and get it themselves if they want it so badly?" Lartaun reached out for her. He tried to take her tormented face in his callused hands, but she pushed him away. "You do whatever you want, but I'm not touching this shit!" she said at last.

At a loss, Lartaun tried to explain. "I told you about this, back when we were on the mountain. I made a deal with the man waiting below. He honored his side of it by bringing me back home from Mexico. Now, it is my turn to—"

"You never told me what it was exactly you had agreed to do in exchange!" she snarled at him.

"I agreed to bring the dynamite down from the *zulo* and to help them carry the load to a secret meeting point over the Spanish border where a car will be waiting for us at seven o'clock tonight."

"And then what?"

"He and I will be even. I won't owe him anything anymore."

"How could you agree to such a sick deal?" Faustine asked in amazement, searching his eyes for a viable explanation.

"Only because I got the details of the mission when I was already back in France!" Lartaun could hardly stand Faustine's angry looks, but he owed her an explanation. "Look, Faustine, I'm fully aware that it doesn't make the situation any more acceptable, but try to understand my position. I lost everything on the night that I was forced to flee my country. My past, my future and everything in between! Overnight, I was a man on the run in Mexico. I managed to elude the police, but a free man I sure as hell was not! I was a fugitive, Faustine, and a fugitive, even if innocent, cannot embrace freedom. So what if the bars of my cage were invisible to the naked eye? They were there, all right. I was desperate for a second chance, I wanted out of San Cristóbal! So when my best friend dangled the key to a Pandora's Box right in front of my nose, I ran with it! Yes, I was perfectly aware that the offer came with strings attached, and yes, I realized that my involvement in this operation could get me into all kinds of serious trouble down the road. I knew of the despicable and unethical nature of the job, but at the time I thought, 'how could hell be any worse than my life here on earth?' Look, Faustine, I don't expect you to understand, but I would have sold my soul to the devil for the chance to start a new life as a man with no past!"

"And so you did," Faustine said after a moment of intense reflection. "You're not a bad person. You fell victim to your convictions, and someone took advantage of your desperate situation. Still, for the life of me, I can't comprehend how that sick prick below could have once been your best friend!"

"We were different people back then. I didn't blow up the police station, and neither did he. We were fighting for a better world, but things went sour. Down the road, the hardships in our lives caused us to change and to take different paths. It's not up to me to judge his actions."

"Whatever. Shit happens to all of us, and we don't expect mitigating circumstances for the stupid mistakes we make along the way. Why should he get the special treatment, huh? I say you don't owe him anything. Zero, *zilch, nada!*"

"Actually, I do. That's why I must keep my end of the bargain."

"Wake up, Lartaun! It doesn't take a genius to get the big picture! Refusing to help those deranged weirdos does not make you a weak man or a traitor! If you don't want the blood on their hands to drip onto yours, you must stop them now. Because if you don't, you become instrumental in their destructive plans, and in the end, you're just as guilty as they are!"

"Can't you see that my hands are tied? I can't control their actions! I can't stop fate! I wish I were the knight in shining armor coming to save the day, but I'm just a regular Joe! And yes, if you really wanna know, I'm scared shitless, too!"

"Then, look at it this way. If you must honor the deal you made with them, then so be it. Give them their goddamn dynamite! But you have to promise me that you'll do everything in your power to stop them from putting those explosives to use." Faustine's countenance surprised even her. "You're the only one who knows who they are. Well, one of them at least. Seize the chance to redeem yourself! Only you can stop them before something terrible happens!"

"I wish I could," Lartaun shook his head in despair, "but there's a price on my head. You see, the gendarmes didn't set me free last night. These guys below, they arranged for my escape. I wish I could do what you're asking, but I can't. The police will catch me if I don't leave the country right away. I'm sorry."

Faustine took her head in her hands, admitting defeat.

"I don't blame you for running away. Hell, I would even go with you. But if you can't promise to stop these terrorists first, then I never want to hear from you again. I can't love a man whose hands are stained by the blood of innocent people."

Lartaun's eyes filled with infinite sadness. He caressed her cheek tentatively with his bleeding thumb, then her lips. It was not that he did not want to go after Patxi, but he was running out of time. The manhunt had already begun. And this time around, Lartaun had very little faith that he would manage to stay free, let alone alive, for too long unless he left the country as soon as possible.

"I agree with every word that you just said, *maitea,*" he murmured, a painful smile stretched across his dry lips, "but I can't make a promise I'm not sure I can keep."

38

_ HOGEITAHEMEZORTZI _

01:27 PM ~ Monday, August 29, 1994

"*¡Hijo de la gran puta!*" Patxi cursed between clenched teeth.

He squinted against the sun, trying to figure out why the bags had not yet come to view alongside the cliff. "What's going on up there?" he bellowed with his hands cupped around his mouth. "Are you done loading up the bags?"

Lartaun rushed to the entrance of the cavern and shouted, "I'm almost done!"

He turned back around and set out to work in a frenzy. He unclipped the empty bags from the static rope and set them down next to the stack of dynamite. Careful to avoid Faustine's accusing stare, he loosened the top flap of the first backpack and started filling it with the volatile cargo. He moved on to the next one, then the third, until all four bags were bulging with dynamite.

"What will they do to me when we get back down?" Faustine asked with a tremor in her voice.

"They'll make you promise that you never saw anything. Then they'll let you go, and you'll never hear from them again."

"How can you be so sure?"

"The man below, he is who he is, but he told me that's what he was going to do. So, that's exactly what he'll do."

"I don't want to go back down. I don't want to lose you."

"You'll always be with me wherever I go, *maitea.*"

"That's nothing but a bunch of fucking words, Lartaun, and you know it!" she yelled without warning. They looked away from each other, knowing only too well that they had reached the end of their rope.

Faustine and Lartaun were about to leave the *zulo* when Faustine exclaimed,

"Lartaun, wait! You forgot one!"

She just noticed a lone stick of dynamite lying on the ground. She pointed at it with her index finger. Lartaun picked it up from the floor and set it back with care on the flat rock platform before saying,

"That's OK. Let it be our secret. You and I will be the only ones to ever know that it is there." Faustine shot him a quizzical look, but Lartaun had already returned to the edge of the cavern. "Sending the bags down!" he called out to the men below.

"Be careful!" Patxi shouted back, "I don't know how stable this stuff is!"

Patxi and his two men craned their necks as they watched the bags descend along the face of the mountain, cringing every time they seemed to snag onto rock protrusions. Meanwhile, Faustine secured her abseiling device to a double rope that had seen better days. She started repelling toward belay, then Lartaun followed suit. They repeated the same maneuver once more in order to reach belay number one.

Patxi pounced on the backpacks the very second they touched the ground. He quickly verified the contents of the bags and exhaled with relief. It had been a nightmare, but the explosives were at his feet, at long last.

In four big jumps, Lartaun abseiled down the last pitch and landed between Santutxo and Otsoa. Just to be on the safe side, he had decided to go down first so that Faustine would not have to stand around them alone while waiting for him.

Faustine was busy sorting out the ropes for her last rappel when Lartaun looked up to check on her.

"Coming down!" she warned them.

Faustine zipped down the cliff. She was still a good forty feet off the ground when she noticed, albeit too late, one strand of her double rope was half-severed as it slid through the ring of her figure-eight belay device. She stared at the frayed thread inching away from her with a sink-ing feeling in her stomach. Instantly, she felt a sudden loss of tension on the rope, causing her to suddenly drop a foot or two. She muffled a scream of surprise and peered at the belay fifty feet above her head with growing concern. One of the three anchor points just popped out of the rock. Seconds later, another piton flew off the face with a metallic sound, sending her tumbling down another couple of feet.

"Oh God, no! LARTAUN!" she screamed in terror.

"Get down, Faustine, hurry! The belay's crapping out on you!" Lartaun yelled at the top of his lungs.

Faustine, terrified, released the pressure of her grip on the rope in order to pick up speed, but it was too late. The damaged strand, further strained by the two sudden shocks it just sustained, snapped in two. Faustine seemed to hover in the air for a brief instant as the severed end snaked upwards and slipped through the last of the anchoring bolts. She let out a blood-curdling scream as she plunged at a dizzying speed toward the ground, her hands still clutching the climbing rope for dear life.

Lartaun shut his eyes and pressed his knuckles against his mouth while the three other men watched on, helpless, a frozen look of horror distorting their faces under their masks.

Faustine hit the higher branches of an oak tree growing at the foot of the face before she crashed and bounced onto the ground like a rag doll. Her limp body rolled several feet down the slope, only to be stopped by a large boulder in the way.

"Faustine!" Lartaun leaped to the spot where Faustine lay, still as death. He knelt down beside her, but his trembling hands were not quite able to touch her just yet.

"Is she dead?" Patxi asked hesitantly. He was too stunned to bring himself to turn around and look.

"I beg you, say something," Lartaun murmured in Faustine's ear, his shaking body hunched over hers in a protecting embrace.

"Is she breathing?" Patxi inquired again, inching his way toward them.

Lartaun spun around and bared his teeth at him like a cornered beast, eyes wild with grief and anger.

"Stand back!" he yelled. "Leave us alone!" Patxi complied with the order in silence. Lartaun returned his attention to Faustine. "I'm right here, *maitea*. Everything's going to be fine, I promise. Open your eyes please, wake up. Wake up!" Faustine's eyes fluttered lightly, and then she moaned.

It was the faint, low-pitched sound of a wounded animal. "She's conscious!" Lartaun shouted with relief. She whimpered again, with slightly more energy this time. "Don't move. Just relax. I'm right here. I won't go anywhere without you." Faustine reopened her eyes for a brief instant.

"Pain!" she moaned, "so—much—pain."

"I know, *maitea,* I know. You took a big fall, but you're going to be fine. You're going to be just fine."

"I—can't feel my legs!" she struggled to enunciate the words. In truth, she could hardly breathe at all.

Patxi mustered the courage to approach them again. He tugged at Lartaun's sleeve.

"You should let 'O' take a look at her."

"Who? Him?" Lartaun sneered, pointing his finger in Otsoa's direction. "Why?"

"He did his *servicio* in a Spanish military hospital. He can help, I think."

Lartaun nodded his approval after a second of hesitation, and Otsoa came forward. He knelt by Faustine's side in order to check her vital signs and neuromuscular reflexes. She grimaced in pain as soon as he laid his hands on her to check for broken bones.

"So?" Patxi asked, his hands nervously clasped together in front of his mouth.

"Well, I'm no doctor," Otsoa said, "but she's conscious and she's not vomiting. Her reflexes checked out fine. It seems like her spinal cord may have been spared in the fall."

Lartaun shut his eyes, praying that Otsoa was right.

"She's not out of danger, evidently," Otsoa continued. "She could have a concussion or internal injuries. I can feel broken bones. She needs medical attention right away."

"What are we going to do? It's getting late!" Santutxo muttered after checking his watch. They were expected to meet with Koldobika at seven o'clock on the dot. Should they miss their rendezvous over the border, the driver would assume that the mission had failed, and he would drive away without them. After all the trouble that they had gone through to retrieve the explosives, they could not let that happen under any circumstances.

"Can I talk to you in private?" Patxi asked Lartaun after he quickly conferred with Santutxo. He stepped away from the area where Faustine lay in great pain, and Lartaun followed him reluctantly. "We must go. We're running out of time," he told him, in *Euskara*, so that Faustine could not overhear their conversation.

"You'll have to go without me. Faustine needs me." Lartaun responded.

"That's impossible. How will we get there without you to guide us?"

"I'll show you the way to go. It's really not that difficult."

"But who will carry the fourth backpack?"

"Just look at her! Do you really think that I give a shit about your *goma* right fuckin' now?" Lartaun yelled at Patxi.

"But—"

"Santutxo is strong as a bull. He can carry one in the front and one on his back. When push comes to shove, he'll have to ditch a bag along the way. All things considered, three bags are still better than none!"

Patxi nodded somberly in agreement, and Lartaun gave him the directions to the secret meeting point.

"What are you going to do with her?" Patxi asked toward the end of their exchange.

"I have to get her to a hospital."

"How? There's nothing around here for miles!"

"I'll find a way."

"You know what, *txo?* Santu thinks that I should kill you both. He says I'm nuts to let you go because the gendarmes will catch you the second you get back onto the main road."

"So why don't you? You know you won't stop me from getting Faustine to safety unless you kill me. What would you do if it were Anabel lying there?"

Patxi knew fully well that he would do the exact same thing.

"Just go then," he mumbled, "you've wasted enough time already."

"I'll tell you one thing, though. I won't let the *txakurrak* catch me again. I'd rather kill myself than become their prisoner. Now if you would give it to me…"

"Give you what?"

"The knife, *txo!*"

Last night at Eric's, Lartaun asked Patxi for a weapon once they parted ways. He didn't intend to use it solely for protection, but as a way to take his own life should he be cornered.

"Oh, yes. Right." Patxi produced an ornate pocket-knife, the han-

dle of which had once been carved out of a cow's horn by a skilled crafts-
man. Even folded, it was a good four inches in length. Lartaun recognized
it at a glance because it had belonged to Patxi's father. He had given it to
his son on his deathbed after engraving Patxi's initials, CPA, for Cayetano
Pantzeska Antxustegi, below his own. Patxi reluctantly handed the blade
to Lartaun. "You understand that this is just a loan, right? Take good care
of it."

"*Eskerrik asko*," Lartaun said as a thank you.

"I guess this is the end of the road for us," Patxi mumbled, looking
down at the tip of his dusty combat boots.

"You never know."

"I'll see you in another life. *Agur.*"

Patxi turned around and summoned his men to get ready.

Lartaun stashed the knife in his back pocket and hurried back to
Faustine's side. He never looked over his shoulder to watch the others
depart. Still, he heard them panting like dogs, their steps heavy under the
crushing weight of backpacks half their size. Then silence returned. It was
as if the mountain had swallowed them.

39
—HOGEITAHEMERETZI—

03:17 PM ~ Monday, August 29, 1994

At first, Lartaun thought of building a makeshift sleigh to carry Faustine, but he quickly abandoned the idea. Not only would it take too much time, but the trail was too sinewy and uneven for it to work. There was no viable solution other than to carry her in his arms. Lartaun slid an arm under her armpits and the other under her knees. With the utmost care, he lifted her off the ground, grunting under the strain. Faustine screamed in agony. Ignoring her pleas to put her back down, he staggered onto his feet and began retracing their steps. The trail was treacherous, littered with slippery stones and raised tree roots. Before long, his arms, already spent from the long climb, burned in pain. Beads of sweat, the size of marbles, ran down his cheeks and splattered onto Faustine's chest. He ignored the pain and plowed on, focusing on the path straight ahead.

Faustine lapsed in and out of consciousness. Strands of reddish hair, matted with dirt and sweat, stuck to her temples and forehead. The rosy glow of her cheeks was long gone. The simple feat of breathing with a broken rib cage was torture. Watching her in such misery was so taxing on Lartaun that he almost welcomed her fainting spells. At least, each one of them gave her a few minutes of respite from the pain. Yet, every time she passed out, he worried she would never open her eyes again.

Lartaun reckoned that they were another fifteen or twenty minutes away from the road. He was so tired that he thought he would collapse at any second. His body was thirsty for water, aching for a break. But Lartaun would not stop. He could not stop. If he did, he was not sure he could pick her up and carry her again. His muscles had grown numb and his brain was losing control over them. Come what may, he was determined to reach his destination, as fast as his wobbly legs would allow.

Without warning, the sun stopped beating down on them. The sky darkened and threatened to rain. The air they breathed became thicker and charged with static, causing Lartaun's hair to stand up on end. In the distance, the first flashes of lightning tore through the sky like cracks on a windshield, followed by boisterous rumbles of thunder. The ambient light soon dimmed so much that it might as well have been night. One after another, fat raindrops splashed on the trail, leaving wet circles, the size of saucers, in the dust.

"Why? Why now?" Lartaun cursed at the skies.

The rain started to fall upon them in torrential sheets. Faustine's feverish forehead glistened with a mixture of sweat and rain. Her skin had turned so translucent and pale that it seemed to shimmer under the purple sky. She started to shiver uncontrollably, and her teeth began to shatter. Lartaun was terrified he would never get her to the hospital in time. Finally, he saw a patch of black asphalt piercing through the foliage of the forest undergrowth.

There it was: RN-134.

"Hold on tight, *maitea!* I see the road! I'll get you to a hospital! And they'll give you morphine, and you won't feel pain anymore. Do you hear me? No more pain, Faustine!" Lartaun saw that Faustine was trying to say something, but the words did not get past her lips. He gently laid her down on the road shoulder. "Hang on tight a little longer. Just hang on!" he whispered in her ear, while using his upper body as a shield to protect her face from the pounding rain.

It was almost six o'clock when two bright yellow headlights came into view, slicing through the dark curtain of rain. Without hesitation, Lartaun stepped into the middle of the road, yelling like a crazed man, agitating his arms high above his head. The pickup truck reduced its speed, even though it was quite clear that its driver had no inclination of stopping. Instead, he honked repetitively with the hope of scaring the demonic apparition out of his way. Lartaun stood his ground, determined to stop the vehicle at all costs. It swerved a couple of times in a desperate attempt to avoid him before it finally jolted to a halt. An older man, probably in his seventies, stuck his wrinkled face out of the window. The leathery texture of his skin, more tanned and weathered than a blacksmith's apron, spoke years of hard work in the mountains.

"What in da 'ell you t'ink you doing?" he shouted with a less-than-confident voice.

"Please, sir! Don't drive away! There's been a rock climbing accident! My friend over here needs help!" He pointed to Faustine who was writhing in pain as her clothing soaked up the water-logged gravel on the side of the road.

The old man stared across the passenger window and immediately recoiled in his seat upon seeing her. "Shit. I can't 'elp you. Gotta go!"

Lartaun held on to the side of the truck just as the driver attempted to step on the gas pedal. "You must help us! She took a big fall down the mountain! She needs to get to a hospital right away!"

The old man seemed to consider his options. "How bad she 'urt? She bleeding? She isn't going to die in my truck now, is she?"

"No, sir! Thank you! Oh, thank you!"

"OK. But no funny business, aw'right? I know everyone and 'is brodda in dis valley, including de police."

"I can never thank you enough, mister…?"

"Name's Léon. I can drive you as far as Sarrance, but no fur'der."

"We live at La Goutte d'Eau, past Cette-Eygun."

"What, the 'ippie place? Aw'right, I guess I can do dat."

The old man turned the hazard lights on and cranked the parking brake. He reluctantly opened the car door and hunched his shoulders in a vain attempt to escape the pounding rain. He was of average size, and he still looked strong for his age. The two of them carried Faustine onto the flatbed in the back of the truck. As soon as they were done, Léon hurried back inside the vehicle. He reached over the passenger seat to open the door for Lartaun.

"Aren't you going to 'op in?" he asked upon noticing his hesitation.

"I can't!" Lartaun lied. "I must go back to the cliff and help those who stayed behind!"

Léon, who was not born yesterday, looked at him with suspicion.

"I'm not takin' the gal all by 'meself. You get in de truck or she gets off!"

Their altercation was cut short by a blood-chilling wail coming from the flatbed.

"Can't you see that she is in pain? Come on, old man, step on it and honk the horn as soon as you get to La Goutte d'Eau! Someone will come right out, you've got my word!"

"Aw'right," Léon relented with a sigh.

"I can never repay you for saving this woman's life, Léon!"
Another sigh. "Aw'right."

"Just give me a minute, please." Lartaun hurried to the back of the truck. There were so many things he wanted to tell Faustine, yet so little time. He took her hand and pressed it gently against his lips.

"*Maite zaitut*, Faustine. Be strong. I love you so much."
Faustine smiled weakly.

"Come on, I 'aven't got all day!" They heard Léon shouting from the front seat.

"Go," she exhaled.

Lartaun slapped the rear of the flatbed twice with the palm of his hand. Léon put his truck in gear and drove away slowly, gripping the wheel with both hands, the way old people do.

Suddenly, Lartaun took off running after the pick-up truck, chasing it like a mad dog, and yelled at the top of his lungs,

"I'm going to stop them, Faustine! Do you hear me? So that one day you can look me in the eyes again and feel no shame!"

The truck went around the bend and disappeared out of sight. Lartaun, out of breath, stopped in the middle of the road. He dropped to his knees and broke down, his strong frame bent under the violence of his sorrow. He remained hunched over long after his tears had run dry, and wondered what to do next. Voices in his head urged him to run away while he still could, to rush headlong into the unknown and escape one more time. But he just made Faustine a promise, and he was a man true to his word.

As if the great faucet in the sky had finally exhausted its water supply, the rain stopped as abruptly as it had started.

06:37 PM ~ Monday, August 29, 1994

Eric relaxed in a deck chair, which he had placed just right so he could face the late afternoon sun. He loved to sit on his front porch after a storm and do nothing but watch puddles of mud turn into dry clay while he drank a cold beer. He reminisced about how hard it was to adjust to the simple mountain life at first, and how he grew quite fond of it in the end. His time in the valley was coming to a close. Provided that Patxi and his acolytes met Koldobika in time, his work here was finished. He would pack and head back to Bayonne soon.

A tidy pile of firewood was stacked up against the cabin, protected from the elements by a corrugated iron awning that jutted out from the roof. As soon as winter came, the logs would be fed to the stove to keep the next tenant warm. A rusty axe, the blade of which had been driven into a chopping block, stood nearby. Its sight did not escape Lartaun. He had followed the banks of the Gave d'Aspe to Eric's house, and for the past fifteen minutes, he crouched in the shadows, waiting for the most opportune moment to strike. When the right time came, he grabbed a sturdy log to use as a club, and snuck up on Eric from behind.

Whack!

The hit was so precise that Eric slumped into his chair without making a sound. His fingers went limp, and his hand let go of the beer bottle, which rolled onto the ground, spilling out its contents onto the rickety floorboards.

When Eric regained consciousness, he noticed a revolting taste on his tongue. A kitchen rag was stuffed in his mouth. Worse, he was tied to his favorite rocking chair, and his broken leg was propped up on a chopping block in front of him. "What is this thing doing in my living room anyway?" he thought, still dazed from the blow he received. His temples pounded. His haggard eyes wandered about the room. He jerked in stupefaction when he saw Lartaun standing against the light, smoking one of his rolled cigarettes by the window. He wore a clean pair of jeans and a T-shirt, which Eric recognized as his own. His head was shaved. There he was, running his fingers absentmindedly along the sharp edge of Eric's axe.

Eric struggled with the ropes binding his wrists, chest and thighs. The chair rocked and creaked under him, and Lartaun slowly pivoted his head toward him.

"I was really hoping that I'd never have to see you again, Eric."

"Mphmmph!" Eric started twisting like a worm that had just been stepped on. No matter how hard he pulled and tugged at the binds, they did not loosen. On the contrary, his erratic movements drove the ropes even deeper into his flesh.

"Do you have something to say? Good. I've got questions for you, too." Lartaun said as he walked over.

Eric followed him with his eyes until he stepped out of his line of sight. Helpless, he only sensed Lartaun's presence right behind him. He twitched in alarm as soon as he felt Lartaun's hands touch the back of his neck as he loosened the gag.

"Try to shout once," Lartaun warned him, "and I'll gore you like a sheep after Ramadan."

Eric spat out the dirty rag, retching and dry-heaving in disgust.

"What—what do you want from me?" he stammered.

"I must find Patxi."

"What?" he repeated, dumbfounded.

"Patxi! Where did he go?"

"I don't know, I swear! How would I know if you don't?"

"Don't take me for a fool, Eric. You're doing yourself a huge disservice." Lartaun paced across the room. He picked up the axe with both hands and returned to face his prisoner.

"What are you doing?" Eric stared at him in panic. "Come on, this is—NO!"

Without warning, Lartaun smacked Eric's cast with the axe handle. An acute jolt of pain shot through Eric's leg. He stifled a scream. His dark blue eyes darted in all directions, desperately searching for a way out.

"Tell me where Patxi is and what his plans are."

"Fuck you! I don't know!"

Lartaun hit his broken leg with the axe handle again, harder this time. Eric gritted his teeth in agony. Tears of pain started to roll down his cheeks.

"I don't believe you." Lartaun was unshakable in his determination. He turned the axe around and brandished it again, blade up this time, above his leg. Eric gaped at the axe. "Answer me!" Lartaun was running out of patience. With trembling lips, Eric started to beg for mercy, but Lartaun didn't seem to care. "Don't tell me that I didn't warn you." He lifted the axe a few inches above Eric's cast. "See, there is a tried-and-true technique to wood chopping. First, you cut a notch into the wood to guide the axe, like so." As if in demonstration, Lartaun hit the cast ever so lightly with the sharp edge of the axe, causing the hard plaster to crack on the surface. Eric squealed in terror. "Then, you—"

"They're meeting tomorrow night! Nine o'clock at Anabel's old apartment! The one on Cipriano Larrañaga street, in Irun!" Words could not have spewed out of Eric's mouth any faster. Lartaun stopped.

"Is that where they're keeping the dynamite?"

"No, they're supposed to drop the cargo at the *baserri* first!"

"What *baserri*? What farm are you talking about?"

Eric could not avoid the gripping power of Lartaun's eyes. As if he was being hypnotized, he was lulled into submission by two devilish pendulums of ice and fire. He had no choice but to divulge the location of their secret headquarters.

"It's in the mountain, right on the border, not too far from Roncevaux." Eric said. He gave Lartaun directions how to get there.

"Then what? What will happen at the meeting?" Lartaun asked.

"They'll decide when to head out to Madrid."

"Madrid? What for?"

"You're putting me on, right?" Eric chuckled in disbelief. Lartaun raised the axe above his head again in a menacing stance. Clearly, Lartaun had no clue about Patxi's plans. "OPERATION ASKATASUNA!" Eric cried, scared witless.

"Operation *what?*"

"'Operation Freedom!' That's the name they picked for the *ekintza!* I can't believe that Patxi never told you about it?" he replied, astounded.

"What are they going to do with the *goma?*"

Eric lifted his head slowly toward Lartaun. "You don't know that either?"

"SPEAK UP!"

"Patxi is planning an attack in Madrid!"

"You're lying!" growled Lartaun. "Patxi would never be crazy enough to do something like that. Not in the city! Not where people could be hurt!"

"Oh, no? Think again!" Eric snarled in his turn. "Your best friend is on his way to blow up the Spanish Parliament!"

The news knocked the wind out of Lartaun. He let the axe drop to the floor.

"The—*Congreso—de los Diputados?*"

"The plan calls to carry out the attack when the Parliament is back in session. But I don't know the exact date, I swear!"

Eric feared that Lartaun was going to take out his anger on him, but Lartaun was in no condition to do that. He was too stunned to fully grasp the gravity of the situation.

"I need cash," Lartaun mumbled after a long pause.

Eric gave him a baffled look. "What?"

"I need to borrow cash from you," Lartaun repeated impatiently.

"In my wallet, by the kitchen sink."

Lartaun opened Eric's wallet and scanned its contents. In it, there was a fifty-franc note plus change. "I'm gonna need more than that."

"Look in the tin box. Inside the stove."

Lartaun did as he was told. He removed the grille of the stove. Inside, he found a rectangular cookie jar full of French francs and Spanish pesetas. Lartaun helped himself to a wad of bills and stashed the box back in its place.

"Consider this your contribution to avert a disaster from happening."

"Take all the money you want, but don't hurt me! I swear I won't say anything to Patxi! Let's pretend that none of this ever happened, all right? Please!"

"Do you seriously think that I would take your word for it?" Lartaun stifled a cynical laugh. "I should kill you!" Lartaun picked up a large kitchen knife from the rack above the sink. Eric, whose eyes were suddenly intent on the sharp object in Lartaun's hand, swallowed with an audible gulp. "Quite frankly, that was the first thought to cross my mind when I came here. But then, that would make me a despicable, lowlife person just like you," he added like an afterthought. "I was wondering what else I could do to prevent you from running straight to Patxi about this, and then 'Surprise!' I found this in your room." Eric followed Lartaun's finger. He was pointing to a spot atop the ramshackle library shelves bolted to the far end wall of the living room.

"Son of a bitch!" Eric muttered in awe. The red light of his personal camcorder blinked right at him. Lartaun had been recording their whole encounter on video. "What's your deal? You turned informer for the fuckin' police?"

"I've never cooperated with the police, and I'm not about to begin now. This is a personal matter between me and Patxi. As for this tape," he added, ejecting the videotape from the device, "it's my guarantee that you'll keep your mouth shut about our conversation. See, I'm going to seal it in an envelope addressed to the gendarmerie in Pau. I'll entrust it to someone with instructions to throw it in the mail should anything bad happen to me in the next few days. Don't waste your time wondering who's got the tape, though. I won't give it to Faustine or anyone you know. Just remember this—if you talk, I'll fall. But I'll make sure that you fall with me."

"You're a sick bastard!" he hissed.

"Would you prefer it if I killed you on the spot?"

Eric remained silent.

"My thoughts, exactly," Lartaun continued. "Just forget everything that's happened here tonight. And this time, I hope that we are parting ways for good." Lartaun cut through the rope to set Eric's right wrist free. Next, he balanced the kitchen knife across Eric's cast. "Don't make any sudden moves. If you drop the knife, you won't be able to free yourself."

Lartaun dropped the videocassette inside a plastic bag and exited the house quietly.

As soon as Eric heard the front door close, he grabbed the kitchen knife and sawed off his bindings as fast as he could. Frantic, he hopped on his good leg toward the window. He yanked it wide open and yelled once, at the top of his lungs:

"TRAITOR!"

40
—BERROGEI—

08:02 PM ~ Monday, August 29, 1994

Lartaun found a hiding spot behind a large boulder alongside an old smuggler's trail cutting across the slopes of the Somport Mountain. Here, he would await nightfall to cross the border unseen and continue his journey to Irun via Spain. Obviously, traveling through the Vallée d'Aspe was no longer a viable option. The people at La Goutte would have already rung the alarm upon finding Faustine in the back of the old man's pick up. The gendarmes summoned to the scene would have been quick to match Léon's description of the man he had seen with that of Lartaun. By now, the manhunt would be in full swing. Gendarmes and volunteers alike would be intent on catching the dangerous fugitive before he could harm any more innocent souls.

From his vantage point on the mountain, Lartaun saw a gendarmerie road block set across RN-134 near the tiny electric power plant of Les Forges d'Abel, a couple of miles before the customs post. Without a doubt, there were more of them stationed along the road heading north toward Oloron-Sainte-Marie. His plan required that he walk overnight to Jaca, a town twenty-five miles south of the Spanish border. From there, he would hitch a ride west to Irun. Even if traveling on foot at night was the most sensible option at this time, Lartaun knew that it was no guarantee of a safe escape. Most likely, every gendarmerie station in the valley had dispatched patrols to hunt him down on the mountain. Even though he had spent a lot of time hiking the slopes of the Somport to familiarize himself with its topography, Lartaun was no match for the gendarmes on their own turf. Most of these men were natives of the valley: they knew the area like the back of their hand, from the days when they tracked the booze, drug and cigarette smugglers who crossed the Spanish border on a daily basis as a means to supplement their meager farmer's income.

Darkness started to fall, at last. Birds of prey soared high above Lartaun, carelessly performing their aerial acrobatics in the darkening sky. How envious he was of their freedom! Not even the flamboyant sunset could alter his brooding, nor could it shake his immeasurable melancholy. Perhaps Faustine had not made it in time to the hospital. What if she was dead? Lartaun hit his forehead with his fists to make that thought go away.

At last, he took one long hard look at the valley below, knowing that he could never return. He patted Patxi's knife through the fabric of his jeans for comfort. Once again, it was time to move.

09:46 PM ~ Monday, August 29, 1994

Anabel spent the day alone at the *baserri,* anxiously waiting for Patxi, Santutxo, Otsoa and Koldobika to return with the dynamite. Since there were no telephone lines reaching the farm, she only speculated that everything went as planned. Rather than waiting around and worrying all day, she set out to work around the farm and keep her mind occupied. She erased all evidence of Faustine's recent incarceration and continued to prep the secret area where Koldobika and Mikel would be making the bombs. They had built a double-wall partition at the far left corner of the barn in order to keep Koldobika's "devil's workshop" out of sight. It was genius, because anyone who ignored the exact location of the atelier would never be able to find it.

Eventually, Anabel ran out of things to do. She plopped down amidst the bales of dry hay and crossed her arms behind her head. Everywhere, fine particles of dust danced in the beams of light that came down from the displaced tiles on the roof. The air was warm and fragrant with the scent of fodder. She closed her eyes and let her imagination wander to her endless summer holidays at the *pueblo,* back when she was a child, back when life was a lot less complicated.

Out of the blue, the distant, yet familiar, noise of a car engine woke Anabel up with a jolt. To her surprise, the room was plunged in darkness. She sat up in a daze and plucked the tiny pieces of straw sticking to her hair, wondering how long she had been asleep. The vehicle approached the courtyard. She felt her way out of the barn and ran outside to meet with Patxi and his men.

41
— BERROGEITABAT —

04:45 PM ~ Tuesday, August 30, 1994

Lartaun's trip from the mountains to Irun had been surprisingly easy. The quirky Italian lady who picked him up at the crack of dawn on N-240, twenty miles past the town of Jaca, adored him so much that she agreed to drive him all the way to his destination, even though she was originally planning to go no further than Pamplona.

Lartaun picked the locks of Anabel's old digs on Cipriano Larrañaga street and let himself in the apartment. He quickly found a hiding spot underneath the bed, which allowed him to peek into the living room, provided no one closed the door. Lying on his stomach, he smelled the mold impregnating the quilted bedspread. The odor was revolting, but he resigned himself to wait there until nine o'clock. As disappointing as it was to spy on his former friend, Lartaun knew he had no choice, or he would be just as guilty as they were of the horrific attack they planned.

Before long, Lartaun realized how much his mind and body had been driven beyond endurance over the past few days. The physical exercise and the continuous lack of sleep had taken its toll on him. In addition, the once-familiar sounds of Irun, a cacophony of car horns, police whistles, chatty pedestrians, speeding cars and backfiring motorcycles permeated the room from the street below. Like a comforting urban lullaby, they had a soothing effect on him and, in spite of his perilous predicament, his eyelids felt heavier than lead. Before he could count to ten, Lartaun was sound asleep.

The sound of a key rattling in the front door disturbed the oppressive silence inside Anabel's apartment. Lartaun jerked awake as Patxi and Anabel walked in, not suspecting that anyone was there with them. Minutes later, there was a knock at the front door. Patxi's henchmen rolled in, one after the other. Lartaun immediately recognized Iñaki walking in. He was the same bearded messenger with the mousy face he had met, nine months prior, in San Juan Chamula, Mexico. Then appeared the big hulk of a man he saw the day before at the *zulo,* Santutxo, flanked by Otsoa, the guy who had examined Faustine after her fall. He looked at their faces for the very first time. Another man he had never seen before followed suit. His name was Mikel. Finally, the last member of the secret posse showed up. The bald and stocky young man looked strangely familiar to Lartaun. Could it be that they knew each other? The answer came in the form of a flashback, taking him back to the *Sanfermines* in Pamplona nine years ago. Koldobika! That was him, no doubt. How had he and Patxi become so close when, as far as he could recall, they only briefly met once, on the day Lartaun was attacked by the bull? It suddenly dawned on Lartaun that Patxi had kept him out of the loop about the real extent of his activism for the past years. He took the news like a stab in the back. It hurt him immensely to realize that no matter how devoted they had been to each other, Patxi still managed to keep many secrets from him. Lartaun pushed the bitter thought to the back of his mind. After all, it did not really matter anymore.

By the time nine o'clock struck, everyone was in attendance. Patxi opened the meeting with the pose of a confident leader.

"We've come a long way since you answered my call to arms. You put your unwavering faith in me. Together, we created ZORROTZ TALDEA, *Euskadi's* most secret and radical cell ever, with one goal in mind: to make history by forcing the imperialistic state of Spain to relinquish its sovereignty over *Euskal Herria,* once and for all. We are going to do what ETA never had the guts to do! The attack of the Spanish Parliament will be by far the biggest blow that Spain has ever experienced in its historic struggle against us, the Basque people!"

Lartaun heard a rumble of approbation.

"Monday, September 5th will be a date to remember. A plenary sitting has been scheduled at the *Congreso de los Diputados.* At least half of the deputies plus one must be in attendance at the seat of the Parliament on that particular day. They are expecting a full house, given that the congressmen will be back in full force after the long summer break."

"How much time are you planning on giving these people to exit the building from the moment that we place the call to the media?" Anabel ventured.

"There will be no phone call to the press before the attack," Patxi answered with a solemn voice. There was a collective gasp in the assembly.

"That wasn't part of the original plan!" Koldobika interjected, unable to hide his surprise.

"Without prior warning, hundreds will die!" added Mikel.

"I am aware of that. People, we are not ETA, we are ZORROTZ TALDEA, and we will live up to our name! We're not afraid to step on razors and take radical action to free our people. And yes, we're dangerous!" exclaimed Patxi. "We must set a radical example! This is the only way to alter the course of history! That is why I have decided that we will strike the Parliament without any advance warning."

They all looked at each other uncomfortably, but no one had the courage to voice their opposition to Patxi's final decision.

"When will we leave the *baserri?*" Santutxo asked calmly, breaking the uneasy silence.

"Any day between this Friday and Sunday," replied Patxi. "Our departure is contingent upon the completion of all six bombs. In other words, it is up to Mikel and Koldo."

The more Lartaun listened to Patxi talk about OPERATION ASKATASUNA, the more he understood that no detail of the *ekintza* had been left to chance, from the way they would transport the bombs to Madrid to the exact location where each one of them would be placed inside the Parliament building and the synchronized time of their detonation. As horrifying as it was, Lartaun had to admit that Patxi was a brilliant strategist. His checklist was ready to go. Each task would be ticked off according to a precise schedule. Less than a week to go, and the *Congreso de los Diputados* would go up in flames.

The countdown had begun.

After two hours, the meeting finally approached an end. Patxi produced a stack of passports from a manila envelope.

"Every one of you has a solid alibi to explain your absence from your usual routines, starting tomorrow. Also, I have provided you with your own itinerary. After the *ekintza,* we will each travel our separate ways at different times. I will contact all of you two days after the attack. Provided that you have not gotten yourself in trouble, I will disclose to you the secret location where we are to meet again. From there, we will claim the attack and make our demands." Patxi held the passports in his hand the way he would hold a deck of cards and addressed the small assembly again. "There they are. Pick the one that belongs to you. And don't come bitching to me about your new names because I didn't pick them. Just keep these documents in a safe place until the time comes to use them."

Santutxo was first to take possession of his precious booklet. He thumbed through the pages and let out a whistle of admiration. This was undeniably the work of a skilled counterfeiter.

"These things must be worth their weight in gold."

"More than that, actually," replied Patxi, "they were forged from a batch of stolen virgin passports. They're the real thing, *txo.* You can't find anything better on the black market."

When everyone had grabbed their documents, one passport was left on the coffee table.

"Who is that one for?" asked Mikel.

"That one was meant for Lartaun," Patxi replied quietly.

"You made a big mistake by letting him go," Santutxo pondered. "We should have killed them both, him and his girlfriend. We could have made it look like a real climbing accident."

"You're right, Santu. I should have, but I did not. And you know why? Because I never told him a thing about OPERATION ASKATA-SUNA, let alone about ZORROTZ TALDEA. He knows nothing at all. He would never know where to start looking for me, even if he wanted to."

"Where do you think he is right now?" asked Otsoa.

Lartaun, who was only a few paces away from them in the adjacent room, cringed.

"His escape made the headlines today," said Patxi, "but it says nothing about him being recaptured."

"So you think that he managed to escape?" Anabel chimed in, a flicker of hope passing through her eyes.

"It's too early to say. Honestly, his chances are slim to none."

"I'm glad to hear that," said Mikel. "Good riddance."

Patxi turned to Mikel and stared him down long and hard. "Show me that chain around your neck!" he suddenly demanded.

There was an awkward silence in the room. Mikel's temples turned beet red.

"It's, uh, Lartaun's chain," he stammered. "I found it in the envelope that he left in the car the other night. I thought you wouldn't mind if I took it. I mean, I can give it back to you if you want me to."

"Keep it, for all I care," Patxi said with disdain, "just don't make me look at it again."

Mikel was mortified that he was just scolded in front of the others, but he knew better than to lock horns with Patxi tonight. He tucked the medal inside his shirt instead.

"What will you do with it, then?" Otsoa drummed his fingers over Lartaun's passport again, eager to turn the attention away from Mikel.

"I guess I'll throw it in the dumpster on my way out," mumbled Patxi. "I don't think Lartaun will need a passport in hell."

11:50 PM ~ Tuesday, August 30, 1994

Anabel's apartment was plunged in darkness. Everyone had left a good half an hour ago, including Patxi and Anabel, who were the last to depart. Lartaun was still hesitant to leave the safety of his hiding place for fear that someone might return and stumble upon him, but he had to make a move. He slithered from under the bed and hugged the walls of the flat until he reached the front door. He cracked it open and surveyed the staircase landing. Everything was dark and silent. He hurried down the stairs, not daring to click on the switch to light up the stairwell, and veered to the right upon reaching the first floor. There, he found what he was looking for: a tall trash can standing against a recessed wall in the main hallway.

Even though Lartaun's eyes had fully adjusted to the darkness, he could not rely on sight alone to find such a small item inside the large container. He would have to get his hands dirty. He lifted the dumpster lid with his elbow and gagged upon smelling the revolting stench of its contents. It was a nauseating mixture of soiled baby diapers and rotting vegetable peels. He grimaced and waited a few seconds to get used to the odor. Breathing through his shirt, he hunched over the can and started to sort through torn grocery bags filled with household trash, empty bottles and other cardboard items. He was careful to make as little noise as possible so as to not attract the unwanted attention of the neighbors.

After several minutes of tedious work, he neared the bottom of the dumpster. Lartaun refused to give up hope. As he pushed a flattened card board box aside, he heard something slide down the side of the garbage can. He leaned over the edge and stuck his left arm down as far as it would go. With his face pressed sideways against the foul-smelling plastic bags, he rummaged around until the tips of his fingers pinched something that felt like a small notebook. He inched it up, ever so careful not to let it drop again. He brought the dark green booklet close to his eyes to examine it. Printed in golden brown-embossed letters were the words "MEXICO," and further below the coat of arms of the United Mexican States, "PASAPORTE."

The ridiculousness of the situation almost made him giggle. He had put his life in jeopardy to get out of Mexico, only to become a bona fide citizen of that country!

Lartaun ran his fingers over the grained cover of the official document and flipped it open to the second page. A recent picture of himself stared straight back at him behind its protective plastic film, along with data stating his new identity, place and date of birth. He whispered in a barely audible voice,

"My name is Javier Núnez Obregón. I was born in Mexico City on June 22nd, 1970, and I'm a Mexican citizen."

Lartaun wiped the passport clean against the front of his jeans, stashed it in his pocket and left the building in a hurry.

42

- BERROGEITABI -

02:25 AM ~ Saturday, September 3, 1994

Madrid was a suffocating furnace during summer, and today was no exception. An endless ribbon of cars, trucks and buses moved at a snail's pace along Calle de Alcalá. Out on the curb, subway stations disgorged carloads of white-collar workers whose shirts were already pit-stained with sweat though it was still early in the morning.

Rob and his young wife Erica, newlyweds on vacation from Liverpool, England, were on their way to admire Pablo Picasso's iconic "Guernica" at the Centro de Arte Reina Sofia. They decided to make a quick detour to see the Parliament first. They were pleased that they had taken the time to see it as the neoclassical palace was one of the recommended tourist stops. The building, fronted by a portico adorned with six Corinthian columns and topped by a triangular pediment sculpted in bas-relief, brought the famed Acropolis' temples in Athens to mind, and along with it, good memories of their recent honeymoon in Greece.

"Hey, luv! Fancy a picture of you with the lion?" Rob asked his wife while he pointed at one of the two identical bronze sculptures of lions at guard that flanked each side of the building.

Erika wrapped her arms around one of the massive animal's legs and smiled candidly for the camera. The shutter clicked.

This was the last thing they would ever know as the Congreso de los Diputados exploded at that very moment, pulverizing Rob, Erica and the statue she was holding into a thousand bloody pieces.

Lartaun's forehead dripped with cold sweat. The nightmare was so vivid that the stench of blood and burnt skin was still teasing his nostrils. He stumbled to his feet and peered over the crumbling wall of the abandoned shepherd's refuge. The *baserri* below was lit by a near full moon. He checked the time on his watch and looked through the binoculars that he purchased with Eric's money. The same watchman he observed a couple hours earlier was still patrolling the compound. Lartaun hoped he would fall asleep at some point.

In order to get to the farm, Lartaun hitched a ride east toward Pamplona, then north past the historic village of Roncevaux toward the border between Spain and France. From there, he continued on foot along a small road cresting the mountain's ridge to the Col d'Arnostéguy. At the pass, he changed course onto an abandoned smugglers' dirt trail, which, in turn, led to a dilapidated refuge, and further below, to the farm. While it had only taken a few hours for Patxi and his gang to drive there, it had taken Lartaun two and-a-half days to cover the same distance. The grassy mountain slopes were wide open, save for the occasional Scotch pine or cluster of eroded boulders, and offered zero chance of a stealth approach, forcing Lartaun to travel at night. Now that he finally made it to the shepherd's refuge, he was intent on chancing a blitz raid on Patxi and his men that same night.

Lartaun opened his knapsack and took a few sips of water to stave off his hunger for as long as he could. He resigned himself to wait with the patience of Job until three o'clock in the morning. He figured that he would have better luck sneaking up on the security guard at that ugly time of the night, when even the most alert and zealous watchmen tend to get sleepy and let their guard down. He planned to knock the guard out and disarm him before he had a chance to ring the alarm. Then, he would catch Patxi by surprise and announce that he and his men had only thirty minutes to disappear before the police would be summoned to the *baserri* to arrest them. It was a far-fetched claim, but Lartaun hoped that the surprise factor would give him the upper hand and that Patxi would be so stunned that he would comply with his orders, abandoning the explosives in his haste to beat an arrest.

Lartaun was well aware that he had no room for error because

Patxi would certainly not spare his life a second time around. But his night-mares had made it abundantly clear to him that he had no other choice but to stop them, even if it cost him his life.

Lartaun was startled by an incongruous smell coming from down wind. It was the unmistakable scent of feminine perfume.

"ANABEL!" his mind screamed at once. "What is she doing here?"

All his senses on red alert, Lartaun recoiled into the shadows of the crumbling wall and held his breath, cursing himself in silence for his terrible negligence. How could he have not heard the sound of her foot-steps until she was right upon him? All that separated her from Lartaun was a broken-down wall, not even five foot tall at its highest point. Anabel screamed with fright when she saw Lartaun. Clearly, she did not expect his presence any more than he expected hers. In a flash, Lartaun jumped to his feet, pulled his knife and pinned Anabel to the ground before she could react.

"Don't hurt me!" she cried in panic just before Lartaun closed his hand over her mouth. As much as he hated the thought at first, taking Anabel hostage made too much sense to pass up. With her at his mercy, he would not only be able to get precious information, but he could also use her as a bargaining chip to blackmail Patxi into aborting his plans in Madrid. He quickly patted her down, and slowly released his grip once he realized that she was not armed.

"What are you doing here, all alone?" he asked, puzzled.

"I—came here because," she panted, "never mind. What are you doing here? How did you find us?"

Lartaun, who was not about to tell her that he had crashed their secret meeting in Irun, ignored her question and interrogated her instead. Anabel did not come all the way up here in search of someone. Rather the opposite, in fact. She came here to be alone so she could calm down and think. Lartaun sat down by her side with his back to the wall and listened to her as she opened her heart to him.

"I can't do this, Lartaun! I can't!" she wailed. "I tried to bring Patxi to his senses. I begged him to abort the operation but he won't listen!" As strange as it sounded for her to confide in him, Lartaun was not surprised in the least. Back in the day, they held no secrets from each other. And in Anabel's eyes, he was still one of them. "I should have warned you not to accept Patxi's deal, back when you were in Mexico," she said in a low voice.

"Somehow, I feel responsible for all this."

"What are you talking about?"

"I should have told you that Patxi was going insane. You know, he became a different person after the night of the riots. You weren't there to see it happen. When the *policía* released Patxi after you escaped, I could hardly recognize him. He was so full of hate, so angry all the time. That was when he and Bixente joined ETA's ranks."

"I figured out from his correspondence that he had become a *legal*," Lartaun nodded.

"But soon after they joined, the French police arrested ETA's leaders in Bidart, and it quickly drove the whole organization to a standstill for a while. Patxi stayed put, at first, but you know him. Enforced idleness was not what he had signed up for. So he decided to create his own secret organization." Anabel fell silent for a while. When she spoke again, she sounded tired and defeated. "Beware of Patxi. He is not the person that you once cared about. He lost his soul a long time ago. Hatred is the only thing that keeps him going these days."

"I know what you guys are up to, and it makes me physically sick just to think about it," Lartaun said. Anabel shot him a surprised look, but again, she did not comment on how he could have possibly heard about OPERATION ASKATASUNA. She went on talking instead.

"I'd be lying if I told you that I was never in favor of the *ekintza*. But as things moved along, I started to have doubts, especially after Bixente's death."

"What do you mean, Bixente is dead?" Lartaun stared at Anabel in shock.

"Oh, Lartaun," she whispered, "I'm so sorry, how could you have known?"

"When did it happen? How?" Lartaun stammered, grief-stricken.

"It'll be two weeks on Monday. They were after this one hot shot industrialist in San Sebastián. Somehow, the son-of-a-bitch got tipped off that they were coming, and his bodyguards opened fire on Bixente and his men as soon as they entered the compound. They shot my brother in cold blood, Lartaun!"

"I'm so sorry," Lartaun said in a comforting tone. He put his arms around Anabel's shoulders and held her tight.

"I know how much you two liked each other," she said after a while.

"He was like a brother to me."

"I know."

"You must be so angry. Do you want revenge?"

"No, just the opposite, in fact."

"I don't understand."

"It's quite simple, actually. The policeman believed that by killing my brother, he fulfilled his duty to protect and serve the good citizens of his country. In his eyes, Bixente was nothing but a member of ETA, and ETA is the enemy. I, on the other hand, think that the guy committed nothing short of a senseless act of barbarism. So, you see, one event, two points of view. It just depends on which side of the fence you're on, I guess."

"True." Lartaun tried to follow her train of thought.

"And now I realize that we are setting out to do the exact same thing. We have targeted the Members of Parliament as our enemy. As a consequence, we believe that they all deserve to die. But do they, really?"

"Someone's foe will always be someone else's friend," Lartaun replied with a sigh.

"That's what I'm getting at! We have no right to decide who lives and who dies. Only God has that privilege!" she blurted out, utterly distraught.

"Listen to me, Anabel. I am no Judas. I won't be the one who sends Patxi to the gallows, but rest assured that I'll do everything I can to stop him from carrying out this attack."

"How?"

"I've got a plan, but I need your help to make it work."

43

-BERROGEITAHIRU-

09:44 AM ~ Saturday, September 3, 1994

The sound of an engine resonated in the mountains. Lartaun hurried back to his post and adjusted his binoculars. A grey station wagon spat thick clouds of exhaust in the middle of the courtyard. People exited the main building. Lartaun recognized Patxi and Santutxo. They opened the back doors of the van and disappeared inside. Seconds later, Iñaki came into view. Then out came Otsoa, walking alongside Koldobika. Gripping his binoculars, Lartaun zoomed in on the driver, who stuck his head out to adjust the side mirror. It was Mikel, of course. How could he forget the despicable man who had stolen his chain? Lartaun quickly ran a mental list of all the passengers. "Patxi and Santu, that makes two, three, four, five, six with Mikel. Damn! Where's Anabel? She must have been the first one to climb into the van," he reasoned. "I must have missed her."

Everything proceeded according to plan. The entire posse piled up in the station wagon. That morning at breakfast, per Lartaun's instructions, Anabel convinced Patxi to organize a last-minute trip to Pamplona so that everyone could run their final errands before they went to Madrid to carry out OPERATION ASKATASUNA.

Lartaun hid behind the uneven stones of the wall as the vehicle and its occupants passed him and jolted along the bumpy trail. He anxiously waited for it to disappear behind the mountain ridge. Then he sprung into action and broke into a mad run toward the deserted *baserri*.

Lartaun followed Anabel's instructions and found the key to the barn which was attached to a rusty hook by the chimney in the main room. He retraced his steps across the courtyard, opened the padlock with unsteady hands and let himself into the barn. The heavy door creaked on its hinges, and he headed straight for the secret workshop.

The room furnishings consisted of a long Formica table flanked by two simple chairs on either side. Two powerful architect lamps, tapping electricity from the farm's generator, were clamped onto each end of the table to provide adequate lighting. A wide array of tools, pliers and wire cutters, designed for watch-making and similar works of precision, laid atop stainless steel trays. This reminded him somewhat of a surgeon's operating table. Rolls of duct-tape and electrical wiring hung from hooks on the wall, organized by diameter and color.

And there they were, resting inside foam-padded coolers at the far corner of the room: five finished Improvised Explosive Devices. Each time-bomb contained about fifty pounds of dynamite. Two of them were outfitted with five pounds of nails packed around it as shrapnel. By the looks of it, Koldobika started making another one before he had to interrupt his work to go on the trip with the others. The dynamite that was yet to be used was stored inside wood fruit crates, piled up one atop the other, underneath loose floor boards alongside the wall.

Lartaun glanced at what would soon become the time-delay mechanism on device number six. It was nothing but a basic countdown cooking timer, deceptive in its simplicity. With the tip of his fingers, he grazed the device that Koldo had been working on that very morning. He swatted it hard with the palm of his hand, sending it crashing against the wall.

He opened the lid of the cooler closest to him with extreme caution. Lartaun stared at the bomb inside with morbid fascination. In a flash, visions of screaming people, oozing wounds and rivers of blood passed before his eyes like a bad psychiatric aversion therapy experiment. He pressed his fists into his eyes to make the haunting images disappear.

Lartaun was on a mission, and he had no time to lose. The sooner this nightmare was over, the better. He reached for the timer attached to the bomb. Koldobika had placed it into a small insulated case to muffle the ticking sound so that the bomb would become undetectable once it had been set. He put his fingers on the dial and rotated it as far as it would go without a trace of hesitation. One hour was the timer's maximum allotted time.

Seconds started to click away. Lartaun figured he would have plenty of time to run for cover before the explosion would occur. Just the same, he turned around and exited the barn in a hurry.

09:52 AM ~ Saturday, September 3, 1994

Had Lartaun looked at the side window of the main farm building, he would have realized that Anabel did not leave the *baserri* with the others. Peeking through the drawn curtains, Anabel anxiously waited for him to exit the premises. As soon as the area was clear, she hurried to the barn.

She was frantic with dread, but she had made up her mind. Even though she understood that she and Lartaun were doing the right thing, she was also double-crossing Patxi and her fellow members of ZORROTZ TALDEA. She knew Patxi would never forgive her. She was betraying him with the man who once was his best friend. She would not be able to look into Patxi's eyes ever again. The thought alone was heart wrenching. No matter what her lover had become, he had been, and always would be, the love of her life. Without Patxi's trust and devotion, life was not worth much to her. All things considered, it would be a small price to pay, a painless way to end it all.

In order to make her own plan work, Anabel pretended to become violently sick overnight, and she managed to convince Patxi to go to Pamplona without her. The bomb that Lartaun had set ticked away in front of her eyes. Fifty minutes to go. To Anabel, it seemed like an eternity. Afraid that she might lose her nerve while waiting for death to come, she opened a second cooler. She pinched the dial with trembling fingers. All she needed to do was to rotate it clockwise to start the countdown on the other bomb. She took a big breath, hesitated, and let go of the timer at the last second. How long should she set it for, she suddenly wondered? Ten seconds? A minute? Judging by the speed with which he had left the barn, Lartaun must be out of reach of the bomb by now. She shut her eyes tight and turned the dial to the right at random. When she opened them again, she could not help but smirk at the irony of it all.

She just drew a lucky seven.

From now on, she was one among the precious few who could predict the exact time of their death:

-10:08 in the AM-

10:04 AM ~ Saturday, September 3, 1994

Lartaun was running across the field, eager to put as much distance between him and the *baserri* when he heard a vehicle in the distance. Why were Patxi and his gang returning so soon? It made no sense. He crouched behind a cluster of boulders and frantically searched for his binoculars.

"They must have forgotten something," he thought with worry. He checked his watch. There were still over forty-five minutes to go before the explosion, so he relaxed a little. Hopefully, they would just pick up what they needed and leave again right away. He followed the progression of the grey station wagon through his lenses, brake pads screaming in protest as it descended at slow speed along the steep grade of the dirt trail.

10:06 AM ~ Saturday, September 3, 1994

The familiar roar of the vehicle engine shook Anabel out of her petrified trance. She opened her eyes in surprise and froze in terror as she grasped the situation. Patxi was coming back! Frantic, she looked at the bomb. She had a little less than two minutes to go on the countdown timer.

She stood up so quickly that she sent her chair crashing backwards with a metallic bang.

10:07 AM ~ Saturday, September 3, 1994

Lartaun caught sight of Anabel as she sprinted up the trail toward the station wagon, gesticulating like a fury. What was she doing at the farm? Were they coming back to get her? He quickly adjusted his binoculars to get a close-up of her face. She was yelling at them, but he could not hear what she was saying because the wind was blowing in the opposite direction. Judging by the way she was waving her arms, it seemed that she wanted the vehicle and its occupants to turn around and to go back the same way they came from. Lartaun was at a loss. Why was she so frantic? Her behavior would give everything away. All she needed to do was to get in the van and convince them to get out quickly. What was going on?

Mikel spotted Anabel first.
"Is that Anabel? What the hell is she doing?"
"No idea," replied Otsoa with a genuine look of surprise, "but it

looks like she's trying to tell us something."

"Then why don't you roll down your freakin' window so that we can hear her!" Patxi's aggravated voice rose from the back of the truck. Mikel immediately complied with his order.

"...*going to blow up! Go away!*" Anabel screamed at the top of her lungs.

10:08 AM ~ Saturday, September 3, 1994

The bomb detonated, followed a fraction of a second later by four more. The explosion was astounding. It sent a shock wave that rocked the whole mountain. Lartaun felt as if a giant rug was being swept from under his feet before the tremendous force of the blast threw him to the ground. When he dared to look up after some time had elapsed, it was as if his ears had been stuffed with cotton. The sheer intensity of the detonation actually deafened him temporarily.

"What was that? What the hell happened?" he stuttered out loud, stunned in part by the thought that he could not hear his own voice, but mostly because nothing made sense to him. "The bomb was not supposed to detonate for another forty-five minutes! Why did it explode before it was supposed to?"

The answer came to him in a flash. Anabel! She plotted her own suicide because she could not stand the idea of betraying Patxi. But then, why had the others decided to turn around and head back to the *baserri* at the worst possible time? Was that part of her plan too?

Lartaun staggered onto his feet and forced himself to take a look at the farm below. He saw a picture of doom and destruction. A black crater lay right where the sturdy stone buildings had been standing less than a minute ago. From where he stood, Lartaun could see the circular patterns of destruction caused by the bombs, like ripples stretching across the surface of a disturbed puddle of water. The grassy slope surrounding the crater was littered with debris. Trees within a fifty-yard radius from the zone of impact had been vaporized. Instead of grass, the ground was covered with rubble made of construction stones and old mortar, slate shards and wooden beam splinters. Within the next hundred yards, the outward pressure produced by the explosion had neatly flattened the vegetation to the ground.

Lartaun's disbelieving eyes traveled again toward the epicenter of the explosion. Outside the edge of the gaping crater, the shattered carcass of what had once been a station wagon lay toppled on its roof. Above it, a thick column of smoke, the color of soot, reached up for the sky. As for Anabel, Patxi and the other people in the car, it was as if they had never been there. Even the dirt trail was gone.

10:14 AM ~ Saturday, September 3, 1994

As reality settled in, so did the cold, irrefutable truth that they had all perished. Lartaun would never see Patxi or Anabel again. Immeasurable sorrow washed over him. Fate had played a hideous trick on them, turning them into the protagonists of a modern-day Greek tragedy. They devoted their whole lives to the separatist cause, striving to achieve their ultimate goal, independence for *Euskal Herria*. Sadly, their actions and the decisions they made along the way brought them formidable misfortune, causing their collective downfall and costing them their lives. The punishment was harsh, and such became their cruel destiny, but there was no escaping the will of the Gods.

Before long, people would come from the valley to search for the cause of the terrifying explosion. Lartaun walked over to where his knapsack had fallen to the ground, scattering its contents over the grass. He picked up his binoculars, whose lenses had shattered, and stuffed them inside the bag, along with his water bottle and passport. There was no point in staying any longer. He wiped the dirt off his face with his T-shirt and cast one last glance at his lost friends below. There was nothing he could do, no help to be offered. For them, at least, the nightmare was over.

From now on, Lartaun had to think about himself. If he wanted to survive, he knew he had to leave France and Spain behind as soon as humanly possible. He set off at a fast pace toward the Col d'Arnostéguy, resolutely turning his back against a past that seemed buried for good, this time.

44

-BERROGEITALAU-

08:05 PM ~ Saturday, September 3, 1994

"How's our 'Lady Luck' doing tonight?" the nurse asked with a jovial smile. Ever since her arrival at the hospital in Pau on Monday night, the entire medical ward had given Faustine this moniker for having survived such an incredible ordeal. "Looks like you found your appetite again! Unless your mother helped you finish the chicken and mashed potatoes?" she added with a wink.

"I did not touch my daughter's food. She ate it all herself!" Vivienne replied with a hearty laugh.

"Doctor Hemelin will be happy to hear that."

Faustine was lucky, indeed. Broken bones aside, she sustained no trauma to the head or the spine and, with physical therapy and patience, her surgeon expected her to make a full recovery.

Vivienne spent every waking hour by her side and, so far, did an excellent job at keeping Major Boréda at bay. Yet, she knew that it was only a matter of time before the comforting haze of the morphine would evaporate and her daughter would face the haunting prospect of stepping back into the real world. With the physical pain receding a little more each day, so did the daily concentration of opiates dripping into her body.

Vivienne put the eight o'clock news at low volume to keep Faustine company before she left her daughter's hospital room for the night.

"...Basque country: a violent explosion occurred around ten o'clock this morning at a remote farm on the Spanish side of the Pyrenees near the Col d'Arnostéguy, between the villages of Arnéguy, France, and Roncevaux in the province of Navarre... The Spanish police are currently investigating the scene to determine the cause of the blast, which is believed to be accidental. We are not sure if the incident has claimed any victims. Stay tuned for more information as it develops."

08:25 PM ~ Saturday, September 3, 1994

"What weekend? You mean tomorrow? You should know by now that I have no life, *maman!* Yes, yes, I know. Ah-ha, yes, I'll be there for lunch next Sunday. Promise! Bye, now. *Yes!* I will!"

Jean-Claude Boréda hung up the phone and immediately regretted being so curt with his mother. The past two weeks had been the most taxing and humiliating weeks of his entire career. As he poured himself a generous glass of Pinot Noir in the kitchen, he wished the world would forget he existed, at least for an hour or two. He was bringing the glass to his lips when the shrill ring of the phone startled him again, causing him to spill some wine on his shirt in the process. Cursing, he marched to the phone.

"WHAT?"

"It's me, Frédéric Blanchard. I'm sorry to bother you on a Saturday night, but—"

"But what?" he spat.

"Pack an overnight bag. We're going to Pamplona."

"Are you kidding me? Where are you?"

"At the hotel. I'll be waiting for you by the reception desk in twenty."

08:58 AM ~ Sunday, September 4, 1994

Alfonso Masa Palancar of the Pamplona police received the Major and DST agent Blanchard in his office at nine o'clock the following Sunday morning. Nicknamed *El Buey*, "The Ox," by his coworkers, Palancar was an imposing man whose puffy face seemed to have been screwed straight onto his broad shoulders. His uniform was cinched tight around his expansive belly, and while he seemed jovial at first sight, most knew better than to crack a joke at his expense. After a quick greeting, Palancar proceeded to fill his visitors in about their current investigation.

"We've already come to the conclusion that the explosion was caused by the detonation of several potent Improvised Explosive Devices. We also found assault weapons. There's no doubt that the farm was being used as a secret arsenal, a "zulo" as they call it. It was a perfect location, if you ask me. Completely isolated from civilization."

"What about victims?" asked Blanchard.

"Forensic pathologists are assuming that there were at least six of them."

"Assuming?" Boréda challenged sarcastically.

"Yes," Palancar confirmed sharply, "we're talking bits and pieces, here. Even the victim's teeth have been scattered all over the place. It's going to be a nasty job trying to sort out what piece of burnt flesh belongs to whom. All we know is that the victims were sitting in a vehicle near the compound when the explosion occurred. The station wagon itself has been reduced to shrapnel."

"Wow," Blanchard said in shock.

"Obviously, there's a possibility that we will discover more bodies as the search of the pile of rubble goes on. I mean, that was a nasty explosion." Señor Palancar opened a folder and spread out a thick set of photographs across his desk. He cleared his throat loudly and said, "Take a look at these. Let me warn you, it isn't pretty."

Boréda took the stack in his hand. He examined the glossy pictures, one by one, with great attention before passing them on to Inspector Blanchard. The first set of snapshots showed charred mutilated limbs as they had been found in and around the carcass of the van. The body parts were all in shambles amongst twisted sheets of metal and burnt upholstery. Palancar had not exaggerated. The scene was gruesome.

"They were keeping busy out there," Palancar continued while they were perusing the photos. "We found evidence of four detonated bombs so far, and counting."

"I dread to think what they were planning to do with them. I doubt that a mass suicide was what they had in mind," commented Boréda.

"So much for all the banter about ETA running out of steam," added Palancar.

"What makes you think that the arsenal belonged to ETA?" asked Blanchard. Alfonso Palancar gave the DST inspector a funny look from behind his thick glasses. He shrugged his shoulders in a dismissive gesture, as if the question was not remotely worthy of an answer. "Well? How can you be so sure?" Blanchard asked again, undeterred.

"Because, Inspector, I've investigated their dirty work for the past thirty years and change. I like to believe that it gives me an edge to make an educated guess. But if it is hard evidence that you're after, I'll tell you that we've found several detonators in the wreckage. They were all made of aluminum, which is the kind ETA favors over copper detonators. As for the two assault weapons we found in the rubble, they originated from a large consignment batch delivered to ETA by the Soviets a few years back. The list of incriminating evidence goes on and on. Do you want to hear it all?"

Blanchard was about to put him back in his place, but he thought best to keep his mouth shut. He came here with the intention of getting answers, not making enemies. It had to be expected that the two men would dislike each other from the moment they met. Indeed, Palancar was from the old school, and half of his police career dated back to Franco's era. He was not the kind of man to let a snot-nosed French upstart question his judgment, let alone in his own office, and especially not on a Sunday.

"Sir, I don't mean any disrespect here," Blanchard said, even-keeled, "I was just thinking out loud. What if this was the work of an independent cell? Say, a rogue separatist group? Ex-ETA die-hard *guerrilleros* who, one day, decide to play God and plan some bombing of their own?"

Palancar let out a dry laugh. "That's just what we would need, huh? A new terrorist group to contend with on Spanish soil! Nah, that is doubtful." He brushed Blanchard's comment away as if he were swatting an annoying fly. "What I was about to say is, standard ETA detonators aside, we were stumped by the type of explosives they used this time. I can't tell you what it is at this point, since we're still waiting for Explosive Ordnance Disposal's conclusions, but it isn't the kind we're accustomed to."

"What type are you accustomed to?" asked Boréda, careful not to ruffle the man's feathers.

"Goma-2 ECO, or Goma-2 EC, usually. It's a nitro glycol-based high explosive that's manufactured in Spain, near Burgos to be exact. Even though its fabrication and transport follows high-security standards, 'shit happens' as they say, and sometimes the cargo falls into the wrong hands."

"Tell me about it," Boréda replied with a sigh. "If the analysis of the explosives reveals that we're talking about the F19 NOBEL kind by any chance, we will need to be notified right away."

"You're referring to the batch that was stolen in the Vallée d'Aspe, correct? Well, we'll know in due time, but I've got a hunch that if you ever wanted to see the kind of damage French dynamite is capable of, you should make your way to the Col d'Arnostéguy and see for yourself," Palancar replied.

"What about the bodies?" enquired Blanchard. "What are the chances of identifying them within the next forty-eight hours?"

"We bagged up all the body parts we could find and sent them to the Hospital Donostia in San Sebastián yesterday so that autopsies and forensic tests could be performed by expert pathologists. They've been working around the clock trying to identify the remains. It is no small task for them. Honestly, I think that we'll have more luck waiting for the families of the dead to come and claim the corpses when the story goes public. It'll be faster than—"

"What is this?" asked Boréda out of the blue. He was tapping his index finger on a tiny white patch on a black-and-white picture. "Would you have a magnifier so that I can take a closer look at this?"

Palancar leaned over to see what he was referring to.

"Oh, that. Yes. Actually that's something that might help us identify one of them. It's melted pretty badly but we believe it was some kind of a medal. Keep on looking through the stack of pictures, there should be a close-up of it somewhere in there."

Boréda thumbed through the photos until he found the object that originally attracted his attention. His eyes grew wide after he recognized it.

"What is it, Major?" asked Blanchard.

"See for yourself. Tell me if I'm crazy," he replied, astounded. Blanchard took the snapshot from his hand and gasped in his turn. He too, just recognized the chain, melted into the mangled torso of its owner.

"Izcoa! That is Izcoa's medal!" Blanchard exclaimed. "Damn, could it be that he was in the van?" he wondered aloud.

"Say what?" asked Palancar, looking at the two of them with sudden concern. "What are you two talking about? How can you be so sure?"

"Izcoa was wearing the exact same medal when we arrested him last week," said Boréda, unable to contain his excitement. "We took it away from him while he was in custody, but we gave it back to him, along with the rest of his personal belongings, on the night of his transfer to jail. It's the Basque cross! See how you can still notice one of its curved points, right there, where it did not melt?"

"Are you sure? Because if you are, this would be fantastic, gentlemen. Just fantastic!" exclaimed Palancar. "Do you realize what it means if we are able to identify Izcoa as one of the victims?"

"Hmmm, one less terrorist stomping around our planet?" ventured Blanchard.

"Amen to that! Good riddance! This man has given us enough of a hard time over the past few years. Not to mention that it will help us identify the other members of his terrorist cell."

"Evidently, we must confirm that we are correct before we jump to conclusions," Blanchard cautioned. "I bet that Izcoa wasn't the only *Euskaldun* walking around with a Basque cross pendant around his neck."

"That goes without saying. I'll pass on the info to the forensic experts to see if they can validate your allegations. We'll also wait for the lab results to confirm the exact composition and origin of the dynamite," continued Palancar, "but if the explosives turn out to be of the 'Nobel' kind, it leaves little doubt in my mind that we've found our fugitive."

"Also, I've been waiting for the doctors' green light to interview Izcoa's girlfriend. She was kidnapped a week ago on Saturday the 27th. I'm hoping that she will be able to provide us with a somewhat accurate description of her abductors," added Boréda. "We are currently creating Photofits of the four men who attacked our officers during Lartaun Izcoa's transfer to jail. I want to run them past her to check whether she recognizes any of them."

"*¡Hombre!* Am I glad that you came over today!" exclaimed Palancar, tapping his belly with content. "So, do you still want to take a trip to the site, or should we cut to the chase and call the media for a press conference right away?"

Blanchard and Boréda exchanged an uncomfortable glance. The Chief of Police let out a coarse laugh and leaned over his desk to slap Blanchard on the shoulder.

"Don't forget to breathe, son! I was just messing with you!"

While it was one thing to look at pictures, it was yet another to face the harsh reality in person. Jean-Claude Boréda walked side-by-side with detectives and specialists of all trades the entire afternoon, scouring the debris below the Col d'Arnostéguy. He watched as they packed bag after bag of morbid evidence. Save for a pair of television news helicopters scavenging for exciting evening news footage, the whole southern side of the mountain had been roped off to keep both media and onlookers at bay.

06:22 PM ~ Sunday, September 4, 1994

Boréda was lost in his thoughts, barely paying attention to the traffic on their way back to France, when Blanchard spoke for the first time.

"I can't believe Izcoa's dead."

"So, you think that it was him too?" answered Boréda.

"As much as I hate jumping to conclusions, I must admit that Palancar has a valid point. Anyway, we'll find out soon enough. If the pathologists end up identifying Izcoa, and the Explosive Ordnance Disposal's experts can confirm the origin and composition of the explosives as being ours, then, *voila!* Case closed for you. I bet that it is music to your ears, huh?"

"Hmmm. I don't want to think about it right now; we might jinx ourselves," replied Boréda. "Too many questions remain unanswered. I mean, who were these guys? Are there more of them lurking in the shadows? And what were the bombs intended for?"

"Boy, I dread to think of the carnage they could have generated had they exploded in a crowded place. It is a good thing they detonated where and when they did. Makes you believe that there is a higher righter of wrongs somewhere after all," pondered Blanchard.

"Amen to that."

"Look, Jean-Claude, you have to talk to Faustine Laroche. We can't delay her interrogation any longer. We need to find out whether she can help us identify the people who kidnapped her." Boréda threw Blanchard a sideway glance in genuine surprise. The DST inspector had never called him by his first name before. "Be sure to send me the full deposition," he continued. "I'd love to hear it in person, but I must fly back to Paris tomorrow. Vilorain already left this morning. Believe it or not, I think that they're missing us at the DST office!"

Blanchard let out a hoarse laugh and Boréda smiled in sympathy. It suddenly dawned on him that he, too, was going to miss him. Life at the gendarmerie would seem rather dull after what they had gone through together over the past few days. He dreaded returning to his boring routine. After a short pause, he said, almost to himself,

"I feel terrible for this young girl and her mother. They'll be scarred for life."

"I hear you, Jean-Claude. The real victims aren't always the ones who wind up dead," Blanchard replied with a sigh. "Nevertheless, they should count their blessings to have had someone like you in charge of the investigation. You were there for them, not only as an enforcer of the law, but also as a human being. You went beyond the call of duty, and believe me when I say it is a rare occurrence these days. Some of us in the force could take a few pointers from you when it comes to treating people with humanity and decency, no matter who they are or what they have done."

"Thanks for saying that, Frédéric, really," said Boréda.

"I mean it. It's been a pleasure working with you."

"And you."

"I'm gonna miss this valley of yours. It's pretty."

"You'll forget all about it as soon as you land in Paris."

"You're probably right. I don't know if I could survive here for long. The silence of the mountains gives me insomnia and besides, I'm desperately addicted to noise pollution and exhaust fumes."

They kept to themselves the rest of the drive.

45
-BERROGEITABOST-

05:43 PM ~ Monday, September 5, 1994

"Brigade de la gendarmerie de Pau. Who would you like to speak to?"
said the receptionist taking the call.
"Chief Masa Palancar of the Pamplona police, here. Put me through
to Major Boréda, please... Yes, I will hold."

This was not Jean-Claude Boréda's first discombobulated investigation. Still, it never ceased to amaze him how one tiny piece of evidence, like a melted medal, could turn a seemingly desperate case around. He visited Faustine at the hospital that morning and her interrogation, as expected, proved to be demanding for them both.

First, he was greeted by a less-than-friendly Vivienne. She fiercely guarded her daughter's room like Cerberus, the much-feared three-headed dog protecting the gates of Hades.

"Don't you even think of upsetting my daughter," she said in a menacing tone. "It's only been a week since the accident. She's very weak and still in pain."

"I understand, Miss Laroche. I will keep that in mind."

This was the Major's second visit with Faustine. He had been granted a three-minute official interrogation the day after her admission to the hospital, but Faustine had barely been able to talk. She still managed to tell him what had happened to her in a few sentences. That she had been kidnapped and then brought to a mountain where a group of armed hooded men had forced her to climb a cliff. She had blabbered something about Lartaun being there, against his will, as well and that her climbing rope had torn while she was abseiling, sending her crashing to the ground. That was pretty much all he had gotten out of her.

"Have you found, you know..." Vivienne lowered her voice to a whisper, "Lartaun Izcoa?"

"No. Not yet," he lied.

"Any idea where he could be hiding? Any leads at all?"

"I cannot disclose any information at this time, Viv—Miss Laroche. Sorry."

"Which basically means that you have no clue where he is," she hissed. "Whatever, I hope he rots in hell! Just don't tell my daughter I said that." Vivienne reluctantly stepped aside to let the Major through the door.

Even though he had previously seen her, Boréda was still shocked upon seeing Faustine. Most of her body was wrapped in plaster casts, making the black and purplish bruises on her exposed skin even more obvious. A cannula had been inserted into her nose, delivering supplemental oxygen to relieve her laborious breathing. Faustine was awake when he walked in. She acknowledged the Major's presence with a flutter of her eyelids.

"Good morning, Miss. The hospital personnel must be doing an excellent job here. You look a hundred times better than when I saw you last!" he said with a forced jovial tone.

"What about Lartaun?" Faustine asked at once, a flicker of hope in her eyes. "Has anyone heard from him?"

"I cannot upset this young lady," he reminded himself, so he offered her hope. "No, I have not. But I'm sure he's hanging in there, wherever he is."

"Chief Masa Palancar? This is Major Boréda. Sorry for the wait."

"I hate to disturb you, señor Boréda, but this is one piece of news that cannot wait. We've formally identified Izcoa's body! I've got the official report right in front of me!" Palancar's booming voice echoed into the phone.

"This is great news!" Boréda replied, trying to match Palancar's excitement. "What does it say?"

"We're faxing it to you and your colleagues at the DST as we speak.

In a nutshell, it confirms that the pathologists were not able to establish a match against the suspect's dentition. This was to be expected given that, after all, his head was virtually vaporized. Nevertheless, they succeeded in taking a blood sample off a piece of his torso. The analysis revealed that the sample was of type B. We checked the results against Izcoa's medical records, and it so happens that they matched his blood type."

"Well, isn't it a little preposterous to formally identify Izcoa's body based on a blood test alone?" Boréda asked cautiously.

"Indeed, the results would not mean much had Izcoa belonged to the O or A type. But given the fact that only 4% of the entire Basque population share the B rhesus, versus 51% of type O's and 44% of type A's, they judged the test to be conclusive."

"Look, I am sorry to put you through this ordeal one more time, but I must ask you a few more questions," the Major looked straight into Faustine's eyes. "Are you up for it?" Faustine nodded affirmatively with a feeble smile. She was in a great deal of pain, and yet she looked alert and capable of answering his inquiries. "Can you tell me anything that you can recall about the people who kidnapped you and the place where they kept you prisoner?"

To Boréda's surprise, the details she relayed to him were staggering. Although she never saw the outside of her jail because she was blindfolded, Faustine relied on her other senses to paint a vibrant picture of its general location. She also described the inside of the barn in painstaking detail.

"We checked the facts the victim gave you this morning against testimonies of locals who happen to be familiar with the lay of the land over at the Col d'Arnostéguy," said Palancar over the phone. "One man, in particular, knew the place inside and out. It's very likely that Miss Laroche was being held prisoner at the baserri."

Faustine willingly broached the subject of her kidnappers. She had very limited contact with anyone, except for a female who was kind to her. Even though she never saw her face, she clearly remembered her stature, the sound of her voice, and her piercing black eyes. While the presence of a female terrorist did not make any sense to Boréda, he politely listened to her, just the same.

"Our experts at the crime scene turned up evidence of another body

early this morning during their search of the fringe of the impact zone," Palan-car went on. "Once again, we're talking about bits and shreds of human tissue, but the forensic experts are certain. Our seventh victim was a female."

Faustine told Boréda about the two men she traveled with in the truck. Because she wore a blindfold the whole trip, she did not have the chance to see the driver. However, she described the other man they called "O" in detail, despite his attempt to hide his features. She spoke of meeting Lartaun on the trail, flanked by two other hooded men.

"What was Lartaun doing there?" asked Boréda.

"I don't know. I was so surprised to see him. I thought he was in your custody! He told me later that those guys orchestrated his escape on his way to jail. He had no idea it was going to happen."

Boréda presented her with Photofits of the four suspects who attacked his men during Lartaun Izcoa's transfer. The composite sketches were created based on the physical descriptions given by people who witnessed the scene from their street windows. Faustine perused the documents with interest.

"It's tough, because I never got to see any of their faces," she said.

"They were wearing hoods the night they attacked the convoy as well. Still, try to focus on their frames, their posture. Perhaps you can remember a distinctive sign, like a limp or a tic. Anything that would help me single them out. I am trying to establish whether your abductors were the same individuals that attacked the police convoy."

One of the Photofits appeared a bit more detailed than the others. Indeed, Boréda told her that the suspect threatened this particular onlooker with his gun, providing the witness with a closer look. Faustine tentatively matched it with one of the terrorists she saw at the *zulo*. She would never forget the man's gargantuan size and brute strength, and the composite picture she was looking at immediately reminded her of him. She pointed at another portrait depicting a shorter, stocky guy and mentioned that it could be the man the others called "O". The third sketch was that of a tall, skinny man.

"This could be Lartaun's friend. I never saw his face and Lartaun never told me his name, but he did say that they had known each other forever."

"Are you sure?" asked the Major.

"Positive. I remember wondering how he could have ever been

friends with such a sick lunatic."

It took the forensic experts less than an hour from that point on to identify the bodies of Cayetano Pantzeska Antxustegi and that of his missing girlfriend, Anabel Zubizarreta.

"We've had our eyes on Antxustegi, a.k.a. 'Patxi,' ever since he was detained and questioned with regards to the bombing of the police station in Irun. We always suspected that he belonged to an ETA secret cell based in Guipúzcoa, but he never gave us an opportunity to take further action. As for the woman, she was his longtime girlfriend. She was never openly accused of having active ties with ETA, but her family tree speaks for itself. She had two brothers, and both of them were etarras. One, Jose Maria, is in jail, and the other is none other than Bixente Zubizarreta."

"The ETA member who died a couple weeks ago in San Sebastián, correct?" asked Boréda.

"Yep, the very man whose death involuntarily led the Spanish authorities to find out that Lartaun Izcoa had returned to Europe, and to subsequently identify him as a prime suspect in the explosives robbery at the Somport."

"Well, I'll be damned!"

Finally, pieces of the puzzle were fitting together. While they did not have the chance to positively identify the other four male bodies found at the scene, Palancar was confident that it was only a matter of time before they would solve that riddle too.

"There's something that escapes me still," Boréda said to Faustine after a pause. "Why did these guys want you and Lartaun so badly?"

Faustine hesitated for a moment, as if she were pondering how her answer might affect Lartaun's situation.

"There is no time for lies," Boréda pressed on at once, reading her mind. "If you want to help your boyfriend, you must tell me the truth."

"They wanted us to climb that face, and only Lartaun and I could climb it."

"Why in hell would they want you to do that?"

Two big tears started rolling down Faustine's cheeks. "So that we would bring the dynamite they had stored inside a cavern near the top down to them."

THE DYNAMITE. But of course.

"Any lab results with respect to the dynamite?"

"Not yet, señor Boréda, not yet. Hopefully, by the end of the day..."

Boréda learned more from Faustine than he could have ever hoped for. He looked at the young woman with concern. Beads of sweat formed on her forehead as she was breathing laboriously. She exhausted what little strength she had.

"I'm sure you can't wait for me to leave, and I can't blame you," he said as he stood up from the chair he had pulled close to Faustine's bed. "I must thank you for your coop—"

"Wait!" she interrupted. "I'm not done yet."

Boréda immediately sat back down, all ears. "I'm listening."

She struggled to talk between shallow breaths. "Lartaun saved my life. Without him, I would have died after my fall. He is not one of them. Yes, he is a Basque who wants independence for his country, but there are tens of thousands of people just like him out there in *Euskadi*," she rasped with effort. "That does not make them all terrorists, does it? Lartaun never believed in violence to solve the Basque conflict, but somehow, trouble always knew how to find him."

"I'm sorry to say, Miss, but your boyfriend was a criminal well before he came to live in the Pyrenees," Boréda said as diplomatically as he could, given the circumstances.

"Bullshit!" she blurted out. "If you are referring to the bombing in Irun, Lartaun and his friends had nothing to do with—" She could not finish her sentence. She started gulping desperately for air, her chest suddenly rising and falling erratically under the hospital sheets.

"Someone, come help! Nurse!" Boréda found the alarm button atop Faustine's pillow and pressed it several times.

Within seconds, a nurse practitioner barged into the room. She pushed Boréda out of the way unceremoniously and ordered,

"I must ask you to leave, sir!"

"Of course," replied the Major, who was visibly upset for causing Faustine so much stress. "Is she going to be all right?"

"Give me room to work here!" She leaned over Faustine to check on her vital signs.

"Yes, I'm so sorry," he mumbled. "I'll be waiting outside." He headed for the door.

"Sir!" Boréda turned around upon hearing Faustine's struggling voice again. "He is—innocent! He promised me that he—was going to stop them! I know the story! I'll tell—"

Faustine dropped her head back against the pillows. The door swooshed closed behind the Major.

Boréda barely made it down the hallway when he heard Vivienne's accusing voice behind him. He let out a sigh, stopped in his tracks and waited for her to catch up with him.

"What happened in there?" she shrieked. "Didn't I ask you not to upset my daughter?"

All Boréda could do was shrug his shoulders in resignation as he laid his piercing light blue eyes on her. After so many years of service, he had grown accustomed to being the person blamed when things went wrong, and the one nobody thanked when things went right. He built a tough skin over the years, but Vivienne's mean remarks and accusatory looks cut deep under his skin this time. They hurt him like never before.

"No matter what I try to do to solve this case, I'll always be the bad guy in your eyes," he said, "so go ahead, Miss Laroche, take it all out on me; blame me for everything that's happened to you and your daughter. After all, I'm just a cop. That seems to be reason enough for you to think I am a lesser man, right?"

Vivienne stood with her mouth gaping like a fish out of water in front of the Major, so taken aback that she lost her tongue. When she tried to speak again, the proper words would still not come out, so she did something that spoke a thousand words instead. She stood on her tiptoes, wrapped her arms around the Major's neck and kissed him furtively at the corner of his mouth. Then she let go of him, turned around quickly before he could see her blush or attempt to hold her back, and retraced her steps up the hallway toward her daughter's room.

Back at his desk at the gendarmerie, Boréda felt the onslaught of a violent migraine. He lowered the blinds to filter out the late afternoon light and popped a couple of pills. He should have been ecstatic about the way the investigation progressed today. Instead, he felt miserable. There was no pride or joy to carve out of others' misery, that of young Faustine, in particular, who continued to protect her criminal boyfriend come hell or high water. In the back of his head, Boréda wondered whether there was a sliver of truth in what she told him about Izcoa. Indeed, the theory of the accidental explosion of the time-bombs at the *baserri* made little sense to him. These men knew how to handle dynamite. So, how and why would they blow themselves up, unless someone else had detonated the dynamite on purpose?

The phone rang at his desk. It was Palancar, again. It took the Major a great deal of self-control not to let the call go unanswered. "Check your fax machine, Major. I've just sent you the final press release that we're about to send to the media. Izcoa's death will make headlines tomorrow. The public will be glad to know that the world is rid of dangerous ETA terrorists."

"Isn't it a little early to establish Izcoa's direct affiliation with ETA?" ventured Boréda.

"What do you mean?"

"I understand that these are just allegations at this point, but Miss Laroche affirmed that Izcoa was—"

"What? Innocent?" Palancar let out a guffaw.

"Allow me to finish my sentence, please. Miss Laroche affirmed that Izcoa was never connected to the terrorist group at any point in time. She even said that he had left her on the night of the rock climbing accident with the intention of, well, stopping the others from carrying out their mission."

"Come on, Major, don't tell me that you would even consider listening to the tall tales of Izcoa's own *girlfriend?*"

While Palancar had a point, Boréda did not appreciate his condescending tone. He bit his lips to channel his irritation.

"She's been a tremendous help to us today. Why would she lie now if she wasn't lying then?"

"Women go to great lengths to protect the people they love."

"I would never bring it up if it weren't for what happened at the *baserri*. I mean, doesn't the accident theory seem a little odd to you? These people obviously knew a thing or two about handling explosives. I find it hard to believe that the bombs could have exploded by accident. Someone had to set them up."

"Explain to me then what Izcoa was doing in the van with the others? Taking a hit for the team? Playing kamikaze to save us all from doomsday?"

"It might not be out of the ques—"

"Major, don't waste any more of your time looking into this! Whatever she claims his motives were, it does not change the fact that he is still the monster who carried out the attack of the *comandancia* in Irun, killing and injuring valiant policemen in the line of duty. In my book, he is an *etarra* and a cold-blooded murderer, with or without your seal of approval. Mark my words, Major Boréda. People will be dancing on his grave, and I'll be one of them."

46

-BERROGETTASE1-

08:40 PM ~ Tuesday, September 6, 1994

Lartaun heard the news of his violent death on his way to Patras, Greece, aboard a Minoan airlines ferryboat. He watched television at the bar along with tourists who, thankfully, were well on their way to drunken oblivion.

The anchor was reporting an accidental bombing at a farm in the Basque Pyrenees when Lartaun's passport picture took the screen. The ETA symbol of a snake wrapped around an axe appeared in the upper right corner, undoubtedly to add to the drama factor. The picture faded into an archive documentary showing a smoldering police station minutes after the 1992 bombing in Irun, followed by an aerial view of the mountain where Patxi, Anabel and the others had perished near the Col d'Arnostéguy.

Lartaun could not peel his eyes off the screen. It could have been a nightmare, but it was all too real. The news said he was dead. The news said he had been a dangerous terrorist, a heartless cop killer who had been at the top of the "most wanted" list of the Spanish secret service for over two years. Lartaun wanted to scream, but instead he could only shake his head in disbelief.

Anger set in. And shame. His family would have heard the news by now. And Faustine too, provided that she was still alive to see this grotesque travesty of justice. How could any of them know that the media had the story all wrong? That what they heard on television was simply not true? Frustration and helplessness were eating Lartaun alive, gnawing at his entrails like a hungry beast as he thought about the loved ones he left behind to fend for themselves while he made, yet again, his escape. They would have to endure public humiliation as they mourned the death of a son, a brother and a lover who had fallen from grace. And save for Faustine, they would have no means to retaliate, because they had no way to know whether Lartaun was indeed a terrorist. Even after his return to Europe, he did not communicate with his family for fear of compromising his mother and sisters. It would have been too much of a risk to take, a move that would have most likely put them all in danger. While it hurt him immensely, he resisted the urge to contact them and in the process, he never got the chance to tell them the truth about Irun and to come clean about his past. Now it was too late.

It was unfair to let them suffer, but there was little he could do about it, unless he turned himself in to the police. And just like he had told Faustine at the *zulo*, he was only human and his freedom was sacred to him. After everything he had been through, he was painfully aware that a life without freedom was one he simply did not want.

10:15 PM ~ Tuesday, September 6, 1994

Lartaun reminded himself to breathe deeply and to stay away from television sets for the remainder of the crossing. He could not run the risk of being recognized.

The ferry would reach Patras the next day at three o'clock in the afternoon. From there, Lartaun would cross the Peloponnese Peninsula and travel west past the Isthmus of Corinth, the narrow land bridge connecting the Peninsula to mainland Greece, to the Port of Piraeus, near Athens. Once there, he would look for temporary work on the docks. He would take on any job he could find. And after that...

Lartaun stood up from his seat and crossed the lounge area with his head down, back to the promenade deck. He had booked a deck ticket, the cheapest passage available with what was left of Eric's money. As a result, he had no cabin or berth. The rattling plates of painted iron that made up the promenades along the top decks smelled like engine oil, but they would have to do. He was relieved to see that night had fallen when he stepped outside. Still, the temperature on deck remained unbearable, and the rumble of the huge ship engines was as loud as ever. Youngsters traveling in groups already claimed the best sleeping spots. They drank moonshine out of plastic water bottles, and all kinds of music blared from their battery-operated boom boxes.

Lartaun finally found a quiet area toward the bow of the ship where the air, albeit sticky and hot, seemed to be moving a bit. Realizing that there would be no escape from the permanent vibrations or the rolling motion of the boat over each passing wave, he settled down against the throbbing bolted metal floor and stuck his knapsack under his head. Within minutes of lying down against the hot iron deck, his T-shirt and the back of his jeans were drenched in sweat.

Lartaun seized the moment to review his options: *A,* he could throw himself overboard and be done with it once and for all. *B,* he could turn himself in and spend the rest of his life in jail, or *C,* he could accept his own death and rise from the ashes as Javier Núñez Obregón, the name printed on the passport stashed in his pocket. He shut his eyes.

When he reopened them moments later, millions of stars shimmered against the inky sky above him. There were so many that his eyes could not focus. A shooting star crossed the sky. It made him think of Faustine. Until he had met her, the pain caused by the forced separation from his family had slowly grated his heart away into tiny crumbs, shriveling it into a ball the size of a plum and leaving him feeling as if the world was festering on its own rottenness. Thanks to Faustine's unwavering lust for life, his heart swelled in his chest again, reddened to a bright pulsing crimson hue and started pumping life into his anemic body with renewed vigor. She was the catalyst that made him appreciate life again. And yet, all he ever gave her in return was deception and sorrow. Well, that, and love too. So much love! He hoped that she would somehow remember that.

Suddenly, everything became clear in his mind. It was his destiny to move on and travel far, just like Patxi had once advised. He would roam the world until he found the perfect place to settle down and rebuild his life. Then, he would look for Faustine, wherever she might be. And if she wished, she would join him, and they would be together again.

Until that day, he would ride the rails and carry the pain caused by her absence like a heavy bundle tied up to a stick.

417

BERROGEITAZAZPI

11:25 AM ~ Friday, September 23, 1994

Faustine found out about Lartaun's death on Saturday, September 17th, exactly two weeks after his passing and one day after his official burial in Irun. Vivienne did her best to shield her daughter from the outside world while her condition was still critical, but there came a point when she could no longer cover up the truth, no matter how devastating it would be. Good thing she did, because Faustine received an unexpected visit less than a week later.

"Hey, 'Lady Luck,' guess what?" Faustine's favorite nurse said cheerfully as she poked her head in the door. "You've got a visitor today! And it isn't the police!"

Faustine cocked her head to see past the nurse, a curious look on her face. "Who is it?"

"Surprise!" She stepped aside to let the mystery guest in.

"Hola amiga," the gorgeous lady said with a less-than-assured voice, "I'm Haizea."

Faustine did not need a formal introduction to figure out who the woman was. The way the words danced out of her mouth and the inflection of her voice immediately reminded Faustine of Lartaun. As soon as she got over the initial shock, she waved her in. Haizea's stature commanded attention. Her limbs were long, slender and toned, and her proportions were stunning. She had thick, lustrous, chestnut hair and the same supple sun-kissed skin as her late sibling. Her ultramarine blue eyes, while not quite as striking as her brother's, had earned her a fair amount of cash in the course of her part-time modeling career.

Haizea approached Faustine awkwardly and sat down next to her. They did not say a word for a long time. When they spoke, however, they did so without holding back.

"You'll never know how jealous I am of you," Haizea said, breaking the silence.

"What is there to be jealous of?" Faustine replied with a perplexed chuckle, "look at me!"

"I mean, of you and Lartaun. He gave you all his love and attention. As for me, it's been two-and-a-half years since I last heard from him. I never got a chance to kiss him good-bye before he ran away—and now it's too late because he's dead." Haizea's facial features contorted in stark agony, but she quickly regained her composure. She was not about to break down in front of Faustine, who was, after all, a complete stranger.

"Haizea, I would be lying if I told you that I was aware of your existence until now."

"Oh," she replied, looking deeply wounded. Faustine's forthright comment cut her to the quick.

"But I always knew that Lartaun had a family he loved very, very much, even though he did not talk about it. I know he did so to protect you."

"Really?" A pretty smile stretched across Haizea's face again. "You see, my brother and I were only a year apart. We were like two peas in a pod, inseparable. He was always there for me. When he left, part of me died. I tried so hard to hate him for all the grief he caused our family. But no dice. I'll always love him with all my heart, no matter what."

"Me too. I miss him so much."

"Cross my heart and hope to die," Haizea continued, "I did everything I could to get in touch with Lartaun after he disappeared, but the only man who knew what had become of him was this guy Pa—"

"You mean Patxi, right?"

"Did you know Patxi?" Haizea asked in surprise.

"Yes and no. I met him, but I didn't know his name until I heard it in the news. I couldn't tell you what he looked like either. It's a long story."

"Well, Patxi would not tell us where he was, for my brother's sake and ours. The police were on our tails the whole time, checking our every move, reading our mail and listening to our phone calls. All I knew then was that he was alive. And now that he and Patxi are dead, I will never know what really happened. I was hoping that maybe you—"

"I am jealous of you too," Faustine said before Haizea could even finish her sentence. "You got to spend most of your life with Lartaun, when all I got was eight months. I never had the chance to say good bye to him either. No one told me he was dead until after the funeral."

Haizea took Faustine's hands in hers and squeezed them hard. Their eyes started to shine with fresh tears at the same moment, making them laugh in embarrassment. The two young women felt instant relief sharing their grief and realizing how much they had loved Lartaun in their own respective ways, and how much he had loved them both in return.

They became instant friends that day, companions in tragedy.

When Haizea came back the following afternoon, Faustine confided in her. She repeated what Lartaun had confessed to her about his past, back when they were on the mountain. She explained to Haizea what had happened to them from the day they met until the day he saved her life after her fall. She told her new friend how Lartaun had promised he would find a way to stop Patxi from using the explosives they had brought down from the *zulo*. Hearing herself tell this story out loud left no doubt in Faustine's mind that the explosion at the Col d'Arnostéguy had been Lartaun's way of stopping Patxi. She and Haizea took great comfort in believing Lartaun had sacrificed his own life to save hundreds of innocents.

From that day on, Haizea returned as often as she could. Together, they followed the media circus in the newspapers and on television. They listened to the fabricated tales meant to destroy the reputation of the man they both loved so much. The fact that they could rely on each other for support gave them the strength to withstand this ordeal.

During that time, Faustine also received frequent visits from Major Boréda. As the days went by, they became less and less official. Major Boréda turned into plain "Jean-Claude." While Faustine suspected that something was going on between him and her mother, she respected their wish to let it go unnoticed. She had not seen Vivienne that happy in a long time and she was grateful that she, too, had found the right person to love.

Just like any other story, the public quickly lost interest and before long, Lartaun was no longer news. Still, Haizea and Faustine argued with Jean-Claude about the necessity of reopening the case. The Major struggled to explain that, absent the corroboration of unbiased witnesses, their testimony would not stand in a court of law. In the end, Faustine stopped caring about exposing the truth altogether. Lartaun's mother and sisters, along with Vivienne and Jean-Claude, understood that he died trying to do the right thing. Deep down, that was all that mattered to her. Besides, whether justice would be done or not, nothing could fill the void left by Lartaun's departure. Nothing ever would.

Faustine had her whole life in front of her, and no one understood that better than her old friend Graziella. Without being asked, she answered Faustine's silent cry for help and invited her to move into her two-bedroom apartment in Nice. Graziella hoped her grieving girlfriend would embrace her chance at a life she once dreamt of and envied. A radical change of pace was just what Faustine needed to help her forget the past. To Vivienne's relief, she jumped at the chance, and joined Graziella within days of her release from the hospital, on Saturday, October 22nd.

02:12 PM ~ Saturday, October 29, 1994
   Eight weeks after Lartaun's official death

   "Whoa, take it easy, girl! Can't you see that everyone is looking at us?" Graziella moaned in protest.

   Faustine could care less. Her late application had been accepted, and she just enrolled at the University of Nice. She browsed every single item on the shelves of the stationary aisle at the department store. Her shopping cart was already half-full with binders, notebooks and pens in every color of the rainbow, when she grabbed another useless gizmo and threw it into the pile.

   "No, no, no!" Graziella squealed as she caught up with her. She plucked the gadget from the cart with a disgusted look and replaced it on the shelf. "You won't need that. This is university, Faustine, not primary school!"

   "You're not as fun as I thought you'd be!" Faustine replied, laughing.

   Graziella rolled her eyes at her like a big sister before adding with a wink,

   "Let's check out the women's department. We've got a ton of shopping to do, still!"

   Two hours later, Graziella and Faustine giggled with delight as they strolled down the Avenue Jean Médecin with their arms full of bags.

"Girl, now that I've introduced you to the vain, yet insanely gratifying, world of mass consumption, we must match those cool duds we just purchased with your handsome face," exclaimed Graziella. "Off to the hair dresser!"

"Why? What's wrong with my hair?"

Graziella did not give Faustine the chance to argue her case.

"I won't even start to explain what's wrong with that terrorist-slash-ER massacre that you're passing for a haircut these days!" Faustine laughed good-heartedly as Graziella dragged her by the sleeve to the next Franc-spending haven. "Shut up and let's go, sister. You'll thank me after you've made out with all the hot guys I'm going to introduce you to at 'La Villa' in Cannes tonight!"

A black mini dress, strappy heels and a three-hundred-franc-champagne-blond-bob job later, Graziella introduced Faustine to her army of friends. She was intent on proving to her that "living-the-good-life-on-the-French-Riviera" was indeed all it was cracked up to be.

Faustine needed to write off her past. In order to do that, she took the plunge into the deep-end without a trace of hesitation. In a matter of weeks, she immersed herself into a brand new world, learning the ropes of the academic world by day and prowling the clubs at night. In fact, the constant chaos generated by her new lifestyle suited her just fine to help her cope with her grief. Anything would do, as long as it did not give her a respite to stop and think. She avoided idleness or solitude like the plague these days, because the demons of grief would invariably choose those dreaded moments to rear their ugly skulls and mess with her fragile sanity.

49

— BERROGEITABEDERATZI —

10:39 AM ~ Monday, October 31, 1994

Within a week of Jean-Philippe's quiet burial in Biarritz, on the first Saturday of September, Eric left the Vallée d'Aspe for good. He returned to his apartment in Bayonne and tried to get on with his life. Every single member of ZORROTZ TALDEA had passed on except for him, and they had all taken the dark secret to their grave forever. As a consequence, no one would ever know what OPERATION ASKATASUNA could have been. In spite of this, he still feared that the police would come knocking at his door because there was a Damocles sword hanging over his head—the videotape that Lartaun had made of him. Eric would not get any respite until he found and destroyed it.

"Hello?"

"Hey there. Could I speak to Faustine?" asked Eric.

"Who?"

"Er, Faustine? Is she there?"

"You mean, the girl who fell off a cliff? Well, she doesn't live here anymore." There was a short pause at the end of the line. "Hang on a minute, let me get Mina on the phone. She might be able to help you. I'm new here."

"Thanks. I appreciate this," Eric replied, on pins and needles.

There was a muffled noise as the young man dropped the receiver.

Eric heard him walk away and shout for Mina. Mina's voice came on shortly after. She sounded a little out of breath.

"Who is this?" she asked.

"Mina? It's me, Eric. We met before. I used to live at the cabin in Urdos."

"Eric!" she exclaimed with relief, "of course I remember you! Sorry if I sound weird, but with all the shit that's happened around here lately, we've had all kinds of people calling in. You know, journalists, stalkers… All of them asking for Faustine."

"I can only imagine."

"How are you? It's good to hear from you again."

"Good, I guess. Same old, same old. I was hoping to talk to Faustine, but I was just told that she doesn't live there anymore."

"No," she replied with a deep sigh, "she left, along with pretty much everyone who used to live here, actually. It feels like I'm the only one left. Well, I exaggerate, of course, but you catch my drift."

"Who left, then?"

"Well, Vivienne for one. After Faustine's accident, she moved to Pau to be by her side at the hospital. I mean, Faustine was there for well over a month!"

"Holy sh—! A month?"

"She had the luck of the angels, man. She walked out of the damn hospital on her own two legs! It was a miracle, really. Anyhow, rumor has it that while Faustine was there, her Mom got cozy with one of the cops working the case. I mean, Vivienne with a cop! At any rate, she broke up with Etienne over the phone and came back the next day to pick up her stuff. Three days later, it was Etienne's turn to leave. He went to Amsterdam I think, but I'm not totally sure."

"Wow."

"Yep. That being said, no one can blame them. I mean, we've been to hell and back over here. A lot of people couldn't take the pressure. I thought of getting out too, but someone had to stick it out and man the fort. So, I'm still here."

"You're a strong lady, I always knew that. So, where is Faustine, then? Still in Pau?"

"Nah. When Vivienne came back to pick up her stuff, she said that even though Faustine had recovered from her wounds physically, she was still—well, pretty fucked up in the head, if you know what I mean. With her boyfriend's death and all, it's going to be a while before she gets better.

The doctor said that Faustine needed a radical change in her life, something new to focus on. Last I heard, she was going to enroll at university this fall. She already shares an apartment with a good friend of hers in Nice. Actually, you might even know the girl. Does Graziella ring a bell? Massimo Bianchi's daughter?"

"No, sorry."

"Why did you want to talk to her, anyway?"

Eric hesitated before giving Mina an answer. "I wanted to give her my condolences, and see how she was doing, I guess."

"How cool of you. She did not have that many friends around, you know? Raf—, I mean Lartaun or whatever the hell his real name was, he had become her whole world." She paused for an instant, and sighed. "No matter what he's done, he was a great friend to me too! We all pitched in to send flowers for the funeral. So freakin' sad."

"I know. It's been terrible for those of us who counted him as a friend."

"Come visit me some time, all right? It gets lonely here, you know?"

"I will Mina, I will," he said at last, even though it was a lie.

Eric replaced the phone on its cradle, baffled. Clearly, Faustine, or anyone else living at La Goutte for that matter, had never seen, let alone been in possession of the videotape. They would have used it against him already. Who else would have it, then? Lartaun's family? After all, he returned to Irun on the night of their grim encounter. He could have easily passed it on to one of them. Still, it was mind-boggling. The media had the entire story wrong from start to finish. If anything, the contents of the tape could have only helped to clear Lartaun's name. If given the chance, his family surely would have leaked the videotape to the media. Yet, they had not. Perhaps, Lartaun never intended to use the recording at all. Come to think of it, Lartaun never crossed him. They were never friends for sure, but Lartaun carried him down the trail when he broke his ankle, though he could have very well left it all up to Jean-Philippe. Plus, he never said a word of complaint to Patxi about their feelings of mutual aversion.

Perhaps he had just played with his mind? What if he had never given the tape to anyone? That would be just like him. Eric wished that he could bring Lartaun back from the dead and ask him that simple question, just so he could sleep again at night.

50

– BERROGEITAHAMAR –

01:23 PM ~ Friday, December 16, 1994

"Haizea! Look my way, girl. Yeah! Gorgeous. Give me that hot mysterious look of yours. Superb, now that's what I'm talking about!"

Techno music blasted from the stereo inside the studio. Haizea moved in sync with the beat in a purple floor-length gown under two fierce spotlights. As soon as the photographer ran out of film, he stopped the music.

"Two-minute break, everyone!" he announced to his small entourage while his assistant set out to reload his camera.

Haizea stepped away from the décor. She threw herself back into her work lately, accepting every job that she was offered, regardless of the pay. She was rewarded with moments of peace without the pain. Not to mention, the extra cash came in handy to cover the expenses of her rekindled taste for heroin.

She sat in front of a vanity mirror in the dressing room and inspected the dark circles under her eyes. She had lost a lot of weight and looked unhealthy.

"Soon, Lartaun, I'll stop. I promise." In the span of two short months, she turned into a junkie and it showed. "Just look at you," she snarled at her pathetic-looking reflection. She spat at the mirror in a sudden surge of rage.

"Excuse me, Miss Izcoa?"

Haizea jumped from her seat, startled. She turned around to face the photographer's assistant standing over the threshold of the make-up room. If he saw what she did, he possessed the tact and decency not to let it show.

"Yes?"

"We're ready whenever you are, Miss," he said politely before he disappeared.

"I'll be there in a second!" she replied in haste. She grabbed a tissue and wiped the spit off the looking glass. Haizea reached inside her purse and pinched Lartaun's melted medal hard between her fingers. She shut her eyes tight and asked her brother for the strength to keep on fighting, or the opportunity to die soon, whichever came first.

05:43 PM ~ Friday, December 16, 1994

Faustine inserted her key in the lock and held the front door open with her foot. She juggled a heavy load of groceries in her arms.

"Faustine, is that you?" Graziella called out from the living room.

"Yeah! Come give me a hand!"

"Guess what!"

"What?"

"Something came in the mail for you today!" Graziella skipped to the door, brandishing a letter over her head. She relieved her of a few bags and inserted the envelope between Faustine's lips, since both her hands were full.

"Thanks!" Faustine managed to reply. She dropped everything in a heap on the kitchen table and went straight to her room. She inspected the envelope first. It was postmarked from Irun. At a glance, she recognized the exquisite calligraphy of Haizea, who invariably wrote her missives with a purple ink fountain pen. She tore it open and looked inside. It contained a short note from her, along with a second envelope covered with exotic-looking stamps, which had already been opened. Piqued by curiosity, she unfolded Haizea's letter first and started to read with anticipation.

Irun, 8 Dec. '94

Querida Faustine,

I hope this letter finds you well and that you're living life to the fullest in Nice! I'm doing fine, but I'd love to see you again soon. I could use a little cheer in my life!

Check out the letter I've enclosed. I don't know who would go out of their way to play a mean prank on us, especially from so far away. I don't mean to upset you, but I thought that you should take a look at it, too. Do you know anyone who lives in Istanbul? Anyway, I was wondering if this made any sense to you at all. It sure doesn't to me.
Hoping that your studies are going well,

Un besote,

Haizea

Faustine put down Haizea's message. She fished the second letter from within the main envelope. It was all wrinkled and water-stained in places. Its postmark read November 25th, 1994. The sender's contact information read J.N.O, c/o Suleyman Mansur, along with a street address in Istanbul, Turkey. She found a single sheet of paper inside. She unfolded it with nervous fingers, and almost fell off the edge of her bed.

It was a rough sketch of a mountain drawn with a felt pen. It depicted two stylized climbers, a male and a female, tethered to a rope. An arrow pointed to each one of them, with the initials *L* for the man and *F* for the woman. The letters had been cut out of a magazine and glued onto the sheet of paper, so that the sender would remain anonymous. There was a circle drawn in the middle of the mountain, with the crude drawing of a dynamite stick inside of it, and to the right, also in cut off letters, a message that read: "ONLY ONE LEFT."

The cavern in the mountain…
The lone stick of dynamite left inside the *zulo*…

Who could have drawn this picture, when only she and Lartaun knew about this? It just did not make any sense at all. Or could it be that…

"Holy fuckin' shit!" Faustine bolted out the door to grab the phone in the living room. She ran away with it, locked herself inside the bathroom and dialed Haizea's number. Her fingers were trembling so much that she had to punch the numbers three times in a row before she could get it right.

At last, the phone started to ring.

05:51 PM ~ Friday, December 16, 1994

Haizea was sprawled over the couch, staring at the white ceiling with eyes that did not see. She contemplated the blandness of the parallel world she was slipping into with a beatific smile on her lips. What was the point of swimming against the current, when Charon was gently leading her down the River Styx to Hades' underworld? A bloody syringe stuck out of a vein on the inside of her elbow. From far away, the shrill ring of the phone seemed to bounce off the walls like a distant dream. She was so high, so stupendously baked.

"Goddamn you, Haizea, pick up the fucking phone!" Faustine vociferated between clenched teeth. The line finally connected with a click. "Haizea? Is that you?" Faustine almost screamed into the phone.

"*¿Quien es?*"

"Sorry, I was looking for Haizea Izcoa. I must have dialed the wrong number," she stammered, taken aback by the stranger's voice at the other end of the line.

"Who is this?" said the voice again.

"Faustine Laroche. I'm a friend of Hai—"

"Faustine? Oh my God, it's Itxaro!" Haizea's sister shrieked into the phone. She sounded terrified.

"Itxaro, are you all right?"

"No! It's, oh God, it's Haizea! I stopped by her place after school to say hi and—*Joder*, she's passed out on the couch! She's—I think she's OD'ing!"

"Itxaro, listen to me! Call EMS right away!"

"I already called the police! They're sending an ambulance. I didn't want to get her in trouble by calling the cops, but I didn't know what else to do!"

"You did the right thing. They're going to take good care of her."

"What if she dies on me?"

"Speak to her, Itxaro! It might seem like she can't hear you right now, but she can, I swear!"

"What should I say?"

"Anything! Tell her to hold on!" Faustine heard the front bell ringing in the background. "Go get the door, Itxaro!" she urged her, "but don't hang up! Put the phone by Haizea's ear so that she can hear my voice!"

"OK!"

Faustine heard static noises over the phone, followed by Itxaro's footsteps as she rushed to get the door.

"Haizea," Faustine began to say with a shaky voice, "it's me, Faustine! Hang in there, you hear? Listen, I received your letter! I know what it means! I must talk to you! Don't die on me now. This is too important! Don't give up! Don't—"

There was more static as someone moved the phone away from Haizea. Faustine heard male voices blurting out instructions in the background. The line went dead shortly after.

"Hello? Hello? *Hello?*"

Faustine pressed her knuckles against her mouth to stifle a cry.

Moments later, there was a rasp on the bathroom door.

"Faustine, what's going on in there?" It was Graziella. "Open the door, please! You're scaring the shit out of me!"

After a moment of hesitation, Faustine turned the small bolt to the left. Graziella slowly pushed the door inward and looked in, speechless and in shock. Faustine's teary eyes met her friend's. She wiped them with the back of her hand, smearing black eyeliner all over her cheeks in the process.

"I have a huge favor to ask," Faustine simply said.

"Anything, girl."

"Can you drive me to Irun?"

09:12 AM ~ Saturday, December 17, 1994

Faustine woke up next to Graziella in Haizea's bed. She pushed back the covers and tiptoed to the window. The street below was empty and it was raining outside. Her throat was hurting. They stayed up most of the night, consumed with fear, chain-smoking cigarettes with Itxaro, and waiting for news that was not coming fast enough. Graziella stirred in her sleep. She looked at the empty space next to her and propped herself up on one elbow in sudden panic. She relaxed a little after spotting her friend standing by the window.

"C'mon, Faustine," she moaned, shielding her eyes from daylight, "close the freakin' curtains already!"

"Itxaro is up. I heard her in the shower. We've got to get ready too. Just in case," she replied nervously.

Graziella plopped her head back down on the pillow. "I feel like I swallowed an ashtray last night!" she said in a crackly voice.

The phone rang and Faustine jumped, startled. By the time she entered the living room, Itxaro already pounced on the receiver.

"*Mama?*" Itxaro exhaled into the phone, gripping it with both hands as she stood stark naked and dripping wet in the middle of her sister's apartment. Faustine, meanwhile, grabbed the living room door frame for support, anxiously awaiting the news. Graziella joined her seconds later.

"And?" she whispered in Faustine's ear.

"Dunno yet. Hush!" she whispered back.

"She made it! Haizea is going to be OK!" Itxaro exclaimed a minute later.

The three girls screamed with relief before they slumped into each others' arms.

10:25 AM ~ Saturday, December 17, 1994

Haizea sounded as pitiful as she looked, but at least she was alive. Faustine sat alone by her side, holding her friend's skinny hand.

"I thought I was toast last night," Haizea explained. "It felt so right; so easy at first, you know? There was no pain. I just wanted to go along with it. I was in this long white hallway with all these doors, and I was opening them one after the other, looking for Lartaun. But I could not find him, no matter how hard I looked. After a while, it was like something switched inside my head. I could hear this voice telling me that he was not there. I must sound like a total freak to you right now, but it got me real scared. All of a sudden, I didn't want to die anymore. Not like that. The problem is, I couldn't stop it. It was like I was being dragged away by something much stronger than me."

"Thank God your sister arrived when she did," Faustine said reproachfully, even though she silently thanked the grim reaper for sparing her friend's life this time around.

"I know. She's always been my little guardian angel. Oh, Faustine, I feel so ashamed right now. I can't tell you how sorry I am for letting you all down. My poor mother needed that like she needed a hole in the head."

"Maybe that was the kick in the ass you needed to see the light. You have to get a hold of yourself!" said Faustine, caressing her friend's feverish forehead.

"I already spoke with the doctors. They're sending me to rehab. I'd be lying if I told you that I was looking forward to it, but I have to get better."

"I got your letter," Faustine said after a long pause, "including the note from Turkey."

"Oh yeah, the letter. I had almost forgotten about it. Creepy, isn't it?"

"Haizea, there's something I must tell you about that letter, but after what just happened, I'm not so sure that I should bother you with it right now."

Haizea's piercing blue eyes lit up at once. "You've talked too much or too little, Missy! Did you make any sense of the *puto* drawing, yes or no?"

"I think I have, but it's probably best for me to wait until I really know for sure."

"Talk to me, *coño!* You're killing me!" It was Haizea's turn to tighten her grip around Faustine's hands.

"Promise me first that you won't tell a soul. Not your mother, not your sister, not anyone. Because I know he wants it that way. At least for now."

"He who?"

"Swear first."

"I swear!"

Faustine took a big breath.

"I'm flying to Istanbul on Monday. I think Lartaun's alive."